CRIME COP
•••••••••••••••••
BODY OF THE CRIME
•••••••••••••••••
LORENZ HELLER

INTRODUCTION
BY PAUL BISHOP

Stark House Press • Eureka California

CRIME COP / BODY OF THE CRIME

Published by Stark House Press
1315 H Street
Eureka, CA 95501, USA
griffinskye3@sbcglobal.net
www.starkhousepress.com

CRIME COP
Originally published by Pyramid Books, New York, as by
"Larry Holden" and copyright © 1959 by Almat Publishing
Corp.

BODY OF THE CRIME
Originally published by Pyramid Books, New York, as by
"Larry Heller" and copyright © 1962 by Larry Heller.

Copyright © 2021 by Stark House Press. All rights reserved
under International and Pan-American Copyright
Conventions.

"Introduction" copyright © 2021 by Paul Bishop

ISBN: 978-1-951473-38-9

Book design by Mark Shepard, shepgraphics.com
Cover design by Jeff Vorzimmer, ¡caliente!design, Austin, Texas
Proofreading by Bill Kelly
Cover art by BenWohlberg from the original edition
of *Body of the Crime*

PUBLISHER'S NOTE
This is a work of fiction. Names, characters, places and
incidents are either the products of the author's imagination or
used fictionally, and any resemblance to actual persons, living
or dead, events or locales, is entirely coincidental.
Without limiting the rights under copyright reserved above, no
part of this publication may be reproduced, stored, or
introduced into a retrieval system or transmitted in any form
or by any means (electronic, mechanical, photocopying,
recording or otherwise) without the prior written permission of
both the copyright owner and the above publisher of the book.

First Stark House Press Edition: June 2021

7
Introduction
by Paul Bishop

13
Crime Cop
by Lorenz Heller

191
Body of the Crime
by Lorenz Heller

322
Lorenz Heller
Bibliography

INTRODUCTION
CRIME COP / BODY OF THE CRIME

PAUL BISHOP

Hello and welcome to the introduction for this collection of two hardboiled police procedurals, *Crime Cop* and *Body of the Crime*, by Lorenz F. Heller...

Who?

Ahh, I can understand why you might wonder who this hidden gem of a crack mystery writer might be—and I promise I will tell you. But first, I must beg your indulgence as I take you on a short tour down a proverbial rabbit hole of my own devising.

I've been extremely lucky in life getting (among many other blessings) to have simultaneous careers doing the two things love most—putting villains in jail by day while, under the cover of darkness (so to speak), putting words on paper that eventually ended up on bookstore shelves. In the course of pursuing these vocations, I spent thirty-five years with the Los Angeles Police Department—thirty as a detective; twenty-five investigating sex crimes; the last twenty of which I spent supervising a crack unit of thirty detectives responsible for investigating sex crimes from soup to nuts (indecent exposure to sexual homicide) in the most crime ridden parts of the city. During that time, I also wrote sixteen published novels along with writing for both episodic television and feature films. I often get asked how I found time to work fifty to sixty hours a week, be on call 24/7, and still find time to write. As an answer, I sometimes offer a phrase borrowed from *The Treasure of Sierra Madre*, but with a personalized twist—*Sleep? We don't need no stinkin' sleep...We don't have to show you no stinkin' sleep*—Hmmm, that works a lot better in the original when it referred to *badges*...but you get the idea. To this day, I still don't sleep more than four to five hours a night (although, at this juncture of life, I have discovered the infinite joys of the twenty minute power nap).

Hopefully, I haven't arrested any of you who are reading this (which is possible since I once collared a suspect and during a search of his home found a copy of my latest book half-read next to his bed). But maybe there are a few of you who might have read one of my crime novels. If you have, then you would know I write police procedurals. You might even refer to them as *realistic* police procedurals—or at least as *realistic* as possible without letting the facts get in the way of a good story—and therein lies my problem...

I love reading hardboiled private eye tales, great *high adventure* stories, and even the Christie-style classic mysteries. For whatever reason, I have no problem suspending my disbelief while reading those types of stories—I just go with the flow and turn the pages. But, when it comes to the police procedural genre, I often can't get through the first chapter before glaring errors of procedure or nomenclature drive me to distraction.

Most of all, the illogical concept of a homicide detective who only works one case at a time with unlimited resources is such a real world fallacy, it makes it impossible for me to read on and causes me to throw the book violently across the room. Well, perhaps that's a bit dramatic. In reality those transgressions simply cause me the reader's equivalent of heartburn and I toss the book—without reading further—into the pile I will eventually surrender custody of to the Friends of the Library—like a bounty hunter preferring to bringing a felon in dead rather than alive.

When it comes to reading the novels classified as police procedurals, I simply know too much about how things really work for my suspension of disbelief to remain intact. Trust me, in the real world, my detectives juggled a full caseload of current crimes; cold cases that suddenly became hot because of an unexpected DNA hit; cases to be filed at the DA's office; cases necessitating being in court to testify; and a plethora of other details incessantly demanding attention despite whatever else is of immediate importance.

It's funny what people will believe. I have two cousins in England who are coppers with the London Metropolitan Police Force. When I go to visit them, they think what I do as an LAPD detective is a lot like what they used to see on *Starsky and Hutch*. I try to tell them there is no training class for sliding across car hoods in the LAPD police academy, but they won't buy it. When I ask them if what they do was anything like *The Sweeney*—Britain's equivalent of *Starsky and Hutch*—they laugh uproariously and say, *of course not, that's a TV show*. But somehow, they still don't get the connection since they appear to think *Starsky and Hutch* was a documentary series.

I've found it to be true that if a TV show or book series is popular, it has absolutely nothing to do with it being realistic—it's all about the appeal of the characters. However, like doctors pulling their hair out watching medical shows, I cringe watching cop shows. The current reboot of *SWAT*, or the ludicrous *Tommy* (featuring the first female chief of the LAPD), or the outrageously idiotic *The Deputy* (a rogue officer who by the most convoluted set of circumstance possible finds himself in charge of the Los Angeles Sheriff's Department), and so many more are unwatchable for me—yet the great majority of viewers follow these shows loyally.

Under her pen name Dell Shannon, Edgar Award winning mystery writer Elizabeth Linington wrote a series of very popular police procedurals (she was arguably the first woman to write in the subgenre). However, when Linington began describing her protagonist, LAPD Homicide Lieutenant Luis Mendoza, as a millionaire who drives his Ferrari to crime scenes in the hood, and then leaves it parked at the curb while he investigates, I almost wet myself laughing. Linington's plots may have been twisty and her character admirable, but I never found out because I couldn't read any further.

The whole premise of the millionaire, flashy car driving, LAPD detective was also championed by the TV show *Burke's Law*, which starred Gene Barry as a millionaire LAPD detective who drove his Rolls Royce to crime scenes. So, according to TV shows and mystery novels, the LAPD is apparently made up of millionaires who have no worries about somebody seeing their ridiculously expensive cars and opening a police corruption investigation.

There is also a never ending list of little things that could have been correct if only the author had done even a mote of research. If a novel about an LAPD detective has the main character turn up at the *precinct house*, I'm done—LAPD doesn't have *precincts*. The LAPD is geographically broken up into what today are referred to as *areas* because their original designation as *divisions* was considered too militaristic and scary for the current woke generation. I won't argue that point, but I will assure you LAPD does not have precincts. Nor does LAPD have anyone with the rank of *inspector*. And let me just mention that no female detective—no matter what department they work for—is going to run around in six inch heels while on duty, despite what you see every night in prime time. And unlike the TV show *The Closer*, LAPD does not take Deputy Chief lateral transfers from other departments—nor do Deputy Chiefs ever investigate cases or interrogate suspects (even if they do look like Kara Sedgwick).

And speaking of interrogations, the good cop/bad cop routine you see over and over again on TV is illegal—it's a violation of our civil right not to be intimidated, and cops have gone to jail for using it. I now teach interview and interrogation seminars to law enforcement agencies across the country, which means when I watch even supposed reality shows like *48 Hours*, I end up yelling at the screen because I see everything the cops are missing. Fortunately, my wonderful wife changes the channel before I begin frothing at the mouth.

Now you may point at my first cop novel *Citadel Run*, in which two pairs of LAPD cops in the late '70s get involved in a race to Las Vegas and back...in their patrol cars...while on duty. *Come on, Paul*, you may well scoff, *how realistic is that?* My response would be to show you the pictures...Well, show you the pictures after the statute of limitations has run out.

There are a few authors of my acquaintance who make a real effort to get their police procedural right while still telling a great story. Both Michael Connolly's LAPD detective Harry Bosch, and Lee Goldberg's Los Angeles County Sheriff's Department detective Eve Ronin are at the top of my personal short list. I believe it when Harry Bosch or Eve Ronin investigates a case—other police procedural writers, not so much...

Keep hanging in there with me as I'm about to bring this soliloquy (perhaps *rant* would be a better choice of words) full circle. When I was approached to write this introduction for this Stark House collection of *Crime Cop* and *Body of the Crime* by Lorenz F. Heller, I had to think about it. I was admittedly unfamiliar with the author and needed to do some background before I commented on his two police procedural-style novels, which clearly is a very touchy area for me. So you can imagine what my first reaction was when I came across the following synopsis of Heller's novel *Murder In Make-Up* from 1937—*Peg-legged, scar-faced, blind, wearing a macaw on his shoulder, tiger hunter Von Leeuw comes from India to work with the New York police. His first case is the murder of a once famous actor—and Von Leeuw catches the criminal with a hunting cheetah.*

Uhmm, after reading that, I really have no idea where to start...A bizarre civilian NYPD consultant who uses a hunting cheetah to catch criminals—there has to be a violation of rights there somewhere. That said, I have to admit to the writer side of me having a strong desire to read *Murder In Makeup* simply because I really, really want to know how Heller pulled this story off...As odd as this may sound, the creativity of the synopsis, made me commit to writing this introduction. If Heller could get away with a character like tiger hunter Von Leeuw, what was he going to do in *Crime Cop* and *Body of the Crime*?

And I'll tell you what Heller did right up front—he wrote two of the best police procedural paperback original novels to come out of the late '50s and early '60s. If you are as big a fan of Ed McBain's far better known 87th Precinct novels as I am (McBain is top notch at getting the procedure right while telling complex and engaging stories), then you're going to love *Crime Cop* and *Body of the Crime,* and hate the fact Lorenz Heller never wrote any more in what—like the 87th Precinct novels—is a loosely connected series featuring the cops and the detectives working out of the 7th Precinct station house in the Hudson section of Jersey City...If you want a real crime, there's one right there.

Like Michael Connelly, Heller has a newshound's eye for detail and the instinctive ability to write terse, propulsive prose filled with an inner tension that rachets up tighter than a pair of handcuffs. There is no doubt in my mind, Heller spent time inside *cop shops* observing the ebb and flow of humanity. His cops are flawed humans, driven by something beyond simply solving a crime, no matter how heinous. They are driven by an innate sense of justice and furious with a world where justice can never be completely attained.

In *Crime Cop* a strangler is at work and detectives Jeff Flavin and George Gilman are hot on his trail, but the key to the killer's identity is in the hands of a beautiful and seductive woman (is there any other kind in fiction or real life?). Heller's gifts as a writer are on full display here. His focus is not on the crime, but on the characters—whom he captures with deft strokes of nuance and subtly unique psychological quirks. Heller clearly knows readers care far more about the people populating the stories than the revealed whodunit at the end. Give readers someone they can root for and identify with and they'll come back to spend time with those characters again and again.

In *Body of the Crime*, the new Homicide Squad top dog Lieutenant Ben Tutchek—who put in an appearance in *Crime Cop*—finds dealing with the death of a woman who has been kicked to death, or solving the locked room style murder of a business man who appeared to have been slipping into dementia, a lot easier than gaining the trust of his team of detectives. Not only does Tutchek have to prove to them he's competent, but also that he make his detectives his top priority over toadying up to his superiors.

I've seen this latter squad room dynamic close up in the real world from both sides, and Heller gets it exactly right. One of the first questions the rank and file will ask when a new boss takes over is, *would you follow him/her up the hill?* This is a concept fraught with land mines...It's not just about is this new boss going to be a pain in the ass or somebody we can work with, but when it's crunch time following somebody *up the hill* means they are leading the charge and getting in the muck and bullets right along with you. As a snotty-nosed and persnickety critic of the police procedural genre, the highest praise I can offer is, as a reader, I'd follow Lorenz Heller up the hill any time.

—March 2021
North of Los Angeles

Novelist, screenwriter, and television personality, Paul Bishop is a nationally recognized behaviorist and expert in deception detection. He spent 35 years with the Los Angeles Police Department where he was twice honored as Detective of the Year. Co-host of the weekly *Six-Gun Justice Podcast* (www.sixgunjustice.com), he has written sixteen novels, numerous scripts for episodic television and feature films, and three non-fiction Western reference works: *52 Weeks—52 Western Novels, 52 Weeks—52 Western Movies,* and *52 Weeks—52 Western TV Shows.*

CRIME COP
LORENZ HELLER

writing as Larry Holden

Headquarters

Police headquarters was housed in a four-story red brick building on Jackson Street next to the Lyric Burlesque Theatre. There were many larger and newer buildings, but Headquarters dominated the neighborhood. It had a gray slate mansard roof, innumerable tall narrow windows and thick oak entrance doors over which hung a green glass globe the size of a basketball.

The first floor belonged to the uniformed branch of the police department. On the second floor was the Detective Bureau, its large general squadroom surrounded by small offices, interrogation rooms, the locker room and two inadequate toilets which had been installed when the pace of living was more leisurely.

The press room was also on the second floor. It was a narrow cramped den beyond the toilets, beyond the janitors' supplies closet, beyond the freight elevator, beyond everything, and the reporters knew they had been stuck there on purpose. The Authorities wanted the press room as far away as possible; if they could have hung it out the window on ropes, they would have done so. As far as they were concerned, newspaper reporters were trained observers from a hostile country with which an uneasy truce existed.

The Records & Identification filing cabinets made a cold green steel maze of the third floor, but this particular maze was not designed to entertain weekend guests with innocent merriment. In those drawers was a package on every person convicted of a crime in the city. The package was the record. It contained every scrap of information possible to assemble—name, alias, color, date of birth, description, scars, tattoos, birthmarks or other physical peculiarities, dental history, occupation, names and addresses of associates and relatives, previous criminal record, method of operation, personal tastes in clothes, women and other forms of entertainment, pictures and fingerprints. Professional criminals are basically more afraid of the record than of a cop. A cop is, after all, only a man. You can run from him, shoot him dead or confuse him, but you cannot run from the record, shoot it or confuse it. If you committed a fresh crime, the record could and often did lead a team of detectives directly to you, and when you were convicted, it told the court how bad you were and what should be done to you and for how long. It was a stupid criminal who did not fear the record, but then the stupid ones did not last very long.

Here, too, on the third floor was the Crime Laboratory, which employed highly skilled technicians who examined and analyzed a crime with the dispassionate tools of their various sciences. The Crime Lab dealt in tangible, provable facts—the facts of ballistics, photographs, fingerprints, plaster casts and the intricate miracles found in the eye of a microscope.

A large part of the fourth floor was occupied by the detention cells and the drunk tank, a twenty-by-thirty iron-barred enclosure known as the Zoo. Nights were usually lively in the Zoo, a regular sideshow, if you wanted to look at it that way. Some detectives, like big Harry Muir, came up here for a laugh when they were bored, but to most cops a rummy was not funny.

Down the corridor was an auditorium with a small stage at one end. In here the players on the stage were assured of undivided attention if not applause. This was the daily lineup and the players were known criminals, trouble-makers and other undesirables gathered by the police during the past twenty-four hours. They were scrutinized sharply by a capacity house of police officers as they were forced to stand in the bright light against a white wall which was black-ruled in inches and feet to show their height. They blinked or squirmed or stood sullenly tight-lipped, knowing that hundreds of police eyes were cataloguing them for future reference. That was the purpose of the lineup: to strip the criminal of every vestige of anonymity, to make him known to as many policemen as possible, to bleed him of self-confidence.

Police headquarters, layer by layer, laminated for strength. There was not another building like it in the city of Hudson. Even ordinary citizens looked at it and obscurely feared it.

One

It was eight-thirty a.m. and there was a sluggish muttering quiet in general squadroom A of the Detective Bureau Police Headquarters, City of Hudson. Dust motes flickered crazily in rafters of sunlight slanting from the windows; noises seemed muted and remote—the tac-tac-tac of typewriters, the opening and closing of doors, footsteps on linoleum-covered wooden floors, the metallic groans of the old elevator, droning voices. Men moved and talked as if they had yet to shed the remembrance of warm beds, big breakfasts and comfortable homes, reluctantly left. The start of a workday was no different here than in the shipping room of the Acme Paper Box Company on Railroad Avenue or the wet wash department of the Sno-Wite Laundry, Service Is Our Motto. Even the huge presses of the *Hudson Evening News*, straining with headlines and bulletins, did not leap to full velocity the moment a switch was thrown. They had to be warmed up gradually and with care. That was the only sensible way to treat a machine. It caused less stress and strain and, after all, a big machine represented an important investment. It was financial idiocy to slam them around. A policeman represented an important investment also. It took time and money to train him and too there was the cost of maintaining the police school and gymnasium on Bank Street. There were fifteen hundred men, or employees, on the Force, counting technicians of the Scientific Investigation Division, clerks, Police Chief Earl Sharkey and Commissioner Willie Quinn's bouncy blonde secretary, and as any comptroller could tell you without thinking twice, the investment involved to put such a group in the field was many times the cost of a whole battery of two-story printing presses. So obviously the Force had to be given more painstaking consideration than all the presses in the basement of the *Hudson Evening News*. You can't argue with IBM facts and figures.

But a cop would get his tail chewed out by the first officer who caught him warming up gradually and with care, and the hell with stress and strain.

On the average, seventy-five crimes were committed in the city of Hudson every day, or about one every twenty minutes. If a cop took twenty minutes for setting-up exercises and deep breathing, it meant that a criminal would get away with a heist, a mugging or murder in general. Therefore, the sluggish quiet of the squadron was a delusion. The men may have yawned and scratched themselves but they were intently at work. Some were goofing off, of course—there's dead freight in every organization—but most were plugging away at the endless job of seeing to it that nobody got away with anything.

It was several minutes before they noted the unusual amount of hustle and bustle in and out of Captain Mackenzie's office. Captain Mackenzie was Chief of Detectives, known as Foxy or Foxy Grandpa. He was shrewd, but whoever laid that label on him was only half right. The other half was still Iron Pants Mackenzie, his tag when he was the toughest precinct captain down at The Point. The Point was the toughest precinct in the city. You had to be an Iron Pants down there or wind up with no pants at all. Or in the morgue with an identification label tied to the big toe of your right foot.

One by one, the men looked up from their desks and watched the procession disappear into Mackenzie's office—bristling Lieutenant Haas of Homicide with Detectives Harry Muir and Ben Tutchek, both huge men, the biggest in a Bureau of big men; Sergeants Ochs and

Nairn of Burglary and Safe and Loft respectively; then, coming from the elevator, Captain Frank Rhodes of the 15th precinct, trailed by two of his detectives, Urquhart and Jenner. Mackenzie's secretary, Joyce Ames, followed swiftly, carrying a bundle of packages from Records & Identification. This was her third trip to and from the floor above and her appearance in the squadroom was a down-tools-stop-work event at any time. The attention given her was usually more personal and speculative than professional but today there was a strong blend of both. She was a quiet, sweet-looking girl, slender but definitely not too slender, and she walked with a light and completely feminine step; she did not galooph along or jiggle in bow and stern as did many girls when in a hurry. Her hair was light brown, her smile a sudden photoflash brilliance. She was more than just another nice girl, although no one could have told you exactly why. Around Headquarters, certain persuadable girls were known as quiff. Joyce Ames was anything but quiff.

Neither did she usually run errands. Therefore, her rushing up and downstairs to Records could mean only one thing; the conference in Foxy's office was triple-A, top priority urgent.

Voices began to buzz from one end of the squadroom to the other. Something had busted loose for sure or Cap Mackenzie would not have summoned such an array of police talent to his sanctum. Within a few minutes there were several authoritative explanations, all different. The Detective Bureau was neither better nor worse than any other organization when it came to creative gossip.

On one thing everybody was agreed: there was hell to pay somewhere in the city.

Detective 2nd/grade Jeff Flavin, a compact six-footer with sandy hair and quick gray eyes, watched the parade pour into Foxy's office and soon had a fairly general idea of what was going on, judging from the kind of men who had gathered. A murder had been committed during a burglary in the 15th precinct by an armed thief. A safe had been opened or blown and probably looted. The burglar possibly had an armed-robbery record. The angles were being checked. The identity of the killer was not yet known. If it were, the investigation would have been routine but intensive with Homicide in charge. The killing had taken place last night or this morning and the victim was probably a V.I.P. The Chief had called this emergency meeting because somebody had goofed—possibly the boys from the 15th precinct—and things had to be pulled together fast. The chewing-out, the rushing around, the detective details called in—all these told Flavin approximately what was going on. You didn't have to be a Sherlock to see that much.

But there were other explanations.

A lanky detective named Kiler stopped at Flavin's desk to bum a cigarette. "What a hassle," he said. "I hear they're going to clean up The Point."

"The Point?" There was always a small grin somewhere in the vicinity of Flavin's mouth. "Is that why Cap Rhodes of the Fifteenth is here? I thought the Fifteenth was the Stone Bridge section."

"Malone lives in the Fifteenth, old buddy, and Malone's political boss of The Point. Get it?"

"Is Malone in wrong with City Hall?"

"This is an election year, Jeff," said Kiler wisely. "The Point always gets cleaned up in an election year."

"That's right. I forgot."

"I wish to God we could keep The Point cleaned up but they won't give us enough men, they won't give us enough money, they won't give us enough anything. So every election year we go through the motions." He pointed his chin at Mackenzie's office. "I feel sorry for Foxy. He's a good cop. I'll bet it gripes the hell out of him."

Flavin said, "I'll bet." He didn't argue. In the next twenty minutes he'd hear twenty more theories, all plausible. Or at least as plausible as Kiler's.

Kiler strolled on. Flavin's phone rang. He picked it up and recognized the voice of his "pet pigeon," Birdie Burdson. Stool pigeons were generally despised but, as Foxy had once remarked dryly, they were the backbone of the police department. This was not entirely sarcasm. A stool pigeon was the bridge between the police and the underworld. Some pigeons were petty thieves or petty operators themselves but were given a sort of dubious immunity in exchange for information. And at times honest citizens, the ones who squawked the loudest when the crime quota rose, could have given the same information but did not want to become involved, or thought they were protecting a friend, or simply did not want to be bothered and were really "too busy." Oh, there was a reason for stool pigeons. Just ask any cop. If you want to hear some strong language.

Burdson was an ex-con man, now a sometimes bookie, tout, errand boy or whatever he could pick up, including an occasional ten dollars for finking. "Fink" was a contemptuous synonym for stool pigeon.

"Mr. Joe Reilly?" he asked when Flavin answered the phone. Finks did not advertise their connection with a cop, for known finks did not live very long.

"What is it, Birdie?"

"I believe I have something in the third at Hialeah which may interest you, Joe. Something very very choice indeed, if you don't mind my saying so. A bit of a surprise, Joseph, a real surprise package. A bundle of joy, you might call it." The voice was still smooth and rich but Birdie was becoming long-winded in his flabby old age. Long-winded and anxious.

In a way, Flavin felt sorry for the old fraud; not too sorry but sorry enough to be patient. Some bulls gave their finks a bad time. "What is it?" he repeated.

"A tasty little tidbit, Mr. Reilly. That particular item which is always a delight in the sport of kings. It is called the sure thing and what more could a man ask?" This may have gone over big in the old days when Birdie's specialty was "the wire," or fixed horse race con, but today it was a pain in the neck.

"All right," said Flavin wearily, "I'll bite. What is it?"

"If you will allow me—"

"Come to the point! I'm busy."

Cut short, Birdie said glumly, "Whiskey Johnny Goss blew in from Philly and made a touch at Bergman's. Two cameras."

"He sell 'em yet?"

"T.B. But his kip seems to be the Birdcage."

"Got anything else?"

"I understand there's a new heavy in town but—"

"There's always a new heavy. Or do you have a real make?"

"He's most elusive, I fear, Mr. Reilly, and the cost of specialized research becomes prohibitive when you consider the—"

"I'll take care of you if Goss pans out," said Flavin, and hung up.

His partner, Detective 3rd/grade George Gilman, back from the can, asked, "That Birdie? Him and his new heavies."

A "heavy" was a thief with a record of violence and Birdie used the new-heavy gag whenever he was short. No one had bought it yet and no one would. Birdie couldn't con a mark in the Bureau.

"Johnny Goss lifted two cameras from Bergman's," said Flavin. "Birdie drew a total blank on the sale but said Goss is practically living at the Birdcage. It's something but not much."

Gilman nodded. He knew of Goss, a petty grifter, and he knew the Birdcage, a big all-night cafeteria on Broad Street. It used to be a hangout for queers, but the Vice Detail put the sneeze on that. It was still called the Birdcage although the queers had moved to The Point and it was now used by thieves, finks and visiting firemen. The police did not clamp down because sometimes a plant or a fink got a real make in the place.

"I'll go upstairs and pull Goss's package," said Gilman.

"He took a fall under the name of Gauss, as I remember. Big deal."

He moved away with that fast duck-foot walk of his. Flavin frowned, puzzled. He couldn't figure George at all, even after six months of working with him. He was a good man, slow but sure when it came to assorting routine details and applying them as he went along, but he had been a timeserving beat cop for twelve years and had just earned his promotion by cleaning up a bunch of would-be muggers, high school kids, in the quiet Brookville section around South Branch Park before they really hurt anybody. It was not an accident; once in a while a timeserver did run into something; but Gilman had worked on the deal and used his head to stop those kids before they tasted blood. This, after twelve embalmed years on a beat. It was a mystery. He was a wide, homely man with a jutting, almost frog-like mouth, bald, a little awkward and self-effacing in a funny way—something to do with his being raised by a stinker of an old maid sister, about whom George had dropped a few unintentional remarks.

Flavin pulled a crime report pad to him and used it as a scratch pad to jot some notes on Goss. Flavin was on the Pawnshop Detail and shoplifters weren't his business but Goss had fenced his loot in a hockshop before and that was Flavin's business. He called several pawnbrokers and told them to watch for Goss and then walked to the water cooler. The day was stuffy and humid and sweat crawled down his ribs like tired ants. The cooler was beside the low wooden fence which separated the squadroom from the waiting room where Detective Desk Sergeant Bauer processed visitors. Right now Bauer had a complainer, Mrs. Mankey, a thin, gray, worried woman. Mrs. Mankey was a chronic complainer. This was her fourth time in.

She had a son Raymond, aged seventeen, six foot three, two hundred pounds. Handsome as a blond Gregory Peck, to hear Mrs. Mankey tell it. He delivered meats and groceries for Nivens Food Mart, a fancy supermarket in the Stone Bridge section. According to Mrs. Mankey, Raymond was being seduced regularly by a married woman on his route. She'd heard him tell another boy about it. Or thought she had. She'd tried talking to Raymond but he said she had it all mixed up and he'd only been talking about girls and there was nothing to that either.

"But a mother knows, mister," Mrs. Mankey told Sergeant Bauer mournfully. Being a mother was not a bed of roses.

"Raymond is twenty, not seventeen, Mrs. Mankey," said Bauer.

"Yes, so young, too young. She'll be arrested, this woman?"

"An investigating officer is working on it." This was the standard brush-off. "You don't have to keep coming back."

"You don't know what it is to be a mother, mister. Raymond, he's a good boy, only seventeen, a baby, and she's no good, that woman. It ain't right now, is it?"

She was pleading with Bauer, begging him to agree, beseeching him to give Raymond back to her, but all her possessive clinging and desperate maneuvers could never make Raymond her baby boy again. The kid was twenty years old, for Godsake. Maybe he was getting it from some bored married woman. The world was full of bored married women and twenty-year-old kids didn't have to be beaten over the head with a club when a toss was there for the taking. Not any twenty-year-olds Flavin had ever known. All things considered, you just couldn't pity Mrs. Mankey. It was time she pulled in her apron strings.

Flavin drank a second cup of cold water and slouched back to his desk. This was going to be one bitch of a day and the ceiling fans only flapped at the dripping heat and gave it to you in soggy waves.

Sergeant Gill, head of Pawnshop, appeared in the doorway of his office, looked around and strode straight across the squadroom to Flavin. "I've been calling you," he said irritably.

"I've been goofing off," said Flavin. "I had a drink of water."

You could joke with Gill. But not this time. "Report to Lieutenant Haas," he said. "And don't stop for any drinks of water."

"I'm transferred to Homicide?"

"Ask the Dutchman—Lieutenant Haas. Wait a minute. You know about those three burglaries out in the Fifteenth?"

"More or less."

"Good. That's part of it. The other part is, a woman was knocked off last night. It's a mess. I don't know where you fit in but the Lieutenant'll give you the rundown. Now beat it."

Flavin beat it.

The Dutchman's secretary, Paul Kropp, was a thickset cop whose heavy exterior concealed a timid, nervous little man. He did not want to be a watchdog at the gate for Homicide's autocratic boss. He did not want to marry a movie star, own a yacht or make a million dollars. He wanted only one of two things—a return transfer to the serene, uncomplicated typing section of Clerical, or the immediate retirement of Lieutenant Haas. He did not want the Dutchman to drop dead, break a leg or go to bed with a lingering illness, as many men might. He merely wanted Haas to go home and not come back.

He gave Flavin a harassed nod and said, "Don't you know better than keep the Lieutenant waiting? He'll clobber you. I'll tell him you're here." He announced Flavin into the intercom box and winced at the answering blast. Sooner or later, all the Dutchman's secretaries winced at the sound of his voice.

Lieutenant Haas was angrily planted behind a desk on which

everything was rigidly lined up like a regiment at attention. He had an inch or two of muscular neck, a hard round head and cropped bristling hair like the movie version of a Prussian field marshal. He regarded Flavin with that pale-eyed stare behind which all Dutchmen seemed to lie in wait. He jabbed a thick thumb at the deskside chair and took a paper from one of the at-attention stacks before him, squaring it exactly in the center of his green desk blotter, which did not have a blot on it. It never did. He demanded and got a new one every morning.

"You took your God damn time," he bellowed.

"I was working on a shoplifting tip, Lieutenant. It had a Pawnshop angle."

"Then Sergeant Gill took his God damn time finding you!"

"I was out of the squadroom, Lieutenant," Flavin defended Gill.

Haas was not interested in Sergeant Gill. He yelled because it cleared the atmosphere and plainly told a new man that Homicide was not a God damn Sunday school picnic. He glowered at the paper in his hand. "Flavin, eh? Safe and Loft Detail one year, Burglary one year two months. Unmarried. Why unmarried? A chaser? A chaser's no damn good for nothing. You know that, hah?"

Flavin was not wearing his trademark grin. He had heard of how the Dutchman went at you. "Yes, sir," he said, knowing no real answer was expected.

"But the record is good," said Haas. "That's what counts, the record, and don't never forget it. You're no good unless it's down in black and white."

"Yes, sir."

"All right. Now we understand each other. You know the burglaries up in the Fifteenth?"

"Yes, sir."

"You do? All right, tell me."

"Three burglaries in four weeks. The thief broke in through a cellar window. A wall safe looted in each case and afterward he made the husband tie and gag the wife, then slapped the husband around. Slapped, with his open hand. The women were not molested."

Haas listened stolidly. "Well," he said, "that's something. Not much, but something. Later you read the reports and find out. There are not three burglaries; there are four. Last night was the fourth and last night the woman was damn well molested. She was molested all the way. She's dead. Same MO, but she's dead."

Flavin said, "Yes, sir," and waited. This was where his part came in.

"On this," said Haas, "I need Safe And Loft and Burglary. That's you. But that's all I need from you, understand? Keep your nose out of the rest of it. Muir and Tutchek're handling that. You do your job and they do theirs. Understand?"

"Yes, sir."

"You do? All right. Tell me."

Flavin thought, Oh Christ, and knew his face was turning red. What did this thick Dutchman think he was, a schoolboy? Nevertheless, he said, "I'm to work the burglary angle and keep my nose out of Homicide"—and suppressed a crackling impulse to ask if he should stay in after school and write it a hundred times on the blackboard. A lieutenant of Homicide wasn't God Almighty but he could damn well close the Pearly Gates on a detective 2nd/grade. He could put a detective 2nd/grade back in uniform and set him to pounding a beat down in The Point where patrolmen did the tour in pairs.

"Very good. Keep it in mind or you won't get your ass in a sling, you'll get it in a plaster cast. Now get out to Twenty-three Park Lane and go to work. Afterwards, you read the reports. Move!"

On the way out, Flavin stopped at Kropp's desk. "Tell me something," he said. "When I turn in my reports, do I salute or salaam?"

Kropp looked up at him. "Wait," he said, "that's all, just wait. If you can still wisecrack at the end of the day, I'll eat it."

Homicide included the personnel, it seemed.

2.

When Flavin walked up, George Gilman was cleaning out the drawers on his side of their common desk while a lanky detective named Pohl stood to one side like a pedestrian waiting for the traffic light to turn green so he could cross the street and get out of the neighborhood.

"What do you think you're doing?" Flavin demanded of Gilman.

"I'm transferred to Missing Persons. Pohl's on this new thing with you."

It took a minute to sink in and then the whole business of Lieutenant Haas exploded inside Flavin. "The hell with that noise!" he said violently.

He turned on his heel and strode across the squadroom He did not know exactly where he was going, but wherever it was, he was going to have this thing out. Not the Dutchman. The Dutchman wouldn't listen. The goddam Dutchman had never listened to anybody in his life. And not Lieutenant Old Buddy Walsh. In that dead voice of his, he'd ask if Flavin thought this the police department or the First Methodist Ladies Aid and stop acting like a kid and go to work. There was only one other place and even as Flavin hard-heeled toward it, he realized it was probably the wrongest place of all.

Joyce lifted her shining light brown hair and oval face in incredulous astonishment. Police Chief Sharkey might stamp into Captain Mackenzie's office and kick the door shut behind him, but not detectives 2nd/grade furiously demanding to see Foxy and "get on that squawk box, sister, this is important!"

Joyce Ames was intelligent as well as decorative but there was nothing in her experience to tell her the standard operating procedure with a wild man. She was saved from stammering idiocy by a loud irritable call from the Captain himself in the private office.

"Send him in, girl, send him in. Don't keep the man waiting!"

She started, automatically, "The Captain will see you—" and turned her head to stare at the office door which still seemed to quiver from the velocity of Flavin's entrance.

Mackenzie growled, "Sit down, sit down. And stop waving your arms. I don't know wigwag. Now who lit your fuse?"

Flavin did not take the indicated chair but he did force a sort of calm upon himself. "I just want to ask one thing," he said. "Why did George Gilman get the boot?"

For the love of Moses, thought Mackenzie, so that's it!

"Relax, Flavin," he said. "Nobody gave Gilman the boot. You're on an important assignment and he doesn't have the experience."

"He was booted into Missing Persons. It's a graveyard. You have to be embalmed."

"Relax, man. It's only temporary."

"I just came from the Dut—from Lieutenant Haas," Flavin did not realize his voice rang like a cavalry bugle; he thought he was speaking in reasonable tones. "He put me straight on the assignment."

"Relax," Mackenzie repeated. He sighed. He knew how Flavin felt. The old Dutchman was his best officer but why, why did he have to affect people this way? All the same, Flavin knew better than to bust in here like this. If he had a legitimate beef, he should have taken it to Tom Walsh. Yet there was more to this than the Dutchman. Flavin was really going to bat for Gilman. The Department was full of men who went to bat for their partners, but how many would have the gall or guts to brace a Chief of Detectives?

Damn few. He watched Flavin with a blend of interest and curiosity.

"And he put me straight on the record, too," Flavin said metallically. "There's nothing like the record. It's the last word. You can be J. Edgar Hoover but if it's not down in black and white, you're no place, and George Gilman got the boot because he's no place. Well, there are things about him you can't put down in black and white!"

"No?"

"No. You can't put down that when he starts plugging he never stops and no matter how many hours he puts in, you get your full sixty minutes' worth, and slogging from one lousy hockshop to another keeping them in line, and the way he remembers every little thing so it's there when he needs it, and maybe those high school kids out in Brookville were only would-be muggers but he broke up the bunch before it got started and that's what counts, not waiting till you can make a flock of high-class arrests for the record."

Of all the officers in Headquarters, Captain Mackenzie was the last who needed a lecture on crime prevention. In fact, when he had to give a talk to Kiwanis, Rotary and all the rest, that was his subject.

But he nodded because he wanted to find out why Tom Walsh had made such a point of putting Flavin on this case with the Dutchman's crackerjack outfit. Tom was a sick boy, sicker than anybody realized. He was worried about Tom. Yet sick as he was, Tom Walsh knew men and had flatly said Flavin when the Dutchman asked for a man. Flavin. And here was the same Flavin fluffing his shanty Irish duff and who threw the overalls in Mrs. Murphy's chowder? Was Tom slipping?

"I know Gilman's record," he murmured.

"But the record doesn't know Gilman. The record doesn't know what goes on inside. The record doesn't tell you that a few more kicks in the pants, and there's a good cop up the rain pipe. The record—"

Flavin stopped. He had not run down. There was a lot more he wanted to say about George Gilman but didn't know how to use the words. Could he say Gilman was flesh, blood and heart? That was silly. Everybody was flesh, blood and heart. Could he tell how George felt about his gold-toothed, frog-mouthed homeliness and that, when he was a kid, the other kids had called him hop-toad and that his own sister, a perfect bitch, unwed and no beauty herself, said just looking at him made her sick to her stomach. But so what? George was on the cops, not in the movies. Who cared if a cop didn't look like Gregory Peck?

So he'd said everything there was to say and at the same time hadn't said a damn thing.

"This Gilman," said Mackenzie at length, "he seems quite a friend of yours."

"Just a cop," said Flavin dully, knowing he'd made a mess of it. "Just a damn good cop."

"I'd like to meet this paragon or whatever the hell he is. I've been on the Force a long time and in all those years there's only two, maybe three men, I'd call damn good cops. There've been a lot of good ones but mighty few *damn* good ones. Look around for awhile, sonny boy, before you start telling people who is or isn't a damn good cop."

"George Gilman is a damn good cop," said Flavin.

"All RIGHT!" Mackenzie shouted. "If he's as good as all that, marry him, but don't bother me with it anymore. I'm sick and tired of George Sherlock Gilman. Tell Pohl to report back to Sergeant Ochs. Tell him to go home. Tell everybody to go home. Tell them you and Saint George're taking over Headquarters. Now are you satisfied?"

"Yessir."

"You're sure?"

Flavin suddenly felt as if the carpet under his feet had turned into the soft and scented grass of Elysian fields. "Yes, sir!"

"Good. I'm glad to hear it. Now I'm going to tell you something, detective. Take your beefs to Lieutenant Walsh in the future. The next time you come yelling in here I'll really give you something to yell about. This is an office, not a Lonely Hearts club for half-ass detectives. Keep it in mind. And another thing. You're damn lucky to be working under Lieutenant Haas. Keep your eyes and ears open and you'll learn more about the detective business in eight minutes than apparently you have in the last eight years. When Lieutenant Haas turns out a detective, he's a graduate. Now let me ask you something." The Captain's manner softened but just barely. "You knew better than come in here with a gripe, so why didn't you go to Lieutenant Walsh?"

"I was sore and, well, thought I'd get more action if I went to the top."

Mackenzie nodded. He saw the real answer in the closed expression on Flavin's face. So the men knew Tom was sick and no longer trusted him. He waved Flavin out of the office.

"And tell Miss Ames that Gilman and Pohl have both been untransferred," he said.

He opened the middle drawer of his desk and took a cigar from a box stamped Tampa Specials. Good cigars. A dollar seventy-five for fifty. Stank like hell but a nice smoke. He bit off the end and spat it into the shining brass cuspidor beside his desk. It had been his own idea to transfer George Gilman, not the Dutchman's. But there'd been no sense bringing that up. Anyway, the Dutchman wouldn't mind another one percent of being thought a son of a bitch. He was a tough old Kraut. He could stand it.

Outside Flavin told Joyce Ames about the status quo of Pohl and George Gilman so she could correct the assignment sheet and later call Lieutenant Walsh's secretary, and have her do the same.

"And look, Joyce," said Flavin, "I'm sorry the way I sounded off at you."

She laughed. It was an extremely pleasant laugh, low and rich. She had overheard the whole conversation in the Captain's office—how could she help overhearing!—and her opinion of Flavin had risen several notches.

"Oh good heavens," she said. "Everybody loses his temper once in awhile. Especially in this madhouse. I'm glad it turned out all right for you and Detective Gilman."

"And I'm glad you're not sore."

"Good. Now we're both glad."

Now why hadn't he noticed how that flashing smile made her oval face seem really incandescent, he wondered? Probably because he'd been too busy making a play for the bouncy blonde in Commissioner Quinn's office. Joyce Ames could give any blonde cards and spades and still score without trouble. She was the most attractive girl around.

"Maybe this is a dumb question," said Flavin, "but what are you doing for dinner tomorrow night?"

"Dinner? Eating, probably."

"Now that's what I call a coincidence," Flavin felt unaccountably antic and gay. "I'm crazy about coincidences. Eating, that's the coincidence. I eat too, so let's make it more of a coincidence and do it together."

She hesitated as a girl does when she's framing a tactful refusal. But she hesitated too long. Although she appeared to be smiling up into his face, Flavin knew she was not really looking at him. The outlines of the smile were slightly hazy, thoughtful, remote, as if the problem involved more than having dinner with him.

Flavin saw it coming and was beginning to feel the inevitable letdown when her smile refocused and she said, "Well, thank you. That's a nicer coincidence than most."

Flavin looked at her, grinning for several seconds. "Will seven o'clock be all right?"

"Seven is just right."

He walked out of the office and grinned around the squadroom. When you stopped to notice, it was really a cheerful place, the way the sun streamed in through the tall east windows and drew gold from the wood grain of the battered oak desks and tables and reflected it in the faces of men bent over their work, gleamed brightly on brass cuspidors and touched everything with a spark of life. At times the old firetrap beamed all over like somebody's grandmother with a glass of wine in her.

He turned with a light step and was confronted by Lieutenant Tom Walsh on his way to Mackenzie with a handful of reports. Up close, Tom looked more gaunt and dead-faced than ever.

Flavin hesitated and said, "Hi, Tom. You—you're busier than Siamese twins in a revolving door, as usual."

"Work," Walsh mumbled. "Up to my neck."

"At this pace, you'll be the next missile launched at Cape Canaveral."

"Huh? What?"

"You'll be the missing missile," Flavin offered, hoping to raise a smile on that necrotic mouth. "You know, Atlas, Thor, Titan, Snark, Thomas J. Walsh. Missiles. Satellites. Satellite is the loneliest lite in the week. The next thing you know, you'll be sabotaged by the Russians and there it is; Tom Walsh, the missing missile. Send us a picture postcard from Moscow."

"Oh. Well—your new assignment, there might be a promotion in it." He nodded, walked around Flavin and went into Mackenzie's office.

Flavin moved slowly into the squadroom. So that was that. Not hello, not goodbye, not anything. Double-O. Blank. Six months ago Tom's wife, Grace, was killed in a car accident. She was buried in Pittsburgh, where her folks lived. Tom stayed out there two months, grieving, and when he came back he looked and acted like—well, this. It was natural for a man to mourn his wife and Tom and Grace had been closer than most married couples. Not lovely-dovey close but living, breathing, flesh-and bone close. People did not come much closer than that, as Flavin knew well. They'd been friends. But what were they now? He didn't know. At times he was almost sure Tom couldn't stand the sight of him. Avoided him, didn't speak except on business. Was it because he reminded Tom of Grace? That was possible. They'd had him to the house for dinner about once a week, went night-clubbing together when he had a date, tuna fishing out of Brielle down on the Jersey coast, parties, picnics. They had their own private jokes, the way friends do when it needs no more than a word or a wink to start them all laughing. Yes, it was easy to see how he'd remind Tom of Grace.

But Tom had to start living again. He shouldn't try to go at it alone. It was getting him and when you pressed maybe a little too hard, just saying let's have a beer or something, an almost menacing darkness came into his face and he cut you off short. Time after time. Yet you couldn't tell yourself, I can't be bothered, and forget it. That was the lousy part of it. Tom wouldn't let you.

Two

A green-and-white patrol car, a black squad car with the police gold insigne on the doors and several others belonging to technicians of the Crime Lab were parked in front of 23 Park Lane. It was a stately white Georgian house and the eight fluted pillars across the two-story gallery stood with the serene dignity of elder statesmen. The wide front door, punctuated by a brass spread-eagle knocker, had the grace of a Thomas

Sheraton creation and over it was a beautifully carved fan light. The windows were capped by similarly carved pediments and flanked by green shutters.

There was a very small crowd of rubberneckers, chiefly idle teen-agers, but then this was the remote, wealthy Stone Bridge section. In any other section of the city, you'd have been neck-deep in rubberneckers. Stone Bridge did not believe in that sort of thing. It was secure and withdrawn from the rest of Hudson and in the heart of it were the drowsing lawns of Old Brook Park.

But 23 Park Lane was not drowsing today. Nothing drowses when the police move in.

Flavin and Gilman did not immediately enter the house. Flavin spotted a Lab technician on his knees beside a basement window and canted his head, telling Gilman to follow him. The Lab man was very carefully spraying a small patch of earth with shellac. He looked up when Flavin and Gilman shouldered through a rhododendron bush.

Flavin said, "Hi, Bert. What is it, a footprint?"

The man nodded and said, "Hi, Jeff, hi, George. Yeah, a stinker of a print. It'd blow away if you breathe."

Flavin hunkered down on his heels. The print was in a mixture of dry loam and leaf mold. Several sprayings of shellac held it together. Bert had surrounded it with a low collar of firm earth to keep the edge of the cast about an inch thick when he poured in the plaster of Paris. Flavin and Gilman bent over the cast as Bert mixed a coffee can of plaster with water, letting the plaster settle through the water, then stirring it carefully to avoid air bubbles. The footprint was deeply patterned with the design of a gymnasium shoe sole. The right side of the sole near the toes was worn almost smooth as was the middle section across the instep.

"This bird does a lot of driving," said Gilman. "That smooth mark on the side's from the gas pedal and the one in the middle's from the brake."

They leaned back as Bert slowly poured the plaster mixture in from one side, allowing it to flow softly into the print. He stopped when the cup of earth was half full, quickly reinforced it with a cross-hatch of thin twigs, then poured in the remainder of the plaster. It would harden fast, for he had added salt to the plaster to hasten the drying process.

"Of course this ain't going to mean a goddam thing," he grumbled as he washed out the coffee can. "You can get sneakers like that by the million."

"Did you work on the other three burglaries?" Flavin asked.

"Yeah, but this is the first print. That boy knew his stuff. He always swept his prints with a broken branch."

Flavin said, "According to what I read in the papers, he always wore sneakers. How do you know?"

"Oh, he left some blurry dust prints on the floor inside the houses but hardly anything you could take a picture of. Such a careful guy. You'd think he was breaking the law or something."

Flavin looked at Gilman. "These Lab scientists," he said, "they get that way from sticking a microscope in their eye too much."

"That ain't where I'd stick their microscope," said Gilman.

Bert listened, unsmiling. "So it's not funny," he said. "I agree. Four jobs this bird pulled and so far all we got is one lousy sneaker print. And I'll give odds he didn't even leave that much in the house. Except what he left on the second floor," he added soberly.

"Take good care of that plaster cast," said Flavin. "Don't drop it."

"I'll handle it like a new-born baby, pal, never fear. I'll take it back to the Lab in an armored truck." He caught their gaze and his eyes were deadly serious. "This is one bastard I'd enjoy throwing the switch on personally.

Flavin and Gilman trudged through the bushes, showed their badges to the patrolman at the front door and entered the house. They were in a magnificent center hall from which a mahogany stairway curved gracefully to the second floor.

A fingerprint man was going over the handrail of the staircase. He looked up, nodded and went back to his powders and brushes, working as slowly and delicately as a brain surgeon. The highly polished surface looked like a perfect fingerprint trap but the technician's mouth was bunched in weary resignation. He knew better. This inviting surface trapped only tired fingerprint men. The very old or infirm would grip a handrail and leave a nice clear cluster of whorls and ridges but the young and vigorous either did not use the rail at all or slid their hands over it, leaving a useless smear.

Generally speaking.

The surest way to pull a blooper in this business was to take something for granted. So you didn't take anything for granted. When you got a handrail you dusted every futile, tedious inch of it. The fingerprint man raised his eyes, grimaced and shook his head at Flavin.

"It's a rough one all round," he said.

"It sounds rough," Flavin agreed. "Getting much, Jerry?"

Jerry straightened up to ease his back and wiped the slow humid perspiration from his face with a handkerchief. "I don't know about the others," he said, "but I'm not. The guy wore gloves. We got that much from the dust around the cellar window right in the beginning, so anything we raise won't be his. Guys like that don't make booboos."

"There ain't no such animal, Jerry."

"Maybe not, but here's his fourth local job and God knows how many others around the country and he still hasn't left us a crumb."

Flavin said, "Luck," and, followed by Gilman, mounted the stairs, both very careful not to brush against the newel post or the handrail.

At the head of the staircase, a man sat cross-legged on the floor with a pad of graph paper on one thigh. Ahead of him stood a bronze gooseneck lamp bent low over a faint, blurred dust print which defined the characteristic sole pattern of a gymnasium sneaker on the light parquet floor bordering the carpet. Beside the man was a pair of calipers and a large round magnifying glass with a black handle. He was painstakingly sketching the print on the graph paper with meticulous strokes of a soft lead pencil, pausing frequently to use the calipers and compare the measurements with his drawing. The print, that of the left foot this time, was too faint to be photographed. The man had the serene, bemused air of a Sunday afternoon artist making a composition of the much-sketched fieldstone bridge in Old Brook Park. His smile was gentle and indulgent when Flavin and Gilman stopped and bent to look at the print more closely. The instep was unpatterned; a clutch pedal could wear the sole as smooth as that. The man obviously did not drive a car with an automatic shift, but then many thieves didn't. When you were in a squeeze, it took the old-fashioned manual shift to move you fast.

"This bird must be a hackie," said Gilman. "I mean, it don't make sense."

Flavin said, "Yeah." He knew what George meant. It had taken a lot of concentrated driving to erase the sole pattern in those specific spots. If the sneakers were merely old, the entire pattern would have been worn down. A busy thief had no time for pleasure driving. So, as George had indicated, this was a bird of a different feather. Whatever *that* meant.

The artist had taken another sketch pad from a cowhide briefcase and was reverently turning each page as if it were an original Rembrandt, pausing now and again to lean back and squint his eyes with cultured appreciation. His fair, thinning hair looked pink and he had the pale, ascetic face of a scholar or an incurable invalid. His name was Hartley Malcolm, a baptismal accident almost unknown outside the payroll department; his Headquarters name was Pimp McGimp or, for the sake of a dubious propriety, just McGimp. You had to be pretty crummy yourself to call a man "pimp" to his face when he really was not—except in a very special and macabre sort of way.

The sketch book—it was really a canvas-bound portfolio—lay open on his lap. "Before you gentlemen enter the chamber of horrors," he suggested in a tranquil voice, "I think it might be helpful if you viewed a study of the lady as she appeared prior to processing."

Flavin said curtly, "That's not our angle," but Gilman leaned over automatically as the McGimp turned the portfolio for his inspection.

It was a startling drawing, bold and sharp as a dry point etching. The woman lay on a twin-sized tester bed. Her head strained back and her teeth bit whitely on the bandana handkerchief bound across her rigid jaws. She was dead, strangled on the gag first thrust into her mouth. It was only a black-and-white pencil sketch but it left no doubt in your mind that the face was blue. You could *see* the cyanosis, typical of strangulation cases. Her arms were tied behind her back. She wore a nightgown but those last desperate struggles had bunched it above her hips. The body was slim but the breasts were full and the thighs deep and rich. She was twisted and convulsed, her back arched, the legs wide and thrusting.

It was vividly drawn, complete in detail, more graphic than a crime report. It told you all you needed to know about the mechanics of violence.

But there was more to it and the rest was not something you could put your finger on. It was implicit, done without exaggeration or distortion. The McGimp's technique was flawlessly photographic, yet in some way he had shamed the young woman. The agony of violent death destroys dignity, tramples pride and makes garbage of the remainder.

The McGimp had gone beyond that, for he also shamed the viewer. His portfolio of death was full of similar drawings, nudes and semi-nudes, male and female, shamed and shaming. He enjoyed exhibiting them. His expression remained gentle and indulgent as he slowly turned page after page and the viewer stared as if in helpless fascination. When he spoke it was only to give the name of the victim, the date and nature of the crime. After that, he had merely to give you a bemused smile in passing and you felt naked and dirty. His drawings were not of men and women who once had breathed warmly, yawned and stretched upon awakening, ate, laughed, kissed, loved and after looked into a mirror to re-apply lipstick or comb their hair. McGimp's men and women had always been the way he showed them and from beyond whatever rim of darkness they had come had also sprung the human race. That was the way he made you feel.

Aside from this, he was one of the best police artists in the state and more valuable to the Department than most technicians in the Crime Lab. *Good* police artists are highly trained specialists and extremely rare.

He permitted Gilman to look at the drawing for several moments, and then murmured, "This, of course, is only an example of simple strangulation. The unfortunate girl choked on a wad of absorbent cotton. Strangulation by rope, on the other hand, may affect the, ah, shall we call her the stranglee?—affect her differently. The face may be suffused with blood or be completely pale, depending upon the position of the knot or pressure point. Now I'd like to show you—"

"Before you go on, Doc," Gilman interrupted, "I just want to say you got this picture all wrong."

McGimp's head jerked. "What are you talking about?" he asked sharply.

"The eyes. I seen a few strangle cases myself and the eyes always bug out like cue balls. The way you put them down, she looks like she's only sleeping and's having a bad dream."

"I drew it exactly as it was!"

"Okay. Maybe some people close their eyes when they can't stand what's going on. But here's another thing. You didn't put in no bruises. You put in everything else, but no bruises. There'd be at least a couple on her arms and legs. She'd of put up some kind of fight—unless she liked being tied and a hunk of cotton shoved down her throat. Or'd you just skip the bruises?"

"Have you seen the woman?"

"No, but the bruises—"

"This is ridiculous!" McGimp closed the portfolio with an angry snap.

"Have it your own way, Doc," Gilman straightened up and shrugged. "You were there. I wasn't. Sorry to keep you waiting, Jeff."

"Don't mention it," Flavin grinned. "It was a pleasure." And then as they walked up the hall toward the bedroom in which flash bulbs were popping, "That's the first time I ever saw anybody give McGimp the needle."

"I wasn't needling him," said Gilman seriously. "Maybe he's right. Some people don't bruise easy. But what an oddball."

"He's all of that, George."

"You know what the trouble with him is?" Gilman chuckled for the first time. "If he's got a girl friend, he's sore because she ain't dead enough."

2.

A fingerprint man was bent over the shaped glass top of a dainty Sheraton dressing table when Flavin and Gilman entered the bedroom. A photographer, his camera dangling from his hand between his knees, sat on the edge of the tester bed, smoking a cigarette. A blanket had been thrown over the bed but the body was gone. At the far window stood big Harry Muir, patronizing the two precinct detectives, Urquhart and Jenner. Muir's banter was the lingua franca of Headquarters—obscene abuse.

Muir turned and glared at Flavin and Gilman. He was hot and sweaty and had worked himself into a lather because the whole damn Department had its eye on this one.

He said, "Just a minute," to the precinct men and strode down the room toward Flavin and Gilman, slapping a wad of bright yellow Evidence Tags against the palm of his hand.

"What the hell you think you're doing here?" he demanded.

"Relax, Harry," said Flavin mildly. "Your boss sent us. We're on the burglary angle."

"I thought you were on Pawnshop."

"The Dutchman asked us to give you and Tutchek the benefit of our superior experience."

Muir scowled. He didn't want to get fouled up with the Dutchman. "Well, what is it?" he asked ungraciously.

"What did the M.E. give you on the Sturgis woman?"

"Time of death. Between two and four A.M. Strangled. Nothing else till the autopsy. This your idea of working on Burglary?"

"It establishes the time, doesn't it?"

Muir grunted. "Anything else?"

"Later maybe. We'll see what comes up as we go along."

"Okay, but if something comes up make sure you ask me or Ben first. This's been messed up enough as it is. Stick to your angle and we'll get along."

Harry turned his back and walked to the window beyond the bed, flexing his big arms. Ah hell, he thought moodily.

Flavin, Gilman, Urquhart and Jenner gathered in the outside corner of the bedroom. Urquhart and Jenner had worked on the other three burglaries.

"And baby," said Jenner ruefully, "did us and Cappy Rhode get it from Foxy down Headquarters this morning!"

"Sure," said Flavin, "but how about Cappy? Did he soft-pedal it for the record? He's a boy who likes the best of it."

"I wouldn't know," said Jenner, closing his face against Flavin after a quick glance at Urquhart. Jenner was a thin, gray man who likes to air his woes; Urquhart was more solid and less talkative. When he said his piece, it was usually to keep Jenner from gabbing too much.

"It's bad, Flav," he said, shaking his head. "This is the fourth, and all by one guy in a six-block area."

"How do you know it's the same guy?"

"Same MO," he said, surprised at the question.

Flavin pointed his chin at the bed on which the woman had died in such agony. "That wasn't the same MO."

"An accident. That's no way to knock off somebody. Takes too long."

"She raped?"

"Don't ask me," said Urquhart warily. "Wait for the autopsy."

"Somebody must have asked the M.E. What'd he say?"

"Just an offhand didn't think so, but that's his opinion, not mine. That end of it, I don't make any guesses."

"That's right. It doesn't pay to take chances."

"Okay, rib me, but you didn't get laid out by Foxy this morning."

Gilman started, "Was there—" but his normally hoarse voice played a trick and scraped out as if the words were a handful of roughly crushed stone. He hawked, looked around for a place to spit, then swallowed. "Was she beaten up any?" he asked finally.

"No-o," said Urquhart. "I wouldn't say so."

"Not a scratch on her," said Jenner. "So no rape, unless like the Chinaman says, she relaxed and enjoyed it."

"That's the no bruises then," said Gilman to Flavin, referring to the McGimp's drawing.

"It's still not enough to make it the same guy," said Flavin.

Urquhart gestured vaguely at the doorway or an obscure and unnamed part of the house. "We got a description. From Mr. Sturgis. He's the husband. It tallies with the first three. The guy wore dark sneakers, dark pants, a dark sweatshirt and a woman's stocking pulled down over his face with two eyeholes cut in it."

"Where's Sturgis?"

"Hospital."

Flavin lifted his eyebrows. "And you still say it's the same MO. I thought this bird just slapped the husbands on the cheek or wrist or someplace. A few slaps don't send you to the hospital. Or did Sturgis have a nervous breakdown?"

"Okay, rib me," said Jenner sadly. "It ain't the first time. But just listen for a change, will you, Flav? The guy started out with the slapsie routine, but Sturgis, he puts up a battle. He's a pretty powerful guy for a rich gee. Takes care of his muscles. Goes down the H.A.C. every day. He should have stood still. The guy laid him out with a jack handle. We found it on the floor of his bedroom."

"A what?"

"A jack handle. I know a jack handle when I see one. A bumper jack handle."

Flavin looked at Gilman, nodding. "The same MO," he said dryly. "The guy fancied it up a little, that's all."

"Variety's the spice of life, like they say."

"If there's anything I hate," crabbed Jenner, "it's the ulcers you birds're giving me. It was the same MO. He got in the same way, he was dressed the same way, he started in to slap the same way, and it would of ended the same way except Sturgis thought he had muscles. It could of happened to any of the first three guys if they put up a scrap. What more do you want?"

"Not a thing," said Flavin. "I was just wondering if Mrs. Sturgis always tried to swallow a wad of cotton when she went to bed, that's all."

"Did you ever see a guy like this before?" Jenner asked Urquhart morosely. "Nobody slips on a banana peel. They're always pushed."

Urquhart looked at Flavin and Gilman without friendliness.

"Shut up and listen, stupid," he told Jenner in a sarcastic voice. "These big time Headquarters dicks know more about the business than you and I could forget in a month of Sundays."

"Including Leap Year," said Jenner.

"And time-and-a-half for overtime," said Flavin, grinning their resentment aside. "That's our graft."

He knew what was the matter. They were afraid they'd pulled a booboo somewhere along the line and were going to be shown up. Men like Urquhart and Jenner depressed him.

"I don't mind being educated," said Jenner. "I like it. I—"

Flavin, impatient with their curdled griping, interrupted and asked if Sturgis' wall safe had been rifled, as had the safes in the other burglaries.

"Of course it was," said Urquhart nastily. "We said it was the same MO from beginning to end, didn't we?"

"In Sturgis' bedroom," said Jenner. "Open and empty. Not being experts from Headquarters, we came across it by accident. We didn't *know* it was there."

Expecting the same treatment, Flavin asked for the names and addresses of the first three burglary victims.

"See, he knows the MO backwards and forwards," Urquhart informed Jenner smugly, "except what it's all about."

"Don't be dumb," said Jenner. "Headquarters dicks're psychic."

It made them feel better to find that Flavin, for one, knew less of the case than they did. They gave him the information in a more friendly fashion. Urquhart took out his notebook and read slowly, spelling each name.

1. Francis Tetley, 11 Stockton Place
2. Henry Bridges, 23 Circle Drive
3. John Harris Copland, 7 Pomander Walk

"Tetley?" Flavin pondered the name. "Any connection with Howards-Tetley Safe and Lock on Jackson Street?"

"That's the joke," said Urquhart. "He owns the outfit and it was one of his own de luxe model safes that was cracked. Opened like a swinging door."

"Where's Sturgis' bedroom?"

"Down the hall. We'll go with you."

"Never mind. We'll find it."

"Wait a minute, Flav," said Urquhart quickly. "You're not sore because we ribbed you a little, are you? Hell—"

"I'm not sore. We work faster alone, that's all. Anyway, we'll be out of here in five minutes."

"As long as you're not sore."

"I'm not that touchy."

Harry Muir did not turn from his window when Flavin and Gilman walked from the room, not even with a characteristic warning not to get their asses in a sling. That was not like Harry but he was trying to get his teeth into this thing. It was not an out-and-out kill like a shooting or a stabbing and he didn't like that. In a shooting, for instance, you could set up the pattern sooner or later. This didn't have a homicide pattern in the usual sense and at the same time it definitely was homicide because it happened during the burglary. Any death caused by the commission of a crime was murder. That was the law. But basically it was a burglary case and he and Ben Tutchek were not burglary specialists. They had to depend on Flavin and Gilman.

3.

As they walked down the softly green-carpeted hall, Gilman asked curiously, "What was the matter with those two anyway?"

Flavin shrugged. "Oh, some precinct guys think Headquarters always give them the crappy end of the stick."

Gilman thought it over. "Sometimes it does work that way," he said judiciously. "Though I don't know as Headquarters gets it so easy. They should be given a dose of it."

"Ever wish you were back on the beat, George?"

"Nope. I wanted to make Sergeant or get this."

"Why?"

"I thought it was time I moved up. I'm thinking of getting married."

Flavin's mouth opened as if to say, married! but thank God it didn't come out.

"You've picked out the girl?" he asked idiotically in his hurry to say *something*. Of course George had picked out a girl. Who else would be have picked out? An alligator?

"She picked me out, to tell the truth." You couldn't blame George for swelling his chest a little. "Not that she picked me *up,* or anything like that. I go to the library sometimes. She works there and one way and another she got me to talking, then I took her out and well you know how it goes. She's a good-looking woman." Gilman's voice deepened and the emotion, the big emotion, came out like a sustained cello note played by Casals.

"I'd like to meet her sometime, George, if you don't mind."

"Well—sure," Flavin felt rather than saw Gilman's quick, narrow glance, and he squirmed, the way *he'd* wise-cracked about women sometimes. "Have dinner with us, but all we do is just kind of sit around and talk."

"I like to talk," said Flavin. "You'll probably have to shut me up." And he swore a heart-felt oath that if this woman was using George because she was bored and wanted to get out of the library, or because he was her last chance for a permanent meal ticket, he'd—he'd what? Bust it up? George wouldn't thank him. Flavin touched his lips and pointed to the doorway ahead. "We'll set up the date later, George."

"Hannah Beale," said George, and this was trusting Flavin all the way. "Her name. She cooks. What do you like for dinner? She cooks anything."

"Meatloaf and potato pancakes. But later."

Another fingerprint and photographer team—the whole Lab was out on this case!—were at work in Sturgis' bedroom while Ben Tutchek leaned against a nearby wall, joking with them and gesturing with a casual cigarette.

Ben was another big man, six feet four, as big as Harry Muir. Externally, they were much alike ... dark brown hair, brown eyes, broad face, heavy bones, big-fisted, big shoulders, thick and deceptively clumsy-looking arms; bold, lusty men. The atmosphere in here was much different from the atmosphere in Carol Sturgis' bedroom, just as Ben was different from Harry Muir. Ben was quiet and pleasant; rough, but that was expected of a Homicide dick.

He acknowledged Flavin and Gilman with a smile and a nod. "Am I glad to see you guys," he said. "The Dutchman called and said you'll take the Burglary off our necks. You're riding the tiger, baby. This bird don't leave nothing for nobody never nohow under no circumstances. No prints, no anything. Unless you brains have a make on him."

"Nothing," said Flavin. "You?"

"Ask the boys. They're the scientists. Lots of prints, all Sturgis. The other crud wore gloves like always."

On the broad, leather-topped Chippendale kneehold desk lay a length of half inch metal rod, spread with rusty-seeming spots—encrusted blood. A bright yellow Evidence Tag was tied to it. It was about two feet long and bent in the middle. Gilman stared intently.

"A jack handle, all right," he said. "And the car was too heavy for it. That bend in the middle."

"It was bent over Sturgis' skull," said Ben dryly, and then to Flavin, "Gilman? He's new. Transfer?"

"From the Ninth," said Flavin. "Patrolman. Ask him a question, any question."

"Don't get on your high horse, baby. I was just asking."

Still, Ben Tutchek regarded Gilman with interest. George was crowding forty, he guessed. Not often an old beat cop was promoted to the Bureau. Too set in their ways; brains stalled.

"Why's he say jack handle right off the bat?" he asked Flavin. "It might be any hunk of half-inch iron."

"One end is flattened to take off hub caps," Gilman pointed out. "Homemade. You can see the hammer marks. Ball peen hammer. Those little cup dents. The other end is scored where it was put in the jack.

"Sherlock," said Ben without sarcasm.

"*I* listen when he says something, Ben."

"I said don't get on your high horse, Irish," Tutchek's voice hardened. "It could be a pinch bar, couldn't it? How's about that, Gilman?"

"A pinch bar's no good without a claw for pulling nails. And there's those marks where it went in the jack. Compare it with any jack handle. They're all dented the same way."

"You're probably right but I'm not taking your word till it goes through the Lab."

"You're a lousy Polack," said Flavin.

"He means I put you through the hoops," Ben smiled at Gilman.

"How's Sturgis doing?" Flavin asked.

"Not good, not bad. He's in Graystone Memorial with a possible fracture. Right front forehead."

"Sounds like he was smacked by a southpaw."

"Not necessarily. A rightie could have given it to him with a backhander. Kicked him in the balls too after he fell, judging from the bruises, according to the M.E. Nice boy, eh?"

"He gave you the description?"

"He was laying on the floor and mumbling away when we got here. Ninety-nine percent you couldn't understand and the rest we coaxed out of him, a few words here, a few words there."

"But he was still able to give you the description."

"He didn't *give* it to us. He was still fighting the guy in his mind. We pieced some of it together and guessed at the rest."

"How come he had a separate bedroom? Were he and his wife on the outs?"

"They got along okay—when they saw each other. He traveled a lot. Consulting engineer. Big time, rich as hell. Never relaxed. Sleeping in the same room with him was like sleeping with a machine shop and he liked to get up in the middle of the night, turn on all the lights and work." Ben canted his head at the big desk.

"He was in bad shape but managed to call the precinct?"

"What's on your mind, Jeff?"

"Husbands have knocked off their wives before and faked the burglary."

"And vice versa," Tutchek agreed. "I know. He's not in the clear, don't worry."

"Who did call in?"

"A friend of the wife—Fay Copland. Her and Carol Sturgis was supposed to drive down to Atlantic Highlands for a day on the beach with friends."

"How'd she get in the house?"

"The front door was unlocked, she said. The Sturgises were like that. If they came home half lit, nothing got locked. We'll check on that, naturally."

"And the girl? It wouldn't be the first time a friend of the wife was playing around with the husband on the side."

"I'll tell you what, baby. You work the homicide and I'll take a whack at Burglary. How's that?"

"Now who's on his high horse?"

Ben waved his cigarette in negation. He remained smiling and patient. He chuckled. "You wouldn't do bad, baby. I mean it. She'd of planked for the husband, or I miss my guess. Maybe she did. That didn't go by for a called strike, Jeff-boy. We're putting a twenty-four hour tail on that sexy little redhead. Rough and smooth. The same goes for Sturgis, when and if."

A rough tail was a man who shadowed the suspect and deliberately permitted the suspect to spot him. In theory and sometimes in practice, this method was designed to panic the suspect into a rash and possibly incriminating act. Of course, the first thing the suspect did was lose the tail. The shadower permitted this to be done and that's where the smooth tail came in. He took over at that point. Again theoretically, the suspect was unaware of the second tail. When the men could be spared, a team of detectives worked the smooth tail, lessening the chance of their being spotted or lost by the suspect. It was seldom the understaffed Bureau could spare two detectives for a tail job, which was long and tedious and most times a pure gamble.

"All I want," said Flavin, "is to make sure this is a burglary. Where's the safe?"

Ben pointed his cigarette at the desk. One end was pulled out from the wall and behind it was the safe in the wall. It was the twin-dial Home-Vault model put out by the Norwich Safe Company, Norwich, Connecticut. A rugged little box.

"Anything on it?" Flavin asked the fingerprint technician.

"A glove print inside. That's all. The rest were just smears as though he rubbed over with the glove."

Flavin turned and looked thoughtfully at Tutchek's broad face.

"Well, what do you think, Ben?" he asked. "You're Homicide. You know about things like this. Does it smell?"

Tutchek lifted one noncommittal shoulder and let it fall. "Hard to say, Jeff-boy."

"It's pretty damn fancy for a homemade kill."

"It's fancy, all right. As fancy and cockeyed as the first three burglaries."

"Then you're not exactly enthusiastic on the Walt Sturgis-Fay Copland angle."

"Putting it that way, baby, no. Too wide-open if they been playing footsie, too obvious."

"Then you think it's straight burglary with an incidental kill."

"Uh-uh. I didn't say that and I ain't gonna. It don't pay to overlook even the outside bets."

"So it's an outside bet."

"Maybe yes, maybe no."

"In other words, it would be a good idea if Burglary got the lead out."

Tutchek winked good-naturedly at Gilman and angled his thumb at Flavin. "He should of been a pepper instead of a mick. All he knows is, you open your mouth and he sticks his fist in it. I'll tell you something, Gilly-boy. A trade secret. One of the most foolproof ways to knock off a guy is to go up to him in a crowd, stick a knife in his back and walk away. Anybody can figure it out if they stop to think."

Gilman, who looked as if he'd been thinking of meatloaf and potato pancakes and ways and means of telling Hannah Beale he was inviting a friend to dinner, said seriously, "It's all up in the air as far as I can see. Until you can say Sturgis was giving the Copland girl a toss and went overboard, we're right back where we started."

It was a moment before Tutchek laughed. He roared. Ben Tutchek laughing was something to see. His face turned a delighted red, tears streamed from his eyes, he slapped his thigh and his entire baggy gray seersucker suit billowed and shook like an Arab tent in a high wind as Gargantuan guffaws rolled out of him. It was a vast, convulsive act of God, like a tornado or an earthquake.

"There, that puts us in our place," he gasped at Flavin. "*Now* do you feel like a mastermind?"

Flavin grinned at Gilman, who seemed puzzled and asked, "Maybe I missed something?"

Ben Tutchek bellowed anew with laughter, "Uh, uh, baby. You didn't miss a damn thing. You put it and me and old Flavin in a nutshell. That's what we get for talking out loud. Hey Jeff-boy, why don't you sic this fool-killer on the walking menagerie?"

"Glad to," Flavin circled his thumb and forefinger at Gilman in a complimentary gesture of you-did-okay-man. "Who is it?"

"Pudge Zoch in Auto Theft. Everybody knows old Pudge." Everybody certainly did. Pudge Zoch was just about the filthiest man in the Bureau. Mouth filthy.

"Pudge?" said Flavin. "I've heard him called a mutt, if that's what you mean."

"It absolutely and positively ain't what I mean. He's the Central Park Zoo in person. He works like a beaver, sweats like a horse, eats like a pig, stinks like a skunk and screws like a rabbit!"

His Herculean laughter thundered and pealed and reverberated long after they left the room and walked up the hall to the stately mahogany-and-ivory-white staircase.

"What a guy," said Gilman.

"His build-ups're always better than his jokes, but you'll like him. Believe it or not, he's a wheel in the Bureau. When the Dutchman retires, Ben's next in line. I got that straight from—" Flavin had been about to say Tom Walsh but finished lamely, "the horse's mouth."

"I believe it. He's a tough man."

"Tougher than you think."

"He couldn't be," said George with emphasis.

4.

At the foot of the majestically curving stairway, two towering white-paneled doors, mounted by a deeply scrolled pediment, opened from the living room and a Homicide cop named Kitteridge walked out, self-consciously bumbling beside a tall girl with embering hair, darkly brown-red. She was not a girl who'd ever have her picture in a *Vogue* advertisement. She was about five feet six and her figure was beautiful but full and deep—breasts, hips and thighs. She had been taught to walk by a very good teacher or her lithe grace was natural. Probably a combination of both.

She was aloof in that special way of the rich, but not remote. Her manner may have been but not her mouth. Definitely not her mouth. Ben Tutchek had called her sexy—Flavin was almost positive this was Fay Copland—but sexy was a meager word. It was hard to describe her mouth. No one word was adequate. It was a wide mouth, generously shaped, tilted just slightly at the ends. A mouth like thousands of others—except for what it expressed.

On impulse, Flavin said, "Miss Copland? I'd like to talk to you before you go. I'm Detective Flavin and this is Detective Gilman, Headquarters."

"But I've already been talked to, Detective Flavin." Her voice was light and cool, a voice with which you talked to detectives.

"Ben Tutchek and Harry Muir," said Kitteridge, flatly dismissing Flavin and Gilman—two errand boys from Pawnshop, in his opinion. He was Detective 3rd/grade Kitteridge, Homicide.

"This is a different angle, Miss Copland." Flavin ignored Kitteridge. "Do you mind?"

"Does it matter if I do?"

"Sorry, but no."

"Very well."

She turned and walked back into a gracious living room which would have delighted the hearts of the 18th Century Adam brothers, architects and Designers Of Furniture For The Gentry.

She sat on a long, slender sofa, lit a cigarette, and crossed her magnificent legs. She was wearing an imported cotton print frock, patterned with adapted primitive geometric angles. It was green in varying degrees of brilliance and saturation, pointing up her tan eyes and hair, now fired by a slashing beam of sunlight. She was bare-legged, as far as Flavin could see, which encompassed a lot of rich territory when he sank into the low chair facing her. She was deliberately oblivious of his glance, and nothing can be more contemptuously oblivious than that. Gilman took up a position at the cavernous marble fireplace and became engrossed in the fascinating weave of his mashed-in Panama hat. He was possibly being true to Hannah Beale.

"Well—" said Flavin, wondering whether he should beat or bed this snooty wench, but neither was practical.

"Well what, Detective Flavin?" she asked, nasty-nice. "Oh dear, I just asked a question. That's *lèse-majesté*, isn't it?"

"You're a movie fan, aren't you, Miss Copland?"

"A— Good lord, no!"

"Don't be ashamed of it. Lots of people are. You've been a fan for quite a while, I'd say. Who's your favorite screen star?"

She stared at him and waved the cigarette smoke from before her face to clear the view. Her mouth drew together and became wary. "I don't understand," she said suspiciously.

"It's very simple. Movies fans have a tendency to type people, themselves included. In detective-suspense movies, on the average, the gal is well stacked and makes wise cracks; newspaper reporters are rummies and never take off their hats and make wise cracks too; hero's a private eye, makes chumps of the police but doesn't have to try very hard because they're all Keystone Cops to begin with. Of course if the hero is a cop, then his partner is the chump. That would be Detective Gilman there by the fireplace. Say something stupid for the lady, George."

"She shows a lot of leg," said Gilman stolidly. "Does she sell snapshots of herself like the fat lady in a side show?"

Fay Copland flushed and automatically pulled her skirt hem down to cover her knees. "I'm sorry," she said quietly. "I deserved that. But it's been a horrible morning and I—I don't know why I'm not hysterical. You may not think so but it wouldn't take much, Mr. Flavin."

"We don't enjoy it either, Miss Copland, but we have to ask questions. People don't tell us things of their own accord. Sometimes we have to drag it out of them. Do you know what a stoolie—a stool pigeon is?"

"An—an informer?"

"You're partly right. His real business is taking bets on horses, running a floating crap game or something on the fringe of the law. We'd like to put him in jail where he belongs but he gives us information that people like you withhold for, let's say, personal or business reasons and give us a lot of worn-out wise cracks instead. Pretty lousy, isn't it?"

"I'll answer your questions, Mr. Flavin," she said in a diminished voice. "I have no personal or business reasons not to. It's just that—" she shook her head as if to clear it of unpleasant thoughts and images. "I'm not accustomed to—to this."

Flavin nodded. He knew exactly what she meant. A strangled corpse is always a nightmarish horror, not a spectacle you'd want to look at every day. But she should see some of the bloated messes they pulled out of the river, especially after the mud crabs had been feeding. Or a knifing victim with her face slashed off and her belly spilling out on the bedsheets. Or what was left of the passengers after a bad DWI smash-up. On the other hand, nobody should have to look at such senseless, sickening debris. Even cops had been known to puke.

Anyway, he had put it to this Copland girl—mildly—and had her in the right mood.

"Your father's house was knocked over before this one," he said. "How much was taken?"

"Nothing he can't afford, although he's furious all the same. About three thousand dollars and mother's diamond necklace. That's what really made him furious. It was new, a wedding anniversary gift. June twenty-fourth. The older jewelry wasn't touched."

"It was all in a home safe?"

"Yes. Behind a Duncan Phyfe drop-leaf table in the south sitting room."

"You've seen this safe."

"Many times."

"What kind is it?"

"What kind? A wall safe. It has three dials and a knob. Not a gadget you can open with a bobby pin, I assure you."

Three dials. Very unusual for a small house safe. That would be, let's see—Flavin pillaged his memory—oh yeah, Howards-Tetley put out a three-dial job, their top grade Guardian model. Burglar-proof as all hell except sometimes.

"Does your father always keep that much money in the house?" he asked.

"Sometimes more. He likes to have money handy. I don't know why."

Flavin had a fair idea. Old Copland was founder and president of the Stone Bridge Republican Club which always elected its nominated councilman and a mayor or two in the past. Copland could give lessons in dirty politics to Lace Malone who ran the Point ward. ("Lace" for lace-curtain Irish, as Malone quipped.) Copland knew how to spend money on elections. Anyway, that was the rumor. "Did the burglar go through the same slapping routine?" Flavin asked.

"Yes, and that was another thing that made him furious. That, and his having to tie and gag mother." She shivered and her hands tightened in her lap at the memory of what she had seen on the second floor in Carol Sturgis' bedroom.

"Aren't there any servants in this house?" Flavin asked quickly. "I haven't noticed or heard of any."

"Carol couldn't keep a houseman for a week, but she's not the only one. Mother's in despair and has to bribe our man with nights off and Lord knows what else. There's no agency in Hudson, you know. The nearest is in New York and they practically demand a bonus to come out here. Carol had a woman do the cleaning four times a week. The Acme

Garden Service takes care of the grounds. There never was a cook. Carol loved restaurants and so did Walt. They hired a caterer for parties."

Flavin filed that, too. This was the perfect set-up for any burglar.

"Were the Sturgises out last night?" he asked, thinking of the unlocked front door.

"*Every*body was out last night, Mr. Flavin. The Annual Nineteenth Hole Dance at the golf club."

"Was Mrs. Sturgis young?"

"My age." Fay Copland did not amplify.

"Attractive?"

"Very."

"Did she get along with her husband?"

"Anybody could get along with Walt. He was the most relaxed man I ever met."

"That's not the story I got. The way it came to me, he had chronic insomnia. That's why the separate bedrooms."

"Oh, pooh. He liked to work at night, that's all. My father is the same. Many men are like that."

"You seem to know Walt Sturgis very well," Flavin said.

Her eyes grew suddenly hard, her mouth angry. "I don't like that, Mr. Flavin," she said icily. "This is what you've been leading up to, isn't it? Now get this straight; Walt Sturgis was the husband of my best friend. They were happily married. I wouldn't interfere. I was not having a mousehole affair with him, which was what it would have amounted to," she said heatedly. "Furthermore, I simply cannot become amorous with short men. He was only five feet eight. In heels, I was taller than he. Does that answer your question?"

"But that wasn't the question." His grin did not disarm her.

"The hell it wasn't," she said, still angry. "You've been weaseling around to this ever since you started. I'm not stupid."

"You're being stupid now."

"Nuts!"

"I just want to find out what kind of man he is."

Her eyes narrowed but all she said was, "That's got nothing to do with the burglary."

"Part of the picture."

"The frame on the picture, you mean."

"That's the movies influence again, Miss Copland. We don't have to frame people, especially amateurs."

"Ah," she said satirically, "now it's a warning."

Flavin leaned forward the squashed out his cigarette in a sterling silver ash tray. "We're not getting anywhere, Miss Copland. You've become too hostile. I'll have to talk to you again another time."

"May I leave now?"

"You might just as well. We're wasting our time."

"Thank you, Detective Flavin. You're very kind."

She rose, threw her cigarette into the fireplace and, turning her back abruptly, strode from the room, her heels stabbing unprintables into the rug.

Flavin looked at Gilman and shrugged. George hoarsely cleared his throat, always the prelude to a long considered statement.

"If you ask me," he said, "she plopped for the guy every chance she got."

"Hell, yes," said Flavin.

Three

At the turn of the century, Mt. Windsor Avenue had been a leisurely, maple-shaded boulevard but now it was a bustling neighborhood shopping center. The rich lived in a confined six block keep; the rest was inhabited by Scots, Irish, English, a sprinkling of dour Sicilians, Germans and several brands of Scandinavians. Business was lively. There was a huge drugstore which sold everything but grass seed and chicken manure; four nationalities of delicatessens with wursts, strings of garlic and plump yellow cheeses, a large cerise salmon, and a pyramid of *limpa* bread in their windows; a Scots bakery, a kosher butcher shop, an Irish fish-and-chip luncheonette named The Dublin; Nivens' fancy supermarket and an I.G.A. supermarket, much less fancy; the Rivoli Theatre, a first-run movie house; a Quik-Serv Laundry And Dry Cleaner; a photography studio; three taverns; a travel bureau and a gleaming hardware store, with a third of its stock displayed on the sidewalk, among others.

And a newsstand. As Flavin and Gilman passed by, the newsboy brandished a paper at passing shoppers like a battle pennant and bugled, "Sex Maniac Slays Beautiful Babel Stone Bridge Socialite Raped!! Sensayshnil Murder Baffles Pleece! Readallabowdut!"

Flavin and Gilman glanced at each other and narrowed their eyes at the news story. Ed Turcott was too smart to put sex maniacs, beautiful raped socialites and baffled police into his report, yet the reader became more and more certain that an orgy of blood and lust had exploded in the Sturgis household. Turcott knew his business.

"Sex maniac," said Flavin. "That son of a bitch Turcott. The hell with him. Look, George, I'm going back to Headquarters. You run over and see what Tetley, Bridges and Copland have to say. There might be more than in Urquhart and Jenner's report."

He took a bus back to Headquarters, relaxing for twenty minutes and letting his thoughts wander pleasantly among the possibilities of his date with Joyce Ames. Dinner, of course. Something special. Maybe in the Esplanade Room on Revere Place. Then a show. A road company was doing *My Fair Lady*—or was it *Early To Bed?*—at the Lyric. A night club afterward? The Deerhead Inn at Rock Ridge near Powhatan Lake. There was a comedian who imitated things. Just things, not people. A hamburger on a soft roll with chili—the hamburger itself hated chili. Crazy but wonderful. He suddenly wanted Joyce to like the old Inn as much as he did.

And now here he was at Headquarters, which was anything but crazy and wonderful. Even if Joyce Ames did work there.

Sergeant McShane was Chief Clerk of Records in the Lab on the third floor and did not look it. Traditionally, Chief Clerks are sparse and sere, like leafless winter trees. Sergeant McShane was a portly man, blessed with creamy marshmallow-white hair, pink well-fed cheeks and the benign you-scratch-my-back-and-I'll-scratch-yours air of a ward leader who could get out the vote. He wasn't. He was wrapped up in the method and logic of his orderly files.

He saw Flavin approaching his desk, sighed and pushed aside the photostated bundle of crime reports on which he had been working. Not that he disliked Flavin. He didn't—but he didn't always understand the things Flavin said. Jokes, he supposed they were. Then, too, he unconsciously resented unpredictable people using his files, which were predictable and precise. Files were files; they shouldn't be disturbed by people.

However, he greeted Flavin with a grandfatherly smile. "Ah, Detective Flavin," he said. "And what can we do for you today?"

"Those burglaries up in Stone Bridge. What kind of job did you do on them?"

"A thorough job," said McShane reproachfully. "A most thorough job. Records and Identification, Known Burglars, Known Safe-crackers, Known Sadists, Known Sex Deviates, Released Prisoners, everything. *Most* thorough."

"How about the MO index?"

"We did that first, category by category."

McShane was happiest when talking of his files. He thought of them as *his* files. He described the Method Of Operation, or *modus operandi*, index, his favorite, the one he personally had perfected. It was a complicated cross-reference file in which every manner of crime imaginable was analyzed minutely, the solved and the unsolved alike. He constantly improved and enlarged it, adding subhead to subhead. The mere correlation of crimes with similar MO's was too elementary, too loose, too unsatisfactory. A crime had to be winnowed, sifted and broken down to its least common denominator or denominators. *That* was method, logic and order. Why, burglary alone had hundreds of subheads—burglars who chewed gum or sucked snuff to calm their nerves; burglars who blackened their faces with burnt cork; burglars who wore dark tight knitted wool caps. If a gum-chewing man held up a bank, the operation was filed under both Robbery and Burglary with subheads correlating other idiosyncrasies or characteristics and might even appear with additional subheads under Muggers, Narcotics (addicts and pushers), Auto Theft, Pickpocket and Vice, not to mention Shoplifting, Homicide, Safe-cracking, Kidnapping, dognapping and catnapping. McShane filed everything of the criminal, from toenails to tooth decay.

But ah, the Stone Bridge burglaries! A burglar who wore dark sneakers, dark pants, a dark sweat shirt, a nylon stocking mask and who was also a possible sadist and safe-cracker that was a new one on McShane, a new one on Communications, a new one on everybody from Los Angeles, California, to Bangor, Maine. A burglar who slapped his victims in their faces. A rare bird. Unique. And now Assault With A Deadly Weapon plus the killing of Carol Sturgis. There was a combination with infinite possibilities.

"Well thanks, Mac," said Flavin, who by this time had heard more of the history of filing systems than he needed to know. "As far as you're concerned, the Stone Bridge mess is a blank. Take down these names and see what you can dig up for me."

McShane pulled a nine-by-thirteen worksheet pad across the desk and held his fine-nibbed pen ready.

> Francis Tetley, 11 Stockton Place, owned the Howards-Tetley Safe & Lock Company, Inc.
>
> Henry Bridges, 23 Circle Drive, business unknown, hobbies unknown
>
> John Harris Copland, 7 Pomander Walk, political leader of the Stone Bridge ward
>
> Fay Copland, his daughter, occupation and hobbies unknown

Walter Sturgis, 23 Park Lane, consulting engineer, hobby trading in municipal bonds (?)

Carol Sturgis, his wife, hobbies unknown

"People like that," said McShane after he completed the list in his clear, neat handwriting, "We probably have no packages on them but there may be something in the Who's Who of local personalities I keep for reference. We'll check thoroughly, nevertheless."

Flavin said, "Thanks, Mac. Shoot it to me as you get it," and walked away before Sergeant McShane could get started on lesson number two: The Importance Of Unofficial Reference Data.

Police Lieutenant Ernest Leitner was a twenty-year man and a Carnegie Tech graduate. In civil life he might have been a top grade chemist. Among other things. But there was something wrong with him. A twist, a quirk or some personal oddity. He preferred the comparatively low-paying job in Headquarters. For two decades he had worked in the large white unhumanly antiseptic Lab at the south end of the third floor.

At the moment he was studying a group of still-damp photographs through a strong magnifying glass. The photographs were of seemingly meaningless smudges. They were far from meaningless. The smudges had been left on various surfaces by gloved fingers. Very special fingers. The fingers of a man who had committed four known burglaries and caused the death of a young woman named Carol Sturgis. On the zinc-topped bench beside him were more photographs, dry and mounted on three numbered sheets of cardboard—No. 1, Tetley; No. 2, Bridges; No. 3, Copland. Number four would be Sturgis.

He would rather have had the gloves themselves but the prints were sharp and clear. He studied the latest photographs and made concise notes on a sheet of paper labeled Sturgis. As the boys said, Ernie Leitner knew his stuff.

Later, when Flavin came to ask about the tests, Leitner had the information ready. The gloves used in burglaries one, two and three were made of light cotton with a close weave known commercially as Suedette. They sold for eighty-nine cents a pair and were distributed exclusively by the Woolworth chain of five-and-ten-cent stores. They were frayed at the fingertips and would probably have burst if worn again. Hence, a new pair of gloves had been used on the Sturgis burglary. The weave was coarse and had a horizontal rib; a workman's or gardening glove. It was manufactured locally by the Atlas Glove Company and the trade name was TufBoy. The retail price was thirty-nine cents. They were sold everywhere—drugstores, cheap haberdasheries, supermarkets, and garden supplies shops. The plaster cast of the sneaker print indicated a size thirteen foot, the foot of a tall man, six feet or over. The depth of the print in that particular loamy soil put the man's weight somewhere between one hundred and eighty and two hundred pounds. The width of the sneaker was E and it was fairly safe to say that the burglar was heavy-boned. As hands and feet usually matched, the killer had big hands. The sneaker itself had been sold by Sears Roebuck for three ninety-five and, except for the wear on the sole pattern, was the same as the pair worn in burglaries number one, two and three. The sneaker laced to the ankle and could be bought in white, gray and black. Half the phys ed pupils in local high schools used them as gymnasium shoes. An inexpensive sneaker like that was worn by at least a half million boys and men throughout the country; approximately ten thousand in the city of Hudson alone.

As Leitner spoke, he sounded as if he knew the tune but, for the life of him, could not remember the name.

"Thanks, Ernie," said Flavin, thinking of a half million men and boys all running around in similar sneakers. "Maybe we better put Woolworth and Sears Roebuck on the case."

2.

Flavin walked slowly and thoughtfully downstairs to the squadroom. He didn't like this one. He didn't like it at all. It had all the earmarks of another package for the Unsolved File. Four strikes in four weeks, and all in the same neighborhood. The take was ten thousand or better. A woman was dead; a man was in the hospital with a possible skull fracture. If the strikes had been made by a professional thief, the boy had long since left for parts unknown. Each job had been a solo, which meant that nobody knew from nothing except the thief himself. All he had to do was fence the jewelry and stay away from the City of Hudson until the heat was off. It took no more brains than that and, except for the Sturgis job, this thief had a brain or two in his head. The last strike had been rushed because the Sturgises had come home earlier than expected.

So there it was. The thief could lie on the beach at Miami and enjoy the fresh sea breezes and sunshine while the police went round and round up here in Hudson. Miami Beach was just the place for a smart thief. The place was full of spenders and he'd be among friends. And thus far, damn it, there was hardly a single bit of physical evidence to link him to any of the strikes. He could wrap the sneakers, gloves, pants, sweat shirt, nylon-stocking mask in an old newspaper, drop it in the nearest garbage can and the early morning Sanitary Department truck would obligingly carry it off to the city dump. A thief wouldn't bother carting such cheap articles around with him in a suitcase. He'd dump them as quickly as possible and get out of town. A twenty-dollar bill would buy him the same outfit no matter where he went—if he were damn fool enough to use the same MO after killing the Sturgis woman. Which he wouldn't. Nobody would. A headline killing scared everybody. There'd be a mess of God-fearing citizens among the thieves for a long while to come. Even the dips would go away and stay there.

And the police? They'd get it in the neck from all sides. That was the nice part of it, thought Flavin sourly.

Lieutenant Walsh was at the reception desk. This was not unusual. Sergeant Bauer had piles and four or five times a day he groaned to the men's room with his jar of ointment and Tom Walsh took the desk. His customer was a large blond boy, about twenty or so, whose face was bunched in the customary unhappy expression. Tom said something to the boy—apparently ordering him to stay there—rose from his chair and intercepted Flavin, taking him to an unoccupied table to the right of the water cooler—far enough away so the thirst-quenchers could not eavesdrop.

"I hear you had a run-in with Harry Muir out at the Sturgis place," he said in a mumbling voice.

"You know me better than that, Tom," said Flavin. "And you know Harry. There was nothing to it except a little loud talk till we got squared away, that's all. It didn't mean a thing."

Tom stood as if waiting irritably for Flavin to finish and then he said, "I don't want you to get in trouble with Homicide. You've got your job and they've got theirs. The Dutchman won't stand for interference and he won't listen to explanations or excuses. Keep that in mind. If you have any complaints, come to me."

Flavin stared in amazement. This was like telling him to act like an office boy, to say yessir and nossir and come running to the office if anybody shot spitballs at him. Did Tom Walsh actually expect him to do this? Or was Tom just plain sick? When you looked closely at him you could see the underlay of gray beneath skin which seemed already to be going slack and there was a kind of, well, you might almost call it a sour smell about it, although it wasn't exactly that. It was something like the smell of a man who'd been sick for a long time and was going to die. Tom wasn't going to die, of course, but he carried an aura of the sickroom wherever he went. That and the cloying odor of spearmint. He was always chewing spearmint gum, two or three sticks at a time. He had a wad of it in his mouth right now and was fumbling the wrapper from another stick. His movements were abstracted and heavy.

So instead of retorting angrily, Flavin said, "Sure, Tom. But there won't be any trouble. There never was."

"Well ... come to me if there is. Understand?"

"Sure," and then with a grin, "Who's the schoolboy you were talking to? Does he want to be a detective in six easy lessons?"

Tom turned his head and looked at the big unhappy blond boy at the reception desk. He shrugged. "Oh, him," he sounded depressed. "His mother made him come in. He's been acting up at home or something and we're supposed to scare him into behaving himself."

"Show him a picture of the Rahway Reformatory."

"Grace always wanted kids but she had that damn hysterectomy ten years ago. We were going to adopt one. A boy. She wanted a boy, but would've settled for anything. It takes a long time to adopt a kid. Too long. Too God damned long!" His face flushed. "She should've had a kid. It's my fault. If I'd pushed on Foxy or the Commission, we'd of had one, but I didn't want to throw my weight around. Other people wanted kids just as bad as us, I thought. We'll take our turn, I told Grace. She agreed. She said it was the right way to do, but I know she wanted one right away. Things'd have been a lot different—a lot different ... a lot ..."

He slouched, hands clenched, brooding at the dead brick wall of the past, and Flavin thought, Oh Christ! This was something he hadn't known before.

"After we knock off today," he suggested, "suppose we go down to the Mick's for a glass of beer and a plate of fish and chips."

Walsh looked blankly at him. "What? What'd you say?"

"I said, later on maybe we can go over to the Mick's for a few brews and his big seafood platter. He was asking for you the last time I was in there."

"One of these days, maybe," said Walsh vaguely. He seemed about to say more, but turned abruptly and went back to the reception desk. Flavin watched as Walsh talked to the uneasy blond boy, and it was worse than anything he'd seen around Headquarters. Tom wasn't being a cop; he was acting like an aggrieved parent. He refused to listen to a word the embarrassed boy had to say, but lectured him and shook a peevish finger in his face.

"What's the matter with you, Mankey?" he demanded in a hectoring voice. "What're you trying to do, worry your mother to death? You've got a good home—or don't you think so? Maybe you'd like to swap it for a room down in the Rahway Reformatory. Is that what you want?"

"No mister, honest, but—"

"Be quiet and listen to me. I've got men around here who make a specialty of turning bad boys into good ones, and if your mother complains to us just once more, I'll let one of them take you in hand. Now go home and behave yourself."

Good God, thought Flavin, he didn't even listen to the kid; tired old Bauer and his piles knew better than that. At least Bauer would listen and if the boy had anything to say, it would go down on the report. Tom hadn't given the boy a chance to open his mouth. That was the important thing. He'd gone off on a tangent of his own imagining. You didn't have to look twice to see he was headed for a breakdown.

And what could you do with a man like Tom Walsh? He was your boss. He gave the orders. You couldn't get close to him. You couldn't make him do anything he didn't want to do. It was heartbreaking when you remembered the big laughing go-to-hell guy he'd been before Grace was killed; a good cop and a real friend.

Flavin walked doggedly to his own desk. It was several minutes before he pulled the phone to him by its cord and called Ryan's Gym where his stoolie, Birdie Burdson, usually hung out with the pugs, the nickel-and-dime managers, grifters and all the other ragtag fast buck angle boys. A thickened punch-drunk voice answered and it was another several minutes before Flavin finally got Birdie.

Birdie said hurriedly, "Joe Reilly? Oh yes, yes indeed. It's been a long time, Joe, a long time. You're still the sportsman, I take it, eh? Ha, ha, ha. Nothing quite like the sport of kings. We do our best to improve the breed, don't we? If you'd like to make a contribution to a worthy cause, I might—just might, mind you—drop a hint about something very tasty in the fourth at Hialeah. Very tasty indeed."

Flavin grimaced sourly. The punch-drunk messenger boy obviously had his fat cauliflower ear right next to Birdie's at the receiver.

"The hell with Hialeah," he growled. "I want faster action. When and where can I see you?"

"Oh dear, I'm sorry, Joseph, indeed I am. It will have to be tomorrow, I'm afraid. Right now I have to pick up some new shirts at Bergman's Bargain Basement and unfortunately prior appointments will keep me busy for the rest of the day."

"Right."

Flavin hung up and glanced at his wristwatch and nodded. George Gilman wouldn't be back for another hour or so and that gave him plenty of time to meet Birdie at the shirt counter in Bergman's Basement.

It was a ten-minute walk to Bergman's Department Store. Birdie was already there, examining the tumble of cheap shirts with the critical air of a connoisseur choosing from among a choice selection of fifty-dollar Hathaway imports. He'd been one of the best inside men on the big con until he started fighting the bottle and lost his store. At a casual glance, he still looked prosperously stout, but there were the sagging cheeks and the general flab, the meticulously clean but worn clothes, and the faded blue eyes in which easy confidence had been dulled by a melancholy which precedes hopelessness. He had white hair and the shifty benign expression of a high Episcopal organist who'd been unfrocked for molesting little choir girls.

He waited until Flavin was beside him, flipping through the skimpy machine-made shirt, and then—ostensibly watching the legs of a passing salesgirl—he mumbled, "I apologize for these cloak and dagger tactics. It makes me feel like a bit player in one of Hitchcock's less notable failures. Indeed it does. But Arthur, the alleged pugilist who answered the telephone, was overcome by a case of momentary curiosity and all but sat in my lap."

"What's all this noise about a new heavy in town?" Flavin demanded.

Birdie hurried to assure him anxiously, "This is, or was, some visiting talent among us and, if you don't mind my saying so, speculation is rife."

"I want to find out who he is."

Birdie sighed. "Yes, I rather thought you might. It's the Carol Sturgis kill, isn't it?"

"Sturgis? I'm not on Homicide. I want to know about all heavies in the neighborhood before they get started."

"Well," said Birdie cautiously—his watery blue eyes had never ceased roving the crowded basement shopping area—"there appears to be some conjecture as to whether or not he made those Stone Bridge strikes. The Sturgis killing was bad news all around. There has been an exodus, Sergeant. The Children of Israel are leaving for the Promised Land, which does not happen to be the city of Hudson."

"I want you to circulate and see what you can pick up. I want anything, you understand? Anything you can get."

Birdie smiled benevolently. Now he was on a very satisfying footing. It cost money to circulate and Birdie was very fond of money, hard or soft, and Sergeant Jeff Flavin had come to him. It was one thing to promote a touch, but it was something quite different when a hardboiled fuzz put it to you as a proposition. *That* was money in the bank. Birdie delicately mentioned the fact.

"Twenty bucks," said Flavin shortly. "That's ten more than you expected, so don't argue. I'm giving you twenty because one of the spots I want you to hit is Billy Lowe's gambling joint on Stuyvesant Avenue. You're going to work, friend, or I'll turn you over to the wrecking squad. Now what's the talk you've been hearing?"

"Just—talk, that's all, Sergeant."

"Who's talking?"

"Well—everybody. You know."

"Give me a name."

Birdie hesitated, whispered, "Emmett Malone," and looked frightened.

As well he might. Emmett Malone was political boss of the Point, Hudson's jungle slaughterhouse.

Flavin was startled at this, but concealed it. "What'd he say?"

Birdie had the appearance of a man who had gotten himself into a mess but was too paralyzed to flee. "It—it really wasn't anything at all," he stammered. "He was up at the Gym. He owns a piece of that light-heavy Young Mickey Ross and was watching the workout. Somebody, well, somebody said something about the four Stone Bridge strikes and Malone said, 'He's a God damn fool!' That's all there was to it."

Flavin palmed a twenty-dollar bill and slid it beneath a pile of shirts. "Call me tonight. Call me tomorrow morning and keep calling me. Now get out there and sweat."

3.

Back in Headquarters, Flavin called Ben Tutchek, who was still working with photographers and fingerprint men in the Sturgis house.

"I might have something, Ben," he said, "but on the other hand, I might not. You'll have to take it for what it's worth."

"That's fine," said Tutchek. "That's just exactly what the boys have been giving me all morning—here's something or maybe it isn't. Well, let's have it."

Flavin laughed. "If it is something, you won't have to buy a ton of coal all winter. It's red hot."

"All right, all right, all right." Ben would stand for just so much horseplay on the job and then he told you off. "Let's have it."

Flavin nodded at the phone. It wasn't as funny as all that, anyway. "A friend of mine was up at Ryan's Gym this morning. Emmett Malone was there. He owns shares in a light-heavy named Young Mickey Ross. That's a good thing to know because you can meet him here or there without making it look official. Anyway, one of the yes-men mentioned the Stone Bridge take and Malone said, 'He's a God damn fool.'"

Tutchek waited. "Is that all?"

"That's all."

Tutchek swore. Malone was City Hall. He delivered the vote. This was an election year and City Hall was very touchy about such things as tangling with people who had the knack of marching citizens to the polls when necessary.

"Who told you this?" he asked.

"A talking dog." Flavin was not being funny. All phone calls went through the switchboard and certain people had been known to have a pipeline into Headquarters, one way or another; so the less said about Birdie the better.

Ben understood, and grunted. "Is this straight?"

"Straight, Ben. Odds on."

"I'll work on it from the other end and God help me if I have to bring him in for questioning. Election year," he added bitterly, "of all the stinking times in the world, election year! And him with The Point vote in his back pocket!"

"That's what I said—it's a headache either way. Another thing, the word is, this is a new heavy in town."

"If he's still in town, which he ain't. But thanks. Flav. It's a bitch, isn't it? How're you coming?"

"Nothing yet."

"Well, it's still too soon to tell. If we've got time, we'll get together later in the day and see if we can come up with something." He swore again wearily, and hung up.

George Gilman plodded in a few minutes afterward and he and Flavin sat down at the desk and George brought out his notebook. He really didn't need it. He had an IBM memory. His report was concise. Boiled down, it was this:

Francis Tetley, owner of the Howards-Tetley Safe & Lock Company, Jackson Street. Howards had been dead for fifteen years and although Tetley now controlled the company, the original name was kept. Tetley was a peppery little man with bristling gray hair, like a bad-tempered airedale. His wife was a fatso and had migraine headaches.

"As who wouldn't, with Tetley yapping around the house morning, noon and night," said Gilman. "He's a guy I can do without."

The burglar entered their bedroom between two and three A.M., dressed in dark sneakers, dark pants, dark sweatshirt and a woman's nylon stocking with two holes cut in it pulled down over his head for a mask. Tetley said he was a big man—six foot two or three, weighed over two hundred pounds, strong as a bull. He forced Tetley to tie and gag the Wife, and then slapped Tetley several times back and forth across the face, called him a "two-faced moneybag," and made him open the safe. A Tetley-made safe, of course. Tetley tried to say it was a custom job with a time lock and the burglar called him a "stinking liar," and said he'd open it himself if Tetley wanted a few lumps first. Tetley opened the safe. The burglar then kicked Tetley's butt and knocked him out with a rap on the side of the neck, after calling him a this-and-that two-faced moneybag again.

The second victim was Henry Bridges, 26 Circle Drive, retired. He was kind of tall and bulky and looked as though he'd cry on your shoulder if you let him. His wife, who insisted on being present, was also tall and bulky, but didn't look as though she'd cry on anybody's shoulder. Both said the burglar was about six feet tall and weighed no more than a hundred and eighty pounds. He was dressed the same and the MO was about the same, except that he didn't call Bridges any names but merely laughed at him "in a nasty, sneering way" before knocking him out with a blow on the side of the neck. Also, he didn't make Bridges open the safe. That, apparently, had been done earlier. It was a Tetley-made safe.

Number three was John Harris Copland, 7 Pomander Walk, founder and president of the Stone Bridge Republican Club. If you believed the talk, he didn't mind paying money to get the kind of vote he wanted from the 15th ward.

"I believe it," said Gilman. "He acts like what he don't own, he can buy, and the hell with you."

Copland was a tall, lean, bald arrogant old man with an aquiline nose. (Gilman called it an eagle beak.) His wife was visiting her sister in Virginia. The MO was exactly the same as in the Bridges' house, and the description was the same, even to the height and weight of the burglar. Copland's safe had also been made by the Howards-Tetley people.

According to the victims, the loot was:

1. Tetley— $10,000 in cash and about $18,000 in jewelry. Some of the pieces were heirlooms and irreplaceable.

2. Bridges—$2,500 in cash and a new diamond and emerald dinner ring insured for $5,000. The older family jewelry was not touched.

3. Copland—$3,000 in cash and a newish diamond necklace insured for $12,000. The older family jewelry was not touched.

Nobody knew as yet how much had been taken from the Sturgis house. On his way back to Headquarters, Gilman had stopped at the Graystone Memorial Hospital. Walt Sturgis did not have a fractured skull but had been badly beaten and was under heavy sedation. So far, however, the MO in the Sturgis place was more or less like the other three, except that Sturgis' safe had been made by the Norwich Safe Company, Norwich, Connecticut.

Flavin tilted back in his chair and regarded the sheet of paper on which he had scribbled a few notes. "Old man Tetley's lying by the clock," he said finally.

Gilman grinned his pleasantly homely frog-grin. "Yeah," he said. "That man mountain that walked in and swang him around like an Indian club. Bridges and Copland put the guy at six foot and around one-eighty pounds and I take their word for it."

"That, too," said Flavin. "But I'm talking about this ten thousand in cash and eighteen in jewelry and family heirlooms. The thief didn't touch the old-fashioned junk in either the Bridges or the Copland jobs. He'd be out of his mind if he did. He couldn't fence it, give it away or donate it to charity."

Gilman smote his forehead. "That went by for a called strike. I didn't even see it. I get it now. New stuff, you can sell; old stuff, it's a trademark."

"It would have to be broken up, and once you start that, you're down on the floor with the nickels and dimes. So Tetley gave you a line about the family heirlooms, and if he gave you a line about that, he lied about the rest of it. Maybe yes on the cash, but I doubt it—ten thousand, my God!—the jewelry, no. On top of that, he sounds like the kind of guy who'd go to Mexico, have a ring made out of a silver dollar and set with a fifty-cent turquoise for the wife, then tell everybody it was made by hand by a genuine silversmith."

"All the same," said Gilman thoughtfully, "he *was* smacked around. He showed me the snapshots. His face was all swoll up. He wants to collect insurance."

"Sure. And let's make a point of checking the insurance claim he put in. But he didn't knock off *his* wife, and that's the hell of it."

"You sure got a grudge in for him," said Gilman admiringly. "Me personally, I'd like to put the arm on the little bastard myself. But what's the rest of it? I know that look. I missed something else?"

Flavin grinned at him. "Ah, go to hell," he said. "No, you didn't miss a thing. You brought it all in. But let's take a look at this one—just for the ducks of it. Tetley, Bridges, Copland—" he counted them off on his fingers. "They all had Howards-Tetley safes. Right? Okay. Sturgis had a Norwich safe but from what we heard, all he kept in it was pencils and erasers. So let's look at the safes for a minute."

He was silent and Gilman was silent. At length Gilman said, "There's a lot of them Howards-Tetley safes around."

Flavin said, "Yeah," and stared at his sheet of blue-lined yellow paper.

George Gilman was modest about his talents and right now he was unhappy because Flavin was scowling fiercely at his sheet of notes. He did not realize that Jeff Flavin was following his usual procedure of heckling an idea out of hiding. His best ideas were usually the result of a no-holds-barred brawl with his stubborn brain.

At long last he grumbled, "Going back to Tetley's fairy story and the few raisins of truth in that bun, would you say the guy had a grudge against the little crud?"

"If I had to stay in the same room with Tetley for a half hour," said Gilman, "I'd have a dozen grudges against him."

"Here's what I mean, George. Aside from Sturgis, who asked for it, Tetley was given a worse time than Bridges or Copland. He was slapped around—you say his face was pretty swollen in the photographs—called names, made to open his own safe, kicked in the ass and knocked out. The other two were just slapped and cooled. Tetley was really given the business. Right?"

Gilman hunched over the desk-edge and thought about Tetley. It was impossible to see how anybody could not have it in for the guy. "Yeah," he admitted, "Tetley was pushed around more than the others."

"And called names, George. I can understand the pushing around, but when you call a man names, it usually means you've got something on your mind. He called Tetley a 'two-faced moneybag.' If I were calling a guy names, I'll call him something like a son of a bitch. But this 'two-faced moneybag' sticks in my mind."

"Sure, but I can name you a dozen guys who hate rich bastards just because they're rich. No other reason."

"That part of it's all right, but 'two-faced,' George, 'two-faced.' That spells grudge to me every time I think of it. Another thing: Tetley was number one on the list and his safe wasn't tapped till after he was slapped around. With Bridges and Copland, the box was opened first, which is the smart way to do things in case our boys had to get out of there in a hurry. Do you know what I'm beginning to think, George? I think this bird's first idea was to give Tetley a workout and that's all. The robbery came as an afterthought because, well, the thief was there and it looked so easy. There's the big difference in the MO. They're all pretty much the same—leaving out the Sturgis job—but I'll gamble that Tetley himself and not the safe was the prime target that night. Think it over."

"I'm convinced," said Gilman. "He knew Tetley's box inside out, so why wait till afterwards."

"That takes care of that. I hope. Now for Bridges and Copland. They had Tetley-made boxes, too. We'll have to leave Sturgis out till we talk to him. Something went sour on that deal."

"We can talk to him tomorrow morning, the Doc told me at the hospital. They put him to sleep for twenty-four hours. I got that from the nurse."

Flavin grinned at him across the desk. "People tell you a lot of things, don't they, George."

Gilman grinned back, showing all his gold teeth. "Hell," he said, "I look so dumb, people think it goes in one ear and dies there, but sometimes I surprise them. To get back to these safes, Jeff. We got one, two, three Howards-Tetley boxes in a row and a grudge against old man Tetley in the first place. I know a little about the safe business. Not much, but a little. It's like the washing machine business. They got to have a service department and you take a guy, he works in the service department, he's gotta know all about safes. Or washing machines. They gotta—or out they go. The way you add it up, Jeff, grudge included, this peterman ain't a pro atall. He works in the Howards-Tetley service department."

Flavin looked pleased, reached across the desk and shook Gilman's hand. "You can be the first to congratulate me, George," he said. "And vice versa. Only I don't think he works there anymore. I think he was canned and that's why he's sore at Tetley."

Gilman thought about it some more. "Being sore at Tetley," he offered tentatively, "that covers a lot of ground, but the service department narrows it down to only twenty or thirty. Not that it matters. I just thought I'd mention it."

Flavin jabbed at the paper with his pencil. "This is all a wild guess, damn it," he said. "One word can blow it away like smoke. Does Tetley run the company or live off the profits?"

"If he owns it," said Gilman promptly, "He runs it, from president to paper clips."

"That's what I thought," said Flavin. "Let's go up and look it over."

4.

McGimp, the police artist, marched to their desk before they could leave. He was in a tizzy. As Medical Examiner Dr. Hector Knight once remarked, McGimp was tizzy-prone.

He levelled his most devastating stare at George Gilman and said sharply, "There were no bruises on the Sturgis woman, none whatever. I went to the morgue and looked. There was not a mark on her. You may verify this, if you wish."

"I don't hang around the morgue very much," said Gilman. "When I have time off, I generally go to the movies. So I'll take your word for it."

"Thank you, Mr. Gilman. Thank you very, very much."

He nodded primly and stalked off, his professional honor vindicated. Or so it seemed. Some of the nearby detectives looked disappointed. This had been one of the McGimp's minor tizzies. It wasn't up to par.

Downstairs, Ed Turcott, police reporter of *The Hudson Evening News,* was talking in what seemed to be a casual manner to the desk sergeant, although those who knew Turcott best stated flatly that, awake or asleep, there was nothing casual about him—he merely looked that way. He was an earnest mousy-looking little man with mouse-colored hair, mouse-colored eyes behind rimless glasses and if skin could be said to be mouse-colored, Ed Turcott had it. He looked and acted as if he would be pleased to sell you a conservative blue knitted necktie if you walked into the Men's Wear department of Bergman's emporium. All this was no more than protective camouflage. He was a shrewd, hard-bitten police reporter and if you needed crucifying, he'd supply the nails and swing the hammer. He'd done it more than once. When experienced officers were cornered—and Turcott was good at that tactic—they invariably prefaced all remarks with, "Well, off the record, Ed—" whereupon Turcott smiled vaguely and sauntered away. Under no circumstances would he listen to an off-the-record statement. It was an inviolate ethic that a newspaperman could not print an off-the-record story until you gave him the green light, no matter if he got it from a dozen other sources in the meanwhile. Ed Turcott had ethics but did not like to be hampered by them.

He somehow managed to move thirty feet before Flavin and Gilman had taken a half dozen strides, and there he was, between them and the doorway. Other police reporters might rush thither and yon to scenes of crimes, but Turcott left Headquarters only when it was time to go home.

"Man," he told Flavin in a wan voice, "I can hardly think straight when the weather turns hot. Are you working on that accidental death up in—wherezit now?—Stone Bridge?"

Gilman faded back warily and watched Flavin's face turn blank and uninformative.

"Not me, Ed," said Flavin, telling the truth. "Did you ask the Dutchman about it?"

"Nobody asks the Dutchman about anything, Jeffrey," Turcott sighed. "You walk in and he *tells* you and that's about the size of it. Or he doesn't tell you. There are moments when I don't think he has a heart of gold. But it's the funniest thing, I'm almost sure somebody said you'd been given a piece of the Stone Bridge disturbance. A practical joker, no doubt." He almost succeeded in regarding Flavin helplessly.

"Deaths are out of my department, accidental or on purpose."

"Of course. The humidity's making me feeble-minded, I think. You and George are working the burglary angle."

"We just started."

"This disturbance up in Stone Bridge. These poor rich people, I feel for them, Jeffrey, I really do. How they bleed if you separate them from a nickel. I'll bet they're yelling as if there'd been forty burglaries instead of a mere four. Why are the rich so noisy?"

"I wouldn't know," said Flavin, deadpan. "I never talked to a rich man."

"If you're working Stone Bridge, you're tripping over them. Or won't they talk to anyone but the Commissioner or the Mayor?"

"You can't prove it by me. We just started."

"I'd rather talk to an honest cop any day in the week. Carol Sturgis was a good-looking woman, I've heard tell."

"So they say. I didn't see her."

"I saw some pictures of her in a bathing suit. Unbelievable. Body and soul. No wonder the thief went berserk. I'd go berserk myself. I'll bet her bedroom was a mess after the poor girl so unsuccessfully defended her virtue."

"It was? They must of had the cleaning lady in before I got there."

"Or maybe she didn't defend herself. Somebody, I think it was Calvin Coolidge, said, 'When rape is inevitable, relax and enjoy it.'"

"She was raped?" asked Flavin with a show of interest.

"It's an over-rated pastime, Jeffrey. It's either noisy or dull and your hair gets mussed. But on these burglaries, I've got a lead for you, and if it pans out, I want my picture in the paper under the two-column cut of you and George. This is gospel. I got it right from the horse's mouth, or even lower. Not mentioning any names, but this particular horse operates our slow but dignified genuine bronze grill elevator from floor one to floor four daily between the hours of eight A.M. to five P.M. He told me that the burglar does not reside within the city limits, pays no city taxes, does not have a permit or license and therefore should not be allowed to conduct a business here. He's quite right. It's a scandal, almost as reprehensible as picking the pocket of an alderman. If I were Mayor, I'd give these out-of-towners a stern piece of my mind, and no nonsense about it. Wouldn't you?"

"If he's from out of town, he should pay taxes or at least buy a ticket to the Policeman's Ball. But how's the elevator man know this bird's from out of town? I didn't know it myself."

"Now, now, Jeffrey," Turcott blinked drowsily, "it stands to reason, doesn't it? Or does it? I can never figure these things out. People have to tell me. And they do. Dear Lord, how they tell me! I get theories the way most people get dandruff. I ride upstairs in the elevator, I get it from the operator; I go out for lunch, a waitress gives it to me with the salad. I'm up to here in theories. If you've got one, get it off your chest if it'll make you happy. It makes no difference to me. I stopped listening during the Harding administration. I had to. The doctor warned me. It's bad for the eardrums, he said."

Flavin smiled blandly. "Well now, I'll tell you, Ed," he said. "Strictly off the record—"

Turcott put out his hand and adjusted the white handkerchief in Flavin's breast pocket. "We don't pull them to points this year, Jeffrey," he murmured. "The well-dressed man shows no more than a half inch of handkerchief in a straight line across the pocket. Nice to have met you gentlemen. Drop in any time, any time at all. If I'm not in conference with the chairman of the board over there in the pulpit—" He glanced around as if in muddled surprise at finding himself in the middle of the floor, and then meandered back to the Desk.

Flavin and Gilman left Headquarters and walked briskly to the parking lot for their car.

"Windy bastard, ain't he?" said Gilman, glancing back over his shoulder.

"First time you met him, George? That's Ed Turcott, police reporter from *The Evening News*."

"Somebody pointed him out to me once and said to watch my step or something. He must of been giving me a shenanigan. Don't fool with Ed Turcott, he said. Funny joke. Is he always as windy as that, Jeff?"

"Windier—when he's really pulling your back teeth. Is that all you think of him—he's windy?"

"He gives you time to think something else?"

Flavin's grin ran crookedly up into his right cheek. "You've put it in a nutshell, George. He's a foxy little man, Georgie-boy and whoever told you to watch your step meant just that."

Gilman canted his head, puzzled. At first he frowned and then, as if at the snap of a finger, his face spread in wide astonishment. "Honest to God, Jeff," he said, "he rocked me to sleep. I mean, he kept grinding away like a busted record but everything he said was loaded. If you answered like he wanted, I mean. Was it accidental death? Was the Sturgis woman raped? Are the rich boys screaming to City Hall? Was the bedroom a wreck? Was the thief an imported heavy? What's your opinion on the case as a whole? The tricky little weasel! Me, I'd of been cold-cocked for fair. What I need is a course in getting smart."

Flavin's half-grin became a full smile and turned into a laugh. "At one time or another, George, Ed Turcott has put it over on everybody from Foxy and the Dutchman on down. So be nice and friendly but start out with, 'Now this is off the record, Ed,' and you'll never be bothered."

Four

The Howards-Tetley Safe and Lock Company occupied all five floors of a red brick building at the south end of Jackson Street. The name of this edifice was carved into the granite lintel—Tetley Building. The name Tetley appeared on two bronze plates flanking the doorway, twice again on the frosted glass doors to the business office inside the lobby, and four more times on the building directory beside the elevator.

"This looks like the right place," said George.

"It pays to advertise," said Flavin.

The service department was on the fifth floor. The manager's name was John Phelps. He was an impressive portly man in an Oxford gray suit, a white shirt and a subdued gray-and-red striped bow tie. He had an office and his name was on the door.

Howards
TETLEY
Safe & Lock Company
John Phelps
Service Manager

All the workmen, standing at benches or crouching before gleaming new safes, wore dark green coveralls on the backs of which was stitched in red:

Howards
TETLEY

Mr. Phelps did not look as if he had ever worn dark green coveralls; he looked as if he had been born in an Oxford gray suit, like the executive vice president. He was very cordial to Flavin and Gilman. He shook hands with them and assured them that he was more than pleased to make their acquaintance. He had the manner of a man who would shake hands and be cordially pleased to make the acquaintance of anyone in an official position of more importance than his own. He would have been proud and honored to shake the hand of a great executive like Mr. Tetley. In short, Mr. Phelps was an accomplished apple polisher.

His office was patterned after Mr. Tetley's but was of course about a fifth the size. There was the steel-and-formica executive desk on which sat an alert intercom box, a pen-and-pencil set standing at attention and an EverReady memo pad and calendar. The matted and framed photographs on the walls proved conclusively that Howards-TETLEY made safes and locks of all descriptions.

Mr. Phelps enthroned himself behind the desk with the pen-and-pencil set standing sentry on one hand, the intrepid intercom box on the other and his businesslike memo pad in the middle. Compared to his resolute bearing, Flavin and Gilman appeared a pair of mendicants slouched in their chairs to his left.

"We need a little information," said Flavin.

"I shall be only too glad to be of assistance," said Mr. Phelps. "Only too glad. What is the nature of this information, if I may ask?"

"It's about some of your workmen."

Mr. Phelps shook his head regretfully. Slowly but firmly. He'd be only too glad to be of assistance, of course, but there were rules.

"I'm sorry," he said, "but our personnel files are not open to inspection. A company policy. For reasons of security. I'm certain you understand."

"I'm glad you're so certain."

"The reason is obvious, of course. When our experts install a vault, it is necessary that they adjust the mechanism. This information we file in that safe in the far corner. It is our Fortress model and I can say without fear of contradiction that there is not a more burglar-proof safe on the commercial market. We also suggest that all Tetley safe owners change their combinations at the beginning of each fiscal year. That information, too, is securely locked within the Fortress model. However, there is a human element involved and—"

"I get the picture," Flavin interrupted. "You don't want anybody to get to your boys."

"Although our technicians are checked and double-checked security-wise, there *is* an unfortunate possibility that undue pressure might be brought to bear through threats of blackmail, physical injury or other forms of mental or bodily violence—"

"By cops, eh?"

A well-barbered flush colored Mr. Phelps' face. "I do not make company policy," he said stiffly. "I'm sorry, but such is the situation. My hands are tied."

Flavin leaned forward in his chair. A small grin ran into his right cheek on the bias. "I'll tell you what I'm going to do, Mr. Phelps," he said softly. "I'm going to bring to bear more mental violence than you've ever seen in your God damned life. Mr. Tetley claims a burglary loss of nearly thirty thousand dollars. Insurance companies are crazy about things like that. There's a killing too but that's only police business. So do you know what I'm going to do, Mr. Phelps? I'm going to get a warrant and turn this place inside out, starting with Mr. Tetley and working down to you—if Tetley doesn't clobber you first. So you can't talk to cops security-wise, eh? Isn't that just too damn bad."

George made a customary throat-clearing noise and looked at the squat Fortress model in the corner. "I know a couple boys who'd give an arm and a leg to have a go at that egg crate," he said. "They're in Atlanta now but'll be out in a coupla months."

Mr. Phelps' flush turned veal-white and he struggled to speak. "Gentlemen, gentlemen, please!" he bleated. "I—I was merely stating general company policy but—ha, ha—rules are made to be broken, aren't they? What I mean is, that is to say, you—you have my whole-hearted cooperation, I assure you. This misunderstanding is no more than a, well, a misunderstanding. And we *are* reasonable men, aren't we? Of course we are. So—so let us sit down and, well, talk this over—reasonably."

Flavin had not moved from his chair, nor had George.

"I don't like to get tough, Phelps," said Flavin. "But don't ever say again that you can't talk to a cop security-wise. Some of the boys might get really mad and take care of you. Ass-wise. Okay. Now I feel better, so let's talk sense for a change. How many of your crew have left the company since the house box numbers were changed?"

Phelps sat unhappily in his swivel chair and his Oxford gray suit appeared but three quarters filled. "Two," he said. "Frank Zinns and Leonard Ferenc."

"Were they canned?"

"Well, eh, Frank Zinns was retired. It is company policy to retire a man when he reaches the age of sixty-five."

"How nice. Was he happy about it?"

"Our retirement plan provides a very generous honorarium. Very generous."

"Half pay, eh?"

"The payroll department can give you the exact amount, Sergeant. Mr. Tetley also presented him with a gold pin in recognition of his long and faithful service."

George nodded interestedly. "One of them gold pins you wear in your lapel? Any hock shop in the city'll give you two bucks for them. I'll bet Frank was crazy at being given the boot. What do you think, Jeff?"

"I think. I'll want his address, Phelps. What about this Leonard Ferenc?"

Phelps lifted his chin and his mouth hardened. "Ferenc was contentious, quarrelsome, arrogant, insubordinate and disrespectful. He was fired."

"When was this?"

"Three months ago, shortly after I replaced Edward Maurer as, uh, superintendent of this division."

"What was Maurer's trouble? Disrespect?"

"Mr. Maurer was offered a position with Dominion Lock in Richmond, Virginia. He and Mr. Tetley did not see eye to eye."

"Well, Tetley's kind of short," said George. "Maurer could of seen eye to eye easy if he got down on his knees."

"Let's get back to Ferenc," said Flavin. "Where's he working now?"

"Philadelphia. The Franklin Sheet Metal Company. I gave him a good recommendation which he definitely did not deserve."

Flavin looked out the window, thinking of all the jerks in the world who had positions of petty power, such as Phelps, but George said, "You shouldn't of done that, Mr. Phelps. It was wrong. It wasn't fair to the Franklin Sheet Metal Company. You should of told the truth. They'll lose faith in you when Ferenc starts being disrespectful all over again. Was it you he was disrespectful to, or Mr. Tetley?"

"He was disrespectful to me," said Phelps primly. "He said—but there's no need to repeat his words. He was a stupid, arrogant young man."

"Yeah. I know the type. He probably said you kissed old man Tetley's butt. Don't let it bother you, Mr. Phelps. Guys like that, they talk too much. You the only one knows the combination to that coffee can over there in the corner, I hope."

Flavin smiled quietly to himself and watched a fly crawl dartingly across the ceiling.

"Naturally," said Phelps in a sharp voice. "It's hardly the sort of information I'd post on the bulletin board."

"Uh-huh. But putting it another way, you got a roomful of safe experts working out there, so just between you and me, they'd be pretty lousy if they couldn't open that thing with a Boy Scout knife. Right?"

Phelps' cheeks puffed and reddened. "Every man in my organization has been screened and rescreened, Mr. Gilman. I saw to that personally three months ago. They are thoroughly trustworthy."

"Where'd you work before this, Phelps?" asked Flavin.

"I was production manager of Hudson Productions, a subsidiary of Tetley Safe And Lock, I'm glad to say."

"Hudson Productions? What'd they put out?"

"Uh—metal trays."

"For inside the safes, eh. How many on the payroll?"

"Well—twenty. But you can't judge by size, Sergeant. The work was very exciting."

"How did you get the job as service manager here?"

"Mr. Tetley interviewed me personally, Sergeant. Personally. I had charts and proved conclusively that he could save at least twenty percent on overhead through time study and systematized schedules for each employee. He was, if you don't mind my saying so, much impressed with my facts and figures."

"Then you don't know a safe from a loose brick in the chimney."

"Whether you know it or not, Sergeant, it is not for an executive to work on the production line level. His echelon is finance."

Flavin nodded thoughtfully. "Finance," he murmured. "That reminds me. How much are you in the hole with the finance people? I mean mortgage, car, TV, washing machine and so forth. You don't have to tell me to the penny. A round figure will do. You don't have to tell me. We can get it on the outside."

"F—fourteen thousand," muttered Phelps, looking ill.

"And how much do you make a year?"

"Seven—seventy-five hundred."

"Hell, you're in the clear. Just stop eating for two years and you'll be paid up. This Ferenc, now. Did he like Mr. Tetley?"

"He did not," said Phelps positively.

"Called him names too, eh?"

"In my opinion, Leonard Ferenc had an exceedingly foul mouth."

"What was Frank Zinns' opinion of the boss?"

"He respected and honored Mr. Tetley."

"Uh-huh. How about your predecessor, Ed Maurer?"

"He also respected and honored Mr. Tetley, although, as I pointed out, they did not always see eye to eye."

"Well, what do you think, George?"

George moved his shoulders, indifferent. "I think we're wasting our time. All the important stuff's locked up in the egg crate over there, only it ain't because any one of them thirty experts out there can open it with a sneeze, and that don't include the three birds that don't work here no more. And yeah, we want this Frank Zinn's address."

"Get it," Flavin told Phelps.

Phelps frowned, pressed a lever on his intercom box and spoke a few curt words. Five minutes later a resigned-looking blonde girl entered the office from a side door, placed a slip of paper on Phelps' desk and left without speaking a word. Phelps wanted to read the paper to George, who had been taking notes, but Flavin plucked it from Phelps' fingers and put it into his wallet.

They'd really put the boots to Phelps, Flavin knew, and the man had taken it pretty damn well, when you came right down to it. Of course, he was a flab, a time-study spy and a bootlicker and you couldn't knock dents in his ego with a sixteen-pound sledge, but all the same, he'd come through pretty well, considering. Flavin wouldn't go so far as to say you had to hand it to the guy, because he was basically a stinker, but at the end Phelps still managed to raise the old personality smile. He insisted upon walking to the elevator with them, shaking their unresponsive hands and telling them to call upon him at any time for information or assistance, any time at all; he was at their service. He made a joke about service managers and laughed heartily, oblivious of the fact that he was the only one who did.

Downstairs, George sighed and said, "You know, Jeff, it's just too damn bad that schmo's such a schmo. I'd love to sock it to him. He's got everything for the perfect suspect except guts. That cancels him out and it's a lousy shame now, ain't it? A guy like that."

"We'll wait a little before we cancel him out, Georgie-boy. The whole thing might have been an act. We got three other birds to look into—Maurer, Ferenc and Zinns."

2.

He called Communications at Headquarters from the lobby phone booth and told them he wanted the Richmond and Philadelphia police to check the comings and goings of Edward Maurer and Leonard Ferenc for the past twenty-four hours. He gave the business addresses. Then he and George went to Mt. Pleasant Avenue in North Hudson to talk to ex-Tetley employee Frank Zinns. Zinns was a slight but spry little man of sixty-five with a steel-wool crop of hair. When Flavin and Gilman stepped out of their car before his freshly painted barn-red house, which had white shutters and white trim, Zinns was teaching three impatient boys, between the ages of ten and twelve, how not to use an air rifle.

"I hope nobody complained about the gun, Sergeant," he said anxiously. "I'm learning the boys to be careful and we haven't fired a shot yet."

Zinns' lack of height and weight eliminated him as a burglary suspect, and Flavin assured him, "Don't worry about the gun. We're here on another matter and all we want is a little information. We just had a talk with Mr. Phelps, service manager at Howards-Tetley."

"Nice fella," commented Zinns. "Very friendly."

"And democratic. He shook hands with us."

"Makes you feel right at home," said Zinns.

It took a while for Flavin's casual ease and Gilman's homely grin to unbutton the little man's caution but after he offered them first a bottle of beer and then a glass of iced tea and lime juice, he talked more freely.

Of course he knew the company policy of retiring coworkers at the age of sixty-five. There were no employees in Howards-TETLEY; everybody was a co-worker. This rule did not apply to department heads or other employees. Zinns was sure he was one of those in line for service manager when Ed Maurer quit, and he was pretty darn disappointed when Mr. Phelps, an outsider, got the post. Ed Maurer was rough and ready, but a good boss and, if needs be, could work right alongside you on the bench. Mr. Phelps was all right, you understand, but kind of a smoothie. Some of the men, Zinns admitted conservatively, were not very fond of Mr. Phelps, who liked to draw lines on pieces of graph paper and take them to Mr. Tetley or Mr. Undercliff, the vice president. It was a funny thing, but after Mr. Phelps took one of his pieces of graph paper to Mr. Tetley or Mr. Undercliff the work had a habit of getting a little heavier day by day, work that was usually done by Repairs in the production department, work with the red tickets from Inspection on it. There used to be quite a few men in Repairs but now there were only five. That was one of the reasons Ed Maurer had quit.

"You mean because they were overloading the service department?" Flavin asked.

"No, them graphs," said Zinns. "They kept wanting him to make graphs, daily reports on the men and all that time study crap and he wouldn't do it. I mean, that's only what I heard. He got a good job down south in Virginia and anyways you can't believe all you hear."

Flavin looked at George and then down into his glass, swirling it to make the ice tinkle. So good old Johnny Phelps had been putting the knife into Maurer for quite a while; until Maurer finally blew up and quit. Which was exactly what Phelps had wanted.

"Ed Maurer," said Flavin, squinting into his glass, "he's a big man, isn't he?"

"Ed? Shucks, no. He's a little feller, like me. Five foot seven but heavy built."

"Maybe I'm thinking of Leonard Ferenc. He's the other one who quit, isn't he?"

"Yah, Len was a pretty big boy. Six foot or better. A young feller."

"That's right. Too bad he took a swing at Mr. Tetley, though."

"You're all mixed up, mister. It was Mr. Phelps. And he didn't really take no swing. A couple fellers grabbed him and Mr. Phelps went in the office. Nothing happened. I was right there and I know."

"This is only hearsay. They said he was sore at Mr. Tetley."

"He had a quick temper, that's all. Not a bad temper, you understand;

just quick. Mr. Phelps, see, he had a habit of going around with a stop watch and you got just so much for a certain kind of job, understand? He had it down pat. Frinstance, you take a dial adjustment on the little Watchman model—that's sort of a cheap box—well, according to Mr. Phelps, a man could do it in seven minutes. But shucks," Zinns chuckled happily, "we all put it over on him. Any of us could do it in five, a cheap box like that unless it was really buggered, and if we wanted to coast, it was always buggered. We all kept a real kabolixed assembly on the bench in case he pulled the watch on us. Me, I had a beaut. A dozen engineers and his brother couldn't of put that hunk of junk together. You never saw anything so kabolixed."

"Some men you can pull a stop watch on, and some you can't," said Flavin. "If I put a stop watch on George here, for example, he'd make me eat it. I don't like the damn things myself and I'll bet young Ferenc didn't either."

"You can say that again, mister. He was a good worker, understand? Almost the fastest in the shop and he sure saw red every time Mr. Phelps started parading around on that time study crap."

"Was it Mr. Phelps' idea or Mr. Tetley's?"

"We-ll, Mr. Phelps *said* Mr. Tetley only wanted to make things efficienter for us and, you know, easier and so forth, and Mr. Tetley probably did. The more safes he put out, the more money he made. That's natural."

"But you didn't have to like it, and young Ferenc didn't like it or Mr. Tetley. That's what they tell me."

"Well yes, that's about the size of it and—wait a minute now," Zinns' face sharpened suspiciously. "You're getting me to say a lot of things against Len Ferenc and most of it don't mean nothing, understand?"

Flavin shook his head and grinned. "This is something else entirely, Mr. Zinns," he said. "We're looking for three petermen named Big Harry Muir, Ben Tutchek and Foxy Mackenzie. There's a lot of interest being shown and George and I are filling in background angles so we'll know the complete picture if anything breaks."

Zinns neither believed nor disbelieved this, but he did know he'd answered a number of pointed questions and he did not intend to answer more. "If you want the picture," he said, withdrawn, "see Mr. Phelps or Mr. Undercliff. They work there. I don't. And I'm no bastard."

That was the opinion which George Gilman stated as he and Jeff Flavin drove back to Headquarters. "He's a nice little guy," he said. "Too bad he thinks we mousetrapped him."

"I'd like to meet this Len Ferenc," said Flavin.

"Yeah. He's the only one of the whole bunch so far."

"Not counting the thirty or forty others in the service department," said Flavin dryly. "They can all open safes and they'd all kick Tetley around the block if they got the chance."

It was quarter to five when they walked into the squadroom. Sergeant Bauer, at the desk, had no phone calls, messages, tips or leads for them, but huge Ben Tutchek was just coming from the Dutchman's office and he joined them.

"This is as good a time as any for a quick rundown," he said. "We got just about as much as you'd expect for the first day. Nothing from the neighbors, nothing from the patrolmen, nothing from the special watchmen. Pohl and Kiler are tailing Fay Copland around the clock but she hasn't left the house all day. Harry Muir's nosing around on the Malone angle. Offhand, I'd say he was just making a passing remark, though you can't tell. The only thing definite from the Lab is the plaster cast of the guy's sneakers. We'll have an autopsy report on Carol Sturgis from the M.E. in the morning. You'll get a copy. That's about it. How'd you make out?"

Flavin told him about Leonard Ferenc and the Howards-Tetley service department angle and the checkups being made by Communications on Ed Maurer and Norwich Safe.

"This is still in the pipedream stage," he said, "so don't count on it."

Tutchek's smile bunched and he canted his head interestedly. "You've been a busy son of a bitch, haven't you," he said. "I like the sound of this Ferenc and I'll like it still better when we can sit down with him and kick it around."

"There are about forty other high-class safe experts in the service department," Flavin warned. "Keep them in mind while you're at it."

"I'll keep them in mind next Tuesday. Ferenc comes first. Tell Philly we want him for questioning. Kitteridge can go down and pick him up. Let me know when he's brought in. He's your baby but I'd like to sit in."

"He's your baby as much as mine, so don't make him sound like a door prize."

"If there's anything I can't stand," Tutchek winked at Gilman, "it's a modest cop. They're always the first to grab the medals and headlines and get their faces in the newspaper."

"I noticed that," said Gilman. "He told me to go the other way if I saw Ed Turcott coming."

"Go the other way and hide," said Tutchek with emphasis. "That newslouse'd poison his grandmother for a two-inch story on the obit page. And do the same if you see the Dutchman coming. He's at his worst on the first day of a bad break like this one. Anyway, let's knock it off for now. Everything's covered and tomorrow can be a bitch if things start breaking, and a double bitch if they don't. Or's there something else before I duck?"

Flavin said, "Well—" and told him about Tetley's $18,000 in family heirloom costume jewelry they were sure the thief didn't lift from the safe.

Tutchek understood the reasons without being told. He nodded. "Mr. Tetley's going to be a pleasure one of these days," he said. "Smart and all that, but he's sure to trip up. Maybe this is it."

"George has a list of the stuff he claims was lifted. It won't mean a thing but we'll pass it along to Pawnshop."

"Okay, but then go home an' relax. We don't, none of us, want to be dragging our caboose tomorrow."

He moved away, a big powerful man, and unperturbed. "Five'll get you ten he's the next head of Homicide when the Dutchman finally blows his stack," said Flavin.

"No bet," said Gilman.

Gilman took the added instructions to Communications and Flavin went to Sergeant Gill of Pawnshop with the list of stolen trinkets. Pawnshop already had a list but Flavin said there'd be additions from the Sturgis job tomorrow. Both knew, without stating it in so many words, that the killing of Carol Sturgis, made this priority.

"I'll light a fuse under the boys," said Sergeant Gill. "Hock shops get a little sloppy if we don't put the fear of God into them periodically. How's it with you?"

"So-so."

"Sure. That's the Dutchman all over. So-so. But still the best cop in the Department, friend, and don't let anybody tell you. You will be informed immediately, sir, if it is within our power to unearth any part or parcel of this purloined contraband. Sergeant Bring-'Em-Back-Alive Gill reporting on the double."

"Ah, go to hell," Flavin grinned.

Birdie Burdson called Flavin's apartment at ten o'clock. He had several bits of nebulous information and his voice was hesitant as if he were afraid Flavin would think it his fault.

"There's hardly a peterman around, Mr. Reilly," he said. "The exodus has been general. They don't like the heat. The consensus of opinion is that anyone who can blow a box might have the Sturgis killing pinned on him."

"You mean the word's gone round that we'll frame the first monkey we get our hands on, is that it?"

"I'm merely repeating the general trend of opinion, Mr. Reilly," Birdie said hastily. "If I had any personal thoughts in the matter, which I do not, I realize they would be completely valueless. The city is hot and those who do not have established businesses are going elsewhere."

"That's not news, friend. But you said 'hardly.' You know somebody who's still around?"

"A rumor, nothing more, Mr. Reilly. The name was not mentioned. I'm working on it."

"Keep working. Anything else?"

"Well.... Some people are saying that none of the known professionals were concerned in those four Stone Bridge strikes."

Flavin said, "They are?" and hunched more intently over the telephone. "Did you hear this from anybody who'd know?"

"Nononono. It was merely idle conjecture. The argument advanced is that a professional would tap the till and leave without further ado. Then, too, there was the rape and killing of the Sturgis woman. The act of a crazy man, as everyone agrees, regardless of the lady's personal charms."

"Like the newspapers say, a sex maniac, eh? That's interesting. See what you can pick up."

"I know very little of amateurs," said Birdie sadly. "But I'll do my best. And, Mr. Reilly ..."

"What?"

"I—I misled you, I'm afraid, and must apologize. I've been thinking it over very carefully and the words I attributed to Mr. Malone were actually spoken by another gentleman who was standing several feet away. I recall it distinctly now."

"Don't worry about it, friend. We really don't think Malone killed anybody yet."

Flavin hung up. He was sleepy. He wished he knew Joyce Ames well enough to call her up and say good night or something. He went to bed.

Five

When Flavin walked into the squadroom before eight the following morning, an envelope containing a carbon copy of the autopsy report from Dr. Hector Knight, Medical Examiner, was lying in the wire basket on his desk.

It told him Carol Sturgis' name, race, age, height and weight and, in medical terms, described the examinations and finally gave the conclusions of Dr. Hector Knight, Medical Examiner. It was a detailed scientific document, and one which most undergraduate medical students could translate with hardly any difficulty at all.

Flavin was not a medical student and this was the first autopsy report ever sent for his personal attention but, aside from the precise anatomical slang, he understood the conclusions perfectly.

Carol Sturgis had died of strangulation after half-swallowing the gag.

She had been drinking heavily before death.

She'd had sexual intercourse before death.

She had not been raped.

The absence of bruises, contusions, abrasions or lacerations proved that there'd been no defensive struggle.

It was possible that she'd been too intoxicated to resist, although the presence of seminal fluid in the vaginal vault showed that she'd been at least partially conscious during the sexual act.

As she was a married woman, it was probably with her husband that she'd had coitus.

George Gilman had come up and stood squinting dubiously past Flavin's elbow at the Report.

"No rape," said Flavin. "This is going to be a big disappointment to Ed Turcott."

"That's too bad."

"You sound as though you didn't expect it to be rape."

"Well, you know, there were no bruises. The McGimp told us that a couple times. But if she was soused, the whole neighborhood could of raped her and she'd never know the difference. But if she was that soused, you wouldn't have to tie and gag her. So—no rape."

"I don't get this tying and gagging business anyway," Flavin scowled at the autopsy report. "The idea is that our bird was working on the safe when the Sturgises came home unexpectedly. So what'd he do? Beat up Walt Sturgis and run down the hall and tie knots in Sturgis' wife? That doesn't make sense. And when did Sturgis and his wife have time for this coitus—with a burglar in the house?"

"Maybe they had it in the car," said George. "Lots of people have it in cars. Only the kind of people who have it in cars don't call it coitus. If the Sturgises were soused, they wouldn't care where they had it."

"Sure, but if they were really having a ball, why'd they come home early?"

Gilman looked pained, as if his crystal ball had suddenly become clouded. "Don't ask me," he said. "Maybe they wanted to have a nice private fight in peace and quiet."

"From what they tell me," said Flavin dryly, "this coitus stuff is supposed to be very relaxing. You can fight like cats and dogs beforehand but later on you just kind of turn over and go to sleep."

"Are you adding it up to maybe she was raped?"

"Uh-uh. Not me, George. Doc Knight is the rape expert and I'm willing to take his word for it. See if Communications has anything for us. I want to talk to Nairn and Ochs for a minute."

Sergeant Nairn was in charge of the Safe And Loft detail. A tall thin man with a tight mouth and dark flat hair. Flavin told him what Birdie had said about the safecrackers leaving town and Nairn nodded.

"There's a couple left," he said. "Nobody for us. Too old and beat up. If your fink gets a live one, let me know."

"First thing. Anything live among the boys who left?"

"Hap Metz is the only one who might fit but he's got a bum left arm and that's not something you'd miss. We'll pick him up anyway. I hear he went to Atlantic City. And there could be some strangers I don't know about. They come and go. If we get anything, I'll tell you."

"I'll keep in touch, Nairn."

Nairn's answering, "Yeah," said plainly that he'd believe it when he saw it.

Sergeant Ochs, of Burglary, bland and blond, sat hunched at his desk. "We got hold of a few for the line-up," he told Flavin, "but I wouldn't give you a dime a dozen for them. I know some that can open a safe if they have to but they haven't been around for a while and they weren't that good in the first place. Those jobs took a real operator. Did you talk to Nairn yet? It's more his department."

"Two minutes ago. Hear anything about an amateur being mixed up in it?"

"I heard that and ninety-nine other pipe dreams. Personally, I think the guy's a hophead, horsing around the way he did, but he's in the trade, all the same."

"A mainliner might still be hanging around, then. If he gets the stuff from a local pusher, he'll stay close to home."

"There's a chance," Ochs agreed. "On the other hand, he probably knows pushers from Chi to Cheyenne. Talk to Ted Erple."

They told each other they'd keep in touch and Flavin left. Sergeant Erple was not in his office and Flavin returned to his desk. Ben Tutchek and George Gilman were talking and, after greeting Flavin, Tutchek sat back, indicating that he'd take his turn when Gilman finished.

Gilman hawked, looked around for a cuspidor and swallowed. "Here's what Communications says," he informed Flavin. "They got in touch with Dominion Lock in Richmond and Ed Maurer—that's Tetley's old service manager—he worked all last night on some kind of new vault job. Him and three others, so he's clean. But Leonard Ferenc is a different story. According to Franklin Sheet Metal in Philly, Ferenc filled out an application and they were ready to give him a job but he'd left Philly for a job someplace else. They don't know where. He lived in a rooming house on Grover Street and the landlady says there's no forwarding address. Left on a Thursday without a word. Owes her four days' rent, she said. That was about two months ago."

Flavin lit a cigarette and watched the smoke twist and weave restlessly in the slugglishly moving air of the squad-room. It was unimportant that Ferenc hadn't taken the Franklin Sheet Metal job. He'd undoubtedly filled out applications in several places. Or had he? Phelps, his ex-boss at Tetley's had mentioned writing no other recommendations. Two months was a long time to go without a job and most companies demanded recommendations. Then there was the business of his skipping out on the rent from the rooming house without warning. Ferenc was young and maybe unmarried. He sounded unmarried. Where had he lived while working in Hudson? In another rooming house? With his parents? He glanced at Tutchek, who wore an expression of pleased anticipation. So Ben, too, thought Ferenc was a hot lead.

"We'll call Phelps at Tetley Safe after nine o'clock," he said to Gilman. "We'll want his old address here. Perhaps he had a mother and father— if guys like Ferenc have mothers and fathers."

Tutchek laughed. "Don't take it so personally, Jeff-boy."

"You do all right in that direction yourself."

"Anything from Norwich Safe? Sturgis had one of their boxes, you said."

"According to Communications," said Gilman, "Norwich Safe ain't hired or fired anybody for the last three years. That lets them out."

"And keeps things simpler," Tutchek nodded. "The more I think of this Ferenc character, the more I like him."

"Ochs came up with another angle," said Flavin. "He thinks the guy might be a pro who's on the hop. I'll talk to Erple of Narcotics. He might come up with a name. Nairn thinks maybe Hap Metz might fit the bill but Hap's got a bum left arm. He was shot in the elbow awhile ago and can't straighten it out. Nairn's having him picked up. Metz can be a bastard when he wants, which is most of the time. He beat the hell out of Steinie Meyn about six months ago and all Steinie did was call him One-Wing. Metz is always beating up somebody, including girl friends. But Hap's a periodic rummy, not a hophead. That doesn't mean he didn't pull the Stone Bridge jobs, though I can't see him, myself. Hap wouldn't work in front of witnesses unless he's nuts, and nobody's said anything about the guy having a crooked left arm. On the other hand, Hap can move around so you'd hardly notice it. We'll keep him in mind."

"We'll keep everybody in mind," said Tutchek. "Except maybe Malone. Harry Muir worked on that till almost five this morning and even talked to Malone himself. Kind of just in passing, if you know what I mean."

"You're taking Malone's word for what?" asked Flavin.

Tutchek shook his head, smiling. "There's more to it than that," he said. "A case like this with the papers yelling bloody murder, it can hurt the administration if we don't clean it up fast. This is an election year and what hurts the administration hurts Malone. He's got a councilman, part of a county commissioner, an interest in a state representative and a few others he wants to get out the vote for. If the ticket takes a dive in November, Malone's got a hungry two years ahead of him. Now here's a pretty lousy killing and already the word's going round that the guy's hiding out down in the Point. Malone can't afford talk like that, and the longer it goes on, the more it's going to cost him at the polls, and that's exactly what Malone told Harry. 'If the son of a bitch was my own brother,' he said, 'I'd burn his ass from here to Headquarters and tear up the return ticket.' And he'd throw in his wife too, if he had to. You can always get a new wife but a gone vote stays gone and in two years Malone can be gone right along with it."

"You know something?" Gilman said to Flavin. "I'm glad I don't own stocks in City Hall. I'd have a hemorrhage every time somebody passed a red light."

"Ah, Malone's not so bad," Tutchek shrugged. "I've seen worse. He's about average. He's got things pretty much under control at the Point and won't give you the knife unless there's a buck or a vote in it for him. What the hell, this ain't a May Walk, it's politics. It stinks, but sometimes it stinks better than other times. All you got to do is know what you're up against."

"But the hell with politics," Tutchek said. "They'll be damn careful this year. This redhead Fay Copland, I got Pohl and Kiler tailing her round the clock." He laughed. "They thought they'd be on the town last night, she's known for it, but what'd she do? She went to bed. So one or the other of them spent the night under a tree with a nice view of old man Copland's front door. That must of been the first night she stayed home since the Hoover administration." He laughed again.

"How's it with her and Walt Sturgis?" asked Flavin. "We think it is."

"Hell yes—so far as I can tell without seeing the movies. But I don't know if it's an angle. She's put it out before, from what I hear, in addition to being married and divorced. And Sturgis, well, he's supposed to be a kind of cold-blooded bastard. He'll take it if it's there on Mondays,

Wednesdays and Saturdays. You know, systematic. Red hot with a slide rule. Anyway, he didn't beat himself over the head with that jack handle. Doc Knight said the angle was impossible."

"Did La Copland leave the party with Sturgis and his wife?"

"She didn't leave till they began stacking the chairs on the tables. She never does. We checked with the bartenders, waiters and cleaning ladies. At six A.M. she was trying to get up another party to go to Lake Powhatan for a swim or something. That's the Stone Bridge summer hangout—Lake Powhatan. It's up the other side of Lake Hopatcong. She didn't get any takers."

Gilman listened with a solemn show of interest. "Too bad Pohl and Kiler weren't there," he said. "They'd of been glad to keep her company. Are they still sitting under that tree?"

Tutchek regarded Gilman with an equally solemn show of interest. "No, they ain't still sitting under that tree, Mr. Einstein," he said. "I thought it was bad for their eyes to keep watching good-looking redheads. I sent them down to the freight yards to count box car numbers. And is the next question why did I have them tail her in the first place?"

There was a flatness in his voice, as if he resented having his methods questioned, but Gilman seemed not to notice it. "Why should I ask that?" he said. "She probably gave you the same malarkey she gave us. Some women, they just can't help it."

Tutchek relaxed and winked at Flavin. "I hate to disillusion you, Georgie, but this one was sleeping around. That was the score on her."

Flavin said, "Yeah," and changed the subject. "This idea of Ochs about the guy being a user. Do you want to see Erple on Narcotics or should we?"

"I better take that one, baby. If—and I say *if*—our boy turns out to be a user, it'll explain why he flipped on the Sturgis job and that'll be Homicide straight through."

He laughed, stretched hugely and, as he moved away, said to Flavin, "If you haven't gotten your report to the Lieutenant, you'd better do it, baby, or you'll hear him from here to Hoboken. See you at the line-up."

Gilman watched him stroll toward the office of Sergeant Erple, who headed the Narcotics Squad. He turned back to Flavin. "Looks like I put my foot in it," he said.

"Don't worry about it."

"But he was sore there for a minute, Jeff. I don't get it. I was only kidding about Pohl and Kiler tailing the Copland girl. Hell, I know he had to put them on her. Why'd he act like that?"

Flavin shook his head, smiling, and dismissed the incident with a wave of his hand. "Forget it, George. That's the way Ben is. He's serious even when he's kidding around, so don't make jokes about the way he operates."

"We were all kidding around a little."

"That's different. Oh Christ, it's almost nine o'clock. I'll type up the report and you call Phelps, that service manager at Tetley's, when I take it to the Dutchman. Get everything you can on Ferenc."

He pulled the typewriter stand to his chair and took three report forms and two sheets of carbon paper from the drawer of his desk. He rolled them in to the machine and opened his notebook on the desk beside him. Then, with a most unhappy expression, began heavily to stab at the keys with the forefinger of either hand.

It was well after nine when he finished and he expected a blast from Lieutenant Haas when he took the report to the office but the Dutchman merely turned the sheets in his hands with dull-eyed disinterest. Despite two whirring electric fans, his face was a loose mask of wet cement. Sweat crept down his fatty ribs like exhausted flies; his hands were slippery from it and the waistband of his pants was sodden. He didn't feel well. There had been too much knockwurst, sauerkraut and dumplings for dinner and he'd been up half the night drinking oil of peppermint like water and in the top drawer of his desk was a fresh bottle of it which Kropp had brought from the drugstore.

"Tutchek says you are doing good," he said heavily. "That's fine, fine. Tutchek put it in his report. That's what counts, the report, the record. Do your work, you have nothing to worry about."

The gas swelled, forcing something hot and painful into what he thought of as a sort of chute from his mouth to his stomach. He dimly heard Flavin's response and continued by rote:

"You are doing good. It's on the record. If you don't do good, that's on the record too. There are no excuses. Remember that. All right. You do your job and when the time comes, the record speaks for itself. That is understood. In this case, a daily report is essential. I am glad to see you have kept that in mind. If I am not here, leave the report with Kropp. He will know what to do. Thank you."

Flavin walked out slightly bewildered. It was the luck of the Irish, he decided. The Dutchman had been in a good mood for once.

2.

George Gilman had a happy little joke and sat at his desk savoring it and beaming upon the telephone with his pleasantly homely smile.

"We might just as well take the rest of the day off, Jeff," he said when Flavin returned from the Dutchman's office. "It don't look like there's much we can do before tomorrow and it's a darn shame, us with all this work."

Flavin's hand, holding a cigarette, stopped short of his mouth and his sandy eyebrows bunched. "Are you feeling all right, George?"

"Me? Yeah, I feel pretty good. This is something else. Our day's shot to hell and we can't afford to lose the time."

"All right, George, what's the pitch?"

"It's not a pitch. I called the Howards-Tetley Safe And Lock Company, Incorporated, and we're just plain out of luck, that's all. Mr. Tetley, Mr. Phelps and a couple important vice presidents named Updergraff or Downdraft or something all went to Camden, New Jersey, to congratulate each other on the new assembly plant Mr. Tetley just had built down there and they won't be back until tomorrow or maybe the day after. So with Mr. Phelps gone, there's nobody to give us the word on this Leonard Ferenc. I mean, his old address here in Hudson, the name of his scoutmaster and things like that. No wonder us poor cops have flat feet, having to contend with stuff like this."

"You mean they wouldn't tell you Ferenc's old address?"

"Well, that's what it come down to, yes. I talked to Mr. Phelps' junior assistant or office boy. His name's Herbert Wiess. Very grouchy. According to him, it's against the rules to give out confidential information without Mr. Phelps' permission. Then he hung up."

Flavin grinned and, unable to smother the joke any longer, Gilman grinned back.

"Did you talk to Herbert again after that, George?" Flavin asked.

"I thought I should call him back for his own good, so I did. I told him to get his ass over here or I'd send a squad car for him. Or should I of been politer? But it's kind of tough to be polite when you're running a bluff. Anyway, he got the idea and said he'd get Ferenc's card from Personnel and bring it right over. I told him to wait if we weren't here and he said he would. He's probably a nice guy but I don't think working for Mr. Phelps is good for his disposition."

"We'll take care of his disposition," Flavin said. "Did Birdie call? He was supposed to have phoned in before this."

"Yah. His usual line about a new heavy. Otherwise nothing."

"He must think he's practicing to get back into the con games. He ever tries it, he'll be an easy make," Flavin muttered.

There was a bright green sheet impaled by the spindle on Flavin's desk when he came back from his enforced attendance at the morning line-up. There hadn't been any possible suspects in the Sturgis case in the crew paraded across the brightly-lit stage, but every officer in the Detective Bureau was expected to be on hand, to spot the men who might, just might, sometime in the future, pull something else. Once Flavin—or any of the others—had seen a man up there, he would know him again, when the time came. If he wanted to keep his badge.

The green memo sheets were not supplied by the Bureau. Sergeant Bauer bought them in the five-and-dime with his own money because, he said, he was sick and tired of the old white paper memos being overlooked and keeping people waiting and having to tell them why the hell Detective Sherlock McJerk was down in the basement looking at the latest collection of dirty pictures confiscated by the Vice Detail instead of attending to business. He was right about one thing: no matter how high your desk was piled with junk, you couldn't miss that emerald green sheet of paper torn from Sergeant Bauer's Woolworth memo pad.

It informed Flavin and Gilman that a Herbert Wiess from the Howards-Tetley Safe And Lock Company, Inc., had been waiting to see them since 10:23 A.M. It was now 11:15 A.M. but before they could reward Wiess' impatient vigil, the telephone rang and Flavin pulled it to him by the cord. It was Joyce Ames and in her light clear voice she told him there'd be a meeting in Captain Mackenzie's office at 11:30 sharp and the Captain would appreciate punctuality.

"Those aren't his exact words, Jeff," she said, "but I don't think he really expected a girl to quote him verbatim."

"Ah, what's a few old-fashioned curses between friends?" he grinned. "All set for the big night out with Detective Second Grade Jeff Flavin, me proud beauty? How's about going to Looie's Portugese Grill on Peshine Street for a tasty bite of fried octopus?"

"I sincerely hope you're joking, Detective Second Grade Flavin."

"But that I am not, my girl. Octopus fried in olive oil is an astronomical delight. I said 'astronomical' not 'gastronomical.' 'Astronomical' means out of this world."

"Really? I'm *so* sorry I'll have to miss it but I forgot entirely to tell you that tonight is my night for washing my hair."

"You're making a big mistake, Miss Ames. It's only on Mondays, Thursdays and Saturdays that octopus tastes like garden hose. On Fridays Looie makes them of nothing but the best rubber cement money can buy."

"I'll be glad to settle for a Nedick's hot dog and orange drink."

"I'll be there at seven exactly. If you wear your Sunday dress, I'll put on a tie."

Joyce laughed. "I'll be ready at seven," she said. "But in the meantime, *you* be in Captain Mackenzie's office at eleven-thirty."

"If you say eleven-thirty, I'll be there at eleven-thirty. I guess I'm just a pushover for a beautiful girl."

She laughed again, repeated, "Eleven-thirty," and hung up.

Flavin turned and flushed when he saw that George Gilman had been standing less than two feet away all the while. But Gilman was not a four-letter-word Harry Muir.

"If something's going on at eleven-thirty," he said tactfully, "we'd better see what this guy Wiess has for us on Leonard Ferenc."

Old Bauer, whose piles were not bothering him at the moment, shook his head in simulated exasperation when they approached his desk.

"The poor guy's been sitting out there for over an hour," he said to Flavin, "and you waste time on the phone with a girl. And don't try to tell me it was the Mayor because I know that dopey look on a guy's face when he's making time with a woman."

"You're right, Sergeant, and I'll tell you a funny joke," said Flavin, whose brief chat with Joyce Ames had raised him to a state approaching elation. "Don't call her a woman—she's a ladle and we're gonna spoon. Ha, ha, ha. You didn't know I could be that comical, did you? I'm a card."

Bauer grimaced. "You're a card, all right—the deuce of clubs."

Wiess was standing at the window, his hands knotted together behind his back. He was big and awkward and his large face would have been dark and surly under any circumstances.

He glared and all but ground his teeth at the humiliation of having had to wait so long. He thrust a five-by-seven personnel form at them as if he wished it were a switch blade and said curtly, "This is all the dope we got on Len Ferenc. What ain't typed on front, I writ on the back." Then curiosity (not solicitude) overcame his resentment. "Len ain't in no trouble, is he? I seen you talking to *Mr.* Phelps yestiddy." He was another whose opinion of *Mr.* Phelps was not very high.

"Routine," Flavin gave the stock answer. "And don't jump to conclusions. Your boss had nothing to do with it."

"Give him a chance, mister," Wiess' contempt curled the words. "That's all, just give him a chance. If he thinks it'll get him a pat on the back, he'll have something to do with it, never fear."

"You don't say. Is something the matter with Phelps?"

Bitter though he was, Wiess realized he had talked out of turn in the wrong place and said quickly, "No, he's okay. All I meant was maybe he'll try to help with more than you need."

"Was Ferenc fired or did he quit?"

"He quit."

"He did? It must have been a split second before he took that swing at Phelps, then."

"He didn't swing at nobody."

"No? Why did he have to be held till Phelps ducked away and locked himself in the office?"

Wiess' features contracted angrily. "Maybe it looked that way to Mr. Phelps but it wasn't. Len and Mr. Phelps didn't get along and Len came in about ten that morning, packed his tools and said he was quitting and Mr. Phelps got mad and said he'd been fired since eight o'clock. There was some loud talk and Mr. Phelps walked away and old man Bjornson, he's shop foreman, took Len by the arm and calmed him down and then went in and talked to Mr. Phelps and Len was allowed to quit and that's all there was to it."

"Phelps dummied on that point but it was right there in the things he *didn't* say. The things people don't say are more interesting than the things they do. For instance, you didn't say you think Phelps a brownnose and a stinker. See what I mean?"

"I don't see nothing," Wiess said calmly. "I didn't say it and I don't think it."

"But he doesn't know much about safes, does he?"

"Maybe not at first, but he sat down with old man Bjornson and inside a few months he could take them apart and put them together again, except maybe the big vault jobs, like for banks, but he knows enough about them, too. He studied at night. I know because I seen all the manuals he still takes home in his brief case."

"That's not what he told us, Wiess. He said—let's see now—he said executives don't work on the production line level. That's when I asked him if he knew a safe from a loose brick in the chimney. If he's as good as you say, he should have admitted it, right?"

"If he was foreman, sure, but he's an executive and some executives, you'll never get them to admit they used to get grease under their fingernails on the job. It's like—well—he's supposed to be bigger and smarter than a screwdriver jockey and they got the idea the men'll show more respect if they don't let on they used to work at a bench, too, unless just to learn the ins and outs like Mr. Tetley in the beginning."

Flavin said, "He did? That was smart," and then, "Were you friendly with Len Ferenc outside the shop, Wiess?"

"With Len? He was only a kid. I'm a married man."

"What was his reputation in the shop?"

"He didn't have none," he said, as if the word meant criminal record.

"Was he easy to get along with?"

"Sometimes yes, sometimes no, and you can say the same about Bjornson and all the rest of us."

"Did he ever take a swing at anybody else?"

"He never took a swing at *no*body," said Wiess with emphasis.

"This is something I can check very easily, Wiess."

"Go ahead and check. You'll get the same answer."

"Uh-huh. They tell me Ferenc used to throw his money around like a drunken sailor—girls, expensive clothes, a flashy car and all that. I mean, you know the way kids are," Flavin improvised.

"Sure, some kids, mister, not Len Ferenc," Wiess looked sourly amused. "The men used to say he was practicing to be a miser, bringing his lunch to work in a paper sack, driving an old 'Fifty-one Chevvy, and as far as clothes went, once a year he bought a new suit in that factory outlet place on Mulberry Street, the one that advertises walk up two flights and save fifteen dollars."

"That's not the way I got it, Wiess. Try again."

"I don't care how you got it," Wiess snapped. "I ain't no liar."

"All right, all right, but why get so hot?"

"You as good as called me a liar and if you think you know the answers, why ask questions?"

Flavin had been listening and scanning Ferenc's personnel card simultaneously, a simple thing to do, since the card held little personal information. Ferenc was twenty-six years old, was six foot one, weighed one-ninety, had brown hair and brown eyes and was checked off as an "M," meaning male. He had worked five years for Howards-Tetley, two years as an apprentice, and prior to that had been a clerk in the Serv-U Super Market on County Road in Elmwood across the river. On the back of the card, Wiess had written jaggedly in pencil, "That's his old address on the other side and never changed it when he moved. He had a room in a boarding house in North Hudson but I don't know where. The Jefferson Avenue address is wrong." Flavin looked up and snapped the edge of the card with his forefinger.

"How come you knew this change of address," he asked Wiess.

"Do you think I made it up?" Wiess demanded aggressively.

"I was wondering why he told you, that's all."

"Sure, that's all. And you had to put it in such a way, I look like a liar!" Wiess gave his head a grimacing shake but as if he were more annoyed with himself. "Okay, I guess I shouldn't take it so personal. That old address, he didn't come right out and tell me, it was just a word he dropped here and there, like for instance he once mentioned the Mt. Windsor diner being so handy to his place and Mt. Windsor Avenue's up in North Hudson."

"In the Stone Bridge district?"

"Just the other side."

"This Jefferson Avenue address, the one you said was wrong, did he live there with his parents?"

"His parents is dead. He was an orphan. He earned his own living since fourteen."

"He'll go places," said Gilman, apparently approving.

"If he was just a little older, he'd be service manager, not Ph— Mr. Phelps."

"Maybe he had that in mind," said Flavin.

"Not a chance. He was too independent. He kept telling us he'd own his own place by the time he was forty. Can I go now, mister? Bjornson's a good foreman but I'm supposed to keep an eye on things."

"I think we got all we need for the time being, Wiess. If you happen to think of anything else, give Detective Gilman or me a ring."

Wiess promised, but without enthusiasm, and left. Flavin looked at his wrist watch and groaned.

"Ten minutes late."

3.

Joyce Ames shook her head when they walked into Mackenzie's outer office. "You don't know how lucky you are," she whispered. "Lieutenant Haas is sick and his report is being prepared. But you'd better get in there quickly."

They grinned their thanks and went through the doorway. The inner office was full of men, heads of various Details working on the Stone Bridge case. Foxy and Police Chief Sharkey stood at the window, frowning over their mumbled conversation. Prominent on Mackenzie's desk was the City Edition of the *Hudson Evening News*.

> *Sex Angle Denied*
> RAPE NOT MOTIVE IN KILLING
> OF CAROL STURGIS, POLICE CLAIM

Turcott knew how to write a news story, and where Turcott went, the *Journal*, the *Dunedin Star-Courier*, the *Elmwood Courier* and all the rest were sure to follow.

Rough-mouthed Commissioner Willie Quinn came from the john, buttoning his fly. He frowned at his wrist watch and glowered around the room. A few minutes later Kropp, the commanding secretary, bustled in carrying several type-written sheets neatly stapled together. He went directly to commanding group, said something in a low voice and handed the papers to Quinn. Kropp had a neat sense of protocol.

(Flavin would automatically have given the papers to his own boss, Captain Mackenzie.) Quinn muttered a reply and motioned Sharkey and Foxy to read along with him to save time. When they finished, Sharkey turned from the window, raised his hand and waggled it for attention.

"This is not going to be a pep talk," he said. "It's going to be short and sweet. You've all seen the newspapers—" he glanced ironically at the *Hudson Evening News* on Mackenzie's desk— "Somebody, mentioning no names, is doing his damnedest to dump a sex killing in our laps, and I don't have to tell you what a mess that can be. *So.* From now on, nobody talks to the press except Commissioner Quinn, Captain Mackenzie and myself. Keep your big traps shut. They're only waiting for us to pull a boner so they can make a front page splash. There will be no boners. Is that understood? *There will be no boners.* Work slower if you have to, but I want no mistakes. That's all. Now Commissioner Quinn has something to say."

Quinn looked at the silent men. "You know your jobs; do 'em. We don't want any excuses for sloppy work. There are none. Enough said. Captain?"

Mackenzie shook his head. "The men have their assignments," he said tersely. "They'll do all right. The Lab's going over those crumbs from the line-up with a vacuum cleaner and if one of them was a stakeout in the Stone Bridge mess, we'll bust it wide open, but don't depend on it. Just let's get going."

Quinn nodded grim approval and strode out of the office with Chief Sharkey. Mackenzie dourly flapped his hand, dismissing the rest of the men. Flavin lingered, and the Captain asked sharply, "Something on your mind, Detective?"

"I—well, I didn't see Lieutenant Walsh here. Is he sick?"

"A touch of 'flu. Are you a friend of his?"

"We were."

Mackenzie grunted. Flavin flushed. Foxy could make a grunt more expressive than spoken contempt. Flavin knew what that grunt meant—*hell of a friend, letting Tom get in this shape.*

He said, "Thanks," and left.

Mackenzie sat at his desk and leaned on spread forearms. Now why didn't I tell him to drop in on Tom, he wondered. Don't answer that, Mackenzie. Stand on the Fifth Amendment. You're the boss. You don't have to be people. We'll see what happens tomorrow. At least make sure Tom gets a doctor. Good assistants don't grow on bushes.

The search for Leonard Ferenc was an intricate thing, spreading feelers into every corner of the country. Communications used all means.

Detectives Pohl and Kiler went to Millville where Ferenc had been born and reared. The suspect's uncle had a machine shop in Dunedin; Detectives Kitteridge and Fogarty went there. The clothing factory where Ferenc bought his annual cut-rate suit, department stores, credit bureaus and whorehouses were questioned by other men. George Gilman and Harry Muir called upon the Howards-Tetley outfit. Ben Tutchek journeyed to Ferenc's old Jefferson Avenue boarding house. Flavin drove to North Hudson because Wiess "thought" Ferenc had moved to that district. There was hardly a squad in Headquarters that was not at work weaving together a tough fiber of facts to make a dragnet. But before they could begin seining, they had to know the shape and nature of their fish.

The Mt. Windsor Diner, a shabby hutch in a shabby neighborhood, huddled between a plastics factory and Johnson's Lumberyard. The owner and counterman was a bony, morose Irishman named Houlihan, who brought Flavin a cup of coffee as if that was all anyone ever ordered in this rancid eatery.

Flavin decided this was not the place to flash his badge. "I'm looking for a friend of mine," he said casually. "His name's Len Ferenc. He used to eat here. You know him?" He briefly described Ferenc.

The counterman indifferently picked his nose, listening without interest. "Ferenc? That's too American for here. All I get is hunkies and ginzos and all their names sound like a sneeze. I call 'em all Joe."

"Ferenc is a hunky," Flavin spelled the name. "I'm pretty sure he ate here. A nice guy, but kind of cheap in some ways. Used to buy his suits in a cut-rate factory, for instance. This was about three months ago."

Houlihan scowled, which meant a thought process was in labor. "Wait a minute. I think I know the guy maybe." He described Ferenc in almost the exact words Flavin had used. "That him?"

"Sounds like him."

"Then cheap's the word. If I had broiled filly for eighty cents on the menu and fried horseshit for semny-five, he'd take the fried horseshit to save a nickel. Sorry he's a friend of yours, but you brought it up first. No offense."

"And none taken. Know where he lived?"

"Nope. He just et here. His girl lives around someplace. Maybe she can tell."

"His girl? What's her name?"

"Name? I dunno. Olga, Alma, Irma. You know, a hunky. They all sound like sneezes. I don't pay no attention no more."

"What'd she look like?"

"Look like? Well—a hunky. Kind of blonde. But you should of seen the knockers on her. Like this." Houlihan made hemispherical gestures and winked lewdly. "Onct in a while when he wanted to give her a big time, he brung her in for a cup of coffee and a jelly doughnut, twenny cents, no tip. That's all I know about 'em, though. A cheap son of a bitch, like you said."

Flavin prodded him with questions but learned nothing further. He cut it short when the counterman started to become irritated. He didn't like being made to think, even about a hunky babe with a pair of knockers. Flavin stopped before the man turned outright hostile; there could be more questions later. He spun a quarter on the counter, said, "Be seeing you," and left. Houlihan picked up the coin and slowly came to the incredible conclusion that he had been left a fifteen-cent tip. Well, how about that now, he thought admiringly.

Flavin felt like a bird dog with more quail than his nose could handle. Of the city's half million population, nearly seventy thousand were shoehorned into the North Hudson precinct, known also as Polack Town. It was not a place in which a foreigner like Flavin could make his way without a native guide and translator. He didn't try. The precinct station house was the place to go.

Captain Siemer, who had a face like a shaven orang-outan, was in charge of the "house." He greeted Flavin profanely, wrung his hand, made good-naturedly sarcastic remarks about Headquarters eggheads, and turned him over to two detectives named Goldstein and Zabriski. Goldstein was tall and lanky and his manner was quick and shrewd. Zabriski, blond and gray-eyed, looked, acted and even sounded like a shorter and stockier *doppelgänger* of Ben Tutchek. They were as unlike the two time-servers, Urquhart and Jenner, as detectives could be.

"Olga," said Zabriski when Flavin told them the possible name of Ferenc's female companion. "Hell, there's an Olga in practically every Polish family. And they've all got knockers," he added, grinning. "Polish girls are the most beautiful in the world."

"Until they start looking like female wrestlers," said Goldstein.

Zabriski's grin spread. "That's fun, too."

"Sure, if you can still do it when the chick throws a hammerlock on you. But getting back to business, there's about ten thousand families in that Polska jungle out there, and that makes about ten thousand Olgas, or so. Right, Zabriski?"

"Leave out the female wrestlers and grandmas. Say two thousand

Olgas or Almas. There's fewer Almas and Irmas. And there's only one that went around with your boy Ferenc."

"That's the way to simplify things," Goldstein pretended to admire Zabriski. "We ought to have her on ice before Nineteen-sixty-one."

"Nineteen-sixty." Zabriski smiled at Flavin. "Or maybe a day or two. Anything else we should know?"

Flavin liked these men the way he liked Gilman and Tutchek. They were with it, competent, ready to go. "One more thing," he said. "If you see a newspaper reporter, you no spik da English. You can put that down as useful information. The Chief and Commissioner Quinn gave us the Word this morning and they meant it."

They nodded and let silence seep into the room. They knew the score on that dictum. If there was a leak anywhere, the men unlucky enough to be in the vicinity would get it in the neck, and Christ only knew where or when a leak would spring. You might even spring it yourself if you got overtired and said the wrong thing in the wrong place.

"Well," said Goldstein at length, "that's the way the mop flops."

On his way back to Headquarters, Flavin stopped at Graystone Memorial Hospital to see how Sturgis was. The Supervisor was Maggie Wrenn, sometimes called the Bulldozer, Old Ironsides or Moustache Maggie. She knew them all. She'd been through twenty years of it. In fact, some of the nicknames were actually terms of affection and as for Moustache Maggie, well, she didn't have to shave but that shadow on her upper lip wasn't a fern.

"Get your pants off my desk," she told Flavin. "We're not too poor to have chairs. Use one."

"Ah now, Maggie, you know the Irish. We still live in trees. These modern conveniences baffle us."

"What's on your mind? I'm busy."

"The pity of it, the things they do to a beautiful and sensitive lady like yourself, Maggie my love. That's what I came to tell you. But so long's I'm here, how's your new guest, Walt Sturgis? Resting comfortably, as you teach the girls to say on the phone?"

"He is not resting comfortably, thank you. There's blood in his urine and his testicles—balls to you, my fine feathered simian friend—are not happy and neither is Mr. Sturgis, for which I can hardly blame him. He'll be here for awhile. Under sedation—in case you were thinking of having one of your exploratory operational chats with him."

"Me? I wouldn't dream of it, mavourneen, me pretty. But now that you mention it, has he said anything about anything atall?"

"Yes, he has," she said with dry satisfaction. "He calls for his wife whenever he's conscious enough to speak. He has an idea something happened to her. We haven't told him, naturally. If it weren't for the sedation, he'd be frantic. *That's* how he calls for her."

Flavin reached up and tugged and kneaded his ear lobe, frowning. This didn't jibe with the general theory that Sturgis and Fay Copland had been in and out of bed more times than a mattress tester in a Simmons factory. It didn't jibe at all.

"You're sure it's not an act, Maggie?" he asked.

"For your information, you illiterate Mick, you have to be fully conscious and in your right mind to put on an act, and Mr. Sturgis is neither. Or perhaps he is crazy. He's an oddity. He happens to love his wife. But I suppose you foul-minded apes down at Headquarters think he plays Cupid's leapfrog as much as you do, come one, come all. He loves his wife and takes his marriage seriously. I know. I've heard him. And, Mr. Flavin, I assure you that I am not easy to fool."

"I never thought so. But on the other hand, I've heard about something called the subconscious or unconscious or whatever-it-is mind which never stops working. Even under sedation. I mean, maybe a psychiatrist might get a different slant on the way Sturgis calls for his wife as though he *knows* what happened to her and's trying to cover up. Or something."

"Or pig Latin!" she said angrily. "Suppose you'd been half mauled to death by a maniac, knowing your wife was in the same house. Wouldn't you be frantic, too? But then, policemen don't have wives, do they? When they're in heat, they just mate like monkeys."

Flavin watched her with more than idle curiosity and it occurred to him that rough old Maggie Wrenn was an extremely moral woman. Not a prude and not austere, but a woman to whom virtue was much, much more than anatomical. That sudden realization came as a surprise.

"When do you think we might talk to him, Maggie?" he asked mildly.

"It'll be at least a week," she said with cheerful satisfaction. "Doctor's orders. Anything else I can do for you, Detective Flavin?"

"Not for me," said Flavin, unfolding from the chair which audibly sighed, like most leather chairs. "But there's something you really ought to do for Sturgis. Adopt him. You'll be a wonderful mother."

"I'd love it. Please drop in again the next time you have a burst appendix. Go away. I'm busy."

Outside, Flavin nodded to himself. He respected Maggie Wrenn's opinions, even if she was a character in a gender which was filled with characters. She was a howling terror. He grinned.

At the same time, what had he learned? That Sturgis loved his wife? Maybe. Actually, it made little difference one way or another. If all the useless information a cop picked up in a lifetime were put together, it would take an asylumful of nuts to think of it in the first place. Yet, now and then, today's sludge made tomorrow's headlines, which was just about where you'd expect to find sludge. As Goldstein, the precinct bull, had remarked—that's the way the mop flops.

4.

Supervisor Margaret Wrenn, R.N., was not the only howling terror who edified the City of Hudson. When Flavin walked into the squadroom at Headquarters it was rocked and shaken by a cyclonic bellowing, which roared out of Lieutenant Haas' office. The tirade went on and on, raging, battering and stomping. Detectives scattered about the room, standing or sitting at desks with clenched faces, looked as if they were doing their desperate best not to listen. These were not tender, callow youths; they'd been hardened on the beat and tempered in the Bureau. Some were savage men and some were as brutal as the worst of the criminals they fought, but with hardly an exception they tried not to hear, for there was something in the Dutchman's voice that seemed to humiliate and degrade the whole human race, or those within earshot.

The exception was big Harry Muir, who lounged on the edge of George Gilman's desk with half a buttock, detached and moody, smoking a heavy cigar.

There was a sound as if the assembled men had simultaneously released a suspended breath when Sergeant Bauer came out of the Dutchman's office five minutes later. His face was the color of old newspapers, but his head was up and he marched, not walked, across the squadroom to his desk. He sat down and remained motionless for a long minute and then slowly began opening drawers and removing small personal belongings, such as his emerald green five-and-dime memo pads, rubber stamps, an old-fashioned silver fountain pen, a bottle of deodorant (which he applied regularly because he did not like to offend the ladies with ungentlemanly odors,) a black leather-bound volume entitled *Criminal Law Simplified*, and several jars of salves, ointments, creams and oils with which he anointed his tired, sexagenarian piles daily. He did this in calm and dignity.

Captain Mackenzie strode through the far doorway, slapping a folded newspaper against the side of his leg. He stopped short when he saw what Bauer was doing. The room was quiet and his voice carried magnificently.

"Just what in hell do you think you're up to?" he demanded.

Bauer replied quietly and Foxy glowered at him. "You God damned jackass. Behave yourself and put that junk back where it came from—" More words were exchanged but in lower tones and no matter how the gathered detectives strained and stretched their necks and tilted their ears, they could not hear a syllable of the conversation.

In the end, Foxy strode on to his office and slowly and calmly Bauer replaced his assorted possessions and the assorted cans, bottles, jars, tins, plastic containers and sprays of hemorrhoid balm. Each was guaranteed to shrink the most stubborn piles, but Bauer's had been reared in Headquarters and naturally they were tougher. He did not sit down again, however. He remained standing until a plainclothesman, one of Mackenzie's aides, came to the desk, glancing back over his shoulder at the Dutchman's lair as if measuring it for a charge of blasting powder. He grinned at Bauer, punched him lightly on the upper arm and made a derisive gesture over the same shoulder. Bauer shook his head, dismissing the subject, marched to the corridor and turned left toward the locker room.

"Well now," said Flavin, "wasn't *that* something. Anybody know what it's all about?"

George Gilman's eyes flickered, moved and elaborately focused on nothing at all. His face had no more expression than a gallon of distilled water in a sterile glass jug. He did not answer Flavin's question. For the time being, he was absent.

Harry Muir took the cigar from his mouth, looked at it with dislike and blew a scatter of ash flakes from the tip. He put the cigar back into his mouth and resumed his brooding position.

"Did I ask the wrong question?" said Flavin.

Harry's jaw bulged slightly at the hinges. His lower jaw was different from most. It did not angle downward to the chin but seemed to run straight across his face like a bar. It was the kind of jaw on which a man could break all the knuckles on both hands. If Muir permitted him to remain conscious, that is. He turned and looked not through and not beyond but all around Flavin. A tightening, vise-like stare.

"Yesterday," he said heavily, "a delivery kid came in and gave Bauer a tip on the Sturgis broad. Bauer just turned up with it, twenty-four hours late or more. Is that what you wanted?"

He ground out his cigar on the desk top, flipped the butt into Gilman's typewriter and headed for the elevators. Without seeming to move with any purpose, men drifted from his path.

"Well, well, well," murmured Flavin. "What was his part in it, George?"

Gilman was no longer absent. "Nothing out of the ordinary," he said. "Harry was just his own sweet sonofabitchin' self as usual. He was on his way to the Dutchman's when Bauer gave him the memo. You know, one of those green pieces of paper he uses. Harry said something about what kind of buggered up description was that and the old guy shook his head and didn't answer. Harry flipped me the paper and made some more remarks you could of heard in Detroit. Nobody paid no attention. That's Harry's way and there's nothing you can do about it legally. Bauer didn't say a word. He just went back to his desk."

"Is that all? Or was Harry only sounding off?"

"Well—the memo *was* kind of screwed up," George admitted reluctantly. "It said—well, I better write it out. It ain't something I ever heard pronounced."

He scribbled several words on a slip of scratch paper, which he handed to Flavin. Flavin read it and frowned. It said, "C. Stgis. House. Dived groc. order. Tl dk man. Shts? U-wear? At hme. She cled Monty. Nvr saw bfr. Dkd fst. Hans Christian Anderson, Esq., Rtd."

"It takes time," said Gilman. "I didn't get it all till the sixth or seventh try."

"What's this one—'she cled Monty.' Something new?"

"I figured it—'she called Monty.' Meaning, 'she called *him* Monty.' If I got the hang of it, I mean. You got the hang of it now?"

Flavin had the hang of it. A loose translation of the note was this: the delivery boy had taken an order of groceries to Carol Sturgis' house and glimpsed a tall, dark man who was wearing either shorts or underwear. The delivery boy had never seen him there before. The man ducked fast when the boy walked in. At least, Flavin imagined that 'dkd fst' meant 'ducked fast.' It was a logical interpretation, at any rate.

"Do you get the Hans Christian Anderson, Esq., Rtd., part of it?" asked Gilman.

"I'm not sure but I think that was Bauer's way of saying he thought the whole thing a fairy story. 'Esq., Rtd.', means 'Esquire, Retired.' Was Bauer soused when he took this, for the love of God?"

"I think maybe his piles were jumping and he wanted to put it down fast so he could go to the can and rub some gunk on them. I can't see him soused on the job, can you?"

"It could have been the piles but— How did Harry know this came in yesterday? Was Bauer dumb enough to tell him?"

"Just as bad. It was dated and he left it there. The old guy must be slipping, Jeff."

"He must be something," Flavin crumpled the note and threw it into an ancient wire mesh wastebasket. "I hate—" he broke off.

Lieutenant Hass had loosed another leather-lunged bellow. This time it was that four-letter present tense Tutchek and where the four-letter present tense hell was he and don't stand there like a four-letter defecation-visaged illigitimate child, get Muir, *ja*, and get Tutchek too, *or somebody*, get him, *get him*, GET HIM!

Kropp came scurrying into the squadroom. He looked frantically around and became still more frantic when he realized that neither Muir nor Tutchek were there. Then he spotted Flavin and loped across the floor.

"The-the-the Lieutenant wants you right away," he managed to say. "It's very, I mean, it's very important. Right away. Right now. You can't keep him waiting. He's in a bad temper and—"

He bit the sentence off, spat it out and ground his teeth. He straightened up rigidly. "I don't have to go back and be abused anymore," he cried in a loud, unnatural voice, "and you can tell Captain Mackenzie I went home. I'll be there." He didn't quite stalk from the room for there was something akin to locomotor ataxia in his gait.

"Why're we hanging around?" asked Gilman. "Everybody's leaving. Well—let's get it over with."

"No thanks. You're not going in there with me, George. Two of us will only make him twice as mad. Anyway, I was tagged, not you, so leave it lay where Jesus flang it."

He crossed to the office, humming an old song that went, "Oh, the Amsterdam Dutch and the Potsdam Dutch, the Rotterdam Dutch and the Goddam Dutch, God made the Irish and they aren't worth much, but they're damsite better than the Goddam Dutch."

Somebody laughed and Flavin grinned around the edge of his shoulder. The Dutchman's private door was closed. Flavin raised his hand, hesitated, flexed the muscles and knocked.

The too-familiar voice thudded, "Come in, come in, come in. It aindt all night."

Haas sat behind the desk, clasping the edge of it with both hands. He was drenched in perspiration. He dipped his head curtly at a facing chair and clenched the desk more tightly, so tightly in fact that his broad knuckles turned white and raised in bony peaks. Several seconds later he opened his mouth and a heavy belch rumbled forth, followed by another and another. The Dutchman's thick hands gradually relaxed their grip and he leaned back in the swivel chair. He closed his eyes. His lips moved wordlessly.

Flavin, too, relaxed, but did not take his eyes from the ponderous figure behind the desk. Finally got control of himself, he thought. Praise God from whom all blessings flow. He wasn't really afraid of the Dutchman but Haas *could* give you a bad time. Several more seconds lengthened between them. Haas either sighed, or drew a heavy breath, and opened his eyes. The flow of perspiration had lessened.

He picked up three sheets of 8½ x 11 paper from his desk blotter and held them out to Flavin. The top sheet was white, the second yellow and the third blue. This was the daily report in triplicate.

"Just what's at the end, please," he said.

Flavin's eyes widened. The last paragraph was a typescript of the note George Gilman had scribbled and this was Harry Muir's report. So Harry hadn't given Bauer's sloppy note to Haas. Here was an object lesson in how to flub your snubbers when jumping to conclusions. And Harry had not dated the note, either. Another snubber flubbed.

"A nice memo," the Dutchman said. "Very concise, very explicit. Except maybe I need a translator, eh?"

"This is our brand of shorthand," Flavin lied. "We all use it. I guess you don't see it in the reports as a rule but we can read it like anything else."

"You can? Good, Read it. I want to hear."

Again Flavin thanked the Lord, this time for George Gilman's assistance in the first translation. Flavin went through it, glibly explaining the foreshortenings. The Dutchman grunted.

"So. Good. Thank you very much. You understand all of this, eh?"

"I read it to you, Lieutenant."

"But you're *sure* you understand it?"

"I understand it, yes."

"You do, eh? Very good. Now explain to me the time this man came in and made the statement. Explain the height and weight and other statistics of Monty. Also the name of the delivery boy. Please. Thank you. Oh, excuse me. Also please the date Monty was seen in the Sturgis house in his underwear. Now, please."

Flavin leaned forward and laid the papers on Haas' blotter. "I don't know that much about it."

"No? I am not surprised. Sergeant Bauer did not know either and he wrote the original note. Very well. Sergeant Bauer is disposed of and we will say no more about it. This Monty in his underwear—"

"According to the note, he might have been wearing shorts. A lot of men wear Bermuda shorts in the summer."

"And parade around the house with a lady? No. Not if she is a lady. Is there a quick way you can find out about Monty? Somebody you can question?"

"If Monty ducked every time somebody came to the house, I'll have to dig and it won't be quick. Wait a minute. If he was a relative, a cousin, say—"

"Ah, a relative. Yes," Haas smiled dourly. "That would be an explanation. Relatives, *schweinhunds*, walk around the house in their drawers, leave the soap in the sink, on the towel shine their shoes, and eat, eat, eat you out of house and home and slobber on the table-cloth and the rug and the next thing you know, it's bugs. Don't talk to me about relatives, please. Thank you. Except Monty. He's a relative, you ask Mr. Sturgis, eh? Very simple. You talk to him."

"We can't talk to Sturgis before the end of the week. They found out he has internal injuries. Kidneys and stomach. I stopped at the hospital and the Supervisor said he's being kept on dope. Doctor's orders."

The Dutchman's face swelled and turned turkey red. He swore violently but stopped unexpectedly in the midst of it and made a visible effort to control his temper.

"Is Mr. Sturgis in danger?" he asked.

"They don't think so but it's too early to tell."

"Good. We hope. We'll wait. For better information we need the delivery boy. Find him. Or if you are working on something else, take anybody you want."

"All right."

"So easy? All right—just like that. You have a tip or a lead, maybe? Or is it a crystal ball?"

"Sorry, but my crystal ball clouded up and began predicting the weather." Flavin knew he was being a damn fool but you could take just so much and the hell with it. If they kicked him back into Pawnshop, it would be a rest cure after this.

To his astonishment, Haas vented a rusty, blatting laugh. A very short laugh. "Very funny, Detective. For the weather you need a crystal ball. In the newspaper, I don't read them, the weather. They put down the first thing that comes to their head and there's nothing in their head to begin with. But all right. The jokes we save for later. Now, how do you find the delivery boy?"

"He delivered groceries so the market is probably in the neighborhood and there aren't many markets in Stone Bridge. Once we have the market Carol Sturgis bought from, we'll have the delivery boy."

"Good, good. That's the way I like. You sit down, you think, and no shenanigans. Pick a man and tell him what to do—"

Haas' face contracted and he clutched at the edge of the desk again. Ferocity was livid in his white face and around a snarl of teeth.

"That's all," he barked, his voice rising. "Do your work. Go on, go on, get out. It's enough talk, damn it. Do your work."

Flavin said, "Right," and left, closing the door behind him. The old Kraut's nuts, he thought; they were going along okay and, *wham*, he started yelling. For no reason. He was crazy.

As he passed Kropp's desk and typewriter stand, he happened to glance down and there in the wastebasket was a crumpled ball of emerald green paper. Bauer's personal memo. Harry Muir must have thrown it there after adding it to his report. Flavin bent over and picked it up. If the Dutchman found it, there'd be another bout of merry hell. Outside at the edge of the squadroom, he glanced briefly at the paper, stiffened and read it more intently. This wasn't Bauer's neat handwriting. It was a scrawl and the lines of spired letters slanted strongly to the right. Those jagged letters were very familiar, he had seen them many times, and now he remembered watching Lieutenant Tom Walsh at the reception desk, scolding a heavy blond kid and wagging a stern finger in his face, telling the boy to go home and behave himself and stop worrying his mother. It was Tom who'd scribbled that sloppy memo, not Bauer, and it was Tom who'd mislaid it, who'd completely ignored that lead on the Sturgis woman. Christ. Tom was one of the best cops in the department. Always had been. He could smell a lead before it happened. And this one, my God, it was a sitting duck. The dumbest cop on the Force would have to be out of his mind to pass this one up. Out of his mind? Cut it out, for crisake! Is this how the Dutchman affects you? Be yourself. You're a tough Mick, remember? Everybody says so.

Flavin felt a little sick.

5.

Flavin told Sergeant Ochs of Burglary what the Dutchman wanted and two teams of detectives were assigned to find the delivery boy and get a more detailed description of Monty and, if possible, to pick up Monty too.

"We'll have a statement or something from the kid in a couple hours," said Ochs. "But why the hell wasn't the kid turned over to one of us when he was right here in the Bureau? This is ass backwards. Bauer's getting old."

Flavin's hand tightened around the ball of emerald green memo paper in his pocket. "There's nothing the matter with him, Bernie."

"He's a pain in the ass to me, you and even himself with his lousy piles. But okay, we'll put it on the road. How're things coming?"

"Nothing definite yet."

Flavin went back to his desk. Gilman paperclipped a piece of foil from a cigarette package to his lapel. "A slight token of our esteem for valor in the field of Field Marshal von Haas," he said. "A medal of honor from the entertainment committee of the Policemen's Benevolent Association."

"He's nuts," said Flavin. "I'm beginning to think everybody's nuts. Do you know if Tom Walsh came in this afternoon?"

"He's sick. A fat Sergeant from Clerical's substituting. Just the paper work, your girl friend told me."

"My girl friend?"

"Yeah, Miss Ames. Remember?"

"Vaguely." His glance found George looking reproachfully at him and he said, "Sorry, George. That was automatic. I don't broadcast things around here. Too many comedians."

"I hear you, man," Gilman agreed. "And say, I and Hannah got things all set. You're coming for dinner a week tonight. Don't ask me why women need a week to fry a couple meatballs and dump Mazola on a lettuce leaf but she said I didn't understand. Why don't you bring Miss Ames? Four meatballs're just as easy to fry as three."

"I'll be glad to bring her. If we're still on speaking terms. I should have warned her I learned dancing from a mountain climber."

"Take the spikes out of your shoes and you'll be all right, Jeff. Me, Hannah says I dance like they're playing the rambling-wreck-from-Georgia-Tech song."

The warm affection between them had grown rapidly and now here was another thing that made them more akin. Flavin was certain that Hannah, or just knowing her, had brought George out of stagnation as a beat cop. Furthermore, through just being there, she was curing him of that self-consciousness brought on by the sister who'd called him frog-face, among a lot of other sadistic needling.

Flavin knew that he, himself, was doing all right in the Bureau. Nothing phenomenal, but okay. Suppose he and Joyce Ames got together. Would it start up a dynamo he didn't even know he had in him? Like the one Hannah had thrown the switch on in George. Jesus, Mary and Joseph! he thought, struck with amazement, this is the way a guy gets himself married! Well—so what? It was better than a smack in the snoot with a wet shad. He was glad their date was for tonight. Tonight was just right. He glanced at the wall clock. A little after five. Plenty of time. He could shower, shave and dress in the elevator to her apartment, if necessary. Over the years, a cop got plenty of practice doing things on the run.

All the same, he got back to business and George Gilman gave him a quick rundown on his time at Howards-Tetley. He and Harry Muir hadn't learned much. Sourpuss Herb Wiess had given them almost everything that morning, but they'd talked to some people at random, from minor executives to workers, and chiefly they'd confirmed Wiess' statements. Ferenc was a hard worker, but headstrong; Ferenc'd bank all his wages, then borrow a ten till payday and forget to pay it back;

Ferenc should have smacked old brownnose Johnny-boy Phelps when he had the chance on account of Phelps connived him out of the job as service department manager like he'd connived everybody else out. Ferenc was quarrelsome; Ferenc ain't never guv nobody no trouble nohow, he was a good boy, and that stuff with Phelps, Phelps ast for it; Ferenc put the bite on everybody and was a couple hundred in the hole when he disappeared; Ferenc was trustworthy, loyal, helpful, friendly, courteous, kind, obedient—

"And the mystery man of the Nineteen-fifties," said Gilman. "They didn't *know* anything about him. All they had was some cockeyed ideas."

Flavin's eyes strayed again and again to the clock. Time was passing. He abbreviated his day's report to four short sentences and was about to leave when George pointed to the Incoming basket.

"There's an envelope from Sarg McShane of Records for you, Jeff. It's marked Important-Confidential-Please-Return."

Flavin swore silently and was about to say he'd take it with him and read it home, but the effects of training were too deeply ingrained. The envelope might contain something vital that George should know.

There were several newspaper clippings painstakingly sealed in transparent cellophane, plus a pompous note from McShane, telling Flavin to handle these carefully and to return them at the earliest possible moment. McShane hated to take anything out of his precious files. You didn't build a filing system just to take things out. The files were there to put things in and leave them there. An exaggeration, of course. When you wanted something from Records and Identification, McShane made his clerks hustle.

Two clippings from the *Los Angeles Graphic* gossip column, dated 1955, concerned Fay Trowbridge, née Copland. The first was about one of Fay's carefree little Adam and Eve parties which had gotten out of hand and into the bushes, or both, and had finally wound up in the police station. No one was booked, the columnist wrote in a style of sly innocence, because the gendarmes were men of the world and realized that such light pastimes were not really subversive or sponsored by Russia. Fay's husband, a wealthy realtor, had flown back to L.A. from a business conference in San Francisco, laughed merrily at the gendarmes' apologetic chagrin and generously wrote a check (amount not stipulated) to reimburse the gentlemen of the law for transporting the party back to the Trowbridges' Beverly Hills Eden. Fay's divorce followed shortly thereafter. The columnist, who knew a thing or two about libel laws, did not call her a nympho but the omission was so slyly contrived that he all but said he'd be content to have Fay until a real nympho came along, his health permitting.

It seemed a lewd and rather nasty column and George Gilman said, "This crud, I'll bet he runs a bargain basement blackmail trade on the side."

"L.A.'s full of guys like that. If a girl looks at a man twice, she's automatically a nymph. I was out there on vacation once and the crap you hear, my God, you'd think the place was a sex factory. McShane collects the damnedest things."

He glanced impatiently at the clock and quick went through the other clippings.

Police recovered Francis Tetley's car two days after it had been stolen from a Stuyvesant Avenue parking lot. Date: 1953.

Henry Bridges was elected chairman of a committee which demanded that habitual prostitutes, like habitual criminals, be sentenced to life imprisonment. Date: 1957.

Janet McKechnie, 26, an unemployed stenographer, fired four shots at John Harris Copland in the living room of his home at 7 Pomander Walk, after he denied fathering her unborn child. The bullets shattered a lamp and two windows. The woman, temporarily deranged, later admitted mistaking Copland for a man named Brown of Melbourne, Australia. Date: 1939.

Interesting, but not very.

"I've got to beat it, George," said Flavin. "Will you take this stuff back to McShane and ask him to send typewritten copies to Captain McKenzie, Lieutenant Haas, Ben Tutchek and us. It might come in handy. If anything comes up, leave a note with the super of my apartment. I'll see you in the morning."

Six

A man does not have to be an experienced sleuth to determine whether or not his date with a lovely girl is sweet or sour. By all the rules, his date with Joyce Ames should have been a quietly satisfying success, but it wasn't and Flavin could not put his finger on the reason. It baffled him. She was glowingly lovely in a deep green frock and the kind of simple jewelry with which smart women ornament themselves. It was obvious that she had dressed with care and taste, and a girl wouldn't go to that much trouble if she didn't care about the date. Furthermore she was charming and interested and the talk flowed between them with none of the sudden empty silences that drop like an asbestos curtain between two people when they're trying too hard or too little. They were in Perrin's Beefsteak Room, the best restaurant in the city of Hudson, and the management had enveloped them in subtle luxury from the moment they entered. An orchestra played with suave elegance. They danced and it was not very successful either.

"I learned dancing in police school," said Flavin. "We call it judo."

"You dance very well, Jeff."

"That's only footwork. They teach us boxing and wrestling, too. And how to break up a street fight."

She laughed and it didn't sound as if she'd been taught by a professional who trained parrots.

So, what was wrong, what was the matter?

Something.

He plodded back to their table with her when the dance set ended. Dismally. A waiter was at his elbow instantly. A cocktail, sir? Or perhaps a dry aperitif sherry? Ah yes, an aperitif sherry and a scotch and soda. Immediately, sir. He moved off swiftly and smoothly, a streamlined faithful family retainer on Timken roller bearings. He was not happy either. They, the two at the table, were having a spat. He knew it. He could always tell. And the man was a tough one. The face on him. It was long enough to use for an apron. Irish. Ugh. Spoiling for a fight. The waiter swore under his breath in prayerful Italian. A couple, they fight, and what do you get for a tip? The minimum. But there was a way. That first scotch and soda—a double. If there was one thing the Irish like better than somebody's throat in his fist, it was a drink. *Bene.* A drink it would be.

He was an astute waiter. The mellow scotch was warm and friendly in Flavin's stomach and slowly it relaxed and spread its warmth. Flavin looked at Joyce and suddenly, miraculously the evening was a success after all. *He'd* been the alien at the table. His day had finished with a sour note with Birdie and he'd been curdled, but it was all right now. He held her in his smile.

Later, the waiter—also a happier man—appeared and offered a menu as if it were a token of esteem from the management. "May I suggest the filet, sir?" he murmured. "It is most excellent."

"He's not giving you a bum steer either," said Flavin.

"Ouch," said Joyce.

"Two filets," said Flavin.

"Rare, sir?"

"Anyone," said Flavin, "who'd eat them well-done should be burned at the stake."

"Oh oh oh!" said Joyce, and smiled at both Flavin and the waiter. "Please. Are you all right, Jeff? Let me help you. Euthanasia."

They consulted the menu and Jeff ordered dinner.

"Thank you, Mr. Euthanasia," said the waiter.

And so the dinner started very well indeed.

They ate slowly, glancing at each other from time to time with the small intimate smiles of a shared experience. Smiles that reached out across the table and touched. Their conversation murmured warmly.

This did not escape the waiter. He was reminded of love, but not exactly romantic love. His attitude was more commercial and realistic. Ah, she's got him hooked. *Bene*. Now small attentions to the lady. The gentleman would show his appreciation later when his change was brought to the table on the little tray. Gentlemen in love were liberal. His measure of love was in what was left on the little tray. No more, no less. It was a very fine thing to be in love and tip the waiter with generosity. To do that was a compliment to the lady. Yes. Love was also a very fine thing when you considered the practical side of it.

Flavin leaned over the edge of the table. "That waiter's got his eye on me," he whispered. "Does he think I'm going to heist the silverware?"

"I think he's afraid we'll eat and run."

"That wouldn't be polite."

"Perhaps you should tell him. He's worried."

"I know what's the matter with him. His feet hurt. I'll lend him my arch supports and a corn plaster."

"I should have brought him my second-best girdle. It's wonderful support for the back."

They smiled at the waiter, who smiled back and made a small ducking bow.

Ah, love, love!

The tip would be at least twenty percent.

It was inevitable that Flavin and Joyce spoke of Headquarters over coffee and a torte for dessert. And inevitable, it seemed, that Lieutenant Tom Walsh's name was mentioned.

"You know him quite well, don't you, Jeff?" asked Joyce.

"Uh-huh. We were pretty friendly."

"He hasn't been the same since his wife's death."

"He changed," Flavin admitted. "They were very close. It knocked him for a loop."

"He's beginning to look old."

"He's only thirty-seven."

"He's lonely," said Joyce with conviction. "Lonely and sick."

"It's more than that. He won't let anybody talk to him."

"Have you tried?"

"Every time I see him at Headquarters, Joyce, I—"

"I don't mean Headquarters. Have you gone to his home?"

"Well, no. I mean—"

"That's what's wrong with him. Think of his sitting in that house alone night after night. It's enough to get anybody down."

"I know, but how can I go to his house when—"

"How?" she leaned forward and looked earnestly into his face. "It's very simple. Just go. You said you were friends. Well, just drop in. Friends drop in on each other all the time. It's the most natural thing in the world."

"It won't work. I've tried."

"How long ago?" she challenged him.

"In the beginning."

"And you haven't gone since?"

"Dozens of times and all I get is the brush-off. His other friends tell me the same. You don't understand."

"But I do understand, Jeff, really I do. At first he wanted to be alone. He alienated everybody. He realizes it but doesn't know what to do. I'm sure he feels badly. Now is when he really needs friends. Do you think I'm wrong?"

Flavin said, "Well, no ..." and regarded her thoughtfully. "You've taken quite an interest in Tom."

"He's a sick man, Jeff."

Flavin thought again of that woeful, neglected memo on the Sturgis woman and a man called Monty. Even a rookie would have passed it along, no matter how crazy he thought the tip. It was a bad sign.

"I guess there are times," he said in a heavy attempt at gallantry, "when a man needs a woman to do his thinking."

"Tom Walsh is merely an example," she leaned over the table-edge to make the assurance more emphatic. "He does have a problem but his friends are the ones who should help him solve it. That's true, Jeff. You can't deny it."

"You're making me feel like a bad Samaritan," said Flavin.

"It's not your fault. This is a situation in which no one is to blame, neither you nor Tom nor anyone else. But—" she stopped and caught her full, generous underlip between her teeth, giving her head a helpless shake. "I don't know what to say but unless you feel Lieutenant Walsh is a total loss to the Bureau, I think something might be done to help him."

"I don't think he's a total loss!" said Flavin forcefully.

"There wasn't a better man in the Department. He was and will be again."

"Yes—with help," was Joyce's gentle reminder. "Today he's sick and except possibly for a nurse—which I doubt—he's home alone. Has anyone been to see him? Is there a visit-the-sick committee?"

"It's, well, kind of voluntary," said Flavin; he was uncomfortable now.

"There is? I hadn't heard of it. Did they send somebody to cheer him up or see if he needs anything?"

"Uh, well, to tell the truth, they chiefly don't do much unless a guy's in the hospital."

She leaned back in her chair, folded her arms and gave him a short cool nod.

"How nice of them," she said. "You have to be practically dying before they come around. Do they bring a priest or minister with them? Do they give the almost-deceased advice about undertakers, pallbearers and cemeteries? Do they ask him if he wants to make a will? Do they make sure his insurance is paid to date?"

"Ah hell, Joyce, it's—damn it, that's not the idea."

"No? Then what is the idea? Aren't sick men interesting enough? Is that the idea?"

"If a guy's sick for a few days, we drop in to see him."

"How nice," she said, "how thoughtful. Four days? Five days? A week?"

Flavin squirmed before her cool, steady eyes. "Yeah, something like that."

"Something like that! If you happen to think of it. But for four days or a week, the poor man lies there at home, building up *esprit de corps*. Building up his strength so he can go back to work and give alma mater the good old college try."

"We're not kids," Flavin mumbled. "Anyway, most of the guys wouldn't be alone. They're married."

"You're not. Tom's not. George Gilman isn't."

Flavin shook his head in a weaving motion like a troubled leopard in a small cage. The evening was off again on a cockeyed tangent and Joyce seemed only obliquely within reach. It wasn't turning out the way he had hoped. It wasn't turning out at all. He could feel the warmth and loveliness of her but it was as if he were seeing her through a thick pane of plate glass.

Why wasn't he out there dancing with her!

At the same time, he was deeply worried about Tom Walsh and it gave him a chill to think of that botched-up memo.

"You're right," he said heavily. "I'll go to see him. I'll go to his house."

The waiter hurried to their table. "A liqueur with the coffee, sir?" he asked, smiling at Joyce; her pleasure and hers alone was the primary concern of the management, individually and collectively; yessir. "May I suggest a green chartreuse, Miss? A brandy, sir? There is nothing like a French brandy to lighten your mouth." The lift of his hand, his smile and the way he hovered at the table expressed his heartfelt desire to make their dinner a beautiful memory.

Joyce shook her head and Flavin asked for the check. The waiter said dismally, "Yes, sir," and plodded away.

Joyce looked sadly at Flavin. "I've spoiled your evening," she said, and impulsively laid her hand over his. It looked very small and slender and defenseless on the tanned hardness of his fingers. "Please don't look like that, Jeff. I'm sorry, truly I am. Let's go to the Deer Head Inn. It'll be fun."

"You haven't spoiled anything, Joyce. I was thinking of Tom Walsh. It's lousy enough to get sick without being alone too."

"I know, but ..."

"And it's a long drive out to the Inn. We both have to be at Headquarters early tomorrow. We'll go—well, next Saturday. All right?"

"Of course, Jeff. Saturday is perfect."

"It's a date. You sewed yourself up that time, woman."

She crinkled her eyes at him. "I can't think of a nicer way to be sewed up, not even in a mink-lined shroud." She laughed. "What a thought!"

"About the movies tonight," he continued, "let's skip them, if we can. The best one in town is a Cecil B. deStinko called The Ten Commandments Ride Again. I can live without it. Let's—stop in for a minute and see how Tom Walsh is."

"Take me home first, Jeff. I think you should go alone—, well, this time."

"I don't think so," he said stubbornly. "It'll look better if we go as a committee."

"It won't, Jeff, it won't at all," she looked as if she wanted to flee; she drew back her right hand and knotted it into her left, glancing distrait at the exit to the foyer. "It really won't. He'll think we were on a date and stopped to see him as an afterthought. He'll resent that. I know."

"All right, I'll come right out with it. I need moral support. I'll hardly know what to say. You will. All I'll do is sit there and say how are you and that's too bad and oh, you'll be up and around before you know it and make some bum jokes because I won't know what else to do."

"You'll know what to do, Jeff. You're old friends. I'll only be in the way."

The waiter returned. The check was face down on a small pewter tray. He set it on the table beside Flavin without enthusiasm—and gaped when Jeff left him a twenty per cent tip. He'd have been surprised if he'd gotten the ordinary fifteen per cent, the way they'd started scrapping again. Anybody could see they'd been scrapping. Or maybe he'd better start taking lessons. But he was a good waiter. He didn't snatch up the tray and dart off before Flavin changed his mind. He snapped out of the gape and gave Joyce the red-carpet treatment. He hastened around the table and drew back her chair as she rose. To Flavin he said, "Thank you, sir. Was everything all right?"

"Oh, fine. We'll come more often."

More often? Then the gentleman had been in before. Make a note of it. Keep it in mind.

"It was nice seeing you again, Mr. Euthanasia," said the waiter, catching the *maitre's* eye and nodding significantly. "And it was nice that you brought a lady this time—" Tact, that was the way to do it, tact. "Was the dinner satisfactory, Miss?"

"It was wonderful," said Joyce solemnly, "just wonderful." The *maitre*, alerted by the waiter, met them in the foyer with a camellia for Joyce.

"A flower," he murmured. "A remembrance. *Our* remembrance."

"Why, thank you," she said, and smiled at Flavin as she pinned it to her dress. "Camille. *La Traviata.*"

But the *maitre* had neither read the book nor seen the opera. "The flower of happiness," he said.

Joyce smiled at him and said it was lovely, just lovely. Outside, she said. "Well, Mr. Euthanasia, I think it very apropos for you to make a sick call this evening."

"*We* are making the call," said Flavin. "You're coming, too."

"Of course, Jeff. But wasn't it nice of the waiter to be glad you brought a lady this time. Who did you bring last time—a female wrestler?"

"I've never been in that beanery before, so help me God."

"Aren't waiters wonderful?"

She did not have much to say when they drove away from the restaurant. She sat beside him in a clouded silence. Apart, but not remote. Separated by unvoiced thoughts.

"You don't have to come, Joyce," said Flavin. "I shouldn't have made a production of it."

"Neither should I. We'll go as a committee."

Tom's house was in the Old Brook section of Hudson. A comfortable house with a verandah on three sides. A house from a quieter era. Lights burned in every room on the first floor and the drawn shades were luminous. The second floor windows were dark and blind. There was a lagging hesitance in Flavin's ordinarily crisp stride as he mounted the familiar porch steps and pulled the bell. It was an old-fashioned bell, operated mechanically by a wire. How often had Grace laughed at that anachronism? But she'd really liked it and the dignified clang it made.

Stop thinking of Grace!

Flavin waited uneasily and Joyce stood close, as if she too were nervous. It was a tense, suspended moment and there was no need for it. A nurse would answer the door. They would not be confronted by a wooden-faced Tom who'd stand in the doorway and tell them he was too busy for visitors.

Tom confronted them. Tom in a crumpled bathrobe, wearing socks but no shoes, unshaven, uncombed. He peered at them.

"Well for the love of mud," he said boisterously, "if it isn't old Flav and— for Christ sake!—Joycie Ames, the Ice Maiden. Come in, come in! Who wants to stand on the porch? Come on."

He made a wide, loose gesture with his arm and led them into the house. He staggered slightly at the living-room arch and caught at the frame to regain his balance. Flavin watched in horror. Tom was drunk. Sloppy, bleary-eyed drunk. His bathrobe flapped open and underneath he was wearing only a pair of torn blue shorts.

The living-room had never been meticulously neat. Clean, yes, but not orderly. Grace had never been a fussy housekeeper, but she and Tom enjoyed the happy disarray. Disarray was no longer the word. The room was a mess of dropped newspapers, empty tuna fish, soup and beef stew cans, unbagged laundry, milk cartons, streaked crockery and dust. The sofa was covered by a carelessly bunched sheet and a blanket. A pillow lay on the floor. This was where Tom slept.

He moved uncertainly across the room and took a bourbon bottle from atop the TV. Other empty bottles stood on the floor in an uneven pattern. It took Flavin a few minutes to realize that Tom had drunkenly used them to form a crude "G." "G" for Grace.

Tom brandished the bourbon, swaying. "A drink, eh, Flav?" he patted the bottle, grinning foolishly. "Jussa minute. Glasses. Need glasses. Inna kitchen. Mind getting them, kid? Inna kitchen. Ice inna 'frigerator. No soda. Onna rocks. Okay?"

"We dropped in to see how you were feeling, Tom," Flavin managed to say; he did not look at Joyce. "Your secretary said you had a touch of 'flu."

"'Flu? Who said so? Never hadda sick day in m'life. Coddle y'self, thass all. The hell with it. You know me, Flav. Right? Right? Let's have a drink."

"A little later, Tom. We ... just had one."

"Okay. What the hell," he fumbled on a console table cluttered with newspapers and soiled clothing and found a glass. He closed one eye, focused the other, and with the stiff care of the very drunk, filled the glass. He tasted it and made a face.

"Wanna know something, Flav?" he said. "This stuff's a lotta crap. An' you know why? Gives you a gut ache. Heaved all over the bathroom. Lookit this," he turned his head and showed a cut on his cheekbone. "Fell inna bathtub, the sonuvabitch. Hey, how's about a drink, Flav? Give ole

Joycie one, too. Do her good. She's a nice kid, know what I mean? She's okay. But do her a favor and get her down off that ole iceberg. A nice kid like her, an iceberg's no place. Bring her down to earth. You gotta get out and live, Joycie. Have a drink."

"A—a little later, Tom, thanks," she said in a stricken voice.

"Sure sure sure. Alla time inna world. You know something? Ole Flav here, sometimes you can't give him a drink. Thassa fact. Cant' give'm a drink. Won't take it. But he's okay—okay—okay ..." He stared moodily into his glass. "I got ideas for Flav," he said darkly. "I'm gonna see he goes places. A place. I gotta place. I'm gonna take care of Flav, unnerstand? All settled. Right here," he waveringly tapped his head. "I know what I'm doing. He's no mutt, Joycie. He'll be right up there next to Foxy Mackenzie. I'll take care of him. Don't worry about that. Soon—soon—"

He swayed, clutched the table and closed his eyes, clenching his teeth.

Joyce whispered anxiously, "He should be in bed, Jeff."

"Yeah."

Tom's eyes opened. "Whattaya mean, bed?" he demanded.

"You've had a touch of 'flu, Tom," said Flavin.

"'Flu my ass. Hadda gut ache. Bed. Hey, that ain't Joycie Ames. Trying to kid me, eh? What's going on?"

"It is Joyce, Tom. We stopped in to see how—"

"Don't give me that crap. I heard all that stuff about bed anna hell with it. She's a whore you picked up down Market Street but you're not getting me in bed with her, pal. I don't want it. Get her out of here. Out, out, both of you!" his face contorted and, raising the bottle like a club, he plunged wildly at Flavin, shouting, "Out, out, out!"

His feet tangled in a pair of pants on the floor and he sprawled forward, striking his head against a wooden chair. He sighed, rolled slowly on his back and relaxed, unconscious.

Flavin lifted him. "Switch on the hall lights," he told Joyce. "I'll put him to bed upstairs."

She nodded and hurried to the arch. She was crying. The tears swelled, fell from her eyes and rolled heavily down her cheeks. She seemed unable to speak and kept her head turned from Flavin.

He carried Tom upstairs. It was fifteen minutes before he returned. His eyes were leaden.

"He'll be all right," he said. "He didn't hurt himself. He'll be out for the next twelve hours. I've seen guys pass out before. I made him drink some bicarb. He won't feel so lousy when he wakes up. I'll take you home now."

"Thanks, Jeff." Her voice was all but inaudible.

He saw her glance move about the room. "I'll come back and clean it up a little before I turn in," he told her. "I want to take another look at Tom anyway."

She answered with a nod. She was crying again.

"He'll be all right," he repeated in a plodding voice. "What he needs is sleep."

He drove her home. They did not talk about Tom Walsh. They did not talk about anything. There was nothing to say. Everything had been said. Perhaps not in words, but it had been said, all the same.

At her apartment, she said, "Good night, Jeff," unlocked the door and drearily walked toward the elevator. He went back to the car. He felt as if he had been scraped hollow with a garden hoe.

She was in love with Tom Walsh. He did not have to figure it out. It was all there. The conversation in the restaurant, their going to see Tom, the way the bleak tears had come to her eyes. She'd be good for Tom. She was the right kind of woman. He did not pretend he didn't mind. He did. He minded very much.

Ben Tutchek was also having some difficulty with love. He and Harry Muir were searching for a girl named Angela Balik. According to neighbors, Angela had once been almost engaged to Leonard Ferenc. Whatever "almost engaged" meant. That was not the difficulty. The difficulty was that Angela Balik seemed to have disappeared.

2

Flavin spent the night in Tom Walsh's house. At six in the morning, Tom was semi-conscious but flushed and drenched in sweat. Flavin found a medical thermometer in the now-clean bathroom. Tom recognized him when he returned, shaking the thermometer to force down the mercury.

"I thought it was you, Jeffo," he said. "Or is this the DT's?"

"Shut up and open your mouth, playboy."

"It's not the DT's or you'd be pink, like elephants. What's that thing?"

"Thermometer. Keep your mouth open for a second."

"You're wasting your time, Jeffo. All I've got is a hangover. How'd you get here anyway? In the Welcome Wagon? Okay. Welcome to my daily hangover."

"Hangover hell. You're burning up. There. Good. Now keep your mouth closed for a minute."

"Three minutes," mumbled Tom around the thermometer. "Read the directions on the box top. This is the first time anybody ever took a reading on my hangovers. Doctor Flavin, I presume?"

"Shut up."

Walsh seemed glad to close his eyes. His gaunt rack of bones seemed to flatten and sink into the mattress. Flavin felt sicker than Tom looked. The alcoholic ward down in Graystone was full of emaciated men. Tom had been a big man but now he weighed no more than a five-foot-seven necktie clerk in Bergman's Department Store. His bones were urgent knobs and slats. The skeleton was pushing through. All this in the few months since Grace's death. Tom was a gum-chewer but Flavin now remembered that there was always the odor of Sen-Sen, peppermint or coffee beans on Tom's breath.

Tom did not open his eyes when Flavin removed the thermometer and held it to the light, his back to the window. Tom had a fever of 103.6°. Flavin immediately called Maggie Wrenn at the hospital.

"I want a doctor, Maggie," he said. "A good one, a guy who knows a patient's ass from his elbow. Tom Walsh is on fire."

"Did you take his temperature?"

"One-oh three point six."

"Cover him with asbestos. I'll get somebody right away."

A doctor arrived in less than twenty minutes. He hurried up the cement walk and introduced himself as Forstenburg. He was short, slight and brisk. "The patient?" he said. Flavin canted his chin toward the second floor and led Forstenburg upstairs. The examination was also brisk. Flavin watched intently. He knew the difference between a real doctor and a hand-holder. But then, Maggie Wrenn would never have sent him a cluck, which was why he had called her in the first place.

"Well?" said Flavin when Forstenburg straightened and pushed back his stethoscope.

"Miss Wrenn said he's a police lieutenant. Is this the way the Police Department takes care of its men?" He looked angry.

"He pushed himself too hard. We didn't know. His wife was killed in a car accident six months ago. We thought it was that."

Forstenburg's "Well—" was a kind of apology. "He needs a nurse around the clock but he'll be better off in a hospital."

"What is it?"

"Malnutrition, too much liquor, influenza. All he needs now is pneumonia. Well, what do you want to do with him? Leave him here?"

"Hospital. Private room."

Forstenburg dipped his head curtly. "He'll live. He must have the constitution of an ape."

"Flu," said Flavin. "I'll be damned."

He drowsed on the sofa after an ambulance took Tom away. His built-in alarm clock did not work very well and it was nine-thirty before he strode into the squadroom of the Bureau.

"Christ," said George Gilman, "you look like you were up all night."

"I've been up since Christ was a juvenile delinquent. I'll be back in a minute."

He crossed the big room to Mackenzie's outer office. Joyce too looked strained. Her eyes were dark and enormous, filled with that one anxious question.

"I went back and stayed the night," Flavin reassured her. "He woke up this morning with a temperature. 'Flu."

Relief washed over her like surf. "So it was 'flu all along. Only 'flu. Does—does he have a nurse?"

"Well, Doc Forstenburg suggested the hospital. It's cheaper and more efficient. If Tom stayed home, he'd have to have a nurse, a cook and at least a part-time housekeeper, and that's too complicated."

"I'll—I'll tell Captain Mackenzie. He's been worried. And, Jeff—"

"What?"

"I shouldn't have nagged last night. I'm sorry. It, well, there should be a more active committee to, you know, I mean to see that a man has proper care when he's sick. I'll speak to Captain Mackenzie about it. Are you angry?"

"Angry? Oh. You mean, the way I look. Uh-uh. I sat up all night with a sick friend."

"Please don't be angry with me," she said in a small, forlorn voice, bowing her head. "I didn't mean to nag. You really are his friend."

"After you pushed me into it."

He grinned wearily. Later it occurred to him that he had not mentioned their Saturday night date at Deer Head Inn. Date! Two people just going through the motions, and she carrying the torch for Tom Walsh. His jaws tightened. It *was* a date and he'd *keep* dating her! They hadn't blown the whistle on him. As the Dutchman would say— the hell with that noise! He strode back to the desk.

"What's going on?" he asked, haunching on the edge of Gilman's desk.

"Everything," said Gilman. "I'll give it to you one at a time. We're bustin' out all over. A precinct bull, Zabriski, from North Hudson called in and said Ferenc's girl friend was a blonde named Esther Veen, but she don't live there no more. Disappeared or something. Worked in the plastics factory, lived alone, no family. They're trying to get more of a line on her. Zabriski said he'll feed it to us as he gets it."

"He's a smart cop. But what's this disappearance angle?"

"Quit her job without notice. Same with the boarding house. Nobody knows from nothing, except she went around with Ferenc. She was last seen two days before the Sturgis job. She's got twelve dollars pay coming from the factory and she left clothes in the boarding house. A couple dresses, underwear, shoes and a Woolworth suitcase. Zabriski says the whole kit and kaboodle's worth about three ninety-eight, if that. Junk."

"Maybe she didn't think it was junk."

"I hope she did, Jeff. I hope to God she did. But—" now Gilman did look like a hard, tough cop, "Ferenc had another girl friend before her. Ben Tutchek dug up the name. Angela Balik. And *she* disappeared about a year ago. It's getting to be a stinkeroo. I hate to think of the newspapers. Anyway, Ben and Muir are working on it."

"Same kind of disappearance as the Veen girl?"

"Not exactly. She left one night and took her clothes but didn't say nothing to nobody. One of the neighbors *thinks* she was a B-girl in a deadfall somewheres but took it back when Ben put it to him yes-or-no. The landlady says she was a nice, clean-living girl and gave her—the landlady—one of them Toni permanents once in a while to help pay the rent. *She* said Angela Balik was a model. Where I come from, every whore you pick up calls herself a model."

Flavin grunted. Ferenc had gone steady with two girls and both disappeared. Ferenc liked the feel of money. How many would it be when they finally caught up with Ferenc? It might have started as a business operation, the first killing an accident, but after awhile a killer could get blood-hungry. Did the girls have money? One was a factory worker, the other probably a hooker, a two bit-lay if she had to give the landlady a Toni in part payment of rent.

"Where's the money angle, George?" asked Flavin.

"Savings accounts, maybe. War bonds. Esther Veen lived alone, no family, mother and father dead. Suppose they left her a piece of property. That's better than cash sometimes. What do you think?"

"We'll have to do a lot of digging."

"I know, but a miser type like Ferenc, there's a money angle. All we got to do is find it. It's there. This is only a hunch, but think Ferenc over for a minute. He promoted every buck he could."

"Were all his friends women?"

"As far as we can find out, he never played pool with the guys, went bowling, played ball or nothing. That ain't natural, Jeff. And with women, he'd go steady with one at a time. He never played the field. That ain't natural neither. He knew what he wanted and went after it—the buck. It's just a hunch, though."

"They pay off sometimes. We'll pass it down the line and put it with the other stuff we have for Communications."

Gilman looked pleased and said, "I wanted to see what you thought before I said anything. I got it all down in notes. Ben's in with the Dutchman. We'll tell him when he comes out."

Flavin said he'd call Zabriski and Goldstein at the Precinct and see what they could do with the new angle. He glanced at the neat stack of notes, memos and reports Gilman had arranged on the desk before him. They made quite a pile, carbon copies of information that had gone also to Foxy, the Dutchman, Chief Sharkey, Commissioner Quinn, Ben Tutchek and the Lab.

Detectives Kitteridge and Fogarty: The name of Ferenc's uncle was Peter Ferenc. He owned the Acme Tool & Die Company, Duneden. Age 76, widower, no children. Leonard Ferenc worked two years for him. Told the uncle to go to hell and walked out. (Footnote from Kitteridge, "Old tightwad paid the kid $20 a week.) Uncle claimed Ferenc was the best toolmaker he'd ever had. Wanted him back. Willing to give him 49% interest in the shop. Ferenc to inherit other 51% when the old man died. Ferenc wouldn't get a penny unless he came back. Old man wanted to retire. Said Ferenc quit because he was girl crazy but could not name girls. Very little available info on Leonard Ferenc. Kept to himself. No known friends or acquaintances. Went steady with a girl named Janet—. Last name unknown. She had subsequently moved from Duneden. Address unknown. Couldn't get any pix of L. Ferenc.

"Went steady," Gilman pointed out. "Moved from the city. Address unknown. Now is that the same MO or is that the same MO?"

"Could be."

Detectives Pohl and Kiler: subject born in Millville. Parents, Joseph and Marie Ferenc. J. Ferenc a day laborer. Lived in slum area known as The Shacks. Subject's school record: unsatisfactory. Said to be smart but cocky. Over-interested in girls. Expelled from Barton Junior High School. Reason: struck Diana Cuthbert with his fists, broke her nose. Alleged explanation: girl laughed and turned down subject's invitation to school picnic. Daughter of wealthy local real estate broker. Girl at college in France. No info on Ferenc available from family. Subject not known to have school friends. Nickname: Lobo. No photographs.

"Lobo" meant wolf in Spanish but it was well known in English, too. Wolf—a chaser. Also lone wolf. Ferenc had started young.

Detectives York and Tellup: found delivery boy who took groceries to Sturgis home. Name: Raymond Mankey. Age: 20. Drove truck for Nivens Food Mart, 812 Mt. Windsor Avenue, Stone Bridge precinct, city. Saw a man Carol Sturgis called Monty in Sturgis home several times during past three months. Saw Monty in Sturgis home four succeeding days of week preceding murder. Mankey does not know if husband was at home. When Mankey made the last delivery, Monty came into the kitchen with a glass of whiskey. He was wearing only walking shorts or boxer type underpants and leather sandals. Carol Sturgis became angry and told Monty to "get back there," R. Mankey testified. Description of Monty: height, approx. 6 feet; weight, approx. 180; age, approx. 30. Monty was further described as suntanned. He had dark, wavy hair and a moustache Mankey called "kind of medium," meaning neither bushy nor thin. Had no scars, birthmarks or tattoos. Wore a dental bridge, upper incisors. Mankey said, "He laughed when she bawled him out and popped them at her." When asked what he meant by "popped," Mankey said Monty "sort of" pushed them out of place with his tongue and made a face and stood his hands up by his ears and wagged them like a rabbit. Monty had a slight limp in left foot. Part of large toe and second toe were missing, Mankey thought. Not sure. The sandals were "open in front, just two straps across. Mankey said Monty walked pigeon-toed and bow-legged but "not so's you'd notice it if he had his pants on." The best the delivery boy could do with a description of Monty's face was, "He looked an awful lot like Gary Cooper, only he didn't have them deep lines." Was lean but had broad shoulders. Walked very erect like a soldier "up West Point." Mankey said, "He looked, well, you know, snotty even when he was laughing." Under questioning, Mankey said he meant Monty looked "high class, like he was born with a million bucks and didn't give a damn about nothing and nobody. He didn't mean snotty like some people were snotty. Mean-nasty-snotty. It was different—high class. Mankey did not know the color of his eyes.

Altogether, it was a better description than most. Flavin laid it aside with Detectives Pohl and Kiler's report on how Ferenc had broken the nose of a girl who'd scorned his picnic invitation, which was interesting also because the girl was the daughter of wealthy parents.

There was a coldly formal report from the Crime Lab. A hitherto unremarked sneaker print had been found in the coal bin in the basement of Henry Bridges, second burglary victim. Bridges had converted his furnace to oil and the coal bin was unused. It had been overlooked during the first investigation because it was at the opposite end of the long basement from the stairway to the main floor.

Two photographs of sneaker prints were stapled to the report. Photograph "A" (Bridge's home) was different from Photograph "B" (Sturgis home.) Under Remarks, Bert Saide, the Lab's footprint technician, noted that the sneakers worn in the Bridges home were almost new, while those worn in the Sturgis home were several months old and had been given constant wear, "particularly in areas which had possibly come into contact with clutch, brake and accelerator pedals of an automobile." Saide added dispassionately that the "Sturgis" sneakers were sold in large quantities by Sears Roebuck and the "Bridges" sneakers in large quantities by Montgomery Ward. Further information was being sought from the Montgomery Ward manufacturer, however.

The Pawnshop, Robbery and Burglary Details had no information on the possible "fencing" or disposal of the stolen jewelry. A memo from Sergeant Gill, Pawnshop, said that the Prudential Insurance people were investigating the heirloom jewelry theft as reported by Francis Tetley.

Flavin grinned over that little sidenote. "The insurance dicks don't believe that little son of a bitch either," he said to Gilman. "Hell, a thief'd be nuts to lift that kind of junk. He couldn't get rid of it. Is there anything important in the rest of those reports? Let's get finished with it."

Gilman picked up the next report. "Detectives Urquhart and Jenner, Stone Bridge precinct," he read, "Questioned neighbors, businessmen and cab drivers for information on Monty. They drew a blank. Here's a note from Sergeant Ochs. None of them wrecks he shoved into the line-up have confessed to being the lookout on the burglaries. Sergeant Nairn, Safe And Loft, says here that none of the petermen that left the city after the Sturgis kill fit the description of the killer in height or weight, and his pigeons give most of them cross-checked alibis."

In his opinion, the burglar came in from the outside especially to make those four strikes, but his pigeons, to date, hadn't gotten a line on the guy. Under the typescript, Nairn had added in pencil, "If you ask me, this bird cooked up that screwy MO just for those jobs. I know I'm a big help. Sorry. We're still in there pitching."

"That's the last of 'em," Gilman said, stretching.

Flavin said, "Thank God." He wanted to start moving. They talked for a moment and laid out a quick schedule. Gilman phoned Bert Saide in the Crime Lab to ask if the two pairs of sneakers had been worn by the same man. Flavin called the North Hudson precinct. Zabriski was out but Goldstein was there. Zabriski had gone to the Mt. Windsor Diner for a talk with Houlihan.

Flavin told Goldstein about the money angle theory on Ferenc and asked if the girl friend, Esther Veen, had been left a house or property or even jewelry when her parents died. Or would Goldstein have to dig for the information?

"I got it right here, Flavin," said Goldstein. "The Veens—mother, father and daughter—lived right around the corner on Irving Street. The name was Vinowski, but the girl changed it after the mother and father died. They never had a dime. I knew them. They were clean, decent people but the old folks couldn't seem to learn English. Or didn't want to. The old man earned thirty-two fifty a week pushing a broom in Hudson Plastics, Inc., so there was nothing to leave the girl but three rooms of furniture. She sold it for fifty dollars but could have gotten two hundred, counting silverware, appliances and a pewter samovar two feet high. It was a real showpiece. Esther wasn't what you'd call bright. Her brains had been kneaded too often."

"Kneaded?"

Goldstein chuckled. "Her brains, Mr. Flavin, were all in her mammaries, I'm certain. She had the most beautiful pair of knockers I've ever seen, and if you watched her walk down the street, head up, chest out, you'd know instantly that her boobies were hard at work sizing up the situation. They fairly quivered. Sheer concentration, of course, and what a concentration."

"Oh, that type."

"You're wrong, Mr. Flavin. She was a high-minded girl. You could admire her mind, but that's all she'd put out this side of the altar. Maybe she wasn't so dumb at that. And she was a good bookkeeper, they tell me at the factory. As a matter of fact, her boss, Emile Benjamin, said he tried to talk her into taking an accountancy course. He told me she had a wonderful head for figures."

"What about Ferenc?"

"Benjamin kind of remembers her saying she was going to get married but she never had an engagement ring."

"If she was a bookkeeper, she must have been doing all right. How much did she make a week?"

"You don't know this Hudson Plastics outfit, friend. They're cheap sharpshooters. She was listed on the payroll as a clerk and made a dollar and a quarter an hour before taxes."

"What about clothes? Girls like that usually have a closetful."

"She owned exactly one wash-and-wear skirt and sweater and she wore it three hundred and sixty-five days a year. The junk we found in her room she wore when she cleaned house. She was a dedicated housecleaner, the landlord told us. She did it every day and over weekends she scrubbed and polished and waxed and all the rest of it. Her room is spotless. There was only one thing wrong. She'd bore the living hell out of you."

"Except in bed."

"Personally, I don't think she was any good at that either, Flavin. All she had was a pair of overstuffed boobies. She was a cow."

"Can you think of any reason why Ferenc might dump her in the river?"

"Flavin," said Goldstein somberly, "I don't want to think about it at all. I know I have to, but I'll wait till I see how things shape up. Actually we don't know anything about Ferenc. It's guesswork, all of it. Except the burglaries. I'd bet on those."

Flavin told him that Ferenc's former girl friend, Angela Balik, had also disappeared. "But I'll go along with you on that angle," he said. "I'll wait and see."

There was a small silence and then Goldstein said sadly, "I just stopped going along. I don't believe in coincidence. I feel sorry for that poor Veen kid. I knew the family. I'll call in the minute we get a break. Zabriski might pick up something at the Diner. Houlihan understands Polska and hears a lot of stuff when he isn't too damn lazy to pay attention."

Flavin dropped the phone back into its cradle. He looked up and Gilman said, "According to Saide, the sneakers could have been worn by both birds. I mean the same bird. The size is alike. The reason he's checking with the manufacturer is that the mold for the sole on the Bridges sneaker—the left one—was pitted and the marks show up. He says they'd catch that on a quantity job and make a new mold. Maybe we can find out where the first batch was distributed, he says. That'll be a help. Ben Tutchek's waiting for us at his desk. Muir's out trying to get a lead on the Balik dame." His voice turned icy when he spoke Muir's name.

Flavin knew why and told him that Harry hadn't turned Sarg Bauer in at all and typed the memo on his own report. He'd sort of covered Bauer, if you wanted to look at it that way.

Gilman said, "Okay. For him, it was a good deed, I suppose. But anybody else would of checked with Bauer first."

Flavin said nothing about Tom Walsh.

There were no jokes in Ben Tutchek today. That was usual. He always became more and more serious as the problems of a case intensified. "How's it with you?" he greeted them.

Flavin quickly sketched his conversation with Goldstein. "The Veen girl had no money," he said, "so if Ferenc knocked her off, it wasn't that. Her right name is Vinowski. She shortened it when her mother and father died. Any leads on Angela Balik?"

"Finding a hooker in this town is a needle in a haystack. There's a million of them and Christ knows what name she's using now. What's the matter? Got a toothache?"

"I just thought of something," said Flavin. "Maybe she isn't a hooker."

"All right, if you've got a better idea, let's have it."

"You told George she used to give her landlady a permanent once in awhile to help pay the rent. She must have been pretty good at it, or was this the landlady's favorite charity?"

"That bitch? She's tougher than the Marine Corps put together. Hey—!" Tutchek stared at Flavin and nodded. "I think you got hold of something. Let's squeeze it."

"Well ..." Flavin felt his way along. "Ferenc wouldn't get himself 'almost' engaged to a hooker, so maybe the girl was an out-of-work beautician. Some of them get fed up with messing around crabby women or try to start a shop and go bust. Beauticians make good money and even little neighborhood shops clean up. I once went around with an operator. She worked in a little three-chair shop and said the owner figured to retire before she was fifty. Now I can see Ferenc in the picture."

"If there's anything I hate," said Tutchek, "it's the damn Irish. They always know twice as much as people. But okay, we'll try the beauty shop operators. They're better-looking anyway. What do you think of this Monty business?"

"York and Tellup got a nice description from that delivery boy."

"I'm talking about how Bauer messed it up," Tutchek growled. "Our two leads are Ferenc and Monty and Bauer almost booted the Monty tip. The guy's getting too old for the job, damn it!"

Flavin glanced involuntarily over his shoulder and saw the wide, heavy back and white head of Sergeant Bauer at the reception desk. Well. So Foxy knew. He wouldn't have put Bauer back on the job unless he knew Tom Walsh had been the one who'd goofed on that tip. Now how did Foxy know? Bauer wouldn't have told him. Mackenzie was either clairvoyant or had eyes and ears all over the place.

Flavin put his finger to his lips, then pointed to the telephone on the desk beside Tutchek. "Watch your tongue, Ben," he whispered. "Foxy's got a concealed mike on every phone in the Bureau."

Tutchek jerked upright. "What!"

"It's a fact. There isn't a phone without a bug. How else would Foxy see all, hear all and know all?" Tutchek relaxed slowly into his chair and regarded Flavin with slitted, speculative eyes. "Is there something on this Bauer hassle I don't know?" he asked at length.

Flavin shrugged and made his expression as bland as he could. He should remember never to underestimate Ben Tutchek. "Just as a guess," he said, "Bauer isn't back in the chair just to keep his tail warm. I've given up trying to figure Foxy out. Sometimes he does things and the reason turns up six months later. You know that."

Tutchek's eyes remained locked a few seconds longer and then they opened a little and Flavin saw a sharp, probing scrutiny come into them.

They opened still wider and Flavin saw that Ben had taken it apart, examined the details, and put it together again, the hidden pieces brought to light. It went no further than that. Ben said nothing about Tom Walsh, although he knew Tom took the desk whenever old Bauer went to the men's room to anoint his burning piles.

"Well," he said, "we're back on the track and that's the main thing. Did you read the report sent in by those two mutts, Urquhart and Jenner?"

"They had only last night to work on it. They might turn up something today."

"You're damn right they'll turn up something today," Tutchek laughed grimly. "They're going to turn up their goddam toes, that's what they're going to turn up. Captain Rhodes is being transferred to The Point and they're going with him. Haas and Mackenzie really blew their stacks, and did Foxy tear into Rhodes! He told Rhodes that if the three of them are still alive this time next month, he'll put them on the honor roll. Just take a look," said Ben incredulously, "here's this Monty guy sneaking in and out of the Sturgis house for three months, every time the husband's away, and Urquhart and Jenner, who ought to know their precinct inside out, can't find anybody who even saw the guy! That's police work, brother; that's real sleuthing. The hell with them."

"George and I'll nose around and see what we can pick up."

"It's your potato but don't let it burn you, baby."

Flavin made no comment. He felt sorry for the three precinct men. But he agreed whole-heartedly with Tutchek. There was no place for goldbricks in a hot case like this one. But worse, it put George and him on the spot. He glanced sidelong at Gilman but George was solidly untroubled.

"We'll look it over and see what we need," said Flavin.

"I hope you're not walking in cold, baby."

"No. We have a couple things. Fay Copland, for instance. She's supposed to have been Carol Sturgis' best friend. She'll tell everything but the truth but between us we might pull her rug out from under."

"That's the Irish for you," Tutchek winked at Gilman, his temper improved. "He goes to see a beautiful redhead, and what's he after? Her rug."

3.

Most cops do not rely on rabbits' feet, four-leafed clovers or horseshoes when working on a case, but there are times when a little luck can save a lot of time and trouble. For instance, if Flavin and Gilman had been a few minutes later they would not have seen Fay Copland come out of the ugly yellow brick house on Pomander Walk and hurry toward a cab parked at the curb, carrying a small suitcase. Gilman angled the police car to the curb in front of the cab. Already seated inside the cab, Fay watched Flavin and Gilman step out of the sternly black law enforcement vehicle. Her eyes were like those of a woman taken in adultery. She did not wait to be ignominiously gaffed. She opened the door and slid gracefully from the seat and stood on the sidewalk, leaving her luggage behind. She gave the scowling driver a dollar bill and somehow managed to smile.

"I'm afraid my shopping will be delayed," she said. "I completely forgot these gentlemen were going to call. Do you mind waiting?"

It was, as they say, a good try.

"You left your suitcase, Miss Copland," said Flavin. He took it from the cab. It was heavy. "I think we can talk more comfortably inside."

"She'll call you later, buddy," Gilman dismissed the cab driver.

The hackie did not argue. He knew a pinch when he saw one and wanted no part of it. He left.

Fay Copland walked into the house, leaving Flavin and Gilman to trail along behind. She was wearing a dark green tropical worsted suit. The severe tailoring did nothing to diminish her magnificent figure. Not even sackcloth and ashes could have done that. She also had on a light green felt hat and ivory colored gloves. These were not clothes a woman would have worn for a short trip to Asbury Park.

She led them into the living room, an uninspired box with a white ceiling, oatmeal wallpaper and heavy furniture of no particular style or period. She stood at the fireplace. Her face looked thinner, possibly because she had tightened her wide mouth.

"You were going someplace, Miss Copland?" asked Flavin.

"To California," she snapped. "My ex-husband is preparing to leave the state and the question of alimony may conveniently slip his mind."

"You'd better let your lawyer handle it."

"But this is ridiculous. I'll be back in less than a week."

Flavin shook his head. "I'm sorry, Miss Copland, but you're an important witness—"

"Do you mean I'm under suspicion?"

"I mean you're a witness. You knew Mrs. Sturgis intimately. You may be able to help us clean up this case. We can't let you go to California or anywhere else when we might need you at any moment."

"I won't stand for it!" she blazed at him. "I won't sit here and lose a thousand dollars a month because you *might* just happen to feel like asking some silly questions. I told you all I know and—" She stopped, looked at the doorway and demanded, "Can they keep me here like this?

Am I under arrest?"

Flavin and Gilman turned automatically. John Harris Copland was standing in the hall, a folded newspaper in his hand. He was a tall old man and had the thin, ascetic face of a judge who could pronounce the death sentence as dispassionately as a sentence of ten days for disorderly conduct.

"Answer their questions and stop acting like an idiot," he said coldly. "Who told you Trowbridge was leaving California?"

"I—I had a letter from Morgan Hull. He's an actor. You don't know him."

Copland's manner became icy, his eyes a gray glacial void, and he revealed no definable expression. "I know you will pardon my daughter's behavior, gentlemen," he said. "She has not been well. Sit down, Faith. Control yourself. You have upset yourself needlessly. I want you to listen carefully to the questions. They will be important. Police detectives do not like to waste time frivolously. Think before you speak. Answer concisely and intelligently. If it will make you feel more at ease, I shall remain."

Fay moistened her lips, nodded and moved to a stiff, high-backed chair beside the fireplace. She seemed dazed. His arrogance had frozen the fire and magnificence that had been in her. She looked dull and just a little fleshy. Copland came formally into the room and stood behind her chair.

"I was and am an attorney, gentlemen," he said. "You will save your time and mine if you confine your questions to the issue."

"Your daughter's not on trial, Mr. Copland," said Flavin.

"Nonetheless, there are proper and improper questions."

"If there's any heckling," Flavin told Gilman, "make note of the questions."

Copland regarded him with chilly interest, smiled remotely and said, "By all means. Shall we continue?"

Flavin looked at Fay. "You said you were Carol Sturgis' best friend. Is that right?"

"We—I saw her quite frequently," said Fay in a low voice.

"How frequently? Every day?"

"Well, almost. Carol loved restaurants. She never ate at home. Walt was the same, but he was away for weeks at a time. Months. He's a consulting engineer—"

"That is not the question, my dear," Copland interrupted. "How often did you see Carol Sturgis?"

"Practically every day. We'd have lunch or dinner together and go to a cocktail party or the theatre. Places like that."

"You never went around with men?" asked Flavin, and waited for Copland to object.

But the old man said nothing and Fay shook her head. "Not very often. We—sometimes a girl gets awfully tired of having the same old passes made at her. So damn tired. We need a rest once in awhile. And—and Carol was happily married. She was very attractive and if she went out alone, there was always some stupid man who'd try to corner her. She hated it."

"You were a sort of bodyguard then. Is that the idea?"

"That's what I meant to say. We actually weren't good friends the way men are friends. Women never are."

Copland said, "Ridiculous!"

Flavin let it go. "What about Monty?" he asked.

"Who's Monty?"

"You never heard of him? That's funny. He was a very good friend of Mrs. Sturgis, we heard. Spent a lot of time at her house recently. Monty. M-o-n-t-y. Strange you don't know him."

"Oh, *Monty*. I—I thought you said Lonnie. Yes, well, I mean, Carol spoke of Monty but I never met him. He was a—a relative, I think."

"He stayed at her house?"

"No, no, just dropped in once in a while. She hadn't seen him for years."

"Was he an older man?"

"Oh, yes. I mean, she called him 'uncle' once, I think. I really don't know anything about him, though."

"No? We were told he made himself quite at home there."

Copland held up his thin octogenarian hand. "Just a moment please," he said sharply. "What is the purpose of these questions?"

"We're trying to get a line on him, that's all, Mr. Copland," Flavin drawled. "He seems to be quite a mystery. He was always there but nobody knows anything about him. Or won't tell us, if they do."

"How do you know he was always there?"

"He was seen."

"By whom?"

"We got the information from a reliable, disinterested source."

"Disinterested? I'm sorry but your source does not sound disinterested to me."

"Why not?"

"A disinterested person, Mr. Flavin, would hardly tell the police that Carol Sturgis was living with another man while her husband was away from home. And that's the core of this alleged information, sir. I'm not stupid, you know. And your informant can't be very reliable either, if you ask me."

"We didn't," said Flavin flatly. "We were questioning your daughter."

Copland's narrow face was old, the lines and wrinkles deeply carved, and perhaps it was incapable of any expression but that of remote cold. "My daughter knows nothing of this Monty person," he said in a stiff, formal voice. "She has already told you that."

"Not exactly. She said Carol Sturgis mentioned Monty. I want to know exactly what Mrs. Sturgis said. Or is that an improper question, Mr. Copland?"

"Tell him, Faith," said Copland contemptuously.

Fay looked drawn and tense, as if this astringent old man were more to be feared than anyone or anything. How many years of arrogant bullying had reduced her to this, Flavin wondered.

"Carol merely mentioned Lonnie," she said hurriedly. "She didn't tell me anything about him."

"Lonnie? Was that the name?"

"No, I—I really don't remember the name. We didn't talk about him."

"She told you he was a long-lost uncle—or did she?"

"I—I don't remember. I mean to say, that's only the impression I got. There wasn't any more to it. What do you want me to do?" her voice rose shrilly. "Invent things? Lie? I won't do it."

Copland angrily threw out his arm. It struck a Lenox china table lamp and knocked it to the floor. It shattered noisily, but he did not give it a glance.

"That is quite enough, Mr. Flavin!" he said. "If the district attorney, a more competent interrogator, wishes to question my daughter further, you may tell him to telephone me this evening. Good day, gentlemen!"

Flavin nodded and said, "Let's go, George."

Gilman's homely but usually easy-going face was the hue of spilled red wine. He glowered at Copland but said nothing. He tore the top sheet from his notebook and threw it, crumpled, into the fireplace. He made it very plain that he hoped it would explode.

Outside in the police car, Flavin said thoughtfully, "That was a funny one all 'round."

"Funny hell. The redhead's a mess and that frozen son of a bitch made her that way."

"Yeah. Maybe that's why she handed us one lie after another straight down the line. I don't think she ever heard of Monty."

"I wouldn't say that, Jeff. I kind of got the idea she knew too much."

"I'd like to talk to her alone."

"Not a chance," said Gilman emphatically.

In the next two hours, Flavin and Gilman canvassed the Sturgis neighborhood. They also talked to the mailman, the newsboy, the beat cop and the milkman, with no more success than the unfortunate precinct dicks, Urquhart and Jenner. Feller with Missus Sturgis? Never seen um.

They checked in at the Graystone Hospital. Flavin asked Supervisor Maggie Wrenn how Walt Sturgis was getting along. X-rays had been taken, she said, and a series of tests were being run. He had a low-grade fever, nothing to worry about, and his innards were probably all right. Physically. His mental innards? Well, depressed. People reacted differently to sedation. Some became jittery, some depressed, others dreamy—or just plain vomiting sick. She'd phone *Flavin* if anything developed. But not Kitteridge. Who was Kitteridge, by the way? A Shylock who held the hospital's mortgage? Flavin told her not to be like that; all Headquarters was working under pressure. Maggie told Gilman she could always rely on the Irish for one thing—they lied like gentlemen.

Flavin phoned Headquarters from a public booth in the lobby. Sergeant Bauer had two messages for him. Number one—Bauer methodically numbered things—call Detective Goldstein. Number two: Detective Ben Tutchek left word for Flavin and Gilman to come to Headquarters as soon as they could; no reason given.

Flavin called Goldstein at the North Hudson precinct house.

"Just to show you how wrong a guy can be," said Goldstein, "Esther Veen was not the dumb blonde I told you. She didn't have a savings account in the bank but we checked the building and loan here and until a week ago she was worth nearly twenty-five hundred dollars. She drew it out, so I don't know what she's worth now. What's it sound like to you?"

"Did she give a reason? When somebody closes an account, the banks usually ask, as a matter of policy."

"She told them it was none of their business."

They had talked to a few of Esther's ex-boyfriends and it was generally agreed that she was a pretty cold proposition. Her interest in the size of their savings accounts was downright embarrassing. She was dumb. When you told her a guy couldn't buy a car and put money in the bank too, her answer was you didn't need a car; it was cheaper to ride a bus and still cheaper to walk. *She* walked twelve blocks to and from work every day and saved $1.20 a week—$62.40 a year. She knew a hundred and one ways to save a buck here and a buck there. She did not approve of night clubs. They were robbers. If you wanted to dance, all right, you could stay home and dance to the radio. It didn't cost anything. She was a creeping ice cube, if there ever was one. You could give her back to the Eskimos.

Goldstein and Zabriski had the whole precinct working on it but the leads were getting thinner and thinner. What could you expect? Female cash registers didn't make friends; they made money. In Goldstein's opinion, she was ripe to be plucked by a shrewd, handsome, tight-fisted operator like Ferenc.

4.

Detectives Ben Tutchek and Harry Muir were better off than Goldstein and Zabriski They had a tall girl, a real beauty with black hair and gray eyes which gave her Slavic features an interesting—very interesting—exotic touch. Her name was Angela Balik. She, Tutchek, Muir, Flavin and Gilman were in one of the better Interrogation rooms. It contained four wooden chairs, a long-legged oak table and a leather sofa, which had a comfortable case of lordosis.

Angela Balik was delighted to talk about Leonard Ferenc, who had given her the brush-off when he found out that the Ballock Beauty Salon was owned by her sister, not her. ("Ballock" was the Anglicized version of Balik.) She had not seen Ferenc for over a year but she was still bitter and her comments were colorful and vigorous.

"Len was only interested in one thing," she said. "And I don't mean what *he's* interested in." She looked scornfully at Harry Muir and pulled her skirt down over her knees.

Muir grinned wolfishly. She had a pair of legs, a real pair.

"So he was interested in the beauty shop," said Tutchek "You mean the money it made?"

"Capital m-o-n-e-y. When I told him it netted about a hundred and fifty a week, his face lit up as though he had a hundred-watt bulb in his mouth."

"Did he try to get any money from you?"

"You mean, borrow it?"

"Let's put it this way—did he try to get you to sell the shop and invest the money in something he had in mind?"

"Well, not quite," she said reluctantly. "But he was after it, mister. He never let up."

"In what way?"

"I just told you. That's all he was interested in. When this one looks at me," she vented her bitterness on Harry Muir, "he sees a pair of legs and all the rest of it. What Len Ferenc saw was a dollar sign. That's hard to take. I don't like wolves and never will, but at least a wolf makes you feel like a woman."

"I'm not a wolf, baby," lied Muir, filing her last remark for future reference. "If I sized you up, it's because you can give us a line on Ferenc."

"A line is right!" she jeered.

"That's enough," Tutchek interrupted in a hard voice. "How did Ferenc try to get money out of you? What as his angle?"

"He wanted to rent a place in a better location," she said sullenly. "To listen to him, he could get space in the Hotel Clinton for nothing down and nothing a month. Supplies and equipment wouldn't cost me a nickel. He'd handle everything."

"The money?"

"Well—" she moistened her lips and shot a quick glance Tutchek's broad face. "He—said he could make a better deal than I could."

It was plain that she'd rather have said something more damaging. She might have gotten away with it had Muir or even Flavin questioned her. Not that they were soft touches. Nothing like that. It was, well, the big one for instance, you felt naked every time he looked at you, the way he kept lifting your skirt with his eyes, giving you a feel with a look. Ben Tutchek was different. He didn't care what was under her skirt or in her brassiere. Not right this minute, anyway. He was all business and God help you if he got sore or caught you in a lie. Oddly enough, George Gilman also made her uneasy, although he had not spoken a word to her.

Vengefully, she hoped Len Ferenc was in a mess of trouble.

"What kind of deal did he offer?" asked Tutchek.

"He kept saying he could get things for half of what I was paying. I mean, he thought I owned the shop. He said he knew the right people."

"Did he?"

"It depends on what you call right. One of them had his 'office' in a cafeteria. A table like all the rest. That was the 'office.' I was scared. I thought he was a crook. Maybe he wasn't, but who else would carry on a business from a cafeteria table?"

"What did you buy from him?"

"I didn't—" but she knew she had talked herself into a corner; there was a law against buying stolen goods. "He wasn't really a crook," she said hurriedly. "And I didn't buy it from him. He took us to the Freightways Warehouse."

"What did you buy?"

"A—an electric vibrator. You know, for massages. Sis needed one. It cost thirty-five dollars, the kind she wanted. Heavy-duty. Pinky—that's the man Len took me to—wanted fifteen for the same make and Len jewed him down to ten."

"That's quite a difference. How did Pinky get it out of the warehouse—through a back window?"

"No, no. The warehouse man was right there. The vibrator had a dented case. That's how Len got it for ten. There was nothing wrong with the way it worked and you'd hardly notice the dent, but it was damaged and you couldn't sell it for new and Len said it cost too much to ship it back to the manufacturer and anyway it was insured. That was Pinky's business, handling damaged goods. He gave Len five percent commission."

"What was Ferenc's proposition to you?"

"He said, what with one thing and another, the way he'd work it, the beauty shop would make two hundred and fifty a week, net. He wanted me to sign a partnership paper. It was all drawn up."

"Did you read it?"

"Let me ask you something," she smiled. It was an ugly smile. "When you're partners with somebody and he drops dead, do you get his share of the business?"

"Sometimes you have an option to buy his share from the estate."

"That's not what Len Ferenc had down. The paper said I'd get his share if he died, or he'd get mine. There was nothing about an option to buy. I thought it was a funny thing to put in."

"It worked both ways," said Tutchek, curbing her spite before it ran away with the facts. "Nothing funny about that. What did you tell him?"

"I—I said I'd have to think it over."

"Is that when he found out you didn't own the shop?"

"I told my sister how she could make more money if the three of us went into partnership but she didn't want to move. We had a fight and I quit."

"And that was that, eh?"

"He called up the shop and asked for me and Sis answered the phone. That's when he found out. I never saw him again."

Tutchek said, "Uh-huh," and went to the door. He looked out into the corridor and beckoned with his forefinger. McGimp walked in briskly, carrying his canvas-bound portfolio.

Tutchek introduced him, "This is Mr. Malcolm, the police artist. He's going to show you some drawings of Ferenc. Look at them very carefully and tell Mr. Malcolm if they need any changes or additions. We want the best likeness we can get."

The girl nodded. "What did Len do?" she asked. Vindictiveness glittered in her voice.

"He didn't do anything. He's been missing for several days and his family's worried that he might have had an accident."

"Now wouldn't that be too bad!" she said, and her smile was ugly again.

McGimp opened his portfolio and spread four drawings on the oak table. Angela Balik looked from one to the other, shaking her head. She didn't like any of them. The expression was wrong. It wasn't mean enough. And the eyes needed changing, too. Ferenc had little squinty eyes, not big ones. In fact, none of the drawings was right. The face should be longer. Not like a horse, but almost.

McGimp groaned as if such criticism were beyond endurance. This was his usual performance. Muttering to himself, he whipped a charcoal pencil from his pocket and went to work on a fresh sheet of paper. His noises and grimaces meant nothing. They were a form of amusement. He was actually an efficient craftsman and patiently erased and sketched, erased and sketched as the girl stood beside him, disagreeing with almost every line he drew.

Of course she was a damn fool like everybody else, but it didn't matter. If the city fathers wanted to pay him to humor these idiots, it was their business. He didn't mind.

Tutchek took Flavin into the corridor. "What do you think of her, baby?" he asked.

"She's got her knife in Ferenc but you kept her in line."

"I hope. She's got a grudge like a hatful of gallstones. I'm wondering about that partnership agreement. It was real cute, the way she slipped it in. She all but put it in writing that Ferenc wanted to kill her for fifty percent of a lousy beauty parlor. What a bitch!"

"Ferenc tried to get her to sign something, Ben. I'll give you odds that there was a joker in it, too. He didn't miss an angle when there was a dollar in it for him."

Flavin outlined what Goldstein had told him about the missing Esther Veen and her equally missing twenty-five hundred dollars. Tutchek listened soberly.

"That bird isn't smart, Jeff," he said, "he's just hungry. He hasn't covered himself once. The Balik girl, the Veen girl—he's wide open. We'll pick him up."

An hour later McGimp had a sketch of which Angela Balik approved. It looked exactly like Len Ferenc, she said, squinty eyes and all. A face she'd never forget, never! She seemed disappointed that her visit to Headquarters had passed so quietly but cheered up when Tutchek said they'd need her later to identify Ferenc. She was glad. She wanted to help. She'd do everything she could. Harry Muir grinned and started her from the room.

"Well," he said, "there's a few things I'd like to fill in." He turned in the doorway and winked at Tutchek. He closed the door.

McGimp sprayed his latest charcoal sketch of Ferenc with fixative so it would not smudge. He smiled contentedly at the three detectives.

"You should have no trouble finding this man," he said. "He's a very unusual fellow. He's quintuplets."

He waved his arm and indicated the five drawings. The first four he had sketched from descriptions given him by Ferenc's fellow workers at the Howards-Tetley Safe and Lock Company. Not one of the five resembled another. They were charcoal portraits of five different men. The sketch approved by Angela Balik showed a myopic, narrow-faced sinister character with a dissipated mouth, about forty years old. Another was of a solemn boy in his twenties; his face was round. The third was an All-American character with a flashing smile and eyes alight with good deeds. The fourth was very broad across the cheekbones and looked more Oriental than Slavic. There was no doubt about the fifth; he was a moron. He had flat cheeks, dull eyes and his mouth hung slightly agape.

"What shall I do with them, my friends?" asked McGimp sweetly.

"Send them all out," said Tutchek. "Maybe you're right. Maybe he is a quint. No, wait a minute. We'll take them up to North Hudson. There has to be somebody who didn't see him as a comic strip character."

There was, and it was the last person Flavin would have picked for the job. Houlihan, the Mt. Windsor Diner's bemused counterman-owner. It may have been one of his better days for he had a quick, discerning eye. He looked at the drawings and said they all had a bit of Leonard Ferenc in them. He pointed—the cheekbones in one, the eyes in another, the chin, the ears. He and McGimp went into a huddle at the end of the counter.

In less than a half hour they had a finished sketch. Ferenc had a high-boned Slavic face which did narrow his eyes. His nose was narrow and straight, his mouth thin and just a shade too small. He was not unhandsome. It was a face in which boldness, caution and shrewdness were mingled.

They showed it to several persons around the precinct—Esther Veen's ex-landlady included—and all immediately said it was the spitting image of Ferenc.

Tutchek slapped Flavin on the shoulder. "Now we've got something, baby!" he said happily. "The case is moving again."

5.

The portrait was not distributed to law enforcement art centers until it had been critically viewed around and about. Even Angela Balik grudgingly admitted that it looked a little like "the stinker when he was asleep." The remark was a dead giveaway and Harry Muir filed it, among other bits of useful information, for future reference. Under the guise of Investigation, he had promoted a date with the feelogenic Angela. Harry was a hard-working wolf in plainclothes.

McGimp's character study of Leonard Ferenc was printed by the thousands and police officers from Seabring to Seattle scrutinized it with the clinical eyes of experts. Especially alerted by the teletype were cities, towns, villages and hamlets east of the Alleghenies in an area between Boston and Baltimore. Ferenc had never lived far from Hudson and it was generally agreed that he would not become a traveling man at this late date.

An early arrest was expected.

But the empty days continued to pass.

A man in Perth Amboy confessed to the murder of Carol Sturgis. When asked if he'd shot Lincoln too, he said modestly, "Not yet." There are crackpots and psychotics who happily "confess" to headline murders. They "confess" by letter, by telephone, by telegram and in person. Year in, year out, the weary police could depend upon the crackpots.

There were dead-end leads and fake tips and every last one of them had to be laboriously traced to its final blind alley. Through some strange osmosis, the name of Monty seeped in and out. Had all the tip-offs of Monty been authentic, the Sturgis house could not have contained them—unless it were enlarged to the size of Rhode Island.

Another mystery was the blonde girl who had been found floating nude in Shackett River. She had been immersed for several days and, in addition to the resultant bloat, the crabs had been at her face. The indented scar of a mastoid operation behind her left ear was the only mark which might have identified her. Esther Veen's ex-landlady said Esther did not have a scar behind her left ear.

Big Harry Muir worked overtime. His intrepid investigations included Angela Balik, the erstwhile paramour of Leonard Ferenc. He went into the matter thoroughly. Several detectives were highly entertained by his verbal reports, but nothing else came of his earnest desire to fill-in that part of the case. Yet, Harry persevered and sometimes seemed a little tired in the mornings. He was possibly to be commended. Of course. So far as the La Balik angle was concerned, he gave his all, didn't he? Yessir.

Sergeant Erple, Narcotics Detail, was unable to report a *sub rosa* safe expert among the known addicts around town. Pushers were brought in, roughed up, questioned, roughed up some more, sent to jail—but nothing was learned of the Stone Bridge burglaries or the killing of Carol Sturgis.

No one had much hope of getting a lead from the stolen jewelry. It was too hot, Sergeant Gill said. A fence might buy it for two cents on the dollar and hide it away, but he'd never attempt to peddle it while the heat was on.

Sergeants Nairn, Ochs and Stein, of Safe and Loft, Burglary and Robbery, had nothing to report.

The Crime Lab had nothing to report.

Nobody had anything to report.

In boldface type, the *Hudson Evening News* proclaimed:

TOO MANY 'MYSTERY' MEN
IN STURGIS KILL HINTED

"Should Concentrate On One,"
Says Investigating Detective

The investigating detective (3rd/grade) was Harold A. Mecklenburg of the Auto Theft Detail, which had little or nothing to do with the investigation. Mecklenburg had been in his cups at the time of this elementary observation. Other bulls had grouched about the same thing in one way or another, but Mecklenburg was unfortunate. He had solemnly imparted his spirituous deduction to news reporter Ed Turcott, who knew a sneak-punch angle from a stereotyped handout.

The *Hudson Evening News* also ran an editorial entitled:

BOONDOGGLING?

Poor Mecklenburg, who really didn't give a hoot in hell about the case, was suspended for ninety days without pay after a furious chewing-out from Police Commissioner Willie Quinn, Captain Mackenzie and Lieutenant Haas. Police Chief Sharkey composed a hurried essay for all newspapers, denying that there were any "mystery men" whatsoever. Certain persons were being sought for questioning, he said, but it was routine procedure, not a mystery. He fooled nobody.

Nerves were in bad shape around Headquarters and in the precincts. The ax had been blooded on Mecklenburg. Who'd be next?

Seven

Flavin went to see Tom Walsh, who had been transferred from Graystone to the private rest home of Doctor August Hauptmann in the quiet suburb of Abington. Doctor Hauptmann was a plump, jolly man with the mien of a summer resort social director. He wasn't. He was the most astute psychiatrist and analyst in the state.

"Your friend is going through the usual melancholy phase," he told Flavin, speaking English instead of the esoteric medical slang employed by some doctors. "He blames himself for his wife's death. He should not have permitted her to drive to Pittsburgh, he says; he should have insisted that she take the plane."

"He tried. He even had the ticket. I was there that night. She didn't like planes. Anyway, she loved to drive. She wouldn't travel any other way if she could get out of it."

"I gathered that. There's more to it, of course. He thinks he's a failure in the Police Department, his position as Assistant Detective Chief notwithstanding."

"A failure! He's one of the best men in the Bureau."

"I know. I made a few inquiries through Doctor Knight, your Medical Examiner. Confidentially, of course. Lieutenant Walsh has a desk job. Detailed paperwork, office routine, personnel supervision, and so forth."

"That's right."

"I'm sorry, but it isn't. It's all wrong. Lieutenant Walsh is not the man for that kind of employment. He regards himself as chief clerk of the Detective Bureau. He loathes paperwork, which he believes a job for women. On the other hand, Doctor Knight told me Walsh is an executive with considerable authority and office routine is a minor responsibility. It is apparent, therefore, that Walsh has placed undue emphasis on the routine which he dislikes. We must shift the emphasis to his more important executive position but it will take time because of his physical condition."

"How bad is he?"

"Too much whiskey, not enough food. That's more or less the story. This melancholy phase is temporary and will probably be followed by a period of elation. He'll pull out of it," Doctor Hauptmann smiled. "If a six-month binge didn't kill him, nothing will."

"Can I see him?"

"I'll go with you."

Tom was sitting alone at the far end of a sunny porch. His face was sunken and dull but his eyes blazed when he saw Flavin.

"What the hell do you want?" he demanded.

Doctor Hauptmann said quietly, "You need clothes, Lieutenant. Tell me what you want and Mr. Flavin will bring them to you."

"I don't want any God damned clothes. Give them to a rummage sale. And get that lousy snoop out of here."

Flavin said, "Sure, Tom," and left with Doctor Hauptmann, who did not seem perturbed by their rough reception. Walsh was not having an easy time of it. The liquor problem. Naturally. The pattern was usual. He wanted whiskey. He'd tried to bribe everybody. Total withdrawal was hard to endure, but necessary.

"Is it all right if I come back tomorrow?" asked Flavin.

"Of course. It might not be pleasant but he should have visitors."

Flavin returned day after day, although Tom was abusive and refused to talk to him. Other visitors from Headquarters, including Captain Mackenzie, fared no better.

A trip to Graystone Hospital was equally unrewarding. Maggie Wrenn telephoned Flavin and said he could see Walt Sturgis. She met him at the door of her office.

"He knows his wife is dead," she said, shaking her head. "Either somebody told him or he read it in a newspaper. He's had a few visitors from Stone Bridge. I think it was Mr. Copland who told him. I could break his neck!"

Sturgis sat at the window in a wicker armchair. An unopened magazine lay on his lap. Flavin identified himself and Sturgis shrugged.

"I'm sorry to bother you," said Flavin. "You've had it rough. But I'm working on the burglaries."

"I don't know anything," said Sturgis in a monotone.

"Can you describe the man who jumped you that night?"

"No."

"About how tall was he?"

"I don't know. I was drunk."

"Don't you remember anything about him?"

"No."

"The smallest detail might help a lot, Mr. Sturgis. Was he a big man?"

"I wouldn't know. I didn't see him."

"Did he hit you from behind?"

"I couldn't say."

"You were in your bedroom at the time. What were you doing?"

"I have no idea. I told you I was drunk, didn't I?"

"You wall safe was empty. Can you give me a list of what was in it?"

"Nothing. I never used the stupid thing."

"Do you know a man named Monty?"

Sturgis turned his head and stared out the window. "Why?"

"There's a chance he may be implicated."

"That's ridiculous. He was my wife's uncle. He was over seventy years old and quite wealthy. He did not have to rob safes."

"He was described to us as a younger man."

"I don't care how he was described to you."

"The man we were told about was tall, had dark hair and was deeply suntanned. Our witness said he was about thirty or so."

"Dark hair? Did this—this witness, or whatever he was, did he get a good look?"

"Yes."

"For your information, Uncle Monty wore a toupee. He is quite athletic and still plays a little polo. He owns a large cattle ranch in Brazil. South of Sao Felipe, I think. It doesn't make any difference. He looks much younger than he is. What's the point of all this? I don't like silly conversations."

"It's not so silly, Mr. Sturgis. Unless we verify things, we waste valuable time."

"What do you want me to verify?"

"I'd like to have our witness take another look at your uncle. Where can we get in touch with him?"

Flavin waited and finally, out of a remote silence, Sturgis said emptily, "He left for Mexico a week ago. From there he will return to Brazil. His address there is the Rancho Peixe, Sao Felipe. Senhor James A. Mockton. Carol always called him Uncle Monty. Probably a childhood mispronunciation of Mockton."

"Do you have a photograph of him?"

"There's a snapshot album around the house somewhere. In the picture he's standing beside a black polo pony. The pony's name was Fanny."

"Where did he stay while he was here?"

Sturgis was becoming restless, but answered, "At our house for awhile and then with friends in Connecticut."

"Do you know their names?"

"No, I don't, damn it! Why— Sorry. I think the name was Revere. I'm not sure. They lived at Long Neck Point or Lords Point or someplace like that. Perhaps it was Great Neck, Long Island. I don't remember."

"Revere? R-e-v-e-r-e?"

"Yes, Paul Revere," said Sturgis peevishly. "He was a horseman and my uncle was very fond of horses. Now please, Mr. Flavin, if you don't mind, I'm very tired."

"Of course, Mr. Sturgis. Another time."

Sturgis moved his shoulders; an expression of apathy. "If you wish. But there's nothing more I can tell you."

On the back cover of his magazine was the picture of a man and woman embracing. It was an advertisement for *Nuit de Lune* perfume. He moved his hand stiffly. The magazine fell to the floor in a brief flutter of white pages.

Detective Ben Tutchek was angry. He didn't shout or make a scene, as the Dutchman might have done. Everyone knew he was angry—it was obvious in his heavy ursine stride—but he did not indulge in emotional orgies for his personal satisfaction or to entertain the General Squadroom. Only an hour before he had been called to the office of Police Commissioner Quinn in City Hall. He'd been chewed-out. He'd been promoted to Sergeant. To Lieutenant. He'd been told to produce—or else. Lieutenant Haas was crazy and Tutchek was in charge of Homicide. Tutchek was to blame for Mecklenburg's suspension. Tutchek was on the way out. Tutchek was Captain Mackenzie's new assistant and Tom Walsh was out. Mackenzie was out. Police Commissioner Quinn was out.

Scuttlebutt knows all, sees all and tells all.

Tutchek took Flavin into one of the unused Interrogation rooms. "What the hell's the matter with you?" he demanded. "I told you to stay away from Walt Sturgis, didn't I?"

"No."

"You're a liar."

"Take it easy, Ben."

"Easy, hell! I told you—"

"I don't give a damn what you told me. I'm on the Burglary and I'll handle it my way."

"Don't kid yourself, baby. In just about two shakes you won't be handling a God damned thing around here. I'll see to that and don't think I won't. Tom Walsh or no Tom Walsh."

Flavin was half-haunched on the table edge and his foot stopped its rhythmic beat. "I won't take that from you or anybody, Ben," he said. "Not anybody!" His face was suddenly pale.

Now Ben Tutchek was a big man—not merely huge like Harry Muir—and this was one of the times he proved it.

He walked to the window and stood snapping his fingers. "We'll scratch my last remark from the record," he said. "I was out of line." He turned abruptly. "But you were out of line too, Flavin. I told you it's Kitteridge's job to keep tabs on Sturgis."

"Up to a point, sure. But not after the hospital staff stops cooperating."

Be it said for both men that further explanations were neither asked for nor given. There was no need for a showdown between them.

Tutchek said, "Yeah, there's that. I should have asked," and dismissed the hassle. There was no question of his authority. "What'd he have to say?"

"Monty was the wife's uncle, like Fay Copland said. His name's James A. Mockton. He's over seventy and plays polo in a wig. He's got a friend called Paul Revere, who's a horse-lover and lives in Connecticut or maybe it's Long Island. We can get in touch with him in Sao Felipe, Brazil, except he might be in Mexico. He's sun-burned and looks younger when he puts on his rug. There's a picture of him and a horse in the Sturgis snapshot album, if we can find it. That Raymond Mankey kid, who delivers groceries, the one who tipped us off on Monty, ought to see an oculist and get glasses."

Tutchek screwed up his nose. "It smells like herring, the way you tell it."

"Oh, there'll be a James A. Mockton in Sao Felipe, Brazil and if he has sisters or brothers, he probably is an uncle. Put Communications on it and you'll get a confirmation. By this time he knows all about being Carol Sturgis' uncle."

"Has Walt Sturgis mailed any letters to Brazil lately?"

"It was old man Copland, if anybody. According to Maggie Wrenn, the old son of a bitch was in to see the patient."

"Uh huh. What makes you think Sturgis gave you the business?"

"That's the hell of it, Ben—I don't know if it was the business. He didn't volunteer this stuff. I had to pull it out of him like teeth. On the other hand, he just might be protecting his wife's good name. There are guys like that. Does she have a family we could check up with?"

"Only a brother Gerald someplace in Australia, which has an area of about three million square miles. I think we'll put the Brazil cops on Uncle Mockton. They're good, those Brazilian boys. I worked with them once before. The only trouble is, he might be one of those uncles. I got one that lives in Newark. He was only a friend of the old man but we always called him Uncle Vlad. We'll pass it along to Communications. If Mockton's a brand-new uncle, he shouldn't be hard to de-uncle. But, as the boys in the back room would say, so what? Monty'll still be one of the monkeys on our back. Was Sturgis snotty about this?"

"He was like a guy who'd been scraped hollow by a garden hoe. Maggie Wrenn says he knows his wife's dead. That'd do it. Copland told him, she claims. He sits there like a zombie. But just in case he doesn't know, I didn't put it to him. We might get more out of him that way."

"You're a cold-blooded Irish flatfoot. But I'd do the same. And speaking of icemen, I wish to Christ we'd write Ferenc off, one way or the other," he paused. "What're you making faces about? You got a hunch or a cramp?"

Flavin patted the air and shook his head, asking for a moment of silence. He made several more faces, mirroring a jumble of thoughts.

"It's what you said back there about Carol Sturgis being dead," he said at length. "It kind of lit a fuse."

"Good." Tutchek grinned. "Explode."

"It's just a fuse, damn it. There's no dynami— Look. We think another girl was knocked off, don't we? I mean, Esther Veen and her twenty-five hundred bucks. Right?"

"How do I know? What's the tie-in?"

"How do I know, too? But let's say she wasn't knocked off. For the sake of argument. Let's say Ferenc wanted to marry her because she was the same kind of thrifty miser like himself. And because she had those fat twenty-five hundred bucks. Does that change the picture? I mean—" Flavin floundered for the moment. "Aside from the killing, I mean."

Tutchek puffed out his cheeks, thinking. It was as if these new considerations filled not only his mind but his mouth as well. "Then Ferenc didn't take a powder; he took a honeymoon."

"No, I—well, can you see a hundred-and-ten-percent businessman like Ferenc spending good money on a Ferris wheel ride like a honeymoon. Can you see Esther Veen *letting* him?"

"Uh," Tutchek examined the notion. "Frankly, if they *did* get married and *did* take a honeymoon, it was to the U. S. Mint to see how money was made the easy way. But what makes you think he married the girl?"

Flavin spread his hands—but still groping. "How else could he get her dough? Was she the kind of swoon-goon who'd have stars in her eyes? Unless he clubbed her with a baseball bat, I mean. What did he want from that Balik bitch? Her money, Ben, the good old moo, not nooky. He might have married her if she'd owned the beauty shop. From start to finish, Ferenc and money were Siamese twins. I'm leading up to something, but don't ask me what."

"He never lost sight of the buck, and that's a fact," said Tutchek thoughtfully. "If he did things like buying himself a suit for a dollar ninety-eight once a year, he had some good solid scratch stashed away. Him and Esther Veen were two of a kind. If it was profitable to get married, they got married. That would be both their MO's. I can see it now. I can see it better than him knocking her off."

"That's part of what I'm getting at, Ben."

"Wait a minute ...." Tutchek began to pace the room, chopping thoughts from the air with the edge of his hand. "Let's say that with him and

Esther Veen it was a case of love at the first bank statement. Okay. The question is, what did he want to do with this dough?"

"Not just sit and look at it," said Flavin, also starting to pace—Tutchek going one way and he the other, tossing comments at each other as they passed. "Listen and see what you think. The kind of guy he was, if a buck wasn't out there working for him, it gave him coronary thrombosis. Heart failure or whatever it is. Right? Right. Okay. I read someplace that the smart thing isn't to try to *make* money. It's the dollars that make money; all you do is find them the right job. And you have to think that way twenty-four hours a day. Ferenc did. He never stopped. So let's put it this way: he wanted to stick his money into something that'd make more money. His money and Veen's money."

"Not in a safe and lock company," Tutchek interrupted. "That needs too much capital. He didn't have big money. And he wasn't what you'd call a financial butterfly. He wouldn't go for anything chancy like real estate. He wasn't a shoot-the-moon operator, and the safe and lock business was the one he knew best, so we're right back there again. We've contacted every safe outfit in the country. If he tried to get a job or buy an interest or even start a little one of his own, we'd get the word in twenty-four hours."

Flavin faced Tutchek across the table. He leaned over and slapped the top of it. "A business of his own! Not safes, not locks. He was a damn good tool and die maker. We've been told that more than once. Compared to carpenters and plumbers, there are damn few high grade tool and die makers. Ferenc had enough money for lathes and equipment like that and there's the kind of shop he'd set up. If that's it."

Tutchek put out an arm and pointed a finger. They were like a pair of actors with their teeth in a dramatic scene.

"Okay, okay, okay," he said, although Flavin was listening, not interrupting. "Now where do you set up a tool and die shop? In a summer resort like Lake Powhatan? Hell no. You set it up in an industrial center where you can get the contacts. Here, look, we know something about Ferenc. Okay. There's money in Newark and Jersey City and so forth, but he'd head straight for a place where the biggest money is. Pittsburgh, Chicago, Detroit, cities like that. Stop me if I'm wrong."

"But he hasn't had time to set-up yet, Ben, unless he bought out an established business."

"Bought out? Listen. Think the way he'd think. Just for a minute. Even if it makes you feel crummy. He's good and he knows it. You buy out a business and you got to pay for the good will. Nuts to that. I'm putting myself in Ferenc's place. Me, Ferenc. See? I'm the best God damn tool maker in the world. Why should I pay for good will? I can run rings around those engine butchers. Once I get the shop going, I'll have a million dollars' worth of good will and it won't cost me a cent. I'm smart. I know all the angles. And take a look at this genuine machined gimmick. It'll run anything from a guided missile to a cigarette lighter. You're a smart purchasing agent, so why buy from an outfit that can't put an Erector Set together when you can deal with the Super Dooper Ferenc Tool and Die Works. I can turn these out by the million, all perfect."

"And why not?" Flavin agreed. "He's supposed to be good."

"Sure. He'll eat the competition alive. And will he buy new equipment? Don't make me laugh. No matter where he goes, inside an hour he'll know where to get everything ninety-nine percent cheaper with the other percent off for cash. We know his MO and that's it."

Tutchek stopped, drew a long nutritious breath and grinned. "Baby," he said, "I think that fuse you lit, we just stuck into Ferenc where it'll do the most good. But here, that's all well and good, but how does it shape up with the Stone Bridge burglaries and Carol Sturgis?"

"Did he make a profit?"

"His take was over fifteen thousand, not counting the Tiffany specials."

"He made a profit."

2.

It was fed into the teletype and the following afternoon at 2:17 P.M. Detectives Bjornson and Royal picked up Leonard Ferenc in Chicago as he was negotiating—or bargaining—with a second-hand dealer on the purchase price of a turret lathe. Tutchek and Muir took the next plane to the Windy City and brought back not only Ferenc but the thrifty Esther Ferenc, née Veen, as well. They were hustled into separate Interrogation rooms, where Ferenc was given the works by Tutchek, Muir, Flavin and Gilman, while Esther was gone over by Captain Mackenzie himself and a motherly-looking police woman, who (as the saying goes) could chew nails, and spit stilettos.

Ferenc looked almost exactly like the drawing made by McGimp from Houlihan's description. He was calm, but extremely wary.

"I don't have to answer anything," he said. He had a surprisingly small, economical voice for so large a man. He was six-foot-one, broad-boned, weight two hundred and ten pounds.

"That's a fact, Mr. Ferenc," said Harry Muir. "You're absolutely in your rights. You don't have to open your trap. Nossir. Sorry you boys have to leave," he added to Tutchek, Flavin and Gilman. "If you'll send in a deck of cards, me'n Mr. Ferenc'll go a few rounds of blackjack."

Ferenc measured Muir, taking particular notice of the jaw that seemed to run straight across his face like an anvil. "Never mind," he said. "I don't feel like having my ribs kicked in. What do you want to know?"

"We hear you're quite a safe expert," said Muir.

"That's right."

"You admit you're good, eh?"

"Why not?"

"You can open anything?"

"Yes."

"Tetley safes particularly?"

"If I couldn't, I'd want to drop dead."

"Something the matter with them?"

"They're crap."

"You don't need the combination?"

"I don't need nothing but these." He contemptuously showed his hands.

"You don't say. Have you opened any in the last few weeks?"

"No."

"How about a certain Norwich Safe Home Vault model?"

"No."

Muir nodded at the other three detectives with bogus admiration. "This guy knows his stuff. He's really on the beam. He can open anything but it bores him and who wants to be bored. Are we boring you, Mr. Ferenc?"

"No."

"That's good. When I bore a guy, I try to liven things up. I hear you and old man Tetley are all love and kisses."

"I'm out of that place," said Ferenc calmly. "It's over and done with."

"But there was a time you wanted to smack him down but good, wasn't there?"

"And be fined for assault and battery? No."

"You took a swing at Phelps, the service manager."

"I told him he brown-nosed Ed Maurer, Herb Wiess, Frank Zinns and me out of the picture and he polished Tetley's apple ever since. They can't fine me for that."

"Some of the men had to hold you back, they said."

"They were a lot of dumb eager beavers. There was nothing to hold. I had no intention of smacking Phelps. It wouldn't of been worth the money."

"Ah, money. That's the thing, ain't it?"

"You're damn right. I wouldn't pay a nickel to smack Phelps with a

Stillson wrench. Anyway, I didn't stand a chance for the job. That's why I quit. The rest of them're dopes. If this is something to do with Phelps getting beat up, it wasn't me. I don't take chances on paying a fine for nothing."

"For nothing at all?"

"Nothing. I wouldn't even own a car. You get too many tickets."

"So you wouldn't lay a finger on anybody, eh?"

"No."

"Women're different maybe?"

"Yes. You get a stiffer fine for smacking a woman."

"In other words, it's a matter of dollars and cents."

"What ain't?" asked Ferenc simply.

"Carol Sturgis was a matter of dollars and cents too, then. I mean, if she squawked that night."

"What night?"

"You knew her on other nights?"

"I didn't know her at all."

"Then it was an accident. Nothing personal."

"Neither. I didn't know her. Still don't."

"An introduction wasn't necessary that night, sharpshooter!"

"What night?"

"The night it was a matter of dollars and cents."

"Not to me."

Muir bunched his big shoulders as he always did when nettled. His hand lashed out, back and forth. Ferenc's head rocked under the heavy palm-and-backhand slaps. Muir's hand whipped upward, snapping Ferenc's chin back. Ferenc braced together tightly but said nothing. Harry smiled and stretched his big arms like a man about to resume a relaxing, familiar job after a period of enforced tedium.

"Okay, you dollars-and-cents bastard," he drawled comfortably, "we'll start right in from the beginning again. On the night of a week ago last Saturday. If that don't work, we'll start again. We got to get this right."

"Just a minute please, Detective," Ben Tutchek made a mild protest. "I cannot permit you to hit this man again."

"Hit him? Not me. I thought he was falling asleep and kind of woke him up, that's all."

"There'll be no more of it or I'll report you to Commissioner Kakiyak. Is that understood? I'm sorry this happened, Mr. Ferenc. It was disgraceful. As for you, Detective, things are piling under Sergeant Bauer. He'll want relief. You're excused. I'll talk to you later."

"And I'll talk to Chief Muir in the meantime," Harry said loudly. "He knows how to soften up these tough birds. I don't care if you are Bureau

Captain, we're sick and tired of you and your God damned babysitting. Every time we bring in a stinker like Ferenc, you pat him on the head and let him go. This is the end. When I come back, it'll be with Chief Muir and we'll take this bird apart like a Thanksgiving turkey." He pounded from the room and slammed the door.

Flavin had seen this I'm-your-friend act in many variations and knew his cues. "Muir thinks the world of him, Captain," he worried. "Don't stick your chin out."

"It's my chin," said Tutchek shortly. "Furthermore, we have nothing against Mr. Ferenc. You know as well as me he's only here to answer a few questions. Important questions, to be sure, but good God, man, we don't beat up people in Headquarters. I've never allowed it and never will!"

"I'm with the Captain on that," said George Gilman. "Ferenc here, he don't mean nothing to me, but I'll stick with the Captain."

"But Chief Muir's a son of a bitch, Captain. You know that. If—"

"I'm a son of a bitch, too," said Tutchek. "And you, Ferenc. If you repeat a word of this outside Headquarters, I'll break your neck. I'll do everything I can for you while you're here—and I can take care of Chief Muir, as far as that goes, even if it means a showdown—so don't worry."

Ferenc's eyes moved to the door, turned, touched Tutchek, Flavin and Gilman. He revealed nothing.

"I want to make a statement," he said.

"Good. Fine," nodded Tutchek. "There's no pressure. I want you to understand that. Just cooperation all around. What kind of statement do you want to make?"

"A stenographer should take it down."

"If that's the way you want it, okay. I'm with you. Get a stenographer, Detective Gilman. And bring back a pitcher of ice water. We're all thirsty."

"A lady stenographer," said Ferenc.

There was not much color in his long bony face. He had a temper and if ever he got out of Headquarters, Flavin thought, it would be a good idea for Muir to watch the mouths of dark alleys for awhile.

And neither Flavin nor Tutchek missed the significance of that request for a female stenographer. There wouldn't be any rough stuff with a girl in the room. Tutchek tilted an ironic glance at Ferenc and said to Gilman, "Get one of the girls from Clerical. And a lawyer, too, if Mr. Ferenc wants one. He's the helpless type."

"Anything else?" asked Gilman.

"A cup of coffee," said Ferenc calmly.

"Sugar?" inquired Tutchek. "One lump or two?"

"Black."

"A quart of coffee from the Squadroom, George. We'll join our guest in a cup of the brew."

Ferenc sat stolidly. There were no questions or conversation until Gilman came back with a quart container of coffee and a small girl, who carried a folded-back stenographic notebook and a pencil. She was completely mousey, even to the wire-thin mousetrap of a mouth. She gave Ferenc a brief, condemning glance, sat at the table and flattened out her notebook, looking up to Tutchek for instructions. She had taken statements before and was beyond surprise, shock or timidity.

"This is an affidavit, Miss Clagg," said Tutchek. "Make five copies when you type it. The, uh, deponent is Leonard Ferenc." He spelled the name. "If he goes too fast, tell him to slow down. Your turn, Mr. Ferenc."

Speaking slowly, Ferenc repeated his name and gave the date and his business and home addresses in Chicago.

"I don't know why I was brought here," he said. "I didn't hit John Phelps or Francis Tetley at any time whatsoever, and I don't know anything about Carol Sterris—"

"Sturgis," said Tutchek. "S-t-u-r-g-i-s. That's for the record. She's dead. Strangled."

Ferenc blinked but gave no other sign of effect. "I never heard of her till just now. On the night of Saturday, August twenty-three—"

"How do you know the date?" Tutchek interrupted.

"Your stooge said a week ago last Saturday. That was August twenty-three." He turned to the girl. "Ready again, lady?"

"I take down everything," she said without interest. "I'm ready."

"On the night of August twenty-three me and my wife stayed in the Lakes Motel in Union City on Route one-three-oh, Indiana. We registered as Mr. and Mrs. Leonard Stanley Ferenc and had to pay eight dollars for the room on account of the bus broke down and it was the only place. Their regular rate was four dollars. I complained to the cops the next morning when the bus was being fixed and got the run-around. They said I'd have to wait two days and appear in court and told me to forget about it, I was lucky to get a room at all. It was highway robbery. I went back to the motel and helped my wife pack."

"How many towels, pillowcases, sheets, ashtrays, and other junk did you take?" asked George Gilman interestedly.

"I didn't take any. The owner stood right there and watched to see. By accident I tipped over a lamp and stepped on the shade. He wanted me to pay for it. I said we were even now, on account of the eight dollars. The cops were outside and got snotty, but my wife had the regular rate card showing the price of four dollars a night and our receipt for eight. They tried to make us miss the bus. We didn't have the right kind of tickets for stopovers, so I said, you make us miss this bus and I'll get a lawyer and sue the motel. I knew the owner would back down and he did. He wanted five dollars for the lampshade. It was worth about a half dollar. You got all that down, lady?"

"Talk faster. You're going too slow."

"I want you to get it all down and not miss nothing."

"If they made you go without breakfast," said George Gilman, "sue them."

"We had breakfast in the Acme Diner just up the road. A cup of coffee and a jelly doughnut—thirty cents apiece. It's twenty cents all over but the price wasn't up, so I had to let it go. When we got in Chicago that afternoon, I found a guy got us an apartment for forty dollars a month. I mean, he wanted forty but there was holes in the walls and I said I'd do the plastering and took the place for thirty. It's twenty now. The ceiling leaked over the bed, so we moved the bed in the middle of the room and I made a deal to plug the roof. I found a contractor was building houses and had some roofing tar and tar paper left over. I fixed his cement mixer and he gave me the stuff for nothing. The plaster and a can of red paint, too. Something fell off the cement mixer and it was lucky I was standing there."

"Yeah," said Tutchek, "and lucky you didn't step on it like the lampshade."

"It was only the sprocket locknut. I fixed up one out of a hunk of inner tube and a regular nut. The old one was all buggered anyway. He let me have some waterproof trinity cement too and I fixed the bathtub in the apartment so we could take a bath once in awhile."

"You must have made a regular mansion out of the place," said Tutchek. "Red walls and everything."

"Only one corner of the wall. It wasn't regular red paint. It was red lead. Like the wife says, red lead lasts forever, you don't have to worry."

"Except when you look at it," said George Gilman.

"Red lead all looks the same. There's only one kind. If you got any other, you were gypped. They call it red lead but it's kind of orange. There's red lead and white lead. You can't buy nothing better."

"All right, all right," Tutchek interrupted. "That takes care of August twenty-third. What about August sixteenth, ninth and second and July twenty-fifth?"

"I went to Dayton, Ohio, on July nineteen. I got a job as helper and went out on a truck. I looked around but Dayton wasn't the place to locate. Chicago's bigger. I got a night watchman job in the Tri-County Warehouse and they let me sleep on an army cot out back. Didn't cost me a nickel. I was helper on another truck going back to Hudson. A Tri-County truck. The driver's name was Lew Orsini. A ginzo, but okay. I got back Wednesday, August twenty. Essie let me sleep in her place. The landlady didn't know or she'd of soaked me a buck a night. Me and Essie got married by a justice of the peace I kind of knew in Millville. I made a new part for his lawn mower that'd've cost him ten bucks, so he married us for nothing and made himself a few bucks on the deal. I should've charged him the difference, but what the hell, he gave me a pretty good suit. We were the same size. Essie darned the holes in the pants so's you'd never notice. He was kind of a cluck, giving a good suit away. He kept calling us Mr. and Mrs. Leonard but it's Ferenc on the license and the register and that's all that matters. We ate dinner at his place, his wife was dead. After Essie made some samwidges to take along—baked beans and meatball samwidges—he drove us to the bus station and the next day was the night we got stuck in Indiana and that's it."

Miss Clagg lifted her mousey head and her thin mousetrap mouth swung loose. "You—spent your first honeymoon night on a bus?"

"I could've got on the trucks again and that've paid Essie's way but hell, you only get married once, so I went with her."

An incredulous silence followed. Tutchek shook his head as if to clear away some lingering spores of fungus. Whatever else you might say or think about Leonard Stanley Ferenc, it was now fairly certain that he had not killed Carol Sturgis nor burglarized the homes of Tetley, Bridges and Copland. Still, it had to be made certain.

"You realize," said Tutchek, "that we'll have to verify all this."

"That's why I laid it all out to make it easy for you. I want to get back to Chicago. I got a deposit on that turret lathe. Twenty bucks. If I lose it, you guys'll have to pay."

"Don't you understand, Ferenc, that if there's a single cockeyed detail in your story, you might be indicted for the murder of Carol Sturgis? You *will* be! Doesn't that make any impression at all?"

"Why should it? With the money I got in the bank and a business getting started, I'd be nuts to kill somebody."

Captain Mackenzie was given substantially the same story by Esther Ferenc, née Veen. He was not incredulous. He had never seen the Ferencs before, of course, but he'd seen everything else. Esther and Leonard merely added another chapter to his unwritten book on human oddities. While Communications were checking with the Millville justice of the peace, the bus company, the Indiana motel, the Chicago Tri-County Warehouse & Trucking Company and the Chicago apartment, he surveyed Esther with genuine curiosity.

She looked like a woman, a guaranteed female. In fact, she was a hell of a lot more female than most. She was young, ripe, luscious—a voluptuous explosion. No other phrase so aptly described her appearance in that sweater and tight skirt. She fairly burst upon you.

But it was exactly, he thought, like concealing a treasurer's report inside the covers of *Lady Chatterley's Lover*. And what a shock you got when you opened it!

"I know I'm a prying old man, Mrs. Ferenc," he said, using his Foxy Grandpa approach, "but did you marry your husband for his money? Or did he marry you for yours?"

"Well, both ways, I guess," she answered as if it were the most natural question in the world.

"Was there no mention of, oh, let's call it love?"

"We got married, didn't we? We're starting up a business. He'll run the shop and I'll take care of the bookkeeping."

"You're crazy about each other. I can see that. Would you have married him if he didn't have a penny outside his job?"

"You mean Leonard? He watches every dollar. He's not like the others. Or were you thinking of them? The others, I mean."

"No, no. I was asking about you and Leonard. Silly question, wasn't it?"

"Maybe you don't know Leonard, that's all. He's got a saying—a penny saved is a penny earned. More people should know about that. They'd be better off." Then, sharply, "You brought us here and you'll have to pay our room and board."

"Of course. We have excellent accommodations. People sometimes stay for years."

"I wanted to get that settled so there'll be no misunderstanding. And you'll have to pay our way back to Chicago. We didn't ask to come here, you know."

"Mrs. Ferenc," said Mackenzie, "this is a proud city and I'll not detain you a moment longer than I can help. We'll be glad, more than glad, to send you back to Chicago. Chicago's loss is our gain and you have my word, I assure you."

"You mean you'll buy the return tickets?" she asked suspiciously.

"Out of my own pocket, if necessary, Mrs. Ferenc. Two of my biggest and strongest detectives will escort you to the train, and I'll fire both of them if it leaves without you."

The spuriously maternal policewoman patted Esther Ferenc's arm. "And he means every word of it, sweetheart," she said. "If you miss the train, God help us, he'll send you back to Chicago in an armored car, locked and bolted."

"Amen," said Mackenzie.

3.

The Ferencs' story was checked out point by point. There'd been little doubt, but it had to be done. Harry Muir and Policewoman Ethel Leary put Leonard and Esther on the 5:23 out of Hudson. They waited on the platform until the train moved over the trestle across the Shackett River.

"You know something, Harry," said Ethel Leary, "Cap Mackenzie's a coward."

Muir grunted sourly. He wanted to go back to bed.

"He's a coward," Ethel Leary repeated. "A brave man would have warned Chicago but he was scared those two cannibals'd have been floated straight back to us. You know, I heard every word that chick said but I'll never believe it. What a beautiful love affair. He gazed tenderly into her bankbook and she gazed into his and it was love at first sight. And the honeymoon on the bus, Harry, just lousy with romance. Let's you and me get hitched and sail down the Shackett River into the sunrise on a garbage barge amid the lovely iridescent scum and the marine wonderland of Hartsung Bay where all sorts of fabulous things float out of the drainage ditch from our slaughterhouse. Ah, what a nuptial journey, Harry. And just think, it won't cost a nickel if we help shovel the sludge when the barge gets out to the dumping banks. Doesn't it *do* something to you, Harry? Doesn't something inside you turn over? If it does, let me know in time so I can duck."

"Drop dead, will you?"

Policewoman Leary nodded. It wasn't funny. It wasn't funny at all. It had never been funny.

Communications received word from the Brazilian police in Sao Felipe. It was to be regretted, but Senhor James A. Mockton was traveling in the most *formosos Estados Unidos e Mexico*. It was possible that news of him might be obtained from the Brazilian consul in *Ciudad Mexico* or *Nova York*.

It was not possible. Senhor Mockton had taken the plane to Lisbon, Portugal. From Portugal he went to Cape Town, South Africa, and was somewhere in the bush, shooting animals. Impossible to find him at a minute's notice, of course. There'd been talk of his going to Tanganyika or perhaps the Sudan. The Cape Town police would cooperate, naturally, but it was one of those things. Africa was a bit larger than the vicar's rose garden. Had a warrant been sworn? No? What a pity. Impossible to extradite without a warrant. Nothing to do but wait and see, what?

The *Hudson Evening News* emblazoned:

POLICE STILL SEEKING
MURDER MYSTERY MAN

Reporter Ed Turcott got no further than that. There were no leaks from Headquarters or the precincts. Only Flavin, George Gilman, Ben Tutchek, Captain Mackenzie, Lieutenant Haas and Paul Kropp knew of Monty, alias James A. Mockton. Communications had been given no information except that Mockton was a missing person.

No photograph album was found in the Sturgis house.

Flavin drove alone to Graystone Hospital and was told by the reception clerk that Walt Sturgis had been released.

Maggie Wrenn's confidential version was slightly different. Sturgis had simply walked out shortly after dinner the night before. The doctor was surprised and annoyed but said Sturgis was perfectly capable of walking anywhere. There was nothing wrong with him. The head wound had healed and there'd been no real internal injuries. He was free to go to Europe, if he wished. After all, the doctor wasn't a bodyguard.

Nonetheless, an orderly was fired and the night nurse temporarily suspended.

Sturgis had a room in the Hudson Athletic Club but had not used it for several weeks. Nor was he at home. He had gone away.

"Can you blame him?" asked Maggie Wrenn. "His wife was murdered and he'd almost gotten the same treatment. Good lord, in his place, I'd go away forever and stay there."

"Did he walk out in his nightshirt?" asked Flavin.

"No. He had clothes in the closet and, judging from what the nurses and orderlies say, quite a roll of money. Five or six hundred dollars."

"Did he cash a check?"

"Not here, Flavin."

Flavin called the bank but no Sturgis checks had come through since the killing. Therefore, someone had brought the money and Flavin had a hunch old Copland knew about it. Flavin turned his car toward the ugly yellow brick house on Pomander Walk. A bland, almost featureless man in a black alpaca jacket answered the door. He was very sorry but Mr. Copland was not at home. This was the hour during which he took his daily walk or perhaps a short drive into the nearby hills of North Abington. Miss Fay Copland? But Miss Fay had not been home for several days. The door answerer identified himself as Underwood, the houseman.

"I have been with the family a number of years, sir," he told Flavin in a bland, featureless voice; the perfect voice for an old family retainer.

"Is Miss Copland visiting friends or relatives?"

"I really don't know, sir. She was here on Sunday but gone Monday."

Flavin showed his badge. "Gone where, Underwood?" he asked.

"I wish I could help, sir, but Monday was my free day. Would you care to speak with Miss Fay's maid?"

Flavin said yes, he'd care. Underwood smiled vaguely, took him into the stiff, disapproving living room, and seemed more to melt away, like the Cheshire cat, than to walk. The living room was furnished with the most uncompromising Victorian furniture Flavin had ever seen. Over the marble fireplace hung a large tinted photograph of a gentleman, whose face was adorned by a gray beard. He looked as if he had bitten off more steel wool than he could chew. It was an unhappy portrait and no matter to what part of the room Flavin prowled, the eyes peered sadly at him from the gloomy decades of an earlier century.

Underwood materialized with a thin woman who looked as if she might be the daughter of the man in the photograph, born out of wedlock and forever shamed.

"This is Margaret, sir," Underwood said mistily, "Miss Fay's maid—ah—and assistant to the housekeeper. This gentleman is from the police, Margaret. Detective Flavin. Is that correct, sir?"

"I hope so."

Underwood's wraith-like smile was the one he assumed when guests made jokes. He said, "Ah—hmmmm—uh—" and again seemed to dissolve. Margaret's eyes pleaded at Flavin.

"What's the matter?" he asked.

"The matter? Why, there's nothing the matter, sir. Nothing I know of."

The pleading glance was her customary expression. "You're Fay Copland's maid, Margaret?"

"Only occasionally, sir."

"What's that mean?"

"I mostly do the cleaning, sir."

"And when you're her maid?"

"When she's going out, sir, I arrange her hair perhaps, apply fingernail polish and help with—zippers." She was embarrassed and behaved as if she'd used a dirty word.

"Did you see Miss Copland on Monday?"

"That was my free day, sir."

"Does everybody have Monday off?"

"Oh no, sir. Mine is usually Wednesday but occasionally I'm shifted. I was once given Sunday. It was very pleasant."

"Don't let them spoil you that way," Flavin growled. "When was the last time you saw Miss Copland?"

"Sunday, sir."

"Did she say anything about taking a trip to California, for instance?"

"No, sir. She was not feeling well and remained in her room."

"Does she get sick very often?"

"Oh but she wasn't sick, sir. She had the blues."

"The blues or a hangover?"

"The blues, sir. She didn't talk to anybody except Mr. Copland. When she has a hangover, she swears."

The door bumped a side chair as it opened. John Copland walked into the room, formal and erect.

"I think that's quite enough, Margaret," he said coldly. "You have work to do, don't you? Very well. Do it."

"Oh yes, sir," she gasped, and scurried from the room.

Copland placed his folded newspaper on a lamp table. "Have the servants been entertaining you, Mr. Flavin?"

"Not especially. They tell me your daughter's been gone since Monday. That's not very entertaining after we told her to stay here."

"It's a damned silly caprice. She'll regret it, I promise you."

"Where'd she go?"

"California, I believe. Or perhaps Florida. She flutters between the two for some idiotic reason I've never been able to fathom. I apologize for her."

"It'll need more than an apology. This time she'll be picked up and held as a material witness."

"I wish you luck. *I've* never been able to find her when she goes off like this. A few years ago she disappeared and it was not until months later that I learned she was in Spain, watching bullfights. Another time she went to Switzerland with a mountain climber or some such idiot. I'll assist in every way possible but unfortunately I am not a crystal gazer. She may be in France, England or, so far as that goes, moping around with alleged friends right here in Stone Bridge. Is your errand urgent, Mr. Flavin?"

"I want to talk to her about this man Monty."

"Mrs. Sturgis' uncle?"

"We don't know if he is or not," Flavin watched narrowly. "We've got a couple different descriptions that need checking."

Copland lifted thin white eyebrows. He made it seem old-fashioned and distant as if he were an ironic Voltaire and men had not lifted their eyebrows in this manner since. He appeared to withdraw in time and space.

"Mrs. Sturgis did have an uncle of that name I assure you, Mr. Flavin.

After your last visit here, I recalled having met him several years ago. Very briefly. His name escapes me. He was a tall man and so sunburned he looked like a Sioux Indian. I'll never know why he saw fit to clad his cranium in a toupee. Possibly because he was about seventy years old, although he did not look it. The sunburn—or suntan—deceived one. As did his ridiculous toupee—until he walked beneath a bright light. Intelligent, however. Except for the toupee."

"So I was told. Do you know anything else about him?"

"Nothing whatever. I saw him only once again before he returned to Argentina or Bolivia where he lived. He was at the country club swimming pool in bathing trunks, leaping around like an imbecile. Vigorously, I must admit. We had no conversation on this occasion. I am very, very unfond of elderly gymnasts."

"He lived in Brazil, not Argentina. He's on his way back to Sao Felipe. We're in touch with the police there. I'd like to get in touch with Walt Sturgis, too. Do you have any idea where he is?"

"Isn't he in Graystone Memorial Hospital?"

"He left last night."

"That's odd. I spoke with his physician and Walt was to have stayed another week."

"Well, he skipped out, to tell you the truth. We think he might be with your daughter."

"No," Copland whispered the word. "Believe me, Mr. Flavin, Faith is the last person on earth to whom he would go. He disliked her. I'm positive of this. I *know*. That is the reason she never visited Carol Sturgis when Walt was at home. He did not want her around."

"Why?"

"Why?" It was several seconds before Copland answered slowly, "She drinks too much, Mr. Flavin. It's common knowledge. Walt is not a teetotaler by any means, but like me and a number of other men, he finds nothing more repulsive than a female sot. She does this only at parties, thank God. It's sheer exhibitionism, that's all. Otherwise she drinks very little. You may search if you wish, Mr. Flavin, but you'll not find Walt Sturgis with my daughter. Never."

"We'll have to pick her up all the same, Mr. Copland. Do you have a photograph of her? You *said* you'd help."

"There's one, yes. I think it's over here ...."

He crossed the room stiffly, no longer erect, but a tired old man, tired to the last flutter of his soul. He opened an ornate cabinet wartily carved with thick grape clusters and vine leaves. He returned with an eight-by-ten photograph in a silver frame.

"I'm afraid it's not very good," he said wearily. "It's a—a photographer's photograph. You'll see what I mean."

Flavin saw. It was an "art study," diffused, highlighted, shadowed—a mishmash. It bore some resemblance to Fay Copland, but it could just as easily have been an unfocussed Kim Novak or Miss Miasma Beach of 1959. But McGimp had seen Fay and there was a long chance that he might be able to retouch some likeness into the photograph. Flavin took it from the frame and placed it between the leaves of a magazine.

"There's something else," he said. "Why'd you give Walt Sturgis all that money?"

Copland's thoughts had moved to something else and it took him a moment to comprehend the question. "Money?" he said, "Money? I didn't give him any money. I cashed his check."

"None of his checks have gone through the bank for over ten days."

"There must be some mistake. I ..." He brought out his wallet, opened it and there was Walt Sturgis' check for a thousand dollars made out to Cash. "I forgot, I suppose."

"That's a lot of money to forget, Mr. Copland."

"I know, I know."

"And it's made out to Cash. Anybody can collect on it."

"It was stupid of me, I realize."

"You must have quite a bit on your mind, Mr. Copland."

Copland closed the wallet and put it into his hip pocket. He lifted his head and regarded Flavin down the narrow planes of his nose. "Are you also a financial advisor, Mr. Flavin? If so, you are more versatile than most policemen. I shall make a point of recommending you for promotion the next time I see Commissioner Willie Quinn. Willie's not so bright but he does manage to understand English if I speak slowly and distinctly. Am I speaking slowly enough and distinctly enough for you, Mr. Flavin?"

The skin tightened around Flavin's mouth. "Yes, thanks," he said.

"And is that all, Mr. Flavin?"

"For the time being."

"Good."

4.

For the first time in over six months, Detective Lieutenant Tom Walsh was a happy man, although he had not yet reached the complete elation phase predicted by Doctor Hauptmann. He looked drowsy and contented as he sprawled in a deck chair beside the goldfish pond, but growing within him was a bubble of glittering gaiety.

Also, there was the matter of an interesting larceny. During his artfully garrulous examination of Lieutenant Walsh that morning, Doctor Hauptmann had hurriedly been summoned from the office to assist a patient who'd gluttonously eaten a full can of pipe tobacco. Tom Walsh, who could open a spring lock with the thin blade of a paper knife, wandered into the dispensary and lifted a 100-tablet bottle of five mg. dextro-amphetamine sulphate.

So now he was full of small elation bubbles and Dexedrine, an exhilarating combination, to say the least. Otherwise he might not have been so delighted to see *Hudson Evening News* reporter Ed Turcott, who came watchfully from the Administration building, walking diagonally across the grounds through a decorative grove of silver-and-black scrub birch, which also offered excellent cover in case Tom Walsh had police visitors from Headquarters. Turcott was not at his news-sleuthing best in a crowd.

But curiously enough, he had not come for that purpose, although it was well known that he'd trade his wife's virtue (if any) for a story, a lead or even a hint. Tom Walsh was one of the few officers both liked and respected by the bawdy, cynical crew in the news room and they all said it was a damn shame he'd almost worked himself into a hole in the ground after his wife's death. So Ed Turcott's visit, his first, was altruistic and self-conscious.

He was astonished at Tom Walsh's gay, friendly greeting—astonished, suspicious, wary and finally warmed by it, and glad, too, that the Lieutenant had gained weight and was in such sparkling high spirits. They chatted of this and that and made jokes but inevitably the talk turned to the Sturgis murder.

"Too bad the Ferenc lead fizzled out," regretted Turcott. "It was a natural for the front page."

"There's a better one coming, Eddie-boy. It'll break wide open. It's about time they sat up and took notice of Jeff Flavin. He's been on top of that case from the beginning. There's, a boy who's going places."

Turcott's ears sharpened. "Flavin's good," he agreed.

"You're damn right he's good. You don't know how good he is. Even he himself doesn't know how good he is. I'm the only one who knows. Hell, he's got the case in his back pocket. I told him what to do, and you know why?" The Dexedrine and elation bubbles were fizzing together. "I'll tell you why—that hatchet-man, Haas. The Dutchman's all right. He runs his department. But he'd have Flavin so deep in reports and triplicates and memos and paperwork that Jeff wouldn't be able to move. 'Do it your own way, Jeff,' I told him, and that's the way it is."

"I'm glad it's moving again," murmured Turcott. "If he's got a real lead, he'll be smart to do what you said. *If* it's a real lead."

Tom was off now—high, wide and handsome, fancy-free—and he juggled the facts like Indian clubs, tossing them about to suit his supercharged mood. He had given Flavin no advice, of course, but he was convinced that he had.

"If it's a real lead? *If?*" he laughed. "I know a real lead, Eddie-boy, and don't kid yourself about that. Listen to this—Walt Sturgis and Fay Copland have disappeared, departed, vanished. What do you think about that!"

"Sorry, but nothing in particular, Tom," Turcott lied. "They're clean."

"Ha, ha, ha! I thought you knew your stuff. Sturgis sneaked out of the hospital. As good old Sergeant Bauer would say, that's Number One. Number Two; Fay Copland tried to skip the state before but Flavin stopped her. I told you he was on top of the case every minute, didn't I? That's just to show you—but he can't be every place at the same time and now she's skipped out clean, bag and baggage, Old man Copland says she's in France or Spain but doesn't really know. He's cooperating with Jeff and, whether you know it or not, that means something. He might be another hatchet-man but he's a shrewd old goat, too. There's your headline— GUILTY PAIR SKIPS ON EVE OF ARREST."

"I hope Flavin pulls it out of the hat, Tom. I really do. I'm with him. But there's no story yet. Ben Tutchek and Harry Muir gave both of them a clean bill and I don't see how Jeff's going to get around that."

"Details, details," Tom had rapidly achieved the seat of the mighty and the omniscient view was magnificent. "The hell with details. It's the overall picture that counts. Don't you know that? Well, Jeff Flavin has it. He thinks big. He knows the details will fall into place later. And he's not letting Hass tie him up in that lousy paperwork. See? He thinks big. You've got to think big."

"You mean he's investigating this on his own, eh? Well then, I agree with you. You can strangle a case in red tape."

Tom Walsh's Olympian smile condescendingly patted Turcott on the head. "Now you're getting the over-all picture and I'll see that Jeff gives you the story first," his face darkened; the Gods were stern. "You're the only news louse to visit me, Turcott. The rest of them sent get-well cards at two bits a throw. They're stupid. So you'll get the story when it breaks and the hell with them. Think big, Turcott, and you'll *be* big."

"You'll remind Flavin, won't you, Lieutenant?"

"I've given my word," said Tom haughtily. "I'm going back to Headquarters next week and there'll be changes made. The Bureau'll be reorganized from top to bottom ...." Grandiose plans sailed into view, an Armada of galleons with silken sails on a jewelled sea. He was the Grand Admiral and had to stand alone as the fleet passed in review. He dismissed Turcott in a friendly fashion, but firmly. He wanted to think. Think big.

Turcott went after the story like a questing mink. He had a quick talk with his managing editor and a tame trustee of the hospital board got the facts about Sturgis and Flavin from Maggie Wrenn, who loyally defended her staff against charges of negligence. The city editor sent out all available legmen. A ten or twenty-dollar bill changed hands here and there. Fay Copland's maid, Margaret, found the offer of ten dollars very tempting. A desk clerk of the Hudson Athletic Club, where Sturgis had a room, became richer by fifteen dollars; a service station attendant, who'd gassed and oiled Sturgis' gray Lincoln convertible on the night of the walkout, was content with five. A Stone Bridge friend of Copland's owed the *Hudson Evening News* an important personal favor. The exchange of a modest sum persuaded a stool pigeon to tell Flavin that Sturgis and Fay Copland were registered in an Atlantic City hotel under the name of Mr. and Mrs. Irwin Stowe of Englewood Heights, Delaware. The Stowes actually were there but Irwin was having too good a time at the Retail Merchants' Convention to notice a tight-lipped detective from the City of Hudson.

A City Hall reporter of the *Hudson Evening News* had a casual sidewalk conversation with Flavin. Fay Copland was mentioned in passing. It was not an interview. The reporter yearned for the old days (before the Sturgis killing) when a man could place a bet on the horses but the town was 'hot' and the bookies had gone elsewhere until it cooled off. Nevertheless, he managed to obtain a few noncommittal quotes from Flavin. The quotes did not look so noncommittal when placed at strategic points in the story.

> POLICE SEEK HUSBAND
> AND 'BEST FRIEND'
> OF MURDERED WOMAN
>
> Pair Missing Since Yesterday
> Wanted For Questioning, Revealed;
> No Warrants Issued, Says D.A.

The bulldog, or first, edition of the *News* hit the streets at 11:00 A.M. Ten minutes later Flavin was summoned to Lieutenant Haas' office. Waiting for him were Commissioner Quinn, Captain Mackenzie and the Lieutenant. All were grim but Haas looked like a man who'd drunk a pint of nitroglycerin. Flavin was not invited to sit down.

A copy of the newspaper lay spread on the desk. "Have you seen this thing?" Mackenzie asked harshly.

Flavin looked at the black, boldface headlines and shook his head. He felt sick.

Mackenzie snatched up the paper. "Is this true?" he demanded. Then read, 'The flight of Walter Sturgis and Faith Copland is being "unofficially" conducted by Detective Jeff Flavin, who is working with the Homicide Squad. When interviewed, Detective Flavin said, "I'd like to hear the explanation." He offered no other comment on the unexpected disappearance of the murdered woman's husband and the attractive red-haired woman.' *Is this true, God damn it?*"

Flavin remembered his casual conversation with the city hall reporter. "That's all I said. I didn't tell him any of the rest."

"Did you take a plane to Atlantic City, as it says here?"

"Yes."

"Did you question Copland, the maid, the houseman, the Hudson Athletic Club desk clerk and Margaret Wrenn at Graystone Hospital?"

"Yes."

"Do you think Sturgis pulled those damn burglaries?"

"No."

"Why didn't you bring this information to Headquarters and make out a report? Why didn't you talk to Lieutenant Haas? Why didn't you tell *somebody*, for the love of Christ?"

Flavin shook his head again. Could he say Fay Copland and Sturgis had been given a clean bill by Ben Tutchek? Could he say that he had a hunch the pair had lied to him about "Uncle Monty?" That he had a hunch Copland had lied to him about Fay's disappearance? What good were hunches? What good was any explanation now that the story was splashed across the front page of the *News?*

He'd wanted to bring in some kind of evidence linking Sturgis with Fay, or either of them with the killing—but that was not an adequate answer either.

Kitteridge was supposed to cover Sturgis at the hospital and other Homicide bulls covered the Coplands. Flavin had not interfered with them. He had followed a hunch on his own time and with his own money. Many a detective had done that before, but they had not been sucked into a front page sensation. That was the difference.

Haas could sit in silence no longer. Flavin had been told to keep his nose out of Homicide and what had he done? Made them all look like jackasses. Set them back weeks, months, maybe ruined everything. Haas raged like a lunatic. His face was purple and dripping with sweat, his gestures violent.

Mackenzie bellowed, "SHUT UP!" It was the only way he could make himself heard through that wild clamor.

Haas clenched his fists. "I want his badge," he said loudly, and walked from the office with stiff, unnatural steps.

Mackenzie look at Flavin. "Suspended indefinitely," he said. "Now get out of here before—get out!"

Joyce Ames met Flavin on the street outside Headquarters. "Call me tonight, Jeff," she said miserably. "Call me tonight. We were to have had a date last Saturday and— Call me tonight. Promise?"

"I'll—call you," his tongue felt thick and unreal. "Something might come up, but I'll try. It's hard to tell right now."

He did not want solace from a woman who was in love with another man.

Eight

There are many experiences that can take the heart out of a man. The number is beyond calculation. A two-timing wife can rob him of self-respect; glaucoma can rob him of sight; cancer can rob him of life.

But the loss of a job into which he has put more than heart is temporary destruction. Flavin did not kid himself. Foxy said, "Suspended indefinitely," but he had seen the cold, oyster-platter eyes of Police Commissioner Quinn and o-u-t spells "out."

George Gilman came at 7:30. His glance brushed the apartment and found no half-emptied liquor bottles. Thank God for that. Gilman had his own opinion of guys who hit the bottle when the going was tough.

This was worse than visiting the sick. He was always tongue-tied when he went to visit a sick guy, even if he'd known him all his life. What could you say to a sick guy? Hope you get better? That sounded like you thought he was going to die. What *could* you say to a sick guy?

Now here was old Jeff, kicked out of the Bureau. No fault of his own. A guy that did his job day in, day out. A guy that lived for the Bureau. It was his *life*. Now what in the name of Jesus could you say to a guy like that?

"I brung you a cartoon of oyster stew," said George, showing a greasy brown bag. "You gotta eat, Jeff. I knew you wouldn't eat. It's got nourishment. The best. Schrafft's."

Flavin said, "Thanks, George," looked around and set it on a magazine atop his small bookcase. "Grab a chair." He walked across the room, took a cigarette from a pack on the sofa and lit it restlessly.

Gilman leaned against the wall. He glanced at the greasy brown bag.

He hadn't really expected Jeff to eat the stew. "You got a bad shake, Jeff," he mumbled.

"I asked for it," Flavin thrust the incident aside with a sharp sweep of his arm. "It was stupid. Why should I mess with Homicide?"

"If you thought Sturgis knocked off his wife you'd of said so, Jeff."

"I know. That's the stupid part of it. Fay Copland didn't have anything to do with it either. She's got witnesses and Sturgis didn't beat himself up."

"Well—they had a reason for running out."

"Sure. Everybody's got a reason for everything. But why the hell am I worrying about it? My old man owns a lumberyard. He's getting old. He's disappointed I didn't take over before this."

"There's good money in the lumber business."

"Damn good. I should step in and let him retire. Maybe I will. I don't know."

"You'll be your own boss."

"Like Tetley? He's his own boss and everybody loves him, which is why he got slapped around that night. It was a simple case of assault and battery disguised as a heist. Only he wasn't slapped around so much. Compared to Sturgis, I mean. You talked to him, George. How bad was it?"

"Nothing. A couple shiners and some bruises, is all. I think. Worse than Bridges or Copland, though. He was marked a little, but mostly the guy just made fun of him in front of his wife. A guy like Tetley, that's what hurt. You think maybe it was one of Billy Lowe's boys? Billy don't like the son of a bitch."

"None of those," said Flavin absently, his mind skipping beyond the gambler. "A pro would have worked him over better and faster. You know how those guys work. If a pro had orders to give him the once over lightly, there wouldn't have been a mark on him, but he'd have had the sorest gut in Hudson and a pair of aching kidneys. And he'd have been let know the reason. A pro wouldn't have played slap-the-wrist with Bridges and Copland. He'd have laid them out cold or not touched them at all, no matter what kind of grudge he had against the rich."

The best thing, Gilman realized, was to keep Flavin talking. He was alive when he talked. "The way you line it up," he said, "the first wasn't really a heist, but the second three were. And you eliminated all the pros. Ferenc looked good till he ticked off alibis by the numbers. So it took a pro to open them wall safes but you say the guy wouldn't just slap Tetley, Bridges and Copland and let it go at that. Sturgis was something different. He put up a scrap and got clobbered."

Flavin half-turned and looked at George around the side of his upper arm. His eyes widened. "That's right," he said slowly, as if each vowel and consonant had a definite meaning. "The slapsie routine stank. It wasn't rough enough. And there isn't a heavy-gee in the country who'd stick his neck out with shenanigans after cranking the box. He'd grab the take and hit the grit. If he wanted to smack those guys, there wouldn't have been any horseplay. You know what? I think he bounced Copland and Bridges around a little to make the whole works look as though he'd been eating goofballs."

George shook his head, shifted his hat from hand to hand and made faces at it. "I don't go for that goofball angle, Jeff," he said.

"Neither do I. Look. In the Tetley case, the burglary was only the cover-up, so he cracked the box. It was easy money. So easy that he must have been flabbergasted and went after the others. Four strikes in a month, George. Four! And all in the same God-damned neighborhood. That's suicide as far as a real box man is concerned. He'd know better. This bird wasn't a pro. He started with a grudge against Tetley. He opened the box and took money and a handful of old-fashioned jewelry he couldn't have peddled if he gave it away. Now I believe Tetley. The guy did take those old time geegaws. Just to take something. You know? He wanted it to look like a burglary, pure and simple. But he trademarked himself as an amateur right there. A pro wouldn't take grandma's tiara for a gift."

"Tetley," said George. "He's the hinge. It began with Tetley. If only Ferenc hadn't been alibied to the eyes."

Flavin pointed tensely. "Get on the phone, George. Call what's-his-name—Frank Zinns. He used to work for Howards-Tetley and lives right here in Hudson. Ask him who was really in line for service manager before old brownnose Phelps knifed him. I'd do it myself but I'm wound up and I'd fizzle like a wet firecracker."

Flavin could not stand still while George was telephoning. He prowled the apartment impatiently. The call took longer than he expected. Old Zinns was huffy and felt that he had been unscrupulously used in the earlier interview by Flavin when Ferenc was suspect number one. George knew how to butter up the old man but it took time, it took time. He finally hung up and slid around on the chair beside the telephone.

"Remember that big sourpuss we talked to from Howards-Tetley? Herb Wiess, Phelps' assistant. Well, he was the old service manager's assistant, too. That'd be Ed Maurer."

"Wiess, Wiess—" Flavin snapped his finger. "Yeah. The guy who tried to give us the run-around about Ferenc till we put the fear of God into him. You made him come down here to Headquarters."

"Well, Zinns says Wiess actually had charge of the service department for a week or two. On probation. Maybe he was trying too hard but he cracked the whip on everybody. Almost messed up the department for fair. Guys threatening to quit, and all that. Then Tetley brought Phelps in and booted Wiess back to the job of assistant. You know the kind of guy Wiess is. He moped about it. Zinns says he's the brightest guy in the department. He invents things and's got a nice little shop in his garage. You know the old-fashioned dial on a safe? Well, Wiess is working on something new. Ten push buttons down the side. Three of them make the combination. He's building a model so's he can take out a patent. From what I managed to squeeze out of Zinns, if Wiess had a grudge, it was for life. He'd never forgive or forget. And he's touchy as hell."

Flavin kicked a small ottoman out of his path and strode to the window. "What the hell am I worrying about," he said savagely. "I'm not a cop. I've been canned."

"Once a cop, always a cop," said George.

"Bullshit."

"I know, but it sounded good, didn't it? Anyways, Wiess had the job, got the boot, and he's sore. I'll bet he fairly ached to smack Tetley in the puss. But why didn't he quit instead of taking a lot of crap from Tetley and Phelps. He must have sludge in his blood."

"The hell with him."

"Add him up," George ignored Flavin's remark. "He could of massacreed Tetley that night, but what's he do? Slaps him in the puss a little bit. See what I mean? Sludge in his blood. But he could open a Tetley-made box. In fact, he opened three of them and the Norwich safe at Sturgis'."

"Maybe."

"It's all maybe. But add him up, Jeff. That's all. Add him up."

It was a long while before Flavin slowly turned his head and looked at the door to the outside hall. "Hell," he said, "it's impossible for Foxy to fire me twice. Get Wiess' address from the phone book."

"I did," said George.

Wiess was working in his garage machine shop. The patent safe model was partially assembled and stood gleaming on the bench. It was a beautifully machined job. Wiess' dour face was almost happy as he took a just-finished part from a lathe and carefully measured it with a micrometer. He almost dropped both when Flavin and Gilman walked into the garage. His expression closed and froze.

"Don't mind us," said Flavin. "We just want to look around."

"What for? Why?"

"Nothing. Nothing at all. Just looking."

"You got a search warrant?"

"Do we look as though we're searching for something? Is that a bag of cement in the corner, George? Has Mr. Wiess been cementing something?"

"Mr. Wiess can do anything, Jeff. He's smart. Don't let us interrupt you, Mr. Wiess. We only dropped in."

"Nothing in here's been cemented lately, George."

"Maybe he's going to cement something tomorrow, Jeff. What do you think of that safe he's making? You can't beat Mr. Wiess on safes. He can open and close them like the dickens. Right, Mr. Wiess?"

Wiess gripped the chassis of the lathe. His fingers were shaking. "Of course," he stammered. "It's my work. You know that."

"Uh-huh. And after hours, too," said Flavin, pretending to admire the model safe. "All kinds of hours, I'll bet."

George looked the garage over very carefully. He got down on his knees and looked under the bench. He opened drawers, peered into cans, prodded the cement bag with a long, thin piece of tool steel. Flavin examined corners, tilted the waste can and scrutinized the contents.

"Now don't let us hold you up, Mr. Wiess," he said cheerfully. "Tonight we're just a pair of sightseers. Stop us if we get too nosy. Can you really open all kinds of safes? You must be an expert."

"He is," said George. "Show him a safe and it's as good as open."

Wiess relaxed a little and leaned against the lathe. "You've poked around enough," he said. "I don't have to stand for this."

"Mr. Wiess doesn't want us in his garage," said George.

"I never did like garages anyway," said Flavin. "I like jewelry stores. And houses. Mr. Wiess has a pretty nice house. Ranch style, they call it."

"I'm not interested in houses," said George, watching Wiess' set face. "And you can have jewelry stores. Everything they sell costs ten times as much as I can pay. The way I like jewelry is to get it for nothing. I'm the same with money. The best way to get money is for free. But nothing less than, say, fifteen thousand. I wouldn't fool around with nickels and dimes. The guy that pulled them Stone Bridge jobs had the right idea—don't horse around with small change."

"I'm sorry you don't like Mr. Wiess' house, George."

"Oh, it's an okay house but there ain't enough grounds. Hell, you couldn't hide a bottle of aspirin in grounds that size. It'd stand out like a keg of beer."

"Don't be like that, George. Grounds show up better in the daytime. But we're in the way here. Mr. Wiess hasn't done a stroke of work since we walked in."

"He's just being polite, Jeff. Or maybe he just stopped for a rest. He's all sweated up. Look at him."

"He'll catch cold in this night air, George. But on the other hand, he's probably been getting around here and there at night. Did you notice his car on the way in? A couple years old, but solid. You should take a good look at that car of his, George. Both of us should—"

He stopped. They looked, hard-eyed, at Wiess. He was the image of death itself.

"He's got a bad chill," said George. "Let's take him down to Headquarters and warm him up. We'll take his car, too. He might get a bad name if the neighbors see him in a police car."

"I think you need some warming up, Mr. Wiess," said Flavin in a flat voice. "There's a cop at Headquarters named Harry Muir. He's six feet four. He can warm anybody up."

Wiess' jaw wobbled and he backed away from them, lurching, as if he had lost control of his legs. His glance darted from side to side but Flavin and Gilman stood between him and the open door.

George grinned and his gold teeth glinted metallically. "I told you he had sludge in his blood," he said. "He's scared witless. The garage, the house and the grounds didn't mean nothing, but the minute you mentioned the car, his guts fell out. It's the car. You'll find the stuff in the car. Maybe the spare tire or hid underneath on the frame. That's the first place these smart guys think of and the first place we look. It's printed on his face. You can see it."

Flavin took the man's helpless arm. "Let's go," he said.

Wiess screamed and George tapped him behind the ear with his blackjack. He did it almost gently, as an act of mercy.

2.

The stolen jewelry and money were found in a metal box expertly welded to the chassis under the motor. Except for the box and welding, it was a very usual hiding place.

Wiess was exceptionally cowardly and became hysterical. It took four big cops to carry him into the Headquarters. Doctor Knight had to give him a powerful tranquilizer before he was able to babble a confession. Just to sew it up, they got a lawyer for him and the prosecutor was there, but he wanted only to confess. The first burglary was incubated in his hatred of Tetley, who, he claimed, had gypped him, demoted him shamefully, treated him like a dog. But he didn't really want to hurt the old stinker. He just slapped him a little.

("A gutless bastard," said Harry Muir sourly, shrugging. If Wiess had not been quite so gutless, a workout in one of the Interrogation rooms would have given Harry some healthful exercise.)

The burglary had not been premeditated. It had been committed because Wiess wanted to draw attention away from his attack on Tetley. He had an almost superstitious fear that the old man had clairvoyant powers and might recognize him.

There had not been $10,000 in the safe, as Tetley claimed, but only $3,000. That was a large amount of money to Wiess. He had the combinations of other Tetley house safes locked in the office, and greedily he went after more, taking $2,500 from Henry Bridges and another $3,000 from Copland. He could not explain why he took the jewelry for he had no way of selling it.

But he had not been near the Sturgis house. He wept, grovelled and pleaded to be believed. He fell from his chair and writhed on the floor. It was not a pretty sight.

Ben Tutchek gritted, "Oh, Jesus G. Christ!" and went out into the hall with Flavin for a cigarette while a disgusted Doctor Knight administered another strong sedative. They lifted Wiess back into the chair and had to hold him upright. He'd worked all that night, he sobbed, honest to God, he'd worked all night in the garage shop. He clutched the end of Captain Mackenzie's jacket and would not let go.

"The cop, the cop on the beat, the cop," he bleated. "He saw me. He was there three, four times. We talked. I gave him coffee. Ask him. Please ask him. Please, please! He'll tell you. His name—his name is ..." a look of terror made slush of his face. He could not remember the cop's name.

Mackenzie pulled away from those horribly palsied fingers and told one of the detectives to get the cop who'd had that tour.

The cop's name was Lewis Kutscher. He confirmed Wiess' story and further substantiated it with the statement that a cab driver called Hersh Mozeltoff had been in the shop also.

Tutchek swore and walked out. The Carol Sturgis murder was hotter than ever. Captain Mackenzie took Flavin into the end Interrogation room.

"You did a nice job on Wiess. I'll admit that," he was flushed and angry. "But I should beat your brains out with a nightstick anyway. If you have any. What the hell was the idea of sticking your fat head in Homicide business? Jesus, Mary and Joseph! didn't you know Haas would crucify you? And Quinn wants you busted off the Force. Pronto. How do you like that?"

"I don't."

"Shut your lousy fat mouth!" Mackenzie ground his teeth into a frazzled cigar. "I won't even try to talk to Lieutenant Haas. He'd pull a gun on me. But maybe—just maybe—the Commissioner will change his mind after he hears about Wiess. In the meantime get back to work. In case anybody asks, you've been transferred to the Missing Persons Detail and if I were you, you dumb hod carrier, I'd get down on my knees and pray that my hunch on Fay Copland and Walt Sturgis pays off."

"I don't think they had anything to do with the killing," said Flavin.

"Then why the stinking hell did—" Mackenzie calmed himself after drawing a long, incredulous breath. "As we used to say, Detective, that takes the cake. But we'll forget it. You've done some digging on them and they have to be talked to. See Ben Tutchek. And work with him, do you understand!"

"Yes, sir."

"Wait a minute. Did you give that story to the *Hudson Evening News?*"

"No, sir."

"That sneaking little creep," whispered Mackenzie, meaning Ed Turcott. "He got it someplace. I wonder where."

"It's no secret that Walt Sturgis skipped out of Graystone."

"Shut up! I'm trying to think. Anyway, that's not the story he printed. I'll find out. See Tutchek."

It was close to midnight and Tutchek and Flavin went to the all-night cafeteria around the corner for a cup of coffee. Mackenzie was right, of course. Sturgis and La Copland had to be found and talked to. There was no getting out of it since the *News* story. Tutchek had no ideas and Flavin had no ideas. Both Sturgis and Fay Copland were accustomed to travel. By this time they might be on their way to Finland or the Belgian Congo. Or Buffalo, N. Y.

"And I'm praying to Allah, not together," said Tutchek.

"I just thought of something," said Flavin. The Coplands have a cottage at Lake Powhatan in North Jersey. She's a drinker and that's just the place a drinker might hole up with a case of Scotch. There's been no mention of the cottage so far."

"Why didn't you say so before? Let's get back to Headquarters and put it on the wire."

Joyce Ames was standing outside the entrance to Headquarters. Tutchek gave her an appreciative glance and said, offhand, "See you upstairs in about fifteen minutes, Jeff. We might have to move fast."

Joyce did not speak immediately and when she did it was in a low, almost inaudible voice. "Congratulations, Jeff," she said.

"Make that a rain check, Joyce. It's not official yet. And by the way, I've been transferred to Missing Persons, otherwise known as the Zombie Nook."

"You'll be all right, Jeff. You'll do well."

"*With* Willie Quinn's indulgence and *if* Lieutenant Haas doesn't have me assassinated. You can't blame him after that *Hudson Evening News* story."

"Liuetenant Haas is a nasty, noisy old man! The *News* didn't get the story from you. You wouldn't do a thing like that."

"I was there, Joyce. I led with my chin and that's against the rules."

They were standing about two feet apart and neither moved closer to the other. A sandalwood-colored dress warmed her finely-textured complexion. Flavin had an unaccustomed poetic impulse to say her light brown hair was honey-and-gold in the glow of the street lamp but there was an uneasy constraint between them and the conversation thus far had the feeling of being conducted through a defective intercom box.

"I—I waited for your telephone call," she said.

"I'm sorry. I got tied up in this Wiess thing."

"Of course. I should have thought. It was wonderful, Jeff!"

"It would be if the Sturgis killing weren't still wide open and anybody's guess. Have you been out to see Tom Walsh yet?"

"Do you think I should, Jeff? I hardly know him."

So she wants me to give her the green light, he thought. "Why not?" he said aloud. "Time drags in a hospital. Get him a box of those bent nail puzzles and stuff from the five-and-dime. He hasn't worked one yet. They make him mad but he loves them."

"I'll go tomorrow. And—good luck in your new job."

"Thanks."

He went up the worn steps to Headquarters and she walked across the street to her 1954 Chevvy two-door.

There was nothing for Flavin, Gilman, Tutchek and Muir to do but wait through the small, furry hours, which could have been lemurs had they belonged to the animal kingdom. They had nothing but a flimsy lead but nonetheless they waited. They talked and Harry told some of his bathroom jokes, but that soon petered out. They weren't in the mood. To recapitulate, they listed everything they had on the murder. The list was damned meager.

1. The plaster cast of a print made by a worn sneaker.
2. Some prints of work gloves which were sold by the millions from coast to coast.
3. Carol Sturgis had been gagged so clumsily that it choked her.
4. She had been tied up loosely and hastily.
5. Evidence of sexual intercourse but none of rape.
6. Walt Sturgis was later attacked and beaten with a bent bumper

jack handle. Sturgis had been too drunk to describe his assailant.

7. A man named Monty—afterward called Uncle Monty—had been seen in the Sturgis home while Walt Sturgis was away.

8. What had been stolen from the Sturgis house? Carol's jewelry? There'd been nothing in the safe, according to Walt Sturgis.

9. Fay Copland and Walt Sturgis had suddenly skipped town at approximately the same time. A coincidence? Improbable. But why had they run out?

10. The MO was an obvious imitation of the Tetley, Bridges and Copland jobs.

"You know what I think," said Muir. "This mutt Monty was laying the dame, the husband charged in gory-eyed drunk and Monty dragged him down the hall and knocked him off. Then Monty came back and tied up the dame to make it look like the old heist."

"And Monty carried a jack handle in his back pocket for such emergencies?" asked Flavin.

"And in the beginning when Walt Sturgis was half out of his head," said Tutchek, "we got enough description out of him to know the guy was dressed the way Wiess got himself up for the other jobs."

"And Monty don't sound like a guy who'd run around in sneakers," said George Gilman. "Tennis shoes yes, sneakers no."

"Ah, go to hell," yawned Harry. "But somebody laid her."

"The husband," said Tutchek. "Some guys get all steamed up on liquor."

"You, you're a guy that gets all steamed up on a glass of water, you dumb Polack."

"Water," Tutchek smiled at Flavin and Gilman. "When I want it, I don't waste time with anything. But you, you poor old worn-out crud, you have to eat Spanish Fly like candy. Before, during and after."

"Don't kid yourself, hot shot. I can get letters of recommendation from dames that'd surprise you."

"Sure. Frannie the Fink, Grandma Katz and Typhoid Mary. But it wouldn't surprise me, Harry. When you're all charged up on Spanish Fly, you'd jump a saw horse, if that's all was handy."

Harry wearily told Tutchek what to do with himself.

This was a fair cross section of run-of-the-mill Headquarters humor. Some worse, some better.

Two A.M.

Three A.M.

Four A.M.

Tutchek told Muir and Gilman to go home. It must be recorded that token protests were made by both before leaving.

At exactly 6:47 Communications got a strike. Tutchek took the call. Instantly wide awake. He kept shaking his head up and down. "Uh-huh—uh-huh—uh-huh—well, I'll be a son of a bitch—thanks, Paul."

He hung up. He gathered his mouth into an odd pucker. "I can be wrong," he said to Flavin, "but we did put Fay Copland on the wire, didn't we?"

"That was the idea."

"I thought so. Well, guess who the Franklin County cops found in one of the Copland guest houses at Lake Powhatan. Walt Sturgis."

"I'll be damned. They *were* together."

"I said Walt Sturgis. No sign of Fay Copland. No clothes, no luggage, no lipstick, no nothing. Just Walt Sturgis. They're holding him in the guest house. Let's go."

It was an hour's drive up Route 12, then three miles northwest on the Lake Powhatan private road. A lanky deputy sheriff met them at the entrance and took them to the guest house. Walt Sturgis—unshaven and filthy dirty—sat groggily in a red top grain leather lounge chair beside which stood a half case of scotch. From the sick look of him, he should have been back in Graystone.

"He was crocked to the eyeballs when we saw the light and walked in," said the deputy. "We sobered him up some. He was holding that thing in his lap. Thank God he was too soused to move." He angled his long jaw at a heavy .45 automatic on a long cypress table in the center of the room.

"I'm not going to use it," said Sturgis dully. "That's all over."

"What's all over?" asked Tutchek.

"Not in front of William S. Hart over there," Sturgis' bloodshot glance of dislike was without humor. "He talks too much."

"The hell with that," the deputy said hotly. "If there's an arrest, this is my end of the county."

"No arrest, friend," said Tutchek. "This man's sick. He skipped out of the hospital. We're taking him back. If you want to check up, call Graystone Memorial Hospital in Hudson and ask for Supervisor Wrenn. But the poor guy's trying to drink himself to death and—well, take a look for yourself."

Tutchek laid his arm across the man's shoulder and, still talking persuasively, led him out of the guest house. Tutchek was six inches taller, seventy pounds heavier and his thick arm was rock-hard. The deputy lost interest in such trivialities as jurisdiction and other inconsequential red tape. He wanted only to cooperate. A hundred per cent. He proved it by leaving the premises. Tutchek returned and helped the staggering Sturgis to the police car. Flavin wrapped the .45 in a handkerchief and brought it, too. Sturgis slumped in the front seat next to Tutchek; Flavin sat in the back. Sturgis' mouth was folded tightly. He did not intend to talk but both Tutchek and Flavin knew how to handle that.

"Fay Copland," said Tutchek. "It's a damn shame."

"A shame nothing, Ben," said Flavin. "She brought trouble with her from California, and she had a load of it out there, too. Some of her lousy parties, the cops had to break them up. That's why the husband divorced her."

"They should have kept her in California. They should have stuck her in San Quentin."

"The way it came to me, she didn't miss it by much."

"Why'd her old man let her come to Hudson? He should've known better."

"Oh, he found out—after it was too late."

These were not exactly shots in the dark. They'd read Sergeant McShane's newspaper clippings from Records and Identification and knew Fay Copland had thrown at least one sexy party which was raided by the police. There had probably been others and if Fay had that kind of yen, a switch in geography wouldn't change it.

"Me," said Ben, "I blame old man Copland."

"That's the whole thing in a nutshell. He should have told her to stay away from Hudson."

A few stalks of truth in a field of generalities. Tutchek stared at their passenger in astonishment. Sturgis was weeping. They'd wanted to start him talking but hadn't expected this.

Two detectives are better than one when it's a matter of extracting the full story from an unwilling witness. They can tell each other what trustworthy characters they are; one can chide the other when the witness balks at a question; and singly or together they can commiserate with their unfortunate victim of circumstances. Thus the witness always has a sympathetic friend and few of them (not under suspicion) could withstand the combination.

But Sturgis held back and Tutchek and Flavin grimly had to pick every bit of information from him. It was like picking bone splinters from a badly shattered hip.

Flavin could not remember a less pleasant job of work.

On the afternoon of Sturgis' flight, Copland came to him with the whole horrible story. It was not a tale for a sick man, but Copland might be excused for he, himself, was distraught. He had locked Fay in an attic room and bullied a confession from her. He'd had suspicions and had caught her in lie after lie.

She was a nympho. Carol Sturgis was merely reckless and lazy. Fay initiated her. There were strange delights in this wide, wide world. Fay showed her. They entertained men in the Sturgis house, any man, anytime, anywhere. Innumerable men—the young and clumsily eager; the suave and inventive; and the old who had to concoct odd bits of manual nonsense. Women? They were an off-beat diversion. Fay was too smart to dally with children, although she admitted it was quite a novelty. You had to go abroad for that. Local parents were stuffy. Naturally there were "circuses," a very special sensation for the performer. Fay and Carol were the performers. They concocted a sex marathon. Fay won, hands down.

In short, the Sturgis house was a super bordello when Walt was away. Come one, come all; no charge. But the gentlemen callers were forbidden the front door. The entrance was through the heavy growth of leafy rhododendron in the rear and into the kitchen door.

(The pixyish old Hollis J. Winslow, the Peeping Tom, had been right about that. The neighbors must have noticed something odd, but kept their mouths shut.)

"Was this Monty one of the boys or really an uncle?" asked Tutchek.

"I never heard of him before Mr. Copland told me of him," Sturgis answered with dreary despair.

"He knew Monty?"

"Not until a police detective questioned Fay."

"Then she knew Monty."

"No. She lied to the detective and Mr. Copland knew she was lying because Fay and Carol were together every day. She created Uncle Monty. That was the first day Mr. Copland locked her in the attic."

"The *first* day! Is she still locked in?"

"I don't know. But he did keep her there several days."

"Mr. Copland sounds like a pretty tough character."

"He is. He said he had to learn everything so he'd know how to protect himself. The Copland name, that is. And you may be sure Fay was not released until she made a full confession of what—went on at my house."

"Did any of these men live there maybe?" asked Flavin.

"Live there? Nobody ever 'lived' there," said Sturgis bitterly. "There were no dishes except a few coffee cups. We had a quarrel and Carol broke all the rest. She refused to eat at home. She threw out every pot and pan except a glass coffee-maker. She loved restaurants, parties and fun. You had to have 'fun.' If you didn't have 'fun,' you might just as well be dead. She didn't need much initiation from Fay Copland. They were two of a kind ...."

Horror and anguish appeared nakedly in his face. He turned and huddled in the far corner of the seat to hide it from them. He refused to say another word.

They delivered him to Graystone Memorial Hospital. He plodded between them, not caring where they took him or what they did. Flavin spoke to Maggie Wrenn.

"Get the biggest male nurses you can find, Maggie," he told her. "Keep them with him day and night. He was ready to do the Dutch but got too drunk to pull the trigger. If he makes up his mind to try again, he'll need somebody to keep him from going through the window."

"The next time he leaves here," she said, emphasizing each word, "he'll sign out like everybody else."

And that was more than a promise.

3.

Tutchek and Flavin drove to Copland's ugly brick house on Pomander Walk.

"Mr. Copland is at church, sir," said Underwood, the houseman.

"Church?"

"Yes, sir. He attends church every Sunday at this hour."

Flavin and Tutchek stared at each other. Sunday? How did it get to be Sunday? This was what happened to your time sense when you worked seven days a week.

"We'll wait," said Tutchek. "Where's the bathroom?"

"On the second floor, sir. The guest bathrooms. I'll show—"

Flavin took Underwood's shoulder in his hand and held it. He knew Tutchek was not interested in bathrooms.

"I want to talk to you for a minute," he said and, like a dance hall bouncer, steered Underwood into the stern living room, depositing him on a sofa that looked as if it had been upholstered with tapestried cement.

"Where's the maid?" he asked—just to keep talking.

"Margaret, sir? She was given a month's salary in lieu of notice."

"Canned because she clacked to the newspaper, eh?"

"It was not her place to act in that fashion before consulting with Mr. Copland, sir."

This went on and on until Tutchek returned. They sent Underwood away.

"Not a soul in the attic," said Tutchek in a low voice. "He probably flew her to a country we can't extradite her from. He's that smart. Damn!"

It was past one o'clock when John Harris Copland walked into the living room. He looked as old as a barbaric Easter Island stone image and just as severe.

"I'm sorry, gentlemen," he said, standing at the doorway, "but my daughter will not be at home for several months. She suffered an emotional trauma and is in a sanitarium which specializes in such temporary disorders. Her physician is Doctor Elkins Crane. It is unlikely that you will be permitted an interview with her at this time."

"Did her breakdown come from being locked up in the attic?" Tutchek threw in his face.

But it was an old granite face which had been without real life or love for countless years.

"Doctor Crane is the physician, not I, gentlemen," his voice was also stony. "That is all I have to say."

"To us maybe. There are bigger wheels in the Department."

"Don't be ridiculous. Good day, gentlemen."

Flavin and Tutchek left and sat outside in the police car for a few minutes before driving on.

"He knows the whole story, more than he told Sturgis," said Flavin. "A Grand Jury could get it out of him."

"Oh, sure," said Tutchek. "But who's going to call a Grand Jury? This is an election year, baby, and Copland's club delivers the vote in this ward. Politics is politics and the prosecutor likes being prosecutor. Let's see if we can get hold of this brain doctor."

It may or may not have been a coincidence, but Doctor Elkins Crane lived on Hamilton Place, not five blocks from Copland's home. He was as polished and smoothed as a well-oiled ball bearing. He escorted them to his study and discussed the case freely in the Esperanto of psychiatric jargon, which boiled down to one thing—neither they nor anyone else could see Fay Copland until her condition improved and it was impossible to say when that would be. Like Copland, he had nothing more to say. Nothing. Nothing whatever. And especially not the name of the sanitarium in which Fay was incarcerated. He, personally, was anxious to be of assistance but really, you know, it would serve no purpose to question Miss Copland. Surely, they did not wish to worsen her emotional imbalance with a pointless ordeal. Of course not. Consider the consequences of complete withdrawal from reality. It was a grave responsibility ....

So Fay Copland was in a private nut house and the prosecutor wouldn't touch her with a ten-foot asbestos pole, even if he could. She was exactly where she belonged. The facts of the case proved that, if nothing else. Ask the American Medical Association. Ask anybody. Doctor Elkins Crane was a very shrewd cookie.

In the beginning, the problem of "Monty" was fairly simple, a matter of routine investigation, but now there were other questions. Was he a man of position and importance? Was there a general conspiracy to protect him? Had he suddenly realized with horror the madness of those Sturgis house orgies? Had he attempted to get out of it? Had Carol Sturgis refused to let him go? Had he killed her?

So far, the Nivens Food Mart delivery boy was the only one who had given them any information which had not first been colored or censored by the Coplands.

"We better turn that kid over to McGimp," said Tutchek. "If McGimp does a portrait, there's a chance we'll get a make on this Monty, or whatever his name is. I have a feeling he's from around here. What do you think, Jeff?"

"Well—I don't think he's that *National Geographic* bird from Brazil, Africa or other parts of Rand McNally."

"That'll be a help," said Tutchek grumpily.

George Gilman was sent after the delivery boy, Raymond Mankey, while Tutchek and Flavin conferred with Captain Mackenzie, whose face was tight with the constricting lines of strain. Foxy called both the prosecutor and Medical Examiner Doctor Knight. The prosecutor was not at home but was expected shortly and would call. After the conservative manner of medical men, Knight would not give an opinion until he had made "certain inquiries." The three men waited, tense and restless. There was very little conversation. The case seemed to be slipping away from them again.

It was an hour before Doctor Knight telephoned. Fay Copland, he said, had been examined in Hudson Medical Centre by Doctors Crane and Samuel Toth, *the* foremost neurologist. The patient was alternately defiant and dazed during the examination and there was evidence of disorientation in time and space. The diagnosis was a Korsalow Syndrome caused by excessive indulgence in alcohol, attended of course by a lack of sustained attention and impressionability and intermittent amnesia. The Korsalow Syndrome was the failure to remember recent events. Strictly speaking, the patient was not insane.

"The distinction," sighed Knight, "is purely academic."

Mackenzie listened gloomily, put a few questions and finally hung up. "She's off her rocker," he said. "Get this—she was seventeen the first time she had to take the cure. Seventeen. My God! Lakeview Sanitarium. It's on the record. Then twice again in California."

"In other words, she can't remember a thing about her and Carol Sturgis," said Tutchek. "What a handy time to go nuts."

"She told the same story," growled Mackenzie. "Only it happened three years ago in California and it was Carl Sturgis, not Carol. On the third time around she said old man Copland forced her and Carol to put on sex shows and Copland was the guy they called Monty. Later on she said Monty was really Walt Sturgis. Then she got crafty and hinted that Copland and Sturgis were in on it with her ex-husband for business reasons. At the end she got hysterical and called them filthy-minded cops. Knight swears up and down it's impossible to fool a specialist like Doctor Toth. He gave her a lot of other tests to confirm his diagnosis."

"But it's the same story and the same people," said Flavin. "*Something* went on. And she was locked up in the attic for days. She wasn't crazy before."

"How do you know? How do you know *I'm* not crazy? The squirrels have been after me all week and, brother, you can't fool a squirrel."

The telephone rang. It was the prosecutor. Mackenzie grimaced, shrugged and briefly repeated the details, knowing it was a waste of time. It was. He hung up.

"Well," he told Tutchek and Flavin, "we can get her out on a court order next year maybe if we guarantee twelve filberts on the jury. Let's see how the McGimp is making out."

They went upstairs to the Crime Lab. McGimp's "studio" was a white-painted cubicle. It contained nothing to distract the witness and even the windows were of frosted glass. A bulky blond boy sat beside the artist at the drawing board. As Captain Mackenzie, Tutchek and Flavin walked in, he held up the drawing and sneered at it.

"This," he said, "is our impression of Cary Grant during a hard day in the coal mines. Please note the contrast of light and shadow."

The sketch showed a tall, athletic man leaning against a door frame. He was clad in swimming shorts and held a cocktail glass in his hand. The 'contrast of light and shadow' covered the face and chest.

"But that's the way he looked," said the blond kid unhappily. "I only saw him for a second before Mrs. Sturgis chased him out."

"That's all right, son," said Mackenzie. "Was that the only time you saw him?"

"No. A few other times. He was inside. That's a kind of parlor," he pointed at the shadows behind the figure.

"He had on swimming shorts?"

"Well—it might have been underpants. I dunno for sure. You know the kind."

"Boxer shorts."

"Yeah, like that. White."

"How was Mrs. Sturgis dressed?"

"A kimono. You know—a housecoat."

"What time of day was this?"

"In the morning. Between nine and ten. Around there."

"Were they going out, or had they just come in, or what?"

"I didn't ask. I just delivered the stuff for breakfast—pancake flour, maple syrup, bacon, eggs and I think a can of scrapple. I mean, that's what she mostly wanted for breakfast. Sometimes it was waffles or sliced ham. Milk, coffee, cereal. I didn't keep track."

"This was the man she called Monty?"

"It sounded like that."

"Was he the only one you saw there?"

"I thought it was him, yes. He was in the other room. It was hard to see."

"Would you know him if you saw him again?"

"I think so. Yes. It don't come out in the picture but I saw him plainer. The shadows were like that, though. That's how he looked."

"What did you think when you saw him there in his underpants?"

"I thought it was Mr. Sturgis. But then the newspaper come out with a picture of the real Mr. Sturgis and I knew it wasn't. That's what I told the detective at the desk. The man she called Monty ducked out fast when I come in. I never really seen him before. I mean, he was in the other room and I guessed it was him. Mr. Sturgis, I thought then."

Mackenzie squinted at the picture. "Can't you do better than this, son? The way the face is, it won't help us much."

"I dunno. He keeps saying Cary Grant and now all I can think of is Cary Grant."

McGimp ignored Mackenzie's scowl. He yawned. "As I recall," he said, "I also mentioned Daniel Boone, William Randolph Hearst and Lassie. How else am I to deal with an incoherent oaf? He sat there gasping like a flatulent sausage until I got him started."

Mackenzie nodded shortly. Tongue-tied witnesses needed prodding but sometimes the McGimp overdid it. "Take the picture home with you, son," he said. "Make notes on where you think it should be changed. Was Monty older or younger, shorter, heavier, thinner or wider in the face? But don't look at it too much. Try to think of the man Mrs. Sturgis called Monty. We'll go over it again tomorrow. You'll only get more confused today."

"I wanted to help out. Honest."

"That's all right. Tonight write down everything you can remember about Monty." Mackenzie glanced outside. "Where's Gilman? Have him take the boy home."

"He's with my mother," said the kid. "She wanted to come along but he said it was better if she waited downstairs." He looked doubtfully at the racks of filing cabinets which made a maze of Records and Identification.

Flavin guided him to the elevator and rode down with him to the street floor. Beyond the desk sergeant's pulpit, George Gilman sat martyred beside a gray-haired woman whose whining voice complained on and on and on. Gilman stood patiently when he spied Flavin and the kid coming from the elevator.

"Here's Raymond now, Mrs. Mankey," he said. "I told you he was okay."

"He's only a young boy," she said querulously. "It ain't right I should sit down here and you take him upstairs alone. You don't know what it is to have children—"

Raymond flushed and mumbled, "It's okay, Ma. They just wanted me to help out."

"Then they should go about it the right way. The other policeman had more consideration. He was older. He realized."

"I'll take you home now, Mrs. Mankey," said Gilman.

Flavin stared after them as they walked through the front doorway. He had seen that gray dissatisfied face before and had heard the thin grind of that voice.

The desk sergeant grinned. "Mama's boy," he said. Flavin shook his head, not in denial, but to dislodge a stubbornly hidden memory. He was almost certain that this was not Mrs. Mankey's first visit to Headquarters.

It didn't make any difference, of course, but it nagged at him—like trying to remember the name of a tune that kept running through your head. As he stepped out of the elevator on the third floor he saw Sergeant Bauer's pained face. The Sergeant's piles were smoldering away again. Flavin's memory stirred.

"Does the name Mrs. Mankey mean anything to you, Sarg?" he asked.

"Oh no no, please. Not again."

"Mama's boy. Raymond. She was sitting here talking to you one day."

"*One day!* She practically lived here."

"Raymond. It was something about Raymond. I was at the water cooler and—wait a minute—she was telling you that some woman was leading Raymond astray. That was it, wasn't it?"

"To hear her tell it, the woman got hold of Raymond every day and twice on Sunday. He drove a delivery truck and it was some woman on his route. She heard him tell another kid about it."

Flavin said, "Sarge, I love you!" and started across the squadroom, not quite running toward Mackenzie and Tutchek at the door of the Captain's office.

He broke into their conversation, "On the morning the Sturgis killing broke, Mrs. Mankey was in here telling Bauer that Raymond was being laid by some woman around Stone Bridge. Her baby boy! She wanted the woman arrested. She knew it was going on because she heard Raymond tell a friend all about it ..."

It did not sink in immediately but when it did, Mackenzie's tough, grooved face opened into a smile. "Detective," he said softly, "do me the favor of getting that overgrown, mealy-mouthed young son of a bitch back here as fast as you can!"

Nine

They had Raymond in Interrogation Room #1. The chair on which he sat was probably the most uncomfortable in Headquarters. During an inventive moment, Harry Muir had sawed an inch from each of the front legs and Raymond had to brace himself to keep from sliding forward. It was a very tiring position. But he was not tired, although Mackenzie, Tutchek, Muir, Flavin and Gilman had been at him for nearly two hours. He looked so fresh, clean and decent that it was almost impossible to imagine his doing anything wrong. Furthermore—according to Nivens—he was a hardworking kid. He had to be. The Food Mart was open six days a week from eight in the morning till six at night. He was honest and trustworthy.

At the moment he looked more embarrassed than guilty. Very, very reluctantly, he admitted that a woman in an apartment house on Circle Drive used to get him into her bedroom, but she moved away. He didn't like her very much but when she got him inside and, well, did certain things, he couldn't seem to help himself. He was glad when she moved away. She had black hair and her name was Anita Bori. He never knew women did such things. It made you feel funny afterwards but there was something about her, you kept going back, even though you felt that way, the things she did.

Trying to trip him up on details, they made him tell it again and again. He blushed horribly—but his story held together.

Kitteridge went to the apartment house and there actually had been an Anita Bori. "She was a whore," the superintendent said uneasily. "I got rid of her the minute I found out." Kitteridge grinned lewdly. "What'd you say you got when you found out, friend?" he asked "And how many times a day did you get it?"

Raymond did not seem to realize he was a murder suspect. He was too embarrassed by their questions, which were brutally explicit. Did he do so and so and thus and so and when and how? He looked as if he wanted to cry, he was so embarrassed, for his answers had to be just as explicit as the questions.

When the Anita Bori incidents were more or less confirmed by Kitteridge, Mackenzie switched tactics, patting the air with quiet hands to calm everybody down.

"All right, son," he said. "Relax. You're not the first boy a mud kicker like Bori got her hooks into. It gives them a big charge or something. I wish I could stick them all in jail and leave them there. So you see, it's not your fault."

"But I shouldn't have kept going back, mister. I shouldn't have done it."

"She had her hooks into you. The Sturgis woman was the same way. We know all about her. She was just as bad as Anita Bori. Now did she get you in her bedroom every time you delivered groceries?"

"She wasn't like that, mister. She was a rich lady. She wouldn't of let a guy like me touch her."

"You should see some of the mutts she flopped, son. You wouldn't believe it. Why, one of them was no better than a crook and I'll tell you his name—Dirty Harry Muir. What do you think of that?"

"I never heard of him, mister," said Raymond, wide-eyed.

"How often was the red-headed girl there?"

"All I ever saw was Mr. Sturgis. I mean, the feller she called Monty that day."

"Was this nightgown she had on the kind you could see through?"

"It was a housecoat. You know, more like a dress. You couldn't see through it at all. It was buttoned right up."

"But Monty was in his underwear."

"I said shorts. I dunno if it was underwear."

"Did he come downstairs or from the big living room the other side of the parlor?"

"I never saw nothing but the kitchen, mister. I set down the box of meat and stuff on the table and she paid me and give me a tip and I left. Only Mrs. Bori ever took me in her house. You know, rooms."

"What kind of uniform do you wear for work, Raymond?"

"No uniform. Khaki pants, khaki shirt."

"You forgot the necktie, sneakers and brown socks."

"Yes, sir. One of them black plastic bow ties, black shoes and, well, just any old socks so long's they're clean. I gotta buy it myself. It ain't a uniform."

"Did the red-headed girl act as though Monty was *her* boy friend?"

"It was just Mr. Stur—Monty there, that's all."

"Mrs. Sturgis was pretty lovey-dovey with him, eh?"

"No, sir. She sounded mad, kind of."

"Then there was nothing funny going on?"

"No, sir."

"Why'd you report him to us, Raymond?"

"She was murdered and I figured you should report it in a murder," said Raymond.

"You wanted to get Monty in trouble, didn't you?"

"No, sir. Gene, he said, what right'd he have there with Mr. Sturgis away, he said."

"Do you do everything Gene says?"

"Sometimes. He's more grown-up. He's twenty-two in November. He knows about things."

Gilman got the office from Mackenzie and slipped out of the room. The Captain threw a few more questions at Raymond and mentioned the sneakers again, together with the rest of the clothes, asking if that was the uniform. Raymond said, "It wasn't a uniform," and sounded as if he were apologizing. "It's just a pants and shirt."

"You wore more than that, son."

"Yes, sir. A black plastic bow tie—they don't wear out—black shoes and clean socks."

"You're sure they were clean?" asked Mackenzie savagely.

Raymond looked surprised at both the tone and the question. "Yes, sir," he said meekly. "Ma saw to that."

"All right, all right, all right!" Mackenzie drew a long breath. He flapped his hand at Flavin and walked to the window.

Flavin grinned at the boy and after a moment's hesitation Raymond grinned back. A small grin; the kind of grin a boy gives an adult of whom he is not sure.

"I want to picture Monty in my mind, Ray," Flavin said casually, "Was he young, middle-aged, old, or what?"

"Well—" Raymond puzzled over it. "Middle-aged, kind of, I guess."

"Like Captain Mackenzie over there?"

"More like you. Not old. The way you said—middle-aged."

"Like me? The poor guy, he must have forgotten his wheelchair."

"I didn't mean it like that, mister," Raymond was unhappy.

"It was only a joke, Ray. You say Monty was standing in a dark doorway and you saw him for only a few seconds. Is that right?"

"No, not dark. There were shadows from a rack with shelves and plants on the shelves. The sun, you know, the way it was, made stripes and, well, shadows all over the door. But I didn't have no trouble seeing him."

"Didn't you wonder why he had to duck out when you came in?"

"He didn't duck out. Mrs. Sturgis said, 'Get back there, Monty,' and he laughed and popped his teeth at her—he had a couple false ones on top—and wagged his hands form his ears like a rabbit. He went in the other room."

"Was he drunk? Did he stagger?"

"He kind of limped a little, that's all. On the left— Gary Cooper!" he blurted, then seemed abashed at the loudness of his voice. "I mean, the guy that drew the picture kept saying Cary Grant and that's all I could think. But it was more like Gary Cooper, only he had a moustache. Younger than Gary Cooper, but like him."

"Well, thanks, Ray. That's a big help. I appreciate it. Do you mind talking to Mr. Tutchek? He needs some help, too."

He faded back and left the room with Mackenzie as Tutchek took over, saying, "I'll tell you something, man. I said to myself, 'People like that man.' The minute they see your grin and that blush, they like you."

Raymond lowered his head, scarlet to the hairline. "I don't like to blush," he mumbled. "None of the guys blush. They call me Rosy and laugh like I'm a fairy."

"The cruds. Smack them in the puss the next time, man."

Flavin closed the door. Mackenzie stumped up and down the corridor, champing on his cigar, swearing through it. "It's a God damn movie," he said. "The Son Of Gary Cooper Rides Again. What do you think of him? Is he a smart punk or just plain stupid?"

"McGimp got him pretty mixed up on that composite drawing of Monty. Let's get McGimp again and go out to the Sturgis house."

"Yeah, that might help, getting him at the scene," Mackenzie turned his head and peevishly spat cigar shreds. "One of these days I'm going to burn McGimp's ass. And his snotty wise cracks."

2.

It was late afternoon. Long, heavy shafts of sun slanted through the west windows of the Sturgis kitchen. It was just as Raymond Mankey had described it. A tall, modern teakwood room divider patterned the doorway to the inner room with arabesques of light and shadow. A man standing in that mottled arch might look like almost anyone—Gary Cooper, Cary Grant, or any of the various Tarzans, depending upon your first impression. McGimp knew this and opened his sketch pad on the kitchen table without enthusiasm. He was, after all, an experienced craftsman. Still ... He tilted his head and slitted his eyes at the doorway to shut out irrelevant details. Well yes, Mankey was a walking liverwurst but he did have young eyes and a quick glance could find the shape of a man's features.

Raymond stood where he had been that day—at the end of the table nearest the door. Mackenzie motioned Flavin to stand in the arch, a figure to help stir Mankey's sluggish memory. Flavin posed, blinking into the dappled sunlight

"Is that where he was, son?" Mackenzie asked.

"Well—" Raymond pushed at the air with both hands. "He was more back, kind of. Not *right* in the door. He was more back, not so much in the kitchen. Like this." He held his palms about a foot apart.

Flavin began a backward step, then slowly lowered his foot to the floor. He stared at Mankey and almost at the same moment, Mackenzie, Tutchek and Gilman turned and stared also, their stares becoming hard and cold.

"What time is it, Captain?" Flavin asked.

"Half past four."

"Mankey said he was here in the morning that day, didn't he?"

"That's right. Between nine and ten in the morning. How about it, Mankey?"

Raymond smiled uncertainly. "Yes, sir. That's around the time I usually made deliveries in the morning here."

"The sun doesn't hit the windows at that time of morning."

Raymond blinked. "Then it must of been afternoon, sir."

"You told us it was morning."

"Yes, sir, but sometimes Mrs. Sturgis called up the store and I had to deliver stuff twice in the same day," Raymond said earnestly. "And it *seemed* like in the morning, the way Mrs. Sturgis was still dressed in a housecoat. I have to make about two hundred deliveries a week all told, and there's no set time like on a regular route. They call up any old time and it's hard to keep track. Mr. Nivens takes the orders over the phone. He can tell you when I came here that day."

Flavin exchanged a sudden, illuminating glance with Ben Tutchek, remembering what Walt Sturgis told them about his wife. Carol Sturgis would not eat at home. She had broken the dishes and thrown out all the pots and pans except a glass coffee maker. Ben opened the refrigerator. It contained only a can of tomato juice, two pears and a half-emptied milk bottle. He opened a few cupboards and found only a half-dozen fifths of bourbon and some glasses. There were no dishes, no cooking utensils.

"She had nothing to cook with, Ray," said Flavin. "Yet you delivered ham and eggs and scrapple and pancake flour and things like that for breakfast. What did you bring in the afternoons? Meat and vegetables for dinner?"

"Yes, sir."

"If she didn't cook, that doesn't make sense, does it?"

"I don't know, sir. Mr. Nivens took the orders on the phone. I only delivered them."

Captain Mackenzie cut in and pointed at a pastel green wall phone over one of the formica-topped cabinets. "Call Nivens," he ordered Tutchek.

Tutchek spoke into the phone. They could all hear the sharp crackling of Niven's voice, the answers and suspicious questions. Yes, he took care of phone orders and kept carbon copies, too. Sometimes Mrs. Sturgis just called up to have a pound of coffee delivered, other times it was a full meat department and grocery order. Why did Tutchek want to know? Was there any trouble about the orders? He had carbon copies and they were all dated. He could show them. He never padded any orders and anyway Mrs. Sturgis paid C.O.D. Was something the matter? If they wanted to see the carbon copies, he'd be glad to—

Tutchek said, "Thanks," and hung up.

Raymond blushed. "I'm sorry I put you to all this trouble," he said. "I didn't mean to make that mistake about coming in the morning. It's hard to keep track."

Flavin looked at Raymond's shoes. "You drive a truck with a clutch pedal and standard shift, don't you?"

"Yes, sir. A dark green Chevvy panel truck."

"Let's see the bottom of your shoes. Those are the shoes you wear to work, aren't they?"

Raymond said, "Yes, sir," and held up his foot.

"For all the driving you have to do, the shoes don't look very worn to me. How come?"

"I just got new soles and heels. I only have two pair. I got to take care of them."

"How much do you make a week?"

"Mr. Nivens gives me thirty-five, but there's deductions. Ma gives me five dollars spending money and an extra dollar to save for clothes. So I have to take care of my clothes."

"She doesn't like you to wear sneakers, does she?"

"No, sir. They're bad for the feet, she says."

"But for work, sneakers would be cheaper and they'd last longer."

Raymond grinned shyly. "I don't like to go against what Ma says. She gets upset."

"Sure. But you want to be a big shot like your friend Gene Meck. It gets under your skin when they call you Rosy, doesn't it?"

Raymond's fair cheeks became the expected crimson. "They don't mean nothing by it."

"You'd like to show them you're not a sissy all the same, wouldn't you?"

"I don't care. I only go around with Gene anyways."

The lies glinted like plate glass windows behind which Raymond Mankey stood revealed.

Flavin said, "Nuts, sonny boy!" and turned to Captain Mackenzie. "Let's go down to Nivens Food Mart. If we look around the back room, I think we'll find a pair of sneakers belonging to Raymond. He didn't *just* have those shoes soled and heeled. They've been worn for awhile. You can see how smoothed the pattern of the rubber heels are. But he hasn't done any hard driving in them because they're worn pretty evenly. Another thing—Mrs. Sturgis might have ordered food but she didn't use it. I think she phoned in those orders to get Raymond here at the house. It was the excuse. He's a big, strong kid and she had a yen for him. And I think she gave the food to him. We'll check the dates on Nivens' carbons and see if he took food home on those dates. His mother'll tell us—"

Mankey whirled and plunged toward the door, almost beating George Gilman aside with a roundhouse blow on the side of the head. Gilman managed to grab the arm and hang on. Flavin and Tutchek sprang across the kitchen. Raymond no longer looked clean, decent and wholesome. He fought furiously, his face lumpy and white, teeth clenched. The tall room divider crashed over and flower pots, earth and plants spewed across the floor. Mackenzie leaned groggily against the wall with blood on his face. The aluminum kitchen table, McGimp and his chair were flung into the debris. Almost blinded from a kick on the forehead, McGimp showed more than a hysterical capacity for histrionics. On hands and knees, he crawled into the tumult of straining legs, clutched Mankey's ankle and sank his teeth into it. Mankey kicked himself free but Flavin staggered him with a hand-edge chop on the right side of the neck. Tutchek's blackjack flicked. It was a small, light motion—but then, you don't swing a blackjack like a tennis racket. You don't have to. The spring in the handle and the loaded end does all the work. When used by an expert, it needs no more than a flip of the wrist. Tutchek did not believe in fighting as a joyous man-to-man exercise. His attitude was possibly not very sporting, but he had more important things to do. He went into a fight with only one thought—end it quickly. He did.

Raymond Mankey was not very bright, but he did know a thing or two. During his term of employment with Nivens Food Mart, he'd had more than his share of women around Stone Bridge. Some, such as Anita Bari, were lecherous experimenters; Fay Copland was an alcoholic nymph and didn't really count; Carol Sturgis was lazy, sensuous and amoral; but most were bored, empty women who desperately wanted to refill themselves at the fount of his thrusting youth.

Raymond knew how to get what he wanted from these women. It had worked for over a year now. It would always work. All he had to do was grin like a bashful Eagle Scout; the blushes came naturally. He had discovered the secret of success. He could win friends and influence people. In a little while he'd have been a big success with even those severe critics, the neighborhood big shots and their chicks. But quite suddenly there wasn't any "little while" left. Time had run out.

The police were not interested in shy grins and bashful blushes. They found his sneakers on a shelf in Nivens' back room where the vegetables were uncrated and packaged. The worn sole pattern matched a plaster mold taken from a print found in the soft earth outside the basement window of Carol Sturgis' house. There had been another faint partial print in the dust on the second floor. McGimp had sketched and measured it carefully. It, too, matched the sole pattern of the sneakers. Photographs had been taken of prints left on other surfaces by a pair of work gloves. Gloves were found under the seat of Nivens' truck. They were sent to the Crime Lab and declared identical to the photographs. Nivens' carbons show that Carol Sturgis had ordered a standing rib roast, potatoes, a package of frozen asparagus tips and two boxes of butterscotch pudding mix on the day before the murder. Mrs. Mankey did not want to answer questions. Policewoman Ethel Leary, who looked maternal, talked to her, mother-to-mother, and it was revealed that the Mankey's dinner on that day had been rib roast and all the rest of it. There was a bumper jack in the truck. It was taken to the Lab. Technician Lieutenant Leitner had the bent jack handle which had first been used to pry open the basement window and later to beat down Walt Sturgis. It was a simple matter to show that the end of the handle could have been marked by no other jack.

Flavin, Tutchek, Gilman and Muir showed Raymond that he was not a success at all and it became too much to bear. He burst out sobbing. After that, only a police stenographer was needed.

Raymond had played around with Fay Copland and Carol Sturgis but, compared to the bright young chicks around his neighborhood, they were too old. He had never been able to impress the guys or the chicks, but he knew how. Money. The Sturgises were loaded and he knew his way around that house. He also knew they were going to the country club dance. It was unfortunate that he could not have foreseen that they would get drunk and quarrel and come home early. It was Carol who caught him going through the chest of drawers in her room. She was too drunk to care. And too angry at her husband. The sight of Raymond gave her a very exciting idea. There was money and jewelry in her dressing table. Raymond could have it—but first he must beat up Walt Sturgis. She knew about the other Stone Bridge burglaries and fixed a nylon stocking mask. Raymond tiptoed down the hall. Walt Sturgis was in his own bedroom standing before the open wall safe into which he was solemnly putting about a hundred dollars in small bills. But he was not too drunk to turn and fight when he heard Raymond open the door. Raymond, big as he was, was not very good at fighting and had to hit Sturgis a few times with the jack handle. Carol stood outside and watched, becoming more and more excited. She hurried the trembling Raymond back to her bedroom and fell across the bed with him, clawing at his clothes. He didn't want to do anything. He didn't want to touch her, but she was so wild that he could not help himself. Afterward, she told him to tie and gag her, as the women had been tied and gagged in the other burglaries. ("Just in case Mr. Sturgis was hurt bad, she didn't want to be mixed up in it," said Raymond dully.)

He hurriedly thrust a gag into her mouth, tied her up and fled the house with less than three hundred dollars in bills. He was afraid to take the jewelry. He thought three hundred dollars was a lot of money.

Flavin left as Raymond mumbled the remainder of his confession. Mrs. Mankey was sitting rigidly at Sergeant Bauer's desk, tears streaming down her face. Bauer was speaking to her but she didn't listen. "You got to let him go," she kept repeating, "you got to let him go, you got to. He's only a young boy. You can't keep him here—"

Bauer jumped up and stopped Flavin in the hall near the elevator. "Get her into one of the rooms, Flay," he said in a low voice. "All she does is sit there and cry and I can't throw her out."

Flavin went back reluctantly. She refused to listen to him. She wanted to talk to Sergeant Bauer. *He* understood. *He* had consideration. *He* knew her Raymond wouldn't do such a thing. He knew what it was to have children. He'd tell those other men. She wanted Raymond to come home with her. Sergeant Bauer would help her. He understood. He realized.

Flavin and Bauer stood helplessly. She'd never believe Raymond had committed a crime, no matter how overwhelming the evidence. Raymond was only a young boy. *Her* boy. They had him mixed up with somebody else. Raymond was a good boy. She said something about the good report cards he got in school, but much of what came on that stricken voice was hard to understand. And it was obvious that she wasn't seeing Raymond as he was; she was looking back, groping for a child.

"Get one of the policewomen, Sarg," said Flavin at length. "This is out of my depth."

He walked downstairs and out into the street. The air was cool, but it smelled of the city and it was an old city. A good city, yes, but there were ancient evils buried in it.

Upstairs was Raymond Mankey, an overgrown, not-too-bright kid, who'd had a moment of feeling like a big shot just because some bored, lazy, sexy women had dragged him into the bedroom. His big moment was over. Now he'd be brought to trial, found guilty and sentenced. Probably to the chair. You're not a juvenile delinquent at the age of twenty. But there were juvenile delinquents in the city. Gangs of them. The Ravens down at the Point, the Mt. Prospect Rovers, the Jinks. There was always a parade of them in and out of Headquarters. And whose fault was that? The fault of some sexy bitches? Fault, fault. What difference did it make? He was a cop and he'd have to go after them when the time came, no matter whose fault it was. He wasn't a jury or a social worker. It was his job to enforce the law and be a good cop and defend all the happy people who sit home and look at TV and squawk about taxes and get sore when a cop gives them a ticket for speeding.

He stopped in the all-night cafeteria on Washington Street and had a few cups of coffee and thought about being a cop. He thought about the good cops like Ben Tutchek and George Gilman and Captain Mackenzie and the bad cops like those time-servers, Jenner and Urquhart, and the dedicated cops like Leitner and McShane in the Crime Lab. Yes, and of Harry Muir, who was a part-time son of a bitch but a hell of a good cop all the same. Flavin shook his head wearily. Just what exactly was he trying to prove? That cops come all shapes and sizes and that he was a cop? That's what it amounted to. He was a cop.

It was six-thirty A.M. when he finally rolled into bed.

And it was four P.M. when he went back to Headquarters. A note on his desk told him to see Captain Mackenzie before he did anything else. Joyce Ames was not in the outer office. Mackenzie greeted him with a tired but friendly nod and told him to sit down.

"Miss Ames was up to see Tom Walsh yesterday afternoon," he said. "She brought back a letter from him and another from Doctor Hauptmann. Hauptmann says Tom is coming along fine and should be back at work in about a month."

"I'm glad to hear that, Captain."

"So am I, believe me. But " Mackenzie spread his hard square hands on the desk blotter and scowled at them. "Tom resigned in *his* letter. He gave reasons. That story in the *Hudson Evening News*, the one that got you suspended. Well, it seems Tom talked a little too much to Ed Turcott, who dropped in to see him at the rest home. Tom only remembers parts of what he said to Turcott—he was high on Dexedrine that day—but one of the attendants heard the whole thing. There's always an attendant around when a patient's out on the grounds. You know Dexedrine. It does funny things when you eat it like candy. Tom thought he was putting in a big plug for you, but what he actually did was foul you up. So he resigned because, as he writes, he irresponsibly gave confidential information to the press." Mackenzie took an envelope from his desk and tossed it on the blotter. "That's the letter of resignation."

Flavin reached out, picked it up, tore it several times across and put the pieces into his pocket. "There isn't any letter," he said.

Mackenzie sighed. "It's your letter, Flavin. I guess you can do what you want with it. You're the one who took it on the chin and it's still on the record, though I've reinstated you without prejudice. You made a nice gesture. Okay. But I want you to think it over. Seriously."

"There's nothing to think over. Tom's been sick and he's still far from well. I'll talk to him before he writes any more letters."

"All right, all right, but do me a favor and don't break his arm."

"Wait a minute—" Flavin's brows came down, puzzled. "How did he find out what happened here?"

"I wouldn't know. Maybe he had his fortune told. Why ask me. You're a detective and detectives are supposed to know everything."

Flavin sat in thought for a long, silent moment and then slowly turned and looked through the open door at Joyce Ames' unoccupied desk. "She went to see Tom yesterday," he said. "She brought back the two letters. She's the one who told him. Why? Why'd she do a thing like that? Why'd she *worry* him with a thing like that? Why?"

"There's something female the matter with her, I imagine," said Mackenzie dryly. "Anyway, when she learned Tom resigned, she resigned, too, and went home. I'm getting goddam sick of people resigning all over the place. There's work to do. But I don't think Miss Ames told Tom about that hassle because she wanted to worry him, so don't be too hard on her."

Flavin stood and seemed not to realize that he was standing. Some strange, bouncing emotions were beginning to jump up and down inside him, skipping rope, playing leapfrog, singing songs. "No," he said, "no ...."

"Uh, Lieutenant Haas is in the hospital," Mackenzie said. "High blood pressure, duodenal ulcers and nearly had a stroke. He's close to retirement age and the Commissioner has given him indefinite sick leave. Tutchek's got charge of Homicide and he asked for you and Gilman on his squad. You've both been given the day off, what's left of it, but be at your desk tomorrow morning. Sober."

Flavin's freckled face split in a wide grin and he thought, *what a break for old Gilman!*

He must have spoken the thought aloud, for Mackenzie said, "And for you too, Detective. Around here we think promotion to Homicide is something better than a slap on the butt with a wet trout. Here. Gilman left a note for you. Now beat it and close the door on the way out. I want to take a nap."

Flavin said, "Yes, sir." He was in high spirits but his mouth tightened when he thought of Ed Turcott. He knew Turcott and there was no doubt in his mind that the reporter had milked Tom for that story. Turcott was the kind of bastard who would milk a sick man. Well—!

Captain Mackenzie stopped him before he reached the door. "Just a second, Detective," he said sharply. "I recognize that expression. Get rid of it. If that newspaper story's on your mind, get rid of that, too. Forget it. And stay away from Ed Turcott. He's a reporter and a damn good one. Remember this—don't ever get sore at an honest man for doing the job he's paid to do. It's stupid. That's all."

"Yes, sir," said Flavin stiffly, but gradually he felt better as he walked downstairs. Old Foxy was not only smart, he was a mind reader, too.

Sitting in his car, Flavin remembered George Gilman's note and took it from his pocket. It said, "Dear Jeff, I didn't forget about you having dinner with Hannah and me but things kept coming up all the time. How's about Friday. Hannah says meatloaf. It's her idea, so don't blame me. George." Flavin's mouth crooked affectionately. He loved a good meatloaf. But of course old George would never have mentioned that to Hannah Beale. It was all a coincidence.

He chuckled and started the car and within a half block he knew where he was going—to Joyce Ames' apartment. Those odd emotions began doing flip-flops again. She couldn't have known Tom had talked to Ed Turcott. But she'd told Tom that he, Jeff Flavin, the dumb mick, was in trouble. He remembered, too, another night when she'd asked him to phone her and he hadn't and later she met him at Headquarters and asked why he hadn't. It began to add up. It began to add up into something very nice.

Now he *really* looked forward to seeing her. Again and again. And again and again and maybe forever. If it worked out that way.

THE END

BODY OF THE CRIME

Lorenz Heller

Writing as Larry Heller

One

It was the fifth of July and a fine day, air-conditioned by a light breeze that came in steady from the east, cooled by its passage over Long Island Sound and the Lower Bay, as if it meant to cool the city of Hudson for the remainder of the month. This was as it should be, for it was doing its duty as set forth by the United States Weather Bureau.

So long as it kept moving.

Otherwise, it was liable to arrest and prosecution either for vagrancy or misprision, according to the provisions of the penal codes of both the State of New Jersey and the City of Hudson—misdemeanors punishable by fines not exceeding two hundred dollars, or by imprisonment in the county jail not more than six months.

Generally speaking, Sergeant Henry Bullen's attitude toward the weather was no different from that of many a tired, wet, freezing, overheated, or otherwise frustrated patrolman: weather was always on the verge of doing something repulsive, was in the midst of a mess, or had just made one. You couldn't even count on weather to assist the forces of law and order. It was a crying shame. Now, for three years at the Complaint Desk inside the 7th Precinct station house, Sergeant Bullen had regarded a variety of weather through the often quite clean windows, and he'd grown tolerant enough to admit that weather had its good points, if you weren't forced to associate with it. However, today was so absolutely perfect that you really couldn't count it as weather at all. Just as white is the absence of black, today was the absence of weather, and if there was one thing a cop on the beat didn't need, it was weather. He had enough to contend with. On the other hand, Sergeant Bullen was fair enough to admit, weather was just about the only thing that ever really did happen here. It wasn't like some of the other precincts—say, the Roaring 20th, for instance, where everything happened.

So, his astonishment was quite understandable when the front screen door slammed. No one ever slammed doors in the 7th Precinct House. It wasn't that kind of precinct. He frowned and leaned over the near edge of his high desk, as if those few inches gave a better view of the noisy intruder. An elderly man stood abashed at the door, and obviously the slamming had been an accident, no disrespect intended. Then, as the man continued to hesitate at the door, Sergeant Bullen nodded to himself. He had seen these symptoms before; the gentleman had left home determined to make a complaint against somebody for some reason or other, but now that he was actually in the station house, he was on the verge of changing his mind and letting bygones be bygones. He didn't really want to make trouble, but at the same time, he'd come this far and didn't know how to back down without feeling like a complete idiot. It was an old story to the sergeant, but even as a rookie cop on the beat, he'd learned how to give it a happy ending: you encouraged them to talk and gave them a sympathetic word from time to time, and before they knew what was going on, they talked themselves right out of it and went home with their dignity intact and the complaint unmade.

It was plain that this one needed some kind of encouragement. "Come right in, friend, it's always open house here."—Sergeant Bullen usually tried to keep it on the light side. "If there's anything we can do, just ask."

The man started, as if he had not expected Bullen to be there, but recovered and said shortly, "Of course."

He did not seem quite so elderly when he walked out of the dimness of the long room and into the light from the windows behind the sergeant's high desk.

He was a big man, well built, and there was a hint that he might have the large, hale and hearty sense of humor usually associated with prosperous senators from Texas. He was no youngster, of course, for his hair showed clear white and wavy from under the jaunty snap-brim Panama he was wearing. His suit was an expensive tropical worsted Glen plaid and had the assured sporting air of a high-class Dallas horse show. At the moment, his eyebrows were drawn down to meet in an oddly puckered frown and he seemed a little unsure of himself. But that didn't surprise Sergeant Bullen, for when you came right down to it, nobody but a cop could feel at home in a station house.

He stopped a few feet from the desk so he would not have to tilt his head to look up at the sergeant. "My name is Meade, sir," he announced, "Stewart W. Meade. I have come to register a complaint. This is contrary to my professional principles, but there is no choice. I wish that clearly understood."

"Sure, Mr. Meade. What seems to be the trouble?"

"I have reason to believe that my wife and a, ah, former business associate named Wesley Buck attempted to kill me last night."

"You—what!" Bullen stared. "That's a funny way of putting it, Mr. Meade. How do you mean?"

"I just told you, damn it. They'd been drinking bathtub gin. I saw the bottle on the night table beside the bed and she was reaching for it. I saw her face quite clearly in the moonlight. There was no mercy in it."

"Did she hit you with the bottle, Mr. Meade? Or'd she just threaten you?"

"I was lying on the ground when I recovered consciousness. There seems to be no doubt that an attempt was made, does there? I'm not lying, sir!"

"I didn't say you were, Mr. Meade. But you accused this man Buck. Is he the one who hit you? Or don't you know which one of them did it?"

"What kind of idiocy is this?" Meade demanded loudly; his face was pale and sweating. "Am I on trial? Do you think I attacked myself? They won't stop until I'm dead, I tell you! They're too confident, both of them. Is that enough for you? *Both* of them!"

"This is a very serious charge, Mr. Meade."

"It was a serious attempt."

Bullen nodded slowly and took a quadruplicate Complaint Report from the drawer. "I better start taking this down," he said, quickly filling in the Complaint number, his own name as reporting officer, and other standard information, pausing for the fraction of a second before writing A.D.W.—assault with a deadly weapon—in the space marked Nature Of Complaint. He looked up from the pad. "Your address, Mr. Meade?"

"My address is the Flamingo Hotel."

"The Flamingo? I don't know that one. Is it in the city?"

"Indeed it is, sir. On the boulevard."

"Uh huh. Now, where'd the attack take place?"

Mr. Meade said, "The attack ..." and his face darkened.

Bullen waited, and when Meade did not continue, he prodded, "Yes, the attack. Did it take place in the hotel?"

That oddly puckering frown pinched at Meade's brows again, giving him an expression of anxiety. "The hotel?" he fumbled. "No, no ..."

"Was it here in the city? I can't take the complaint unless it happened here. You'll have to report it to the local police."

"Yes, yes, it was here in the city. But not at the Flamingo. We lived in the Flamingo. It was at the Palm Terrace on Flagler Street. They had a room under the name of Mr. and Mrs. Wilfred Boyd. Ha!" a small grin slid up the side of Meade's mouth. "They were in bed together, half drunk and having a high old time when I walked in. I put the fear of God into them and they never forgot. Or forgave."

Bullen lifted his pencil from the Complaint pad, spread his forearms on the desk, and leaned over them. "So you found them shacked up and put the fear of God in them. What with? A gun, maybe?"

Meade chuckled. "An old .38 without a firing pin, but they didn't know that. I beat the living hell out of Wes, and chased Viv down into the street, naked as the day she was born. They thought I was just a dumb kid, too young to know what kind of kiss-the-pillow they were playing behind my back. But I showed them, and it was their own fault."

Incredulous, Bullen asked, "They thought you were *what*, Mr. Meade?"

"I was twenty-three and ... or was it twenty-four...." Meade faltered, groping. "I don't recall exactly ..."

Sergeant Bullen had half risen from his chair to bend farther over his desk, and it was as he'd begun to suspect; the expensive odor of fine Scotch rode richly on every breath Meade exhaled. He put down the pencil and leaned back in his chair. "Go home, Mr. Meade," he said, not unkindly. "You've been hitting the bottle and it gave you bad dreams. Nobody attacked you last night. That was about forty years ago. And even then, nobody was after you. It was the other way around. Right? Think it over."

Meade lifted his pale, perspiring face and his expression wavered, unfocused. "Forty ... years? No, no ... I saw her face in the moonlight and ... I didn't realize until too late ..."

"Forget it, Mr. Meade. You've been at the bottle again today. I can smell it. Go home and sleep it off. Don't make trouble. You'll only be sorry when you sober up."

Meade slowly turned his head and glanced around, but not as if he expected to recognize anything. He stared at the wall clock for a long while, and that did mean something to him, for his back straightened, and he looked up at Sergeant Bullen. "My regrets, sir, but I am late for the office, and must leave. You are quite wrong, however, quite wrong, but ... sometimes things aren't always the same."

He walked steadily enough to the door, but had to put out a quick hand to retain his balance, and then he was gone.

Sergeant Bullen was satisfied. This was how he liked to settle complaints, instead of referring them for investigation and possible summary action. He drew an "x" across the Complaint Report, tore the sheets from the pad and tossed them into a bottom drawer, where he kept scraps of paper for memos or notes. Ah, he thought as he slid the carbons between the white, pink, blue and yellow sheets of the next report on the pad, there's one old gentleman who'll feel like a horse's ass when he sobers up. They always do. And will he thank the police for not letting him make a bigger horse's ass of himself? They never do.

Mr. Meade left the station and walked up the street, swearing behind the white fence of clenched teeth. The Goddamned stupid police! If there was one thing you could depend on them for, it was just exactly that— to be stupid. No matter what they did, it was bound to be a hundred per cent wrong.

If you didn't want them, they were in your hair, like dandruff; but if you went to them with a complaint, they laughed in your face and sent you home. Jesus H. Christ! And when they shaved, they were actually able to look in the mirror without cutting their throats. Judas God, it really did take a special kind of moron to make a cop, and there'd never be any doubt about that! He ground his teeth once, but changed the grimace into a bitter smile and contemptuously dismissed all police from his mind. And in the end, when all was said and done, nothing remained but the basic fact of self-preservation, and a man had to look out for himself.

A big yellow midtown-bound bus roared flatulently by, and he winced, squeezing his eyes tightly shut as he clasped his forehead with a convulsive hand. Another of those headaches, and his own fault again, damn it. This was what happened every time he took a drink. It had been years, but he should have remembered all the times he woke up in the morning with a red-hot dagger burning in his brain. He'd never been able to drink, never—

He stopped at the corner, confused by the rush of unfamiliar traffic. He didn't know this neighborhood. He looked anxiously around and saw strange dingy little shops and dirty yellow brick apartment houses he could not recognize. He became panicky and, although he did not exactly want to escape, there was a growing urgency to go away from this place, immediately, right now, but hurry hurry, for it was dreadfully late and soon it might be too late unless he got to his office at once. It was fortunate for the frame of mind he was in that he spied a cruising cab, and when it miraculously stopped for him, his relief was like nausea. Within less than twenty minutes he was delivered at the very door of the high Executive Building on Schuyler Boulevard, in the heart of downtown.

His urgency did not lessen; it was late and he had to hurry. Inside, an express elevator shot him aloft to the twenty-third floor. Three minutes passed, and made him furious. He couldn't spare three minutes. He strode through the foyer of his personal office without a glance at Emily Burkhardt, his private secretary, or at the thin, quick-faced man who'd begun to rise from a russet leather lounge chair beneath a floor lamp at the side of the waiting room.

"Whoa, whoa there, Stewart," the quick-faced man said humorously. "Spare the horses—"

Meade interrupted, "Excuse me, please. I have an appointment." He did not turn his head, but hurried to enter his office.

His secretary called, "But, Mr. Meade, your appointment is with Mr. Babson here—" The door closed, and she looked at the quick-faced man, apologetic. "I guess he didn't hear me, Mr. Babson."

"Perhaps he wasn't listening, Miss Burkhardt." The quick-faced man named Babson gave the door a sharp, narrow glance. "I think there's something on his mind, wouldn't you say?"

"Oh yes. He's never this late, Mr. Babson. There must have been an unexpected delay, or he would have telephoned—"

From inside the other room came the sound of a jarring, muffled thud, as if a big man had fallen heavily to the floor. It was unmistakable, for there is no other sound that so mingles the hardness of bone and the softness of flesh.

Miss Burkhardt jumped up from her chair, ran across the foyer, thrust open the door of Mr. Meade's office, and gasped. She'd expected to see Mr. Meade getting up from the floor, a little shaky, perhaps, after such a fall, but he was still lying there. He was sprawled face down in the middle of the rug about six feet from the desk, his right arm outstretched as though reaching for the Panama hat, which lay canted against a leg of the desk.

"Mr. Meade!" She flew to his side and knelt down. Then she put out a hand, but the gesture was never completed. Instead, she stared at an odd smudge, about the size of a half-dollar, on Mr. Meade's head, just above and to the rear of his left ear. It was not black, yet intensely darker than a shadow.

It took her a long, slow minute to understand that because a splintered inch-round segment of bone was missing from Mr. Meade's skull, she was not looking at the back of his head, but *into* it, and it was then that she screamed.

Two

Lieutenant Ben Tutchek, Commander of the Homicide Division, was at work early that morning. Not bright and early; just early. He had left his dusty 1958 Chewy in the cramped parking lot behind Headquarters on Jackson Street and trudged toward the lowering four-story red brick building that housed the nerve centers of the police department—the vigilant, concentrated gray matter of its cerebrum and cerebellum.

The cortex and tissue of the Department spread through the body of the city in a close-knit network of precincts, each a probing ganglion and a focus of energy and strength. Although it has been stated that the police cannot afford to have a heart, there was one and it was not hard to find. It beat in the ears of men who heard the spurting shrieks crimson violence, in the eyes that had to look down upon the red ruin, and sometimes in the throats of patrolmen and detectives who knew the terrible loneliness of courage. And there was a soul, too, but much harder to find, for it was in the prayers of sleepless wives and in the tears of widows.

Of course, no one in the Department thought of it that way, but they must have thought about it, for now and again someone would say wryly, "What a way to make a living," and punctuate it with a sub-humorous groan, or perhaps just swear, instead.

Lieutenant Tutchek was a big man, six feet four, two hundred and forty pounds, heavy-boned and massive, but the force within those proportions was disguised by the quiet browns of his hair, eyes and complexion. His broad face looked pleasant and relaxed, but that was an illusion, for there was no real expression—it was the kind of neutral face that grew on cops after a while, a basic face, so to speak, a face upon which the necessity of the moment could mold any expression, tough when they didn't feel tough, human when they did not feel human. Ben Tutchek was tough and human and tired, but chiefly tired. He always made an effort to be especially human when he was tired, because he did not trust himself to handle a tough mood.

One of the reasons he was tired was the Fourth of July. Yesterday. Because yesterday was the Fourth of July, he had been in and out of Headquarters until three A.M. this morning. Every year, it seemed, to him, more and more people celebrated Independence Day by getting drunk and having themselves thrown into jail. Since he was concerned with homicide, he did not like to think of those who would sober up this morning with a hangover that would be with them for the rest of their lives. These were the comparatively innocent, if you could put it that way—the ones who started with an innocent drink and ended with the guilty horror.

He turned his mind from that and began to think of the case which had kept him from bed until three o'clock this morning—the body of a young girl found beaten, kicked to death, among the high, dense rhododendron bushes of South Branch Park in the Brookville section of the city. Very young, no more than thirteen or fourteen years old, in the tired opinion of the Medical Examiner. Thin, unformed, a child, with breasts no larger than old-fashioned hemispherical doorbells, tipped by buds that were not yet nipples. Stripped, she lay spread-eagled beneath the dark, glossy leaves. Rape, of course. And the worst kind, for first she had been savagely beaten, and had no face. A slowly turning prowl car of the Park Patrol had caught a flash of white in the sweep of headlights, and when the two patrolmen stopped to investigate, they saw the two skinny legs, stiffly spread, mottled with bruises and shadows. Her clothes had been carried away by the attacker and there wasn't a chance of immediate identification.

It had been one thing after another all day, and Tutchek was still at his desk when the call was flashed to Headquarters just before midnight. This was a bad one, and even if he had not been at his desk, everyone in the Homicide Division had standing orders to call him at home the instant a major case developed. He had been sell-conscious about that order in the beginning, six weeks ago, immediately after his promotion to Commander of Homicide. He called himself an eager beaver and contrived to hide in his office until the men stopped griping or laughing about it among themselves, but now he grimly knew how necessary it was. A commanding officer wasn't Jesus Christ in a box seat; there was a little work attached to the job, it seemed, and one of the details was that he was expected to know everything about everything all the time.

The headlights of a half-dozen green-and-white patrol cars flooded the rhododendron grove, and around the perimeter of light, kept at bay by a score of uniformed patrolmen, were the prowling, bobbing rubberneckers, clad in pajamas, nightgowns, robes, negligees, shorts and even underwear, as if they had sprung straight from the bedroom. Where they lived in the woodwork. Amid this jostling, babbling pandemonium, the skinny, broken body of the dead girl seemed almost unimportant.

Tutchek surveyed the crowd and said sourly to detectives Ike Bierce and Frank Caputo, "I'll clobber the next detective who forgets to bring tear gas. Take Daly, Johansson, Feinberg and Bruns and see if you can find a witness in that pack of morons that can speak English, or anything else. I'll see if the Lab boys managed to salvage anything before the stampede."

He tramped straight at the crowd and shouldered roughly through it. They swore at him and shoved back, but he did not acknowledge them until a nightgowned woman, with gray witch-hair down her face, screeched at him, "Cut the shovin', crud. This is *my* place."

"No, lady," he said, with heavy emphasis, "your place is under those bushes instead of that little girl, but somebody made a mistake."

He paid no more attention to them after that. The Lab technicians, working at and around the body, looked up when he approached, recognizing him with a nod, but that was all. When they said nothing, it meant there was nothing to say; nobody was interested in idle conversation at a time like this. They had the bunched, angry faces of frustrated men. They did not ask much—just one clue, one lead, one thread, one scrap, but there was nothing, no dress, no stockings, no shoes, not a single article of clothing, and the very grass thwarted them, for it was too thick and springy to show, much less retain, a footprint. All they could do was photograph the body and the smudged bruises, which may or may not have been made by fingers. It was impossible to tell in this Walpurgis light. It would be easier, perhaps, when the photographs were examined later, in the Lab back at Headquarters. A search for the clothing had already begun, under Tutchek's orders, and before dawn over a hundred uniformed men would be combing the small park, bush by bush, and probing the small brook that ran through it, with rakes—finding little other than empty beer cans, empty wine bottles, and the discarded elastic residue of alfresco love, also empty....

When old Dr. Hector Knight, the Medical Examiner, arrived and knelt down beside the body, all through the crowd the heads and shoulders of men and women kept shooting up, like popping corn, as they jumped into the air for a better view over the crowns of those in front of them. The doctor disregarded them as he made as thorough an examination as possible. The thin cordon of police could not keep the excited onlookers from darting to and fro before the streaming headlights, and the light on the body shifted constantly. Still, he was a patient man, and did not complain. Also, he was tired and the sacs beneath his eyes were dark with the poisons of fatigue. But that neither retarded nor hastened his examination, and he turned the battered head gently from side to side with slow, careful hands for a more intent clinical scrutiny. At length he finished and rose wearily to his feet, dipping his head at a patrolman to recover the body. As he and Tutchek stepped back into the cover of the bushes, a reporter hurried to join them, followed by a news photographer.

"What's it all about, Lieutenant?" he demanded. "Rape job?"

Tutchek's temper flared into sarcasm. "Rape hell. She just wanted her picture taken at night in the park with police protection." Then, more quietly, "Sorry, son, but it's been a long day and this is a hell of a way to wind it up. I don't know what it is yet. Dr. Knight hasn't told me. Suppose you wait back there while we talk it over."

"Sure, Lieutenant. Okay to take a few pictures?"

"Help yourself. I know you won't lift the blanket unless you can, so don't."

"Anything you say, Lieutenant."

The Medical Examiner waited until the two newsmen were out of earshot, then sighed and said, "She was kicked to death, Ben. Kicked and stamped on. The marks are plain."

Tutchek sucked in a breath. "Before or after, Doc?"

"Before, I'd say. At least an hour before."

"Oh God!"

"Yes. And I won't say, what kind of animal could possibly do a thing like that? We both know. So"—his shoulders moved in a defeated shrug. "I wish I could get used to these things."

"Do you?"

"No. No, I guess not. Who'd want to? Lord!"

Tutchek looked at the milling crowd. "You know, there's a chance he's still here."

Knight nodded. "That would be part of it. If anybody faints or gets hurt, look for him there. I'm going home. You'll have a preliminary report in the morning."

He left. Tutchek spied Ike Bierce questioning a man and woman several yards away, and beckoned. The detective came over a few minutes later. Tutchek told him what the Medical Examiner had said, and added, "From now on take special note of the shoes. If he's still hanging around, he didn't have time to give them a good cleaning. Probably blood on the pants and socks, too."

"He'd be a damn fool, Lieutenant—"

"He's not a damn fool," Tutchek sharply. "He's a maniac. Keep that in mind, and don't take chances. Now pass the word around, but don't advertise it."

Bierce compressed his mouth. He was a dark, lean man with harsh gray eyes. "This is one arrest I'd like to make personally," he said. "I'll tell the boys, Lieutenant."

Tutchek prowled the scene alone, anxious that nothing be overlooked, but the killer had been extraordinarily lucky, and although over a hundred detectives and patrolmen were concentrated in the small park, they did not find another lead. Tutchek waited until the morgue wagon came and the attendants lifted the thin, broken body into their carrying basket, then plodded toward his car. He turned once to look back, and what he saw filled him with a vast, momentary discouragement. In a surge, the crowd had gone through the inadequate line of patrolmen and were tearing down the rhododendron bush under which the dead girl had been found. Souvenirs.

It was three-thirty when he finally arrived home. He went into the kitchen for a cup of coffee, but took a can of beer from the refrigerator instead. Once again he went over everything in his mind, really hoping to find something he'd forgotten, something that might turn up a lead, but every angle had been covered. There were three teams of detectives at the scene, and a fourth in Headquarters was up in Records & Identification, compiling a list of all known sex deviates, and by this time still other men would be out rounding up possible suspects. Stool pigeons were being contacted, and bums and drunks were being pulled in from the streets surrounding the park. Everything was being done. Tutchek closed his eyes for a moment, trying to think—

His wife, Sophie, found him asleep at the Formica-topped table with his head resting on his crossed forearms, the can of beer still unopened at his elbow. The time was six-forty-five.

At ten past eight he was back at Headquarters.

The day men were moving around and getting settled in the big general squad room of the Detective Bureau, on the second floor of Headquarters. Some were typing, some hunched intently over telephones, and even at this early hour, a few goof-offs were already slouching toward the water cooler at the side of the room. The morning sun slanted through the dirty windows, but somehow managed to look clean and fresh. But that would not last long. As the day progressed and the tempo became heavy and steady, it would turn the color of old egg yolks raddled by dust motes. If it were a bad day, that is. On quiet days the lengthening shafts of sunlight seemed gradually to mellow in the soft laughter of relaxed men, and the heat of the afternoon was friendly, instead of a curdled burden.

A few said, "Hi, Ben" as Tutchek crossed the squad room, but most of the greetings were restrained to, "Morning, Lieutenant," and it made him abruptly self-conscious of the fact that he really was Commander of Homicide, a title he still wore awkwardly. He knew there was a tacit *Verboten!* area between the men and executive officers, but he could not become accustomed to it. He missed the easy exchange of casual insults—which was the lingua franca of Headquarters—the jokes and the griping and the shared grins, and he was having a hard time understanding that it was gone. He could not comprehend how something so warm and real and of such long standing might vanish in an instant.

And an instant was all the time it had taken for that *Verboten!* area to spring up between them. It had begun the very day of his promotion, and he'd been acutely aware of it, even in the congratulations of those he'd thought friends. It was as if they and he had each stepped back a pace and were too separated to shake hands, and it had gotten worse since. He looked and listened for it in every greeting, and when it came, it was like having a door slammed in his face. Sometimes it was so marked that he had to tighten his mouth to keep the resentment from showing. Particularly with the men of his own Division.

There was one salient fact he had yet to grasp: he was on probation, not only with his superiors, but with the men as well. As an executive officer, it was in his power to make or break a man. If he put a black mark against a man's record, it stayed there. This was the way the men felt about every new officer promoted to a position above them, and then was a standing question that always had to be answered one way or the other. It was a big question, asked in wary narrow-eyed whispers. It was: Well, what kind of bastard is this bastard going to be?

Most of the men would be pleased and friendly after he proved himself, but there were the goof-offs, the inadequate and the insecure, to whom a boss is always a bastard. To them, it was merely a matter of degree. He might not be so big a bastard as Lieutenant Ochs, Commander of Burglary, who'd chew the living hell out of a man for making a few honest mistakes now and then—*We're all human, ain't we?*—but what can you expect? When you make a guy a boss, you make him an automatic bastard, and there's nothing you can do about it. If you pull a boner or two, the hell with it; just don't get caught, that's all.

Tutchek entered his office from the back corridor at the freight elevators, bypassing the partitioned Homicide squad room and Policewoman Ruth Lund, his chilly secretary and receptionist. He was not intentionally keeping himself aloof from her or the men, but the mumbling quiet that fell when he walked into a room these days made him feel self-conscious and on stage. They acted as if he were the truant officer. What was the matter with them, anyway? They were grown men, not school kids playing hooky. How could you trust people like that? He knew he was oversimplifying the situation—or possibly exaggerating it—but he had been crowded by so many new and strange things during the six weeks since his promotion that he just did not have the time to sit down and think through each of them separately.

His administration officer, Detective Lieutenant Alec Gillespie, looked up from the wobbly oak table that served as a desk in a corner against one wall of the cramped office they were forced to share, like two mastiffs in a suitcase. He was shorter than Tutchek but wide and solid. His gray hair appeared to have been shaved from the same sheet iron as his inflexibly gray suit. He had a square, capable face and the stubborn blue-gray eyes of a man whose quiet sense of humor was gradually becoming mute. He was a shrewd, effective officer who might have gone all the way to the top if he'd had a little more of Tutchek's implied force and drive.

He glanced clinically across the small office as Tutchek took off his jacket and hung it from a nail in the back of the door, stretched his arms and heavily rolled the muscles of his massive shoulders.

"I hear you had a bitch of a night, Ben," he said. "That rape business."

Tutchek nodded heavily. "A real bitch," he agreed. "I hope it doesn't get worse. Anything from Doc Knight?"

"Just the preliminary investigation report. It was here when I got in this morning. Nothing in it that he didn't tell you last night, I don't imagine."

He handed the sheet to Tutchek, who wearily let his eyes scan the too-familiar details: Race, white; Sex, female; Age, 13-14; Height, 5' 3"; Weight, 101; Hair, blonde; Eyes, blue ... then down to the heading *Physical Examination*. This was filled out in the Medical Examiner's precise, economical script, which rapidly catalogued the multiple bruises and contusions and the several depressed skull fractures that had killed the child. She had definitely been kicked to death, and somehow or other, those bleak, factual medical phrases made the brutality and savagery of the attack starkly vivid.

And then there had been the "rape"—although, Tutchek thought wryly, a good "normal rape" would be mere horseplay, compared to this. There had been what seemed like bestial penetration, but the "sexual" act, in the Medical Examiner's opinion, had not been completed, for there were no traces of semen, either within the vaginal canal or on the skin of the thighs or belly. It was not Doctor Knight's job to draw any further conclusions in this report; it was merely a list of his findings during a purely physical examination of the corpse.

An interrupted rape. Tutchek's teeth clamped painfully together. What had interrupted it? The sweeping headlights of the Park Patrol prowl car as it approached along the curving drive? Had it been as close as that? Would the two patrolmen have seen the figure of the fleeing rapist as he plunged into the darkness if they had made that turn thirty seconds earlier? Had they been too slow in leaving the car to see what lay beneath that dark-leafed rhododendron bush? If they had been quicker to raise the beams of their flashlights ... If, if, if! If Eden had been Brooklyn, there wouldn't have been any apple trees, and Adam's name would be Dutch Schultz. Tutchek gave his head a hard shake to rid himself of these useless speculations.

Still, he had an irrational impulse to turn the report over to see if something more had been written on the back of it. It was complete, he knew, but at the same time there was something inconclusive about it—something left out, something not fully explained. But there was nothing the matter with the report; it was just the shifting of elusive thought motes in his own mind, or the first touch of a chilly premonition that there was another front-page killing that might wind up in the Inactive, Not Cleared file. He dodged hurriedly away from the notion. He could not afford any Inactives, Not Cleared.

"Did Bierce or Caputo call in yet?" he asked abruptly.

Alec Gillespie pointed his square chin at the door to the Homicide squad room. "They're outside now, going through some pictures the Lab sent down."

Tutchek groaned. The detectives would not be sitting at a desk looking at photographs if they were not stalled.

"Well—I'll get together with them a little later," he said. "Are the others still trying for an identification?"

"Yes. Nothing."

"What about sex offenders?"

"They picked up three, so far. Checked out their alibis and turned them loose."

Tutchek grunted. He wanted to say, Well, we're holding our own, anyway, but it wasn't so. The minute a case turned static, you lost ground. They'd overlooked something or there'd have been at least one new lead since last night.

Gillespie said suddenly, "Oh Christ!" and snatched up a memo pad from his desk. "A meeting in Foxy's office at nine o'clock sharp. Triple-A priority."

Tutchek felt a small prickle of alarm. "What's it about? Not that damn rape case already," He knew that was wrong, the minute he said it. Foxy was Captain Mackenzie, Chief of Detectives, and he wouldn't call a meeting in the first hours of a case; he'd phone if he wanted information.

Gillespie was saying, "He didn't say why. But you're not the only one. I asked around a little, and Ochs, Nairn and Stein were also invited. There are probably others. If you want me to, I'll—"

"Never mind, never mind. What are you working on?"

"The recap on all absence reports since January. You told me to get started on it first thing this morning."

Tutchek noted the sharpness in Gillespie's voice, but ignored it. He knew Gillespie resented being handed this chore because it was a routine check through the files, which could be done just as easily by Policewoman Lund, or any girl from Clerical. There was no need for Tutchek to explain or apologize, but he did not want Alec Gillespie, too, to fall into an abrupt silence when he entered the office.

"If there's any deadwood in this Division, Alec," he said unhappily, "the Absence Reports is where it'll show up in black and white, and I want to get rid of it. I'll be up the creek if I even try to run a department with goof-offs. That's not the whole thing, but if it lines up with some of the other hoo-ha that goes on around here, I'll have a picture of it."

Gillespie looked surprised. "That's what I thought," he said mildly.

Tutchek stood for a moment, as if about to say more, but realized he'd already talked too much. He was grateful to Alec for passing it off so quietly.

He muttered, "Well, back to the salt mines," and rolling up his sleeves, turned to his desk and grimaced at the stack of unfinished paperwork that awaited him. The desktop looked as if a snowstorm had drifted across it. He was days behind on some of it. Not his own Division's paper—and there were twenty different kinds of those reports that he could name offhand, not including fifty-seven varieties from the Lab upstairs. He had to keep up with those every single day, or be sunk, and that was a job in itself, following the cases personally, then checking the reports that followed.

It was the other papers that snowed him under—the bulletins, readers, advertisements and out-of-town letters from other police departments with requests or answers to requests, notes, directives, inter-department memos, general orders, receipt requested. The sheer mass of it appalled him, and he was dismayed by the unfamiliar complexity. It had been like this for the five weeks since his promotion, and each day there was more of it and each day he fell a little further behind. He spent a few minutes straightening the mess on his desk, then bent to pick up a sheet that escaped and fluttered to the floor. It was five days old.

HUDSON POLICE DEPARTMENT
Office of the Chief

GENERAL ORDER

Number-61-017-292

TO: All members of the Police Department
SUBJECT: Personal Injury Reports

ACCIDENTAL INJURY: (until cleared) The additional red copy now attached to be filled out on reverse, following procedure of Description Sheet Form 5, i.e.: check Offense and/or Conviction Record with the Records & Identification Bureau (victim (s) and suspect (s)) Include record of previous medical history of Victim from his personal doctor, if any. Red and yellow copies to be sent to the Homicide Division, Detective Bureau, attention of the Commander, by Platoon Commander. Homicide Division will fill out "Comments" on the reverse of the yellow copy and to the office of the Chief.

ASSAULT CASES: Red copy to be filled out on the reverse as described in Paragraph 1. Red and yellow copies to be sent to ...

The telephone rang. Tutchek groaned. This was what always happened. All he had to do was sit down at his desk to get some of the paper work out of the way, and it was the signal for the phone to start ringing, and keep ringing for the rest of the day. This one was from Detective Kitteridge, sent out by Alec Gillespie to investigate a drowning report that came in a few minutes past eight that morning.

"It looks like a mugging, Lieutenant," said Kitteridge. "A woman about thirty-five, or so. Terrific bruise on the forehead over the right eye and a gash on the left side of the head. There's a scrape on the left wrist where the wristwatch was pulled off. The body was caught on a piling of the dock at the East Coast Fisheries. A tugboat spotted it."

"Sounds more like a holdup than a mugging," Tutchek said.

"Yeah. That's what I meant, Lieutenant. A holdup. I just got off that Peshine Street mugging thing and I guess it's still on my mind."

"Any identification?"

"There's a DeJongg label on her evening dress that cost more than a few hundred bucks, and even De Jongg's don't sell dresses like that by the hundred, so I should get a line on her from there. They're bound to remember her. She's not a looker. She's on the fat side with dyed red hair and teeth that stick out a little."

"How long was she in the water?"

"A few hours. Not long. She's in pretty good shape. Two uniform boys are out there with her while we wait till the M.E. gets here. I'm calling from the East Coast office and—"

"Who else is with you?"

"Nobody. I come alone, Lieutenant. Now, do you want me to stay here or take a run over to DeJongg's for the identification? I might save time if—"

Tutchek swore under his breath, but said quietly, "No, stay where you are, Kitteridge. I'll send somebody over to give you a hand. Cover the angles in the meanwhile."

Tutchek hung up and sat for a few seconds with his hand still on the phone, his mouth bunched in a small frown. This was another one he ought to look at before they took it to the morgue, but there wasn't time. It was half-past eight and the meeting in Captain Mackenzie's office was at nine. Still, it definitely was not a case that should get under way without some supervision. The dead woman obviously had money, or she wouldn't have an evening gown from DeJongg's, the most expensive shop in town, and the papers would be sure to play it up for all it was worth, no matter which way it went. He couldn't afford to let it get off on the wrong foot. He wasn't making a mountain out of a molehill—there *was* something to worry about, but he couldn't be in two places at the same time.

"What's the matter, Ben?" Gillespie asked. "Did Kitteridge get hold of a hot one?"

"Run over and see what's what, will you, Alec? It's that drowning at the East Coast Fisheries. You have the address. Kitteridge has made up his mind it was a holdup, but it can be almost anything. Take Stefano and Koch with you. Clean it up as fast as you can. Sit on Kitteridge if you have to. You know how he operates."

Gillespie said, "Okay, Ben," and was on his way to the door, swinging into his jacket as he went though.

Tutchek still didn't feel any happier about it. Gillespie was a good man, and would clean up every detail as he went along, leaving nothing dangling, but Tutchek preferred being at the scene himself during the processing. He fairly ached to get out there, just to get the feel of the investigation. He'd been one of the best investigators in Homicide, and didn't have to be modest about it. He knew how a case should go; it was automatic with him, step by step.

Kitteridge was a good investigator, too, but he had a few faults: he was impatient, and liked to play a hunch. Which was all right, because he had a nose for it, and his hunches usually paid off. Ninety-eight per cent of the time. It was the other two per cent where the trouble came in. When the hunch didn't pay off, Kitteridge was inclined to run around in circles, trying to get another hunch instead of working with facts as they arose—

The telephone rang ... and for the next twenty-five minutes, exactly as he had predicted to himself, it was one call after another. By that time it was five to nine and he had to leave for Captain Mackenzie's office without having been able to do a thing about the accumulated paper work on his desk.

2

There were eight men in Captain Mackenzie's office when Tutchek walked in, and there was plenty of room for another eight, but the three who stood talking together in low voices at the desk made it seem suddenly very crowded. They were Police Commissioner Willie Quinn, Police Chief Earl Sharkey, and Chief of Detectives Captain Foxy Mackenzie himself. Although Quinn and Sharkey were both big, bulky men, dressed much alike in dark suits, white shirts and conservative black knitted ties, their size had nothing to do with the crowded condition of the room.

It was the weight of high police brass gathered there. It was possible that Mackenzie carried a little more weight within the Department than even the police chief. Where Earl Sharkey was inclined to conciliate for the sake of internal harmony, Mackenzie was known to be as tough as armor-plated nails. When it came to a showdown, he was the most feared or respected officer on the Force, depending upon which side of the fence you stood. He was a thickset man with the muscular face of the hard-boiled, experienced Airedale, who never started a fight because he knew there'd always be one handy if necessary. In earlier years, when Commander of the Twentieth Precinct house—the lethal precinct called either The Point or the Roaring Twentieth—Mackenzie had been known as Iron Pants. You had to be an Iron Pants down there or wind up with none at all. Or dead. The label of Foxy, or Foxy Grandpa, had been tacked on him by a newspaperman shrewd enough to see that the mind behind that belligerent Airedale face was as efficient as a loaded gun.

There was a semicircle of chairs facing the desk, and in them were seated lieutenants Ochs, Nairn and Stein, of Burglary, Safe and Loft, and Robbery, respectively; and Captain Jack Willis and Detective Lieutenant Abe McElroy, both hard-bitten officers from the Roaring Twentieth precinct.

Foxy Mackenzie looked around over his shoulder as he heard the door close behind Tutchek, and he nodded a friendly greeting to put him at his ease. Friendly, but crisp. There were no back-slappers in Mackenzie's league.

"Have a seat, Ben," he said, dipping his head at the empty sixth chair. "We'll get started in a minute."

Tutchek nodded at the seated men, and they nodded back, but no one said anything. Everybody looked a little grim. The three ranking officers talked for a few moments longer, then Quinn turned, half-haunched on the edge of the desk, and looked down at the men facing him. His round face was flushed and he kept slapping a flutter of newspaper clippings in his hand against the side of his heavy thigh. His grin was a little too small and looked as if it hurt his mouth.

"Welcome to the horse's ass club, boys," he said in a painfully jocular voice. "There'll probably be a lot more of us before the election in November, so we might as well get used to it."

He glanced around and the answering grins were pinched and uneasy and the men tried to look at one another from the ends of their eyes for a clue as to what was coming.

"I'm not putting you on the spot, boys," he assured them—unsuccessfully. "All I'm doing is preparing you for what might be rubbed under your nose between now and November. The campaign's been pretty quiet so far but—well, take a look for yourself. This is from this morning's *Courier*."

He held up one of the newspaper clippings. The three-line headline was in bold black type a half-inch high:

> CITY VIOLENT DEATHS
> UP TWENTY PERCENT,
> INS. PREXY CHARGES

Quinn shook the clipping at them, his red face almost incandescent. "That's dirty politics," he said violently. "This insurance prexy they're talking about is Gilbert Maxwell, president of the Hudson Mutual Insurance Company. Now I know Gil personally, and he didn't make any such charge. This damn story was lifted from his semi-annual report to the policy holders of Hudson Mutual, and he was talking about payments on double indemnity policies, which include industrial accidents, plane crashes, traffic deaths, and other forms of non-negligent manslaughter. I'm trying to show you how a simple, innocent statement like this can be twisted around in a dirty political campaign. It's no accident that the *Courier's* bucking re-election of the mayor. This is the worst kind of yellow journalism because the average dope doesn't read his newspaper. He glances over the headline and turns to the sports section or the funny sheet. Now what's the effect of this headline—'City Violent Death Up Twenty Percent'. Don't tell me—I'll tell you. The cops are falling down on the job. We'll all be murdered in our beds. You can't walk the streets after dark. A woman isn't safe in broad daylight anymore. The cops are falling down on the job. That's exactly what Joe Dope will find in his newspaper when he comes home from work all charged up to read the funny sheet. All right, he's a dope, but let's be practical. He's the dope who's going to do most of the voting next November, and if he votes in a Reform crowd, there'll be the Goddamnedest shake-up in the police department you ever saw, and I'll be out on my can, but the hell with that. I'm thinking of the Department.

"Chief Sharkey, Captain Mackenzie and I have been working to make this one of the best departments in the country, but a crowd like that with a lot of half-ass ideas about Reform will wreck it in four minutes, and it'll take eight years to put it back in shape again. I don't want that to happen. And more especially, I don't want the Department to become a punching bag in a lousy political campaign." He stopped and glared around, as if daring someone to contradict him.

In surprise Tutchek thought, *he means it*, and then the surprise evaporated, and he realized that this was something he'd known all along about Quinn, but had thought of him as City Hall merely because that was where the Police Commissioner had his office. He was a politician; there was no doubt about that. He was a hand-shaker, a back-patter, and baby-kisser, a maker of large, florid speeches, a spokesman at almost every inedible testimonial dinner in his ward, a straight-ticket man, and in the early days of hot-dog and beer-barrel picnics and brass-band political rallies, he might even have been known as Honest Willie Quinn, the pork-barrel champ. But whatever Quinn's bread-and-butter politics, there was one thing he was honest about, and that was the Hudson Police Department. He honestly did want to make it one of the best in the country, and he had fought for bigger operating budgets and more men and better equipment and went to all the conventions. In a way, he was a police boff, and it was one of the poignant regrets of his life that he didn't have a uniform (with very little more gold on it than Chief Sharkey's) to wear in the annual Labor Day parade.

All in all, Willie Quinn had kept the Department fairly clean of politics—considering the fact that he was still a loyal party member, but then, you can't have everything.

Right now he faced the possibility that dirty politics might move in on his police department, and was only too well aware that neither would be uplifted by the association. He was unhappy and a bit more than a little baffled, and perspiration ran down his neck and wet his collar.

There were faint rustling sounds in the otherwise silent office as the men stirred, exchanged quick glances in flickers, but maintained stolid faces. Generally, they trusted Willie Quinn. Within reason, and only within reason. They had learned to be wary of his moods, which now were complicated by the possibility of divided loyalties. Uneasy might be the head that wears a crown, but that was nothing compared to the feelings of the heads he might command to the axe.

"I called you particular men together for a special reason," Quinn continued placatingly. "But let's get something understood first again. I'm not putting any of you on the spot. Just keep that in mind. I want to see how things shape up, that's all. If the *Courier* keeps up this damn violent death business, your divisions are going to be the first targets. Now let's see where we stand, and what we're doing about it—"

"Do you mind if I interrupt for a moment, Will?" Chief Sharkey interposed. "I think it might clear the air if you tell the boys what you just told Mac and me."

"How do you mean?" Quinn growled. "Told you what, in particular?"

"That all you're after in this meeting is information, Will. And that there's absolutely no implied criticism of the way things are being run. After all," he laughed softly, we don't commit murders—we investigate 'em. The *Courier* doesn't seem to make that distinction."

"Oh. Oh, yes. I see what you mean, Earl," Quinn nodded and twitched a grin at the men; there had been an echo of a threatening note under his voice, but now it smoothed away and he turned to Captain Willis and Lieutenant McElroy, of the Twentieth Precinct, with determined benignity. "Things have gotten a lot simpler for Jack and Abe here," he told the others with heavy humor. "The boys and girls down at The Point stopped beating, shooting, stabbing, mugging and rolling each other, and for the past few weeks haven't done a thing except fight cops. That's nothing to worry about. So long as these monkeys stay up on the roofs and throw bricks and bottles and water-filled beer cans at patrolmen, it keeps them out of mischief. But the other day they missed and beaned a guilty bystander who was being stuck in the paddy wagon, drunk and disorderly. The picture changes when they start beaning people. We've got to do something about it or there'll be a stink in the papers. How were things yesterday down at The Point, Jack?"

Captain Willis scowled. He was a powerful, round-shouldered bull of a man with furious red-brown eyes, and he did not like jokes about cop fighters.

"Things were lousy," he said bluntly. "Holiday. Big celebration. I got two boys in the hospital, one with a broken shoulder, the other with a fractured jaw. There were three mass assaults during the day and two more at night. We've been averaging two a day for months."

"I'll get you more men, Jack."

"The Chief already gave me an extra fifty. It's not enough but there aren't any more. I need another hundred. There are twenty-five miles of streets down in The Point, Commissioner, and something like sixty thousand people."

They discussed it glumly for a while and a meeting was set up for later in the day with other commanders, to see how many men could be pulled from the precincts without stripping the patrols beyond the danger point. Willis wanted army-issue war surplus steel helmets for his men. Quinn promised.

Tutchek started to cross his legs but the chair squeaked, and he cleared his throat instead. "I was just thinking, Commissioner," he said, "Jack's getting it hot and heavy down there with not enough men, and Abe's even worse off for detectives, and now that this thing's under way, it won't let up till after the hot weather's over. The first cool spell will clear the brick slingers off the roof. That's about how I figure it'll go, right, Jack?"

"Right on the nose, Goddamnit. We're in for two more friggin' months of it and Christ knows what'll happen in two months. Everybody'll be up on the roof."

"I'm short-handed myself with this rape killing last night, Commissioner, but I think I'd better get a team of my boys down to The Point to work with Jack and Abe to familiarize themselves not only with the situation, but the general neighborhood as well. One way or another there's going to be a killing before the summer is over, and I don't want my boys to walk in cold. They'll be clobbered."

"Fine, fine. Glad you thought of that, Ben. Get together with Jack and Abe after the meeting." Quinn hurried to get the problem behind him, and turned to Lieutenant Saul Stein, Commander of the Robbery Division. "You've been having your troubles, too, I see, Saul"—he flapped the collection of newspaper clippings in his hand—"two robberies and the usual muggings. How are you coming along with it?"

Stein composed his long legs in front of him and slouched comfortably on the hard oak straight chair. His dark, lean face was the calmest in the room. No one had ever seen Stein excited, and when asked for the secret by harassed brother officers, he told them, "Well, the first thing to do is go out and be Jewish for a while. After that, nothing'll faze you." He was probably right, for he was the least excitable officer in the Detective Bureau, and one of the few who did not shake all over, like a Chihuahua, when the steam pressure started hissing at the safety valves.

"Oh, we're doing all right, Commissioner," he told Quinn. "Most of that was small stuff, and the boys made three pinches—two muggers and one of the young punks that pulled the Park Liquor Shop stick-up."

Tutchek remembered reading of the stick-up in the *Hudson Morning News*, and it was a bad one because the two kids who pulled it beat up the proprietor after rifling the till of over two hundred dollars. It was a wonder the old man was not dead, for the two young hoodlums jumped on him and broke several ribs after knocking him to the floor. They also smashed almost every bottle on his shelves and made off with a case of Scotch. It was an act of senseless brutality and vandalism and deservedly had made the front page.

"... eighteen years old," Stein was saying in his unhurried voice. "Gave his name as Poochy Ryan. Two of my boys, Alix Uri and Bill Hughes, picked him up about an hour ago, dead drunk in his jalopy parked behind a billboard on Communipaw Street. The case of Scotch minus one bottle was on the floor of the back seat. He had over two hundred bucks in his pants. He tried to tell us he'd gotten drunk at the block dance in Polack Town up in north Hudson, and somebody must have planted the liquor and money on him while he was soused. But hell, the old man's blood was still on his clothes and his fingerprints are all over the liquor shop. He still maintains he was framed while he was soused, but that's a lot of horseshit, and I don't mind telling you I'm going to give that cold-blooded son-of-a-bitch a bad time before I'm done with him, Commissioner."

"You watch yourself with that kind of stuff, Saul," said Quinn quickly. "Rough up a juvenile and the papers'll be all over you like a ton of bricks."

"If that's an order, Commissioner—"

"How bad is the old man?"

"Not as bad as we thought at first, but he still won't be out of the hospital for another two weeks, or more. Those two rats really stamped on him, Commissioner. If you ask me, they wanted to kill him. Maybe they thought they did. He looked it."

"Did he identify this Ryan boy?"

"He's in no shape to identify anything."

"Won't that affect your case?"

"Not a bit. The Scotch case we picked up in Ryan's car had the Park Liquor address on it. The amount of money we found in his pocket tallies with what the old man managed to tell us was stolen. Then there was the blood on the kid's pants, and several sets of his fingerprints in the shop itself. He did everything but sign his name. Even a Philadelphia lawyer won't get him out of this one. This isn't his first offense, Commissioner. He did a year in the Rahway Reformatory for beating up an eight-year-old, stealing his bike and selling it. Ryan's not an underprivileged little kid, Commissioner. He's six feet tall, weighs a hundred and seventy-five pounds, and has a bad reputation. We asked around. He's a mean bastard."

"Then you have all you need to go into court."

"We've got enough to put him away for fifteen years."

"All you want from him now, then, is the name of his companion."

"All!" said Stein. "All!"

"Yes, all!" Quinn snapped. "He's convicted on the evidence, and roughing him up now will only create sympathy for him. I'd rather see him get fifteen years than a punch in the snoot. How about you?"

There was a gleam of admiration in Stein's grave, satirical eye. He nodded slowly.

"You're right, Commissioner," he said. "We'll find the accomplice some other way. But I might have to use detectives."

There was an almost twanging silence, and then it snapped in a great splash of laughter which washed away the tension momentarily, and Quinn catechized Ochs and Nairn, of Burglary and Safe & Loft, in a much more relaxed fashion than he had the others.

Tutchek's turn was last, and Quinn said. "Well, you're our violent death specialist, Ben. Will we all be murdered in our beds? Don't answer that. I might not sleep tonight. How does your slate shape up as of today?"

Tutchek's voice balked and he cleared his throat, then flushed and swore at himself for feeling like that.

"Well, we've got that rape killing in South Branch Park," he said, pacing his words. "Nothing on that yet. No identification. A drowning came in this morning. Too soon for a report. That gin mill knifing last night in the Essex Hill section. Harry Muir and Mick Scanlon dug up a witness and found out the killer's name was Dinny Lennihan. They followed up a lead that Lennihan hopped a freight out of town right after the stabbing and put it on the teletype and kept it running.

"Lennihan was picked up in Wilmington this morning and is being returned here by Wilmington police."

"I didn't see that in the morning paper, Ben?"

"It was too late when we got the flash."

"Has a press release been prepared?"

"I haven't seen it yet."

Quinn frowned, looked down at his hands, then clasped them, one over the other, on his right knee. "Now, that brings up a point I've been wanting to make," he said. "Our policy on press releases is too haphazard. I don't like to keep harping on the election this November, but it illustrates the necessity and importance of good public relations. What does the average voter know about the candidates? Nothing except what he reads in the paper, actually. So when you get right down to it almost, the candidate who wins is the one with the best press notices. That goes for the police department, too, and not just because of the election. We want people to have confidence in the police, but what did they see when they picked up the paper this morning? 'City Violent Deaths Up Twenty Percent. Rape Victim Found Brutally Slain In South Branch Park. Two Hoodlums Beat-Rob Owner Of Liquor Shop. Man Knifed, Killer Flees.' Now, Ben here has that particular killer, and it was fast, efficient police action. Saul's boys—that's Alix Uri and Bill Hughes—did a fine job in putting the arm on the young punk who robbed and beat the liquor shop owner. But people don't know a thing about either of those crackerjack arrests because they weren't in the newspaper and right now they have the impression that there are violent deaths and beatings and rapes and robberies all over the city and the police haven't done a damn thing!"

"Newspapers operate on a strict time schedule, Will," Chief Sharkey protested. "The President himself couldn't get his face in the paper one minute after deadline unless he dropped dead or declared war."

"I'm coming to that," Quinn cut him short. "Our attitude toward press releases has been too hit or miss. *My* attitude. Not yours—mine. Your job is to enforce the law and arrest criminals. And you're doing a fine job. I told you I'm not putting anybody on the spot except myself. I think it's about time for us to have a definite public relations policy and stick to it. We are doing a good job in this city, damn it, and it's about time we let the people know. We're bound to get some negative publicity, like in the paper this morning, but that can be offset by a planned public relations policy. When we make an arrest or a real progressive step forward in an investigation, let's have the press release ready in time to meet the newspaper schedules. Let's not miss any more deadlines."

That was the end of the meeting. Quinn did not say he would hold anybody responsible, but it was understood, and the men drifted gloomily out into the dusty, clattering general squad room. Tutchek and the saturnine Lieutenant Stein walked diagonally across the bustling area of shirt-sleeved men.

"You know, Ben," said Stein, "the trouble with our Willie is that he really does have the good of the department at heart, and that's going to be rough on the rest of us."

"The trouble with Willie," Tutchek exploded, "is that the only thing straight about politics is the straight-party ticket in November."

"Yeah. There's that. But there'd be hell to pay if he caught us trying to get out the vote or stuff ballot boxes. There's going to be hell to pay, anyway. The only news he really wants in the paper is the arrest and conviction of enemy aliens. Can't you just see it? Before we're finished with this public relations crap, we'll be taking aspirin the size of manhole covers. And the damned thing about it is that he's eighty per cent right, in his cockeyed way. So long as we're stuck with the newspapers, let's make the most of it. And why shouldn't we tell the public how good we are? This is something we should have been doing all along and I'm in favor of it. Handled right, it will promote confidence in the police department and do some good. I only wish I didn't feel as if someone had just told me I can order anything I like for my last dinner."

"We'll live," said Tutchek shortly.

"I hope. Well, don't miss any deadlines."

"Yeah. And don't take any wooden Indians."

Stein turned into his office, and Tutchek continued around to the freight elevator corridor entrance to his own. He looked despairingly at the snowdrifts of paper work that mounded his desk, but tightened his jaw and sat down to reread Muir and Scanlon's report on the arrest of Lennihan, the knife killer.

He pulled the typewriter stand to him and in fifteen minutes rapped out a comprehensive press release. He reached over his desktop and flipped the switch on the intercom box.

"Come to my office for a minute, will you, Miss Lund," he said. "And bring your book."

She came in a few minutes later, carrying a green-covered stenographer's notebook. He ignored the cold, closed expression on her young face as she sat on the edge of the hard chair, facing him, notebook open and pencil poised. Tutchek leaned back and stared up at the ceiling.

"Head this 'Important,'" he dictated. "Division Order Effective Immediately. Henceforth, all press releases—underline 'all'—all press releases are to be prepared at the conclusion of the initial processing and will be a primary item as of this date, on the Major Case Procedural Check-Off Sheet. Additional press releases are to be prepared periodically during the progress of the investigation. This applies especially to the investigation of important new leads not classified confidential, and to all formal arrests. Underline 'all.' No press releases are to be discussed outside the Homicide Division or distributed to newspapers unless first cleared by the Commander. There will be no exception to this rule. Signed, Lieutenant Tutchek, Commander, and so forth. Type that in caps, Miss Lund, and thumb tack it to the bulletin board under 'Important.' Keep a carbon on your desk and call it to the attention of the men in case they forget to look at the board. Got that?"

"Yes, Lieutenant," she said stiffly.

"Good. Here's a release on the Lennihan case. Have Muir or Scanlon run it over to the press room. Is either Bierce or Caputo in the squad room?"

"No, sir. They went out about an hour ago. Only Muir, Scanlon, Tussy, Flavin, and Gilman are outside."

"Damn. I wanted to talk to them. Look. When they report in the next time, and if I don't happen to be here, tell them to leave a number where I can call back. Did anything come in while I was at Captain Mackenzie's office?"

"Nothing, Lieutenant."

"Thank God. Now get that Division Order up on the bulletin board before you do anything else."

She said, "Yes, Lieutenant," and marched out of the office her rubber heels stabbing damns on the brown linoleum. Policewoman Ruth Lund was not the happiest secretary in Headquarters.

Nor was Tutchek the happiest Commander. He knew Police Commissioner Quinn would expect a progress-being-made press release on both the rape killing and the drowning today. At the very least. This was the kind of pressure he could expect for a while. He looked again at the scatter of waiting paper work and drew a long, heavy breath. He just had to get to it now, but he felt dusty and tired. He got up and went outside to the men's room and washed his face with cold water. The telephone was not ringing when he returned, but the intercom was buzzing like a swarm of dispossessed wasps.

He flipped up the switch. "What is it?"

"Two calls just came in, Lieutenant. I've been trying to get you. The president of Mead-LaFarge Associates dropped dead in his office, and there's a man out on the window ledge on the fifteenth floor of the Hotel Stephen Crane, waving his arms, ready to jump. I was just going to send Detective Tussy—"

"All right, all right, all right. *Damnit!* Shut up for a minute. Send Flavin and Gilman over to Meade-LaFarge and I'll go out with Tussy on the suicide, or whatever it is. If Lieutenant Gillespie calls in on the East Coast Fisheries drowning, take the message. And get a phone number so I can call him back. And tell him about the new Division Order. And for Christ sake, call me at the Hotel Stephen Crane if anything important turns up ..."

The office door did not close entirely behind him after he strode out, and a small draft crept in and wavered across his desk. A paper stirred, lifted lazily, and drifted in floating seesaws to the floor, and then another, and another ...

Three

Policewoman Ruth Lund quickly typed the meager facts of the assignment for Detectives Jeff Flavin and George Gilman. Her darting fingers stabbed the keys with professional resentment, overriding for the moment her personal resentment at having to type it at all. This was the kind of meatless hash you got when civilians were allowed to phone in reports; it ought to be punishable by law. Under the printed heading, Reported By:, she rapped out, Franklin Todd, off. mgr., as if she were both a jury bringing in a verdict of guilty in the first degree, and the judge pronouncing sentence on Office Manager Franklin Todd—to be hanged by the neck until dead.

Or thirty days for obstructing justice, at the very least.

And this reminded Policewoman Lund that Lieutenant Tutchek's relegating her to the position of typist and watchdog at the outer gate of Homicide was tantamount to obstructing justice also. The place to enforce the law, she had been trained, was on the streets of the city, not on her behind in front of a little black monster with fifty teeth.

She gave the typewriter a last vicious jab, and pulled the sheets from the roller. Two strides took her from her desk to the door of Homicide's new squad room, which Lieutenant Tutchek had had partitioned off from the big general squad room. Four detectives were working at their desks, two were typing, and George Gilman lounged against the wall beside the water cooler, staring down into his paper cup with an expression of pained resignation on his homely face, as if he had just drunk a cup of hemlock by mistake. But it was not hemlock; it was the cooler. It was out of order and the water had the flavor of a steamed shroud.

Policewoman Lund did not call Gilman; it was not necessary. The moment she opened the squad room door, five pairs of eyes turned upon her with the wholehearted approval of men who knew an attractive young female when they saw one. She was not just a watchdog and typist to them. She was blonde and 36-23-34, and a man who demanded more than that was too ambitious for the police department. She nodded curtly at Gilman and went back to her desk, followed by those shrill notes of male appreciation, mistakenly called wolf-whistles. True, experienced wolves don't advertise.

She should have been pleased, even if secretly, but wasn't. Nothing about Homicide would please her so long as Tutchek kept her from the job for which she was trained. She was convinced that never before had she disliked anyone so much as she disliked Lieutenant Tutchek.

George Gilman came from the squad room a few minutes later and she handed him the assignment sheet, saying crisply, "Be sure to phone in when you get the doctor's report on the cause of death. Don't wait until you come back to the squad room."

Gilman looked mystified at her abrupt, businesslike manner, but nodded and glanced down at the sheet. "Well, well, dropped dead," he said, reading. "Where'd he drop from, the roof?"

"Maybe they'll tell you when you get there, Detective."

"Not from the guy that phoned this in. If he gives out any information, we might think something happened, and you know how it is when cops hang around—they could give the place a bad name."

"You'll give yourself a bad name if you continue to hang around here, Detective."

"What kind of bad name, Ruthie?" Gilman seemed innocently curious. "I bet you got one on the tip of your tongue just to surprise me."

She flushed, but ignored the mild rebuke. "Are there any further questions, Detective?"

"Not off hand. But if you think of that bad name while I'm out, write it on a piece of paper so's you don't forget. I think I've heard 'em all, but you never can tell." He nodded, grinned, and ambled back into the squad room, looking for his partner, Jeff Flavin.

Ruth Lund's flush deepened and remained, and she looked unhappily at the closed door. Actually, she did like this wide, homely man, whose parting grin had no more meanness in it than that of an amiable, knowing frog. She was the one who had been mean, and she realized it—and realized also that she would do it again and again, to any of the Homicide Division, simply because she so bitterly resented having to sit at a typewriter day after day as if she had no more police training than any empty-headed blonde borrowed from Clerical.

A green and white patrol car stood at the curb on Schuyler Boulevard in front of the Executive Building. Gilman and Flavin parked behind it, got out of their black squad car, and walked across the sidewalk to the tall entrance doors unhurried. They would have hurried had there been a need to do so, but there was no need. They'd had assignments like this before. A man drops dead in his office, and after a lot of fuss and hysterics, a doctor finally shows up and tells everybody what they knew all along—heart failure. But in the meanwhile two representatives of the Homicide Division must pretend they never heard of such a thing as a man dying from natural causes, and thereupon waste a couple hours solemnly examining the body to make sure there are no poisoned blowgun darts or assegais protruding from it, like Sherlock Holmes.

That's just about what it amounted to, for, according to the rules of criminal investigation, a dead body in an office is a suspicious character. Which is true enough in theory, but in practice it usually turned out that the body committed nothing more suspicious than a nuisance. If more people knew this, they'd stay home and drop dead in bed, which is, after all, the only decent and dignified way of doing it. However, until such a course of public education is instituted, hardworking detectives, like George Gilman and Jeff Flavin, have to go through the motions of suspicion-of-homicide until the local A.M.A. disciple arrives to give the corpse a clean bill of health. In a manner of speaking, that is.

That is why Gilman and Flavin did not rush, panting, to the side of Stewart Meade, so recently deceased. In their language, 'dropped dead' meant a medical history of a failing heart, and that, in turn, meant standing around the office upstairs, yawning at the files and paper clips, waiting for the doctor to come and confirm this final phase. They didn't dawdle, but George Gilman did stop at the newspaper and magazine stand in the lobby of the Executive Building to buy a package of Kents, which he certainly would not have done had he known Stewart Meade was lying on the floor of his office with an unexplained hole in his head. After that, he and Jeff Flavin waited for an express elevator to take them to the twenty-third floor instead of commandeering one. There was no reason to hurry; Office Manager Franklin Todd's telephoned report to Headquarters said nothing about violent death, and consequently neither did the assignment slip, which Ruth Lund had typed.

They were met in the foyer of the executive suite by a plump pink-and-blond man, who peevishly introduced himself as Theodore LaFarge, vice-president of Meade-LaFarge Associates. He was impatient for them to do what they had to do and get out, and scarcely listened when Flavin identified himself and George Gilman.

"I don't know why Todd had to bother you people with this," LaFarge fussed. "Things are bad enough without the police, God knows. The entire office is in an uproar, and your being here isn't helping matters any." There were charcoal smudges under his eyes and his face was flushed, but not from indignation. Theodore LaFarge had a hangover.

"Just a formality, Mr. LaFarge," said Flavin.

"We can dispense with it in this case."

"Did anybody phone for Mr. Meade's doctor."

"Doctor? Todd, probably. He phoned everybody else in the city." Then, as if aware that his hangover was showing, he mumbled, "Uh, yes, he called, but Doctor Coombs wasn't in. His office nurse is trying to locate him, but it might be an hour, two hours. Longer than that, maybe, if he's playing golf. All he does is play golf, if you ask me."

"We'll just have to wait, I suppose. Or I could call the Medical Examiner, if you want."

"Oh God no!"

Flavin nodded. He could see that LaFarge was desperate for a drink, a pick-me-up, and he said, "I'll get the routine out of the way while we're waiting, and save time later. I know you're busy. Was anybody with Mr. Meade when happened?"

"Uh—I don't think so. What I mean is, I heard Miss Burkhardt scream—that's his secretary. Todd got here a little ahead of me. She was having hysterics and Stewart—I mean Mr. Meade was lying inside on the floor. We didn't know what happened. We put Mr. Meade on the couch and were trying to make him comfortable—" He stopped, shook his head, and said shortly, "He was dead when Miss Burkhardt found him and that's all there's to it. I see no reason to make a police case of it, do you?"

Flavin said patiently, "It isn't, Mr. LaFarge. We have to have a report of all deaths for the record, that's all. I know this must have been a shock, so why don't you rest a little. These officers can't go back on duty until I take a copy of their notes. Routine."

"Of course. I—" LaFarge looked down at his pudgy hands; they were shaking. "I'll be in my office." He dipped his head stiffly and walked out of the foyer.

Flavin looked at the two patrolmen, who'd been listening from the doorway to Meade's private office. They shrugged and made their faces as noncommittal as possible. They were well aware that LaFarge had done his best to give Flavin a bad time, and that Flavin couldn't have done anything about it, but it wasn't a uniformed cop's place to remark on the fact that a policeman's lot is not a happy one.

In fact, it was not a uniformed cop's place to remark on anything until asked. Not to a detective, at any rate, and especially not to a detective who'd been holding his temper as long as Flavin had. Some detectives had a bad habit of letting go of their tempers at the first opportunity, and when that happened, it was much better if the uniformed cop didn't breathe, because breathing might make him conspicuous, and if a detective had just been given a hard time, nothing irked his blood pressure so much as a conspicuous cop, and more than likely he'd seize the opportunity to point out the uniformed cop's faults in detail and remind him that a policeman's lot is not a happy one, and if there was one thing a cop didn't need, it was to be reminded. Therefore they kept their mouths shut and tried to look like wainscoting.

Flavin was a compact six-footer with sandy hair, level gray eyes and a tough shanty-Irish air of authority. His mouth quirked in a wry grin. "Well, boys," he said, "did he try to make your ears bleed, too?"

They relaxed and answered with a rueful grin of their own, but did not commit themselves beyond, "Well, you know how it goes." They were smart cops and knew how it went.

Flavin said, "I suppose we'd better take a look," and they stepped aside as he and George Gilman walked into the private office. Gilman winked and whispered, "Chickee, the cops." Less than a year ago, he himself had been in uniform, and knew how they felt.

Meade's body lay peacefully on a long green top-grain leather upholstered sofa against the wall on the windowless side of the office. His face was turned to the back of the sofa and his left cheek rested on a folded chair cushion someone had placed under his head. Gilman and Flavin looked at him, then around the office at the rug, the desk, the drapes at the windows, the walls, but there was nothing to interest them—no blood, no sign of violence, nothing hastily scrubbed, wiped, or dusted and rearranged. They felt vaguely depressed, bored, and impatient, as they might at the funeral services of an uncle they hadn't seen for thirty years and never really knew.

Gilman took the uniformed policemen's notes for his report, and there was not much in those either. According to the patrol car radio log, the dispatcher called them at 10:47 A.M. and ordered them to this address from which an unclassified death had been reported, and to preserve the scene until detectives arrived from Homicide to take charge. At the scene (here) they found the subject, Stewart Meade, on couch in private office. Witnesses present in said private office were Theodore LaFarge, vice-president of company; Franklin Todd, office manager of company; and Emily Burkhardt private secretary to deceased. Emily Burkhardt was in state of hysteria and unable to give information more than follows: heard subject fall to floor in private office, subject was alone, subject did not call for aid or utter any other cry, found subject lying on floor, subject was dead. Questioning discontinued because of hysteria, and sedative administered by T. LaFarge.

"What kind of sedative?" asked Gilman.

The cops shrugged and one of them said, "Pills."

Gilman nodded. It didn't really make any difference, and it wasn't important. He'd asked from force of habit, and what the hell, he had to write something in his report, didn't he?

The cops questioned LaFarge and Todd but did not learn anything further. Todd thought Stewart Meade still alive—or at least did not realize he was dead, and called the police because he thought that the quickest way to get a doctor, but while he was calling, LaFarge cried out, "Oh my God, he's dead!" Todd seemed a sane, sensible kind of guy, but so far as the cops were concerned, LaFarge was a hysterical horse's ass and a rummy, to boot. He had at a bottle in his office and kept running in for a nip while waiting for the detectives to arrive—the kind of jerk, if he went to church, he couldn't wait to get home again and have a drink.

The two uniformed policemen left, and a few minute later Theodore LaFarge peeped into the private office, gave Gilman and Flavin a dirty look, and disappeared again, leaving behind a smoky aura of bonded bourbon.

It was a scant five minutes afterward that LaFarge marched triumphantly in with the doctor, a little drunk from all his pick-me-ups, but Gilman and Flavin were too comatose from ennui to notice or care.

Four

Lieutenant Tutchek, Commander of Homicide, was back in his office. There had been no suicide; no one had jumped out of any window on the fifteenth floor of the Hotel Stephen Crane. But it was not entirely a false alarm. When the squad car, Detective William Tussy at the wheel, braked to a tire-shredding stop in front of the hotel and Tutchek sprang out to the sidewalk, a man *was* standing on a window ledge of the fifteenth floor and he *was* waving his arms—waving them in a very businesslike manner, earning a living. He was the window washer.

Now, there are police lieutenants who become irked and irate after hurtling through the city at seventy miles an hour only to find a window washer at the end of the jaunt. They make loud noises and behave as if someone had made a fool of them. They look around for somebody to chew out, and when they return to Headquarters they chew out the dispatcher, and had there been such a misdemeanor, they'd have clapped the window washer himself in jail on a charge of orderly conduct with intent to frustrate an officer of the law.

Tutchek did not feel frustrated. He climbed heavily back into the car, looked up once again at the man on the window ledge, breathed, "What a way to make a living!" and on that breath rode a small prayer of thanksgiving. No, Lieutenant Tutchek did not feel defrauded. Window-jumping was not his favorite spectator sport, for what happened at the end of a fifteen-story leap was no bed of roses. His stomach had not yet descended to its proper position from his throat when he returned to his office; he and his stomach had attended the scene of a few jumps in the past, and it was a case of stimulus and response; it took time to regain status quo.

"Want me to write up the report, Chief?" Detective Tussy asked.

"I'll do it myself, Bill. Thanks."

"It's no trouble, Chief."

"I'll do it." Tutchek was short. Tussy could write reports. Better than anyone in the division maybe. So what? This was one report he wouldn't know how to write. He'd do it by the book—all the same old stilted phrases—and when he finished it would sound as though somebody deliberately turned in a false alarm, and Cap Mackenzie or Chief Sharkey would read it and frown and wonder if Tutchek were getting soft-headed, not making an arrest. Some things you couldn't trust to anybody but yourself.

Later, when he saw the snowdrifts of paper work still mounded on his desk, he grimaced and half wished he had let Tussy write this one up. But no. He shook his head stubbornly. This was one of the things you had to do yourself, and if there wasn't time, you had to make the time. He sat down at the desk and stared at the untidy heaps of reports, general orders, notes, memos, and all the rest of the crap, with growing dismay. It was easy enough to say, make the time, but what did you make it out of, rubber balloons? elastic bands? old inner tubes? He lit a cigarette, hung it from a corner of his mouth, and reached doggedly for the nearest heap of papers.

The phone rang and he thought, *oh Christ!* He picked up the phone. "Homicide. Lieutenant Tutchek."

"Ah yes, Lieutenant Tutchek," that was the dry voice of Councilman Selig, the powerful supervisor of public works, a thin sarcastic man with a tongue like a garden rake. "Just what the hell do those two storm troopers of yours think they're up to over at Meade-LaFarge?"

Tutchek was caught off base. He knew, of course, that Meade-LaFarge was the million-dollar real-estate development and construction corporation, but could not recall sending any of his crew there on an assignment. And this wouldn't be the first time City Hall was full of escaping gas. Still, you had to butter them up....

He started peaceably, "Hold on a second, Councilman, while I—"

"Hold on hell!" Selig interrupted. "I don't want any Goddamned stalling, or don't you know what's going on in your division Lieutenant?"

"Oh come on, relax, Councilman. I just got back from an alleged suicide and—"

"I don't give a damn if you just got back from Siam! You get those two clowns of yours out of Meade-LaFarge, and get them out now. They've got the whole office in an uproar, and I want them out of there. Do you understand? *Out!*"

Tutchek gripped the phone in his huge left hand and hunched over it, his broad face crimson with the bright blood of anger.

"Just a minute Councilman Selig—just hold your Goddamn horses! I don't know what the hell you're talking about, in the first place, but if those detectives *are* from my division and they *are* at Meade-LaFarge on legitimate business, they can throw the whole damned office out in the street and jump on it, if they have to. And if they do, you can be good and sure the office needs throwing out in the street and I'll go and help them if necessary."

"What? What's that? What'd you say?"

"Maybe your department's full of clowns, but my men happen to know their business. They don't hand out parking tickets. This is the Homicide Division, not Traffic—"

Councilman Selig's voice crackled in a shorted high-tension fury, and Tutchek slammed his phone back into its cradle. He waited a moment until he was sure the roar had seeped out of his voice, then reached and snapped down the lever of his intercom box.

"What's all this about Meade-LaFarge, Miss Lund?" he demanded.

"That's the call that came in when you were on your way out to the Hotel Stephen Crane suicide report. You told me to assign Gilman and Flavin."

"Yes, I remember, but what's it all about, please!"

"A Mr. Stewart Meade dropped dead in his office, that's all. There were no details."

"But that's over three-quarters of an hour ago. Haven't Gilman or Flavin telephoned in since then?"

"Not yet, Lieutenant. Is something wrong?"

"No, no, no, not a thing, Miss Lund. You said 'dropped dead', didn't you? Well, it's beginning to look as though he might have been pushed. I think I'll run over there and see what's going on. Call downstairs and have a car out front for me."

He flicked the intercom switch and cut off the connection. He looked at the scatter of paper work that covered the top of his desk, and groaned. He'd never get through that mess now, never; it was one thing after another.

He pushed up wearily from his chair and plodded out into the Homicide squad room. With a prickle of irritation, he spied Detective William Tussy at the bank of file cabinets across the room, straightening up the folders inside one of the drawers. Not looking for anything, mind you, just neatening them up. That's the reason the boys called him Fussy Tussy; things had to be neat.

Smothering his irritation, Tutchek called, "Say, Bill, make out that phony suicide report, will you. But—uh—hold it till I get back. Don't send it through."

Tussy's neat gray face lightened. "On the double, Chief." If there was one thing he enjoyed, it was making out a report, a nice orderly report with all the facts and everything catalogued and tidy.

Five

There was no uproar at Meade-LaFarge, as Councilman Selig claimed; but then, Tutchek had not expected one. He knew City Hall; when the political dogs wanted to make a stink, they'd howl that Chanel Number Five smelled like sewage, from the belief—gained from successful experiences of that kind—that if they howled loud enough and often enough everybody would come to believe it really did smell like sewage.

On the other hand, though there may not have been an uproar in the executive suite of Meade-LaFarge, things were far from calm. Counting the dead man on the big leather sofa, there were nine men in the president's private office, and the only one who was really calm was the corpse.

First, Assistant Medical Examiner Herbert Winkler was exchanging politely sharp words with a tall man-of-distinction type, who seemed to be some sort of medical boff on his own, possibly a doctor. Butting into the conversation at every opportunity was a flushed plump man in a rumpled charcoal-gray suit, wgray suit, whose interruptions consisted chiefly of, "We don't have to stand for this and we won't, damnit!" To one side of this embattled group stood a slimmer, shorter man, biting his lip as if embarrassed by the repetitive shenanigans of the unfocused plump one.

Watching with cold eyes was another group, formed by detectives Gilman and Flavin and two crime laboratory technicians from the mobile unit truck parked downstairs in front of the building on Schuyler Boulevard. The mobile unit Lab men were Bert Daly and Jerry Straub, all-round experts with photography, fingerprints, moulage, bloodstains, charred documents and almost any form of physical evidence or clues that they or the detectives might turn up during the course of an investigation. The mobile unit truck downstairs was as complete a crime laboratory as could be crammed into so confined a space—a compact darkroom and such scientific equipment for on-the-spot information as reagent chemicals and even a ballistics comparison microscope.

Lieutenant Tutchek did not make an entrance with a fanfare of bugles, but silence fell immediately when he walked into the office. He ignored the corporation men and their doctor and even the corpse, but nodded at Gilman and Flavin, who came forward to meet him.

"Hello, boys," he said. "How's it going?"

Flavin glanced at the other group. "There seems to be a difference of opinion, Ben."

"There does? In what way?"

Before Flavin could reply, the flushed plump man lurched across the office and planted himself before Tutchek, swaying.

"If you're another damn stupid cop, get out," he blustered.

Tutchek looked down at him. "You're drunk," he said calmly. "I think you'd better sober up before you get in trouble, sonny."

"Hah? Hah? Hey, see here, I'm a frenna Councilman Selig—"

"That doesn't surprise me a bit. Sit down and shut up."

He poked out his forefinger and the plump one gasped, staggered backward several feet and collapsed into a leather lounge chair, holding his chest and trying to breathe.

Tutchek turned to the Assistant Medical Examiner. "What's the story, Herb?"

The medical man-of-distinction held up a restraining hand. "A moment, sir. I'm Doctor Coombs. May I say a word?"

Tutchek said, "Later," and dipped his head at Winkler. "Let's have it, Herb."

Coombs turned red and his neck swelled. "This is preposterous!" he exploded, and strode from the office with the high head of a man on his way to a telephone.

To ease the tension, Tutchek asked mildly, "Well now, who's *he* a friend of?"

"A doctor like him, Ben," George Gilman's was voice solemn, "he'd be a personal friend of the Holy Ghost, wouldn't he?"

No one laughed, but there was a sound of several easier breaths being drawn, Theodore LaFarge's not among them. But there were no jokes and nobody was really amused, nor would they be amused until the time came when the corpse could sit up and enjoy the joke also. In the meanwhile, violent death was not funny.

Tutchek nodded at Winkler and the Assistant M.E. reached down and turned Meade's unresisting head so that the full left profile could be seen. Tutchek's eyes widened at the sight of that dark shadow on the lifeless head, just above and behind the left ear, the shadow that was so much darker and more intense than a real shadow that it could be nothing other than a splintered hole through the bone of the skull.

"Just dropped dead, did he?" said Tutchek after a pause. "Just plain ordinary dropped. Oh Christ."

"As a matter of fact, Ben," said Winkler, "it's exactly what happened!"

"With a hole in his head the size of that?"

"Yes, with a hole in his head the size of that. And he's not the first who got up and walked away with part of his head gone, Ben. It doesn't happen all the time, but it happens. You know that as well as I do."

"I've heard of it. But it's different when you see it yourself."

Tutchek glanced quickly around the office. Winkler was quite right—it couldn't have happened here, whatever it was that happened. Head wounds were especially messy, and here there was no blood—no blood on the clothing, no blood on the rug. Hell, not even any blood on the hair, which meant that Meade must have cleaned himself up after that piece was knocked out of his skull. Brrrr, it was enough to give you the willies—Meade was as good as dead the instant it happened. No one could go on living with a crater of bone splinters like that in his head, so it was a dead man who showered, cleaned himself, shaved, dressed himself in a clean shirt and a freshly pressed suit, just so he could go to work and drop dead in his office. These were not idle or morbid speculations, for Tutchek could see that, without the breaks, this could develop into a detective's nightmare—a wide-open investigation.

"Well, let's have it, Herb," he said. "How'd he get it?"

Winkler moved his shoulders unhappily. He was a slight, pale young man with a receding chin, a junior member of the medical examiner's staff who looked as if he could be pushed around by anyone with a louder voice than his own self-deprecating drawl—until you noticed that the iris of his eyes, pierced by jet-black pupils, contained the blue-gray hardness of January ice.

"That's the prize question, Ben," he said. "No matter how I answer it, I'm out on a limb. Joe Blow could come along and say something else happened, and be just as right. In theory. Like, he was taking a siesta in Hialeah and got kicked by a flamingo."

"Only he wasn't."

"Right—only he wasn't. So I'll go out on a limb, and say he was shot. The bone fragmentation is particularly clean, which to my mind proves he was hit with tremendous force by a small object, such as a bullet traveling at extremely high speed. A slower, heavier weapon would have left a more jagged wound, and the edges would not have pointed so decidedly toward the back of the head and in so straight a line. Another thing, the wound is smaller at the point of impact and expands at the exit, a characteristic of bullet wounds. If we're very lucky, a microscope may show metallic traces at the edges of the wound, but that's not a bet I'd care to risk a hard-earned dollar on. It wasn't a contact shot or even close to it, so don't count on any sign of powder tattooing of the skin for proof of the shot. Furthermore, it was a glancing shot, almost a miss, so there's no possible way of telling the calibre of the gun. All in all"—Winkler's apologetic smile barely moved his lips—"he could just as easily have been kicked by a flamingo."

"What theory does Doctor Coombs favor?"

The ice in Winkler's eye glinted up at Tutchek. "Doctor Coombs is in favor of any theory that will not involve a police investigation. If I said the victim fell out of an unmoored balloon and stepped on himself, I am certain Doctor Coombs would approve wholeheartedly. But don't think he's a dope, Ben. He isn't. He knows on which side the dollar is buttered. And that limb I've gone out on, there's room for you, too."

It flashed through Tutchek's mind that he would probably save himself a lot of grief and sweat if he remained neutral and let the Medical Examiner's office fight it out with City Hall, but that's all it did—flashed through and kept right on going.

"Move over, Herb," he said. "And I hope it's a nice big limb, because you're going to have lots of company. I don't suppose there's any way of telling when he took the slug, is there?"

Winkler laughed mirthlessly. "You're going to love me, Ben. I'm going to be a big help to you. I can fix the time of death because there were witnesses. An hour ago. As for the shot—let's see, when did the Chinese invent gunpowder? Hell, how can I tell how long a man can walk around with a hole like that in his skull. A week? Ten days? Ten minutes? Don't forget the bone splinters working themselves into the brain, because that's what killed him. That's the problem: how long does it take a tiny sliver of bone to penetrate brain tissue by millimeters? But here's something you can go on—the cerebellum, or little brain, was damaged and that would affect his speech and general motor activity. In others words, he'd probably act as if he were drunk, and that would hardly go unnoticed for any length of time, so it's a safe guess to say he was shot sometime during the past twenty-four hours. That's all I can tell you till we do a P.M.—if we get to do a P.M. If we have to ask permission, there won't be any. I hope you're grateful for my assistance, Ben."

"Yeah, sure. I can't thank you enough, so I won't."

"Oh—here's just one more thing. This bruise"—Winkler touched a faint bluish discoloration on the left side of Meade's neck with his thin forefinger. "*That* is less than twenty-four hours old. I examined it very closely. It's a round bruise and there's no break in the skin. I think it was caused by a knuckle. Somebody took a swing at him with a fist. That's just about as wild a guess as I could make, but what the hell, when you're out on a limb, you can't get any outer. Anyway, that's only for your information to fix the time of shooting to the past twenty-four hours, as I said before. You know, Ben, speaking of being out on a limb, there's one nice thing about it"—his blue-gray eyes glinted again—"you get a wonderful view."

"Yeah," said Tutchek, "you can even see them sharpening the ax. Order the morgue wagon to pick him up, will you, Herb?"

Winkler looked up sharply into Tutchek's broad face, and whistled. "Isn't that pushing it just a little, Ben?" he asked softly. "Couldn't you stretch out the processing till you see what turns up? Play it safe?"

"Have them pick him up, Herb."

Winkler said, "Hold your hats, kids," grinned to himself as he bent to pick up his bag, and walked out.

Tutchek turned to the two Lab men. "Break out your camera and take some pictures, boys. The show's on the road."

Then to Flavin, "Call Miss Lund, Jeff, and tell her to get, let's see, uh, Harry Muir and Rory Scanlon over here right away. Got your notes together, George?"—this to Gilman—"I'll go over them with you."

He looked across the office with distaste at Theodore LaFarge. The plump man was pale and sweating and looked as if he were about to be sick.

All those bourbon pick-me-ups, it seemed, had now let him down with a jolt. Tutchek tilted his chin at the other Meade-LaFarge executive, who thus far had sensibly held his tongue.

"Maybe you'd better take Mr. LaFarge to a comfort station," he suggested. "I think he could use a little comfort. I'm Lieutenant Tutchek, by the way. You?"

"Todd," said the sensible-looking man, "Franklin Todd. I'm the office manager."

"Do you know anything about what went on?"

"I'm sorry. Perhaps Miss Burkhardt can help you. She found, that is, she heard Mr. Meade fall and—well, Mr. Meade was dead then, of course."

"Miss Burkhardt? His secretary?"

"She was Mr. Meade's private secretary."

"Why isn't she here? Where is she now?"

"I believe she's asleep in the ladies' lounge, Lieutenant."

Tutchek stared. "Did you say asleep?"

Todd's hands made vague, embarrassed gestures. "Well, she was hysterical, you see, and uh, Mr. LaFarge gave her some sedatives. It was really quite necessary, Lieutenant."

Tutchek turned his head to Gilman, who coughed and ducked his head twice. "Two of the uniform boys were here at the time, Ben," he amplified. "They said she was in a bad way. She needed something."

Tutchek turned back to Todd, frowning. "So he gave her some sedatives, eh? What sedatives, and how much?"

Todd flicked a glance at the sagging LaFarge from the ends of his eyes and it was plain that he wished the plump vice-president sober enough to answer these questions himself. He sighed.

"Nembutal, I believe," he said. "Two capsules."

Tutchek's face darkened and Gilman said quickly, "She's okay, Ben. Doc Winkler looked at her. He said let her sleep it off."

Tutchek turned abruptly and strode to the end of the office, stood for a moment with his back to them, then swung around and pointed an iron finger at LaFarge.

"Get that drunken son-of-a-bitch out of here and lock him up some place before I do something he'll be sorry for," he snapped at Todd. "Give him a hand, George, and if you drop him, don't let it bother you."

Quite drunk and barely able to stand, LaFarge protested feebly as Todd and George Gilman walked him from the office between them, holding him upright by the armpits. Tutchek watched grimly.

"I hope they do drop the bastard," he said, "down an elevator shaft. Did you get La Lund, Jeff?"

"Harry and Rory are on their way."

"Thanks. Maybe you'd better take a look at that Burkhardt girl and see how she's doing. And if you run into that fart, Doc Coombs, drag him along with you. *Two* Nembutals. Oh Jesus!"

Tutchek closed the door after Flavin left the office, drew a deep breath, and slowly took a cigar from the breast pocket of his jacket. He put it in his mouth but forgot to light it as he looked bleakly around the office.

Just exactly what would have happened here in this office, he wondered, if he hadn't turned up when he did. He had not forgotten that Flavin and Gilman hadn't called in, and if he'd waited for that call, he might still be waiting. He'd talk to them about that later. And there was Herb Winkler. Herb was a good boy, and now that he'd made his pitch, he'd stand by it, he could be depended on not to back down. But here was the question: would Herb have gone out on that limb if he, Tutchek, hadn't been there to give moral support? Possibly. Probably. But still, it was one of those things you couldn't be sure of. Suppose a call had come from Councilman Selig, threatening death and destruction. What would Herb have done? He was only a young doctor, a junior on the M.E.'s staff, his career still ahead of him. Would Winkler have said, Yes, Councilman, I see what you mean, Councilman, anything you say, Councilman. Tutchek didn't think so, but on the other hand, Winkler did not officially go out on that limb until after he had walked in and taken charge of things.

And so there he was, back at the beginning—if you wanted to be sure a thing was done right, you had to do it yourself. Even Flavin and Gilman had slipped up in not making that phone call to Headquarters— and they were experienced men who knew the score.

And that reminded him—Homicide now had a major case on its hands, and Chief of Detectives Captain Mackenzie had to be notified. That was regulations, and if he was going to run this investigation, it had to be done by the book.

He was halfway across the office to the phone on Meade's desk when he saw the picture.

An artist's drawing, to be exact, in a forty-by-thirty frame, and it hung prominently on the wall behind the desk—a strongly colored elevation of bright, shining modern apartments, grouped around a large central mall in which were shade trees, a walk with benches, a wading pool shaped like a Teddy bear, and a fully equipped playground. A housing project. Beneath the picture was the name of it in bold black script—Mayflower Village.

Tutchek stopped with his hand half raised to his cigar, stopped dead. There wasn't a man, woman, or child in the city of Hudson who had not heard of Mayflower Village. It had been written about, shouted against, portrayed, and applauded in the newspapers, Sunday supplements, and magazines for months. Mayflower Village was more than a nice-colored picture on the wall. It was Slum Clearance, and the city was subsidizing it to the tune of five million, two hundred thousand dollars. No wonder Councilman Selig had gone to bat for dear old Meade-LaFarge. So Meade-LaFarge really did have influence in City Hall. In fact, you might say in a way, that in this instance Meade-LaFarge *was* City Hall, and that included Vice-President Theodore LaFarge, at present sleeping off an early morning bourbon binge in the comfort station.

Tutchek did not have to think twice to realize how major this major case was going to be. He nodded once, sharply, as if to snap down the visor on a battle helmet, then picked up the telephone to call his superior, Chief of Detectives Captain Mackenzie.

What was it Herb Winkler had said—"Hold your hats, kids ..."

Six

Tutchek gave his report in a crisp businesslike manner, giving only the bare facts, for it was much too early in the investigation to offer or even have an opinion. This was not a full official report, anyway. According to regulations, this was *Item 2*, of *42*, on the Major Case Procedural Check-Off Sheet: Supervisors notification, Homicide & Shift Commander Asst. & Chief. Tutchek's presence at the scene was also according to regulations. The book required a commanding officer to oversee the processing of a major case.

As most violent deaths are major, and as violent death is the primary concern of Homicide, Lieutenant Tutchek kept pretty busy attending all the scenes. In fact, the only scenes he was not forced to attend were those at which the cause of death was so open-and-shut that even the witnesses could tell what happened. With a fifty-fifty degree of accuracy, that is. Too, he was the one who had to detail extra men to the case, if necessary, and enlist the aid of other detective divisions when the facts uncovered took the investigation into the field of their specialties. For instance, if it turned out that Meade had been shot after a holdup, Tutchek would call upon the Robbery Division to round up all suspects known to specialize in armed robbery. But no matter who he detailed or who he called upon for assistance, Tutchek alone was responsible for the conduct of the investigation, and if there were a half-dozen other cases being conducted at the same time, he was responsible for them also. Sometimes it seemed to Tutchek that he was responsible for everything in the world, including mumps.

He notified Captain Mackenzie that Stewart Meade had been shot (in the opinion of Assistant Medical Examiner Herbert Winkler) and the investigation was proceeding from there. He did not mention homicide, nor even the suspicion of homicide. Gunshot or no gunshot, there were too many other possibilities, suicide or accidental shooting among them. One of the worst mistakes an investigating officer can commit is to open a case with a preconceived opinion, and the mere thought of a mistake at this time was enough to give Tutchek chills and fever. Anyway, he was too experienced to make that one.

The Captain kept saying, "Uhuh—uhuh—uhuh—" then finally, "Well, thanks, Ben. Let me know how it develops."

Tutchek hung up slowly, frowning, disappointed by Mackenzie's casual responses. Was the Old Man slipping? No questions, no interest, no nothing, except that deadpan "—uhuh—" This wasn't the case of a wino found dead in an alley. Or maybe, just maybe, this was Mackenzie's way of playing it safe, of keeping hands off until he saw which way the cat was going to jump. There was a reason why he was called Foxy Grandpa or Foxy around Headquarters. There'd also been a time when he'd also been known as Iron Pants. That was during the years he was the toughest precinct commander The Point ever had, and when you consider that The Point was the toughest precinct in a tough city, Mackenzie could hardly be called a lily of the field. No one ever made that mistake, not even once, for Iron Pants Mackenzie had not exactly mellowed with the years.

Tutchek turned to the two mobile Lab technicians, who were completing their share of the processing. There was no sense taking pictures of the body, for it had been moved to the big sofa, but the fatal head wound was photographed from several angles, for future reference, if necessary. Bert Daly was folding his photographic equipment and Jerry Straub had the contents of Meade's pockets laid out on a narrow console table at the side of the office—a wallet containing a little over two hundred dollars, driver's license, registration for a 'lt. grn. Cad.,' some business cards, a key ring with five keys, a white handkerchief, and seventy-eight cents in coins.

"The usual nothing," he told Tutchek. "Want to take a look before I package it?"

Tutchek poked at the uninteresting collection with his forefinger, turned over the business cards to see if anything was written on the backs, shrugged, and asked, "Did the clothes tell you anything, Jerry?"

Straub glanced at the head wound which looked so innocuous until you knew what it was. "Well—he put on everything clean and fresh this morning, Ben. You can tell by the wrinkles. Or lack of them. No lint or dust in the cuffs of his pants. White buckskin shoes and not a smudge on them. He changed everything this morning, from his underwear out." He sounded a little awed.

Tutchek shook his head. "Anything else?" He did not want to be awed, he did not want to marvel; all he wanted was to get this one off the Pending hook and into the Solved file.

Straub hesitated but Bert Daly spoke up: "We don't want to contradict, Ben, but Doc Winkler said this must have happened during the past twenty-four hours because Meade might have acted drunk and somebody'd notice. You know? But yesterday was the Fourth, a holiday, and who pays attention to a drunk on a holiday? I mean, lots of guys are sober all week but get plotzed on Saturdays, Sundays and holidays, and nobody gives it a second thought. See what I mean?"

Tutchek saw. "You guys are a big help," he growled. Still, it was something that definitely had to be considered; Meade could have been shot on the evening of the third after he left the office.

And if he was, a pinpointed investigation of the Fourth or as the early morning hours of the fifth would be a merry-go-round. Tutchek thought, *oh Christ*, as if another weight had been added to the load he was already carrying. It just went to show, even the book couldn't keep you from pulling a boner. He'd never have thought of that holiday angle if Daly and Straub hadn't brought it up. What or whom could you trust if you couldn't trust the book or yourself?

He turned as Gilman re-entered the office, followed shortly by Flavin. He took them into a brief huddle and came up with a few bits of essential information: Meade lived in the Sutton, a residential hotel on Park Place, opposite Washington Park, five blocks north of the Executive Building to which he walked to work every morning for the exercise; he was a bachelor without any known family. Gilman had had the forethought to get these necessary facts from Office Manager Franklin Todd, who was beginning to seem the only sane executive in the Meade-LaFarge Associates organization.

"The first thing," Tutchek told Flavin, "is to see if you can get anything else from Todd—where Meade was yesterday and the night of the third, his habits, friends and so forth."

"Girl friends," said Flavin.

"Girl friends? What girl friends?"

"The clothes," Flavin tilted his chin at the once handsome white-maned man lying so still on the big sofa. "Glen plaid suit, white shoes, bow tie. It's a cinch he didn't dress up like that to impress the hired help. Just dig them crazy threads, Ben. When these elderly gents decorate themselves like that, it's usually because they don't want the girls to think they're not as young as they used to be, but still full of juice and juniper. Offhand, I'd say brother Meade's interest in the girls was a little more than academic. Five'll get you ten. A bet?"

"What are you?" asked Tutchek dryly, "A wolfologist, or something?"

Flavin's eyes widened in surprise—and then he understood several things simultaneously: he'd been so stupefied at his blunder in taking it for granted that Meade had died of heart failure, that he immediately committed the second blunder of not reporting the death to Tutchek by phone—but Tutchek had turned up anyway, which meant that City Hall had called him to ask what the hell—now Tutchek was sore and had every right to be. Flavin waited for the blast, but it didn't come, and he understood that, too: the two Lab men in were in the room and Tutchek wasn't the kind of officer who'd chew out a man in front of others, no matter how sore he was. Flavin wished he could tell Ben how sorry he was—and he could have done it had Ben been just one of the men in the Division, like himself, but Ben was the commanding officer now, and this was one of the things you, well, just couldn't say to a commanding officer, that's all. You took your chewing-out when it came, and made damn sure not to pull the same boo-boo a second time.

Tutchek continued, "Find out what you can, but don't concentrate on women just because the guy wore a bow tie. I'm going over to the Hotel Sutton. Call me there if anything comes up, and don't forget." He dipped his head at the two lab technicians and George Gilman, "Let's go, boys."

He started out, but half turned in the doorway to say, "Keep the secretary here till I get back. I might want to talk to her. And one more thing—don't release the body to the morgue wagon. In fact, call up and tell them to forget it for the time being. Or till after I check his apartment at the hotel. In the meantime, keep everything the way it is."

That was better. He was getting things under control. You didn't necessarily have to play the angles, but you damn well had to cover them. All of them. And yourself, as well. He could learn a thing or two just watching how Foxy Grandpa fielded the fast ones. In fact, Foxy was a lesson in procedure all by himself, and ought to be included in the Academy curriculum. What Every Young Officer Should Know.

Seven

Before leaving the Executive Building, Tutchek called Headquarters and spoke to Policewoman Lund.

"Is Lieutenant Gillespie there?" he demanded impatiently.

"No, sir," her voice was unthawed. "He telephoned in about fifteen minutes ago about the East Coast Fisheries drowning."

"Well? What did he say?"

"I was looking for my notes, Lieutenant," the sound of turning notebook pages crackled crisply. "Here it is. Lieutenant Gillespie said the body was examined by Assistant Medical Examiner Harold Casperson, who pronounced the woman dead from drowning. The head wounds, though serious, were not the cause of death. She was struck twice by a heavy instrument. Dr. Casperson was unable to tell the nature of the instrument. She was struck from the front and from the left side. Lieutenant said he took the evening gown to the DeJongg Shop on Madison Place. The dress was identified by Arnaud DeJongg, who designed it and also owns the shop. Mr. DeJongg told Lieutenant Gillespie that the gown was purchased by a Mrs. Helen Widdicomb three days ago, on July the second. Lieutenant Gillespie questioned Mr. DeJongg and learned that Mrs. Widdicomb was divorced several years ago and now lives at 27 Pomander Walk, in the Stone Bridge section of the city, with her sister, Mrs. Esther Langston, a widow. Mrs. Widdicomb is independently wealthy. She is approximately thirty-five years of age. Mr. DeJongg knew nothing of the circumstances of her death, and was shocked when he learned of it."

"Where is Lieutenant Gillespie now? Where can I reach him?"

"He didn't leave a number, Lieutenant. He and Detective Koch are trying to find out where Mrs. Widdicomb was either thrown or knocked or fell into the river. He said he would call back in about an hour or so."

"What are Kitteridge and Stefano doing?"

"Lieutenant Gillespie sent detectives Kitteridge and Stefano to 27 Pomander Walk to question Mrs. Esther Langston. The Lieutenant said it was obvious Mrs. Widdicomb was out socially last night, and he wants to learn the name of her escort."

Tutchek said, "Good." It was a relief to know that Alec Gillespie was handling things in his thorough, methodical fashion. "Did you tell the

Lieutenant about the new Division Order about press releases?"

"Yes, sir. He said, "Oh Jesus, what am I supposed to do if I meet a reporter, say 'No spik English?'" There was a note of flat satisfaction in Policewoman Lund's cold voice. "He said also that he would pass the information along to the men with him and that nothing would be released to any of the newspapers until he discussed the case with you personally."

Tutchek was irritated by her tone of voice, and felt like asking what the hell was eating her, but bit back the words. He was getting just a little tired of her continued chilly hostility, but dismissed it from his mind. He had more important things.

"Did Bierce or Caputo call in yet, Miss Lund?"

"Yes, sir. Shortly before Lieutenant Gillespie. The girl in the rape killing has not been identified as yet and they had nothing new to report. I told them you said you wanted to see them and they are on their way to Headquarters now."

"Oh *hell!* Never mind. Look. Tell them to wait for me. I don't know how long I'll be, but I'll be back as soon as possible. Have them see what we've turned up in the way of sex offenders."

"I checked that, Lieutenant. I thought you might want to know. There's nothing new." That note of flat satisfaction again.

Tutchek tightened his mouth. "Well—thanks. If you need me for anything, I'll be at the Hotel Sutton."

He hung up and went out into the lobby, where George Gilman and the two Lab technicians, Bert Daly and Jerry Straub, were waiting for him. Tutchek went in the squad car with Gilman and the Lab men followed in the compact green and white mobile unit truck.

On the way, Tutchek thought about the press release situation again. He grimaced, half-wishing he hadn't bitten everybody's head off back there in the Meade-LaFarge office, and maybe he should not have let the Assistant Medical Examiner make such a point of that wound in Meade's head being from a gunshot. Doc Winkler himself admitted that he was sticking his neck out on that diagnosis, or opinion, or whatever you wanted to call it. Thinking it over, it was plain he couldn't let it get into the papers that way. There'd be all hell to pay if it turned out not to be from a gunshot, and Commissioner Willie Quinn would be fit to be tied. He'd be fit to be tied, anyway, another bad one breaking like this on top of the rape killing, and it would be worse if he found out Flavin and Gilman had stood around all that time without finding out that Meade had been shot. Or clubbed.

Tutchek sighed heavily. He had been intending to give the two detectives a chewing out for missing the boat—although he could see how easily it might happen—but now he knew he was not going to do it. If Quinn heard about it, he'd howl for their hair, in the mood he was in now. Flavin and Gilman were good men, and Tutchek did not want that to happen to them. If anything came up later on it, Tutchek thought glumly, he'd just have to take the guff himself. But keep his fingers crossed in the meanwhile. Ah well, the news release on that quick stabbing arrest would keep the Commissioner happy for a while, and if Alec Gillespie cleaned up the Widdicomb drowning—and Alec might do just that—Quinn would let them sit in his lap.

"End of the line, Lieutenant," said George Gilman.

Tutchek started. "What? What's that?"

"We're here, Lieutenant."

Tutchek glanced dumbly out the window and saw that they were parked before the hotel—and had probably been parked there for a few minutes.

"I was a million miles away," he mumbled.

Gilman's wide face split in that pleasant, friendly frog-grin of his. "Blonde or brunette?" he asked.

"Both. And a glass of beer."

He ducked out of the car and trudged across the sidewalk toward the entrance of the tall structural glass and steel building. He was tired and his legs felt as if they had been stuffed with wet sawdust.

Inside the doors of the residential hotel was a broad, discreetly lighted lounge, and well-dressed men and women strolled here and there with the smiling, indolent assurance of money. To one side was a restaurant, and beyond that the Bit & Spur Tap Room. At the opposite end of the lounge was the arcade to several expensive shops and the inevitable store.

They were met at the brink of the lobby by a gray-haired bellman—or possibly an under-secretary to the ambassador—who asked skeptically if they were guests of a guest.

Tutchek said, "Police."

The man's eyes widened, but not enough for real interest. "Perhaps you wish to speak with Mr. Manthey, our manager," he suggested.

"Perhaps," said Tutchek.

"Just a moment, please." He went to a black and gold house phone in a wall niche beside the door.

George Gilman watched interestedly. "I hope maybe we can get an appointment, Lieutenant. You think so maybe?"

"Maybe," said Tutchek.

The bellman returned, unsmiling. "Mr. Manthey's office is over here, gentlemen."

They followed him across the broad lounge, and the manner in which they walked left no doubt that they were the police, for several of the strollers turned to look after them in frank surprise, and turned back to one another with whispered frowns.

The office was in a small marble-lined alley and guarded a bank of self-service elevators. Mr. Manthey, a plump jolly-looking man with glacial eyes, met them in his reception room, wearing an Arctic smile.

"Police," said Tutchek.

"Yes. Is there something I can do, gentlemen?"

"You can take us to Stewart Meade's apartment."

"Do you have a search warrant?"

"This is a homicide. I'm Lieutenant Tutchek and this is Detective Gilman."

Mr. Manthey was unimpressed. "I'm sorry, but—"

"I don't give a damn what you are!" said Tutchek violently. "Meade's been killed and there's a good chance it happened upstairs. Now let's go!"

Manthey's eyes blazed at him with icy hatred, and he dipped his head, once.

"Very well. I'll take you up."

He walked out of the office to the elevators, leaving them to trail behind. Tutchek did not say a word, but trudged along. George Gilman smiled happily to himself, an expression of great contentment haloing his homely face. He had a secret, a great big wonderful secret, and he wanted to enjoy it all by himself for a while. A little later, if all went well, Mr. Manthey would be in on the secret, too, and when he was let in on it, there'd be all sorts of fun and games for everybody.

The secret was Tutchek—and when Mr. Manthey found out, oh, what a time there'd be. The Fourth of July and fireworks and everything all over again. All over Mr. Manthey.

Gilman beamed at Tutchek with brimming affection.

The elevator stopped on the twenty-third floor and Manthey led them down the corridor to the corner suite. He hesitated, then unlocked the door and stepped malevolently aside to let them enter. He seemed mentally to be thumbing a name list of judges, mayors and congressmen, who would take care of Tutchek as unpleasantly as possible. George Gilman smiled fondly at him as he passed and went into the apartment, followed by Daly and Straub. Manthey came in behind them and closed the door.

"Do you wish me to show you through the rooms?" he asked.

"I think we can manage," said Tutchek.

"What, exactly, are you looking for?"

"That's not, exactly, any of your Goddamned business. Now sit down over there and keep out of our way."

Manthey stared, unbelieving. Gilman took his elbow and gently steered him toward a small occasional chair beside the door.

"The Lieutenant means, sit down and don't touch anything. Would you like me to get you an ice cube? Just to keep you company, that is."

"This is ridiculous!"

"The Lieutenant also means that if you don't sit down, you might get underfoot and somebody'll step on you. That part of it is up to you."

Manthey did not sit down. He remained standing in the foyer. He should have left the apartment, but didn't. After a while it became untenable and he sat rigidly on the chair and smoked a cigarette in poisoned silence.

The four men walked a few feet into the apartment and paused, turning their heads as they sized it up in slow, partitioning glances. There was a living, or sitting, room, approximately twelve by fifteen, and to the right, through a pair of curtained French doors, now open, was a spacious bedroom, L-shaped to accommodate a chocolate and crème de menthe green-tiled bath. A partially open door adjoining the foyer revealed a miniature kitchenette, fitted into a space the size of a broom closet. It was furnished in a contemporary décor, reminiscent of praying mantises resting. The colors were a bit lush and insinuating, but effective. It had the appearance of a Lord & Taylor window during a home furnishings sale, self-consciously arranged to give it that "lived-in" feeling. The magazines on the cocktail table before the long, wide sofa were neatly squared and the casually scattered ash trays were polished and gleamed like jewels. The slats on the Venetian blinds at a battery of windows behind the sofa were all trimly aligned to throw a soft, reflecting light on the bone-white ceiling.

The interest of the men seemed to sag. Tutchek stared moodily at the mathematically set blinds. George Gilman peered into the bedroom and sadly shook his head at the bedspread, which was as flawlessly smooth as a rink before a hockey game. One of the Lab men ran his finger across the arm of a chair, held it to the light, and wrinkled his nose.

Tutchek swung heavily around on Manthey. "Has this place been cleaned this morning, do you know?" he demanded.

"There's daily maid service, of course," Manthey answered contemptuously.

Tutchek's eyes lingered, thin-lidded, then slowly moved off, like those of a carnivore that had just marked a likely spot for future reference.

"Shake this room down, for what it's worth," he told Daly and Straub. "We'll take a look at the others. Come on, George."

He motioned Gilman to the bathroom, while he, himself, doggedly started on the bedroom. Gilman expected very little of the bathroom. He knew what he was to look for—bloodstains—but this bathroom was not the place he would find any. Whatever else might be said of the management of the Hotel Sutton, its maid service was inflexibly thorough. There was neither blotch nor blemish anywhere. The fixtures gleamed richly like family silverware; the stall shower was dry, clean and bright and there was not a fleck of soap on the opaque glass door; the floor was immaculate to the farthest corner, the shag bath mat looked combed and brushed, the tub so unsullied that it could have been used to brew bouillabaisse for an epicure, and even the crystal doorknobs had been buffed to the glittering sparkle of prismed diamonds. Gilman bent and squinted along the edge of the hand basin, but there was not a smudge to mar the long gleam of polished porcelain. He lifted the lid of the commode and it was impeccable enough to incubate delicate tropical fish.

He opened the linen cabinet and felt along the towels and washcloths, but that's all there was—towels and washcloths. He peered into the medicine cabinet at the shelves of shaving cream, skin lotion, mouth wash, aspirin, tranquilizers, Dexedrine, codeine, numerous other salves and potions, three jars of hormones, and a bottle of dye that pledged to turn gray hair snow white. It was disappointing, but not unexpected. He was patting around on the dark floor of the linen cabinet with the palms of his hands when Tutchek called from the bedroom.

"Hey, George, take a look at this. Daly, Straub!"

The three men hurried into the bedroom, where Tutchek was kneeling beside the bed, an open suitcase on the floor in front of him. On the floor also were some folded sheets of newspaper and a length of brown cord. He sat back on his heels as they grouped around him and pointed to what he had found in the suitcase. Spread on the rug was a tan shirt and the dark brown jacket of a tropical worsted suit. The collar of the shirt was jaggedly marked and spotted by blood, now russet and crusty. They had to lean closer to see that the collar and left shoulder of the jacket were similarly stained.

"I found those wrapped in newspaper and tied with cord," said Tutchek. He looked up at Daly, "See what prints you can raise on the case."

Daly nodded intently and took a small fingerprinting outfit from his pocket. He went down on one knee and carefully turned the suitcase so that the smooth plastic sides were uppermost.

Tutchek touched Gilman's arm.

"There's more," he said. "Tell me what you think of this."

He led the way to a large closet at the far side of the bed, and opened the door. Gilman blinked, puzzled. Hanging inside the closet were several lacy and obviously expensive nightgowns and negligees, and three Persian lamb jackets.

"But Meade ain't married," said Gilman.

"That's right."

"Just living with the dame, eh?"

"He lives alone."

"Wait a minute—"

"He lives alone. I can tell. But there's more. Take a look." He canted his chin at an open drawer in the chest-on-chest that stood against the wall.

Gilman walked over and looked down into it. There were several open gift boxes, marked with the Tiffany imprint, and each contained either a gold compact, lipstick holder, or cigarette lighter.

"The drawer under that," said Tutchek, "is full of very fancy underwear, all lace and nothing else. My wife'd be crazy about it. It'd make her feel like a high-class whore."

Gilman moved his bunched lips in and out, like a baffled goldfish, and poked at one of the gold cigarette lighters with his forefinger.

He opened the next drawer down and stared at the foam and frills of frothy lingerie. There were slips, brassieres, panties—mostly panties—all black. Fascinated, he opened the drawer beneath that. It was filled to the top with boxes of nylon stockings, all sizes. Tutchek leaned forward to look.

"I missed that one," he said. "I guess those lace panties threw me. Well, what do you make of it, George?"

"I thought this guy was in the real-estate investment and construction business. He wasn't running a line of ladies' wear on the side, was he?" Gilman made a face. "He had quite a system, didn't he? Bring the girls up here and show 'em these instead of etchings. He must have done all right. How many women did he have, anyways?"

"He was stocked up for a long, hard winter. Let's see what Manthey has to say."

"I'll watch."

"What?"

"Nothing, Lieutenant. I just said I'll keep an eye on him."

Before they left the bedroom, Tutchek went over and watched Daly at the suitcase. There were many prints boldly outlined in gray powder against the dark, smooth plastic, but the technician looked up at Tutchek and shook his head.

"They're all Meade's, Lieutenant," he said, indicating the raised prints around the handle and lock of the case, and tilting his chin at a print-smudged fingerprint card he'd propped on the bedspread. "I took both Meade's sets over there in his office, and compared them with these on the case, and they're all his. There are some latents, but his overlay, so what the hell. If you want me to dust the whole case I'll go down to the truck for more powder, but I can tell you right now, he's the only one that handled this case recent. Here's the only place you can open and close it and there just ain't no other prints but his."

"How about the inside of the case?"

"It's that grosgrain nylon stuff. You couldn't lift a print from that if it was put on with red paint. Sorry, Lieutenant, but if that shirt and coat were in the case, nobody put 'em in there but Meade himself."

George Gilman understood the significance of that and he shot a startled glance at the folds of newspaper and the brown cord on the floor, then raised his eyes to Tutchek's face.

"There's something wrong here, Lieutenant," he protested. "That doesn't make sense. Maybe there's something the matter with me, but when I see some clothes wrapped in an old newspaper, it means somebody is getting ready to throw them out. And when the clothes are bloodstained it specially means they're going to be tossed in the garbage. Otherwise why wrap them in newspaper? If you're going to take them to the cleaners or send them to the laundry, you'd roll them up or stick them in a pillowcase with the rest of the wash or maybe stick them in a brown paper bag. But you wouldn't wrap them in newspaper unless you wanted to get rid of them. You just wouldn't. Am I right?"

"It doesn't look that way, George."

"But it doesn't make sense any other way, Lieutenant. Let's say Meade was rapped over the head and bled on his shirt and coat. Now why should he come home, wrap 'em in newspaper, and hide 'em under the bed? I can see somebody else doing it—the guy that busted his head, for instance—but I can't see Meade doing it. Why should he do a thing like that? What's he got to hide?"

"He must have thought he had something to hide, George, or he wouldn't have done it."

"Can you think of one reason why he'd do it himself, Lieutenant? Just one?"

Tutchek was tired and growing irritable, but he held himself to a patient calm. "George, isn't it just as cockeyed for somebody else to wrap those clothes in a newspaper and hide them under Meade's bed. *And leave them there?*"

"And you can't get around Meade's own fingerprints, George," said Bert Daly, in his mourning tones. "And that's all we got on the suitcase—

Meade's."

Tutchek said, "This is in line with what Doc Winkler told us in Meade's office. With that hole in his head, Meade couldn't be expected to act rationally. We'll never know what reason he thought he had, so let's not waste any more time on it. There should be pants to go with that coat. Maybe they're in the closet."

Gilman found the pants neatly folded over a hanger. There was a dark stain on the right knee, and Jerry Straub took them to the window for a closer examination.

"Looks like a grass stain," he said. "I'll take them down to the Lab. There's some stuff in the cuffs, too. Lint, dust, some kind of dirt. Loam maybe. Any shoes in the closet, George?"

Gilman rummaged on the floor. "Yeah. About a dozen pair. I'll bring them over—"

The shoes were scrutinized at the light of the window. Eleven pairs were brightly polished or merely dusty, but the twelfth showed traces of dried clay and sand caught between the soles and the uppers. Straub wrapped them carefully in the grass-stained pants.

"That's about it, Lieutenant," he said.

Tutchek nodded, letting them go, and they took the clothing, shoes and suitcase, and left. Tutchek nodded vaguely as they went. He wandered across the room to the chest-on-chest and opened the lingerie drawer, regarding the contents thoughtfully. He held up a pair of black panties.

"Do you know anything about this kind of stuff, George?" he asked.

"Well, I'll tell you, Lieutenant, when I got that far, I wasn't asking questions no more."

"I mean, how much they cost."

"Oh. I don't know. Five bucks?"

Tutchek grinned. George Gilman had the face of an amiable frog with a built-in grin, and if you looked at him often enough, you couldn't help grinning, too. Not at him, with him. There was that about George Gilman: he walked in an aura of contagious good humor. Most of the time.

"Hell, George," said Tutchek, "women who run around with big businessmen wouldn't put five buck pants on their dogs. How much would you say he paid for one of those gold cigarette lighters?"

"You're asking the wrong guy, Lieutenant. The dames I bat around with smoke cigars and scratch the match on their butts."

On a common impulse, they both turned their heads and contemplated the closet in which hung all those chi-chi black nightgowns and negligees and the three Persian lamb jackets. Gilman turned back the jackets from their hangers and gave Tutchek a just-what-we-thought nod.

"Three different sizes," he said. He riffled through the nightgowns and negligees. "These are *all* sizes. This guy wasn't human. He was a production line."

"Could be."

"I wonder what a girl had to do to win one of these fur coats, Lieutenant. The lace panties and other stuff might have been a kind of going-away present or a tip, but a fur coat is first prize. Think it over. What the hell went on up here, anyways?"

"I have been thinking it over, George," Tutchek's dry voice betrayed his opinion of *sub rosa* sexual shenanigans. "Let's see if we can get a line on it."

Manthey was standing at the wide living-room windows, glowering down at the screeching, bleating, snortling traffic of Park Place. He had his hands behind him and the snapping of his fingers sounded like swearing.

"About the guests who live here, Mr. Manthey," Tutchek began mildly. "This *is* a residential hotel and they can have all the company they want, can't they?"

"Naturally."

"I mean, you put no restrictions on it, do you?"

"Restrictions? I don't know what you're talking about. Our guest list is restricted, if that's what you mean."

"No Jews or Negroes, eh?"

"My dear sir, we inquire into the backgrounds of all persons who apply for an apartment, without prejudice. They must be financially responsible, and compatible, should they wish to mingle socially."

"Uh-huh. I get the idea. But now, after you rent them an apartment, do you keep inquiring into whatever it is you'd inquire into, in that case?"

"We do *not* check up on our guests, Lieutenant. We assume—"

"That they're ladies and gentlemen?"

"Exactly."

"That's what I thought. Then you wouldn't know if Mr. Meade threw many parties, would you?"

"Mr. Meade was absolutely free to—"

"I know, I know. But that's not exactly what I asked you, Mr. Manthey. What I asked was, do you know if Mr. Meade threw many parties?"

There was no radical change in the chilly set of Manthey's expression, but it was plain to both detectives that the man had suddenly turned wary, and when he spoke again, his voice was bland, almost friendly.

"Well, yes," he said. "As a matter of fact, Mr. Meade entertained extensively. It was necessary to his business, I believe."

"Oh, I see," Tutchek nodded, not changing his mild manner. "These were just business get-togethers, then?"

"Please, Lieutenant, I have no way of knowing what was discussed. A man of Mr. Meade's position in the business world is expected to entertain socially, but to say what transpired would be pure conjecture. From my own experience I can tell you that many business matters are settled informally long before they reach the boardroom."

"Mr. Meade was a big executive, then?"

"President of his corporation, Lieutenant."

"Oh well now, they don't come any bigger than that, do they. Now I can see why he had to throw so many parties. Just about every night, eh?"

"Well, not quite, Lieutenant, but much more frequently than you or I. Quiet sociable gatherings, you understand. Nothing boisterous. We could hardly permit that, you know. Because of our other guests."

"Sure, sure. I knew you could straighten me out on this. Mr. Manthey. But I guess that's your job, knowing everything that goes on."

"Oh, not everything, Lieutenant," Manthey looked smug. "But pretty nearly everything. Yes."

"That's what I thought. I won't ask you what they are, but I suppose you have your ways and means, just as we have *our* ways and means, eh?"

"In a manner of speaking, but it's not quite the same, you must admit. Our guests are neither guilty nor under suspicion. But, Lieutenant, I'm really quite upset about Mr. Meade's death," Manthey's face showing appropriate concern. "Was it an accident?"

"Maybe."

"How tragic. And he seemed so well when he left this morning."

"You saw him leave?"

"No. Henry, the doorman, did. I telephoned downstairs while you were busy in the other room. He said Mr. Meade left the hotel at eight-forty-five. I thought you might want that information in the course of your investigation."

George Gilman leaned against the wall, his amiable frog-like smile unaltered. He regarded Manthey with growing affection. Manthey was one of his favorites, the kind of cute bastard who got cuter as he went along. He had met a great many of them during his years in the police department. The cover-up artists. Now, this is not to be confused with obstructing justice. Nossir. Obstructing justice is not patriotic. All they wanted to do was protect their innocent friends, acquaintances and relations from unpleasant policemen. It is very patriotic to protect the innocent. Ask anybody. George Gilman knew all about it, for it was also his bounden duty as an officer of the law to protect the innocent. Yessir. And, as everybody knew, it was a sacred civic duty to prosecute the guilty. There was no doubt about that. It was as basic as being in favor of the Ten Commandments and against criminals. And everyone knows who a criminal is. A criminal is someone you don't know or don't like; everyone else is innocent. Now, Mr. Manthey, for instance, would be the first to admit that he was very civic-minded and patriotic and against criminals. And Mr. Manthey would be more than willing to help the poor, hard-working cops if they would do him the favor of going someplace else to enforce the law. George Gilman was positive that Mr. Manthey was in favor of any law that was not enforced in his immediate vicinity. That was why George Gilman regarded Mr. Manthey with such affection. He had become very fond of Mr. Manthey, and it was going to be a positive pleasure when he saw the error of his ways. Lieutenant Tutchek was very good at pointing out the errors of people's ways. Mr. Manthey would come apart like a defrocked alarm clock.

Lieutenant Tutchek was just about ready, but wanted Manthey to tie himself up just a little tighter. "I'll be damned," he marveled, "you even know when they come and go, don't you?"

"It's not that we keep tabs on our guests, Lieutenant. It's not that at all. Nor is there any invasion of privacy on our part. This is just between you and me, but hotel living is a bit more public than most people realize. Not that we spy on our guests, but the staff cannot help but notice things," Manthey condescended to give Tutchek the benefit of his wider and superior experience. "If you live in an average apartment house, let's say, there are no employees on the premises except the superintendent and his wife. Things are entirely different in a quality residential hotel. Here, in order to get the service he expects, and demands, the guest, whether he realizes it or not, is under the eye of one member or another of the staff from the moment he wakes up in the morning until he goes to bed at night. There is the doorman, who notes his coming and going. Then there are pages to do his errands, waiters in the restaurant or for room service. Bellmen are also at his service day and night. Maids and housemen clean his apartment. The maintenance crew paints, redecorates, or makes repairs—carpenters, plumbers, electricians, and so forth. The waiters and chefs know what he likes to eat and drink. We have valet service and take care of his laundry. His telephone calls go through the switchboard operator. If he has a car, a page, or runner, will bring it to the door for him. My secretary has a card file in which is noted, shall we say, his taste in flowers for a 1ady, which brand of Scotch he prefers, and of course the date of his birthday.

"There is always some small remembrance from the management on his birthday. In short, Lieutenant, it is the obligation of the staff to know everything about a guest so that we can anticipate his wishes and give perfect service. As a matter of fact, if a guest asked us to breathe for him, I daresay we could do that, too!"

Manthey patronized Tutchek and Gilman with a small, inclusive smile, and was well aware that he had given these two underprivileged policemen a fleeting glimpse into a world of undreamed luxury, far beyond their imagining, for it was evident that ordinary policemen could never afford the opulent joy of hiring someone to breathe for them.

Tutchek shook his head and looked at Gilman. "Did you ever hear anything like it, George? They know everything." But Gilman had become uneasy. The Lieutenant had set Manthey up for the fall, and that was fine; but now he should have knocked him over, and let Gilman, or Jeff Flavin, or Harry Muir, or some other team of detectives in the Section take it from there. The Lieutenant was acting like he was going to carry the ball all the way, and this wasn't how a Lieutenant should do. From here on in, it was nothing but a routine job for the hired help, like himself.

"Yeah, Mr. Manthey sure knows everything, Lieutenant," he said with false heartiness, feeling like a stooge. "He gave us everything but Mr. Meade's blood test, didn't he?"

"Mr. Meade's blood *type* is 'O'," said Manthey, with almost open contempt. "That's what you meant, I believe, isn't it? That is in the card file—as a matter of routine."

"Yeah, there's nothing like routine," said Tutchek. "It's the same in the detective business, Mr. Manthey. You can't go wrong if you stick to the routine. When you follow the rules, it's the other guy that makes the mistake. I've never known it to fail. Now, let's see, where were we? Oh, yes. These business parties of Mr. Meade's. What business was Mr. Meade in? Do you know?"

"Of course. Mr. Meade was president of Meade-LaFarge Associates, a corporation dealing in real-estate investment and large scale development and construction. They have one of the highest ratings in Dun & Bradstreet."

"Make a note of that for the record, George. But just a few more questions, Mr. Manthey. We police have to depend on people like you, otherwise we'd be stuck. You know what I mean?"

"Oh, perfectly, Lieutenant. I'm at your service."

"Thanks. What we ask is a little co-operation, that's all."

Manthey said, "You have all my co-operation, Lieutenant," and the careless lift of his hand showed that he no longer bothered to hold up his guard.

Tutchek's next question came down like an executioner's ax. "I'm glad to hear that, Mr. Manthey. Now, since you know so much about Mr. Meade and his 'business' parties, suppose you tell me something about *all the girls he brought up here.*"

Manthey gasped, "Girls!" but in that shifting flicker of an instant was aghast to realize that he had talked too much, but obversely was just about to begin to talk. Tutchek had him, as they say, by the balls, and he knew it.

Within a miserable half-hour, he talked. He had no choice. He had boasted too much of knowing too much, and had arrogantly assumed that his word alone would rid the hotel of these nosy policemen. Sweat poured from him in such quantities that he seemed to shrivel in his clothes like a dehydrated potato.

Yes, there had been girls. He tried to plead that it was natural for men to like girls, but it was no use; Meade had liked girls just a bit, quite a bit, more than most men liked girls. As a matter of fact, he liked girls all the time, and because he had the money, he had them all the time. Sometimes two, or even three, together with him of a night. And yes, Mr. Meade had suitably rewarded them for the entertainment thus performed. Whatever *that* meant. Meade seemed to have been a voyeur, among other things, including being a satyr, but of course, he could afford the full gamut of private orgies. And whatever *that* meant.

In the end, it came down to the fact that the president of Meade-LaFarge Associates, Stewart Meade, had a penchant (and the funds) for personal entertainments of a sexual nature. But these were "sociable gatherings, nothing boisterous." Which was understandable. Still, over the two-year period of Meade's residence in the hotel, he had "entertained" a large number of anonymous girls.

Yet, though battered by Tutchek's relentless questioning, Manthey dully and stubbornly denied any knowledge of a call-girl service. The Hotel Sutton had its standards.

Tutchek was willing to take his word for that. There were hotels in the upper brackets that did supply a call-girl service for paying guests, but the Sutton was not that kind of boardinghouse. It did not have to be; it was the quality hotel in the city—just as the Dorchester or the Savoy were the quality hotels in London, the Waldorf in New York, or the Fontainebleau in Miami Beach. Among the luxuries it offered at luxury prices was discretion—and freedom from fear of blackmail. You could bring your call-girls in from outside, but not through the Sutton.

But that made no difference. Tutchek had all he wanted from Manthey. He was exhausted when he put the man out of the apartment and plodded back to set up the next step in the investigation of Meade's death.

He took out a cigarette and put it in his mouth, stared across the room, gathering his thoughts, then stubbed the cigarette in an ash tray without even having lighted it. He did not realize this. There were too many things going on inside his head—the undone paper work stacked on his desk, the rape killing in South Branch Park, the drowned woman found floating in the river against the East Coast Fisheries dock, the cop-fighters down at The Point, yes, and even Lieutenant Stein's problem, the holdup of the Park Liquor Shop in which the owner, Anthony Scerbo, was almost killed.

Tutchek was glad, in a vague sort of way, that Anthony Scerbo had not been killed. As a policeman, he was glad because the killing would have been dumped in Homicides overcrowded lap and, God knows, there weren't enough men to go 'round as it was. That was not all, of course. He was not a machine-made cop. As a human being himself, he was glad that another human being had not been killed. And glad was not really the word. His years as a detective in Homicide had shown him many dead men, and although death might be something a man might become accustomed to seeing, it was not something a man would ever like, in its more violent forms.

He was very tired, and his mind was a turmoil, and it was an actual, physical effort to gather his thoughts. This was the time when police training and discipline helped; once put into motion, his thoughts fell neatly into place. He drew a deep breath, and his hand automatically dipped to his pocket and lifted a cigarette to his mouth.

"Now hear this, George," he said in Gilman's general direction, without actually seeing him, "Have the property clerk send down a couple of boys to take a full inventory of this place. I want to see how much money Meade sank in those fur coats, lacy underwear, and so forth, including the jewelry. I think it'll run into more than a few thousand. Stay here till they come. Tell them to post a guard when they leave, but don't seal the apartment. Somebody might come busting in, and we'll want to know who. You know what I mean. And don't forget this—tell them I'll want that inventory list as fast as possible. Make sure they send somebody who knows how to appraise this kind of stuff. Better still, you stay with them till they finish, then bring me the list. If I'm not in the office, wait for me. Okay?"

Gilman said stolidly, "Okay."

Tutchek nodded and went to the phone and told the switchboard operator to get him Meade-LaFarge Associates. He spoke to Jeff Flavin.

"Meade was a chaser," he said curtly. "You were right about that. He used a call-girl service, looks as if. Find out which one. Also, find out if he fooled around with any of the girls in the office. He probably did, from the way it shapes up. Now listen carefully—if he did fool around with that secretary of his, or any of the other office girls, just get the names. Don't question the girls. We'll take that up later. Who's there with you?"

"Muir and Scanlon."

"Fine. They know the score. They can take care of the call-girl angle. Now, I don't want any of these girls brought in yet, Jeff. Make sure Harry Muir understands that. We're not going to bust up the call-girl racket. That's not our job—" Tutchek's mouth felt a little sour when he said that, because there was nothing he could do about it. "Our job is Meade and I want to find out what kind of shenanigans he's been up to. The girls might be able to give Muir and Scanlon a line on that, if they go about it the right way. Tell them this is just background stuff, and if they can get it without mentioning Meade's name, all the better. I don't think those girls are mixed up in it. Not yet, anyway. Now you get the picture?"

"Yes, sir," said Flavin at the other end of the line. "All you want is for them to talk to the girls?"

"That's *all*," Tutchek emphasized. "And the same goes for you. Find out what you can in the office, then report back to me and we'll take it from there. I'm going back to Headquarters now. If you need me for anything, call me there."

He hung up. His eyes felt grainy and he rubbed them with his forefingers. He felt as if he could sleep for a week, but there was too much work to do. A cup of coffee would straighten him out.

He looked at Gilman and said, "Check with me at Headquarters, George," and left.

Gilman stared at the closed door and after a while he muttered, "Check." Then he plodded toward the telephone to call the property clerk. He felt like an office boy.

Eight

Detectives Bierce and Caputo were waiting for Tutchek in the Homicide squad room.

He said "Be with you in a minute, boys," and stopped at Policewoman Lund's desk. "Anything from Lieutenant Gillespie on that East Coast Fisheries drowning?" he asked.

"Nothing new since I talked to you last, Lieutenant," she answered in that crisp, remote voice of hers. "I spoke to him a short while ago and told him you wanted to see him. He's on his way in now."

His temper rose, as if she had slapped him in the face, but he curbed it and said, "Thank you, Miss Lund," and strode into the squad room, wondering again what was eating her. She was antagonistic. She was like ice. No matter what he said or did, she refused to thaw. He didn't understand it. He'd d never bawled her out for anything. Hell, she had one of the softest jobs in Headquarters. He gave his head a small shake, as if to shoo off a bothersome fly. It really wasn't worth fretting about.

As he strode through the squad room, he said over his shoulder to the two waiting detectives, "Come on inside," and went into his office.

They exchanged a wry, shrugging glance, gathered up some papers and envelopes, and followed him, without enthusiasm.

Tutchek hung his coat on the back of the door, grimaced again at the paper work stacked up on his desk, and walked slowly toward his chair, rolling up his shirt sleeves. It wasn't a steamy day, but he felt hot. Hot and tired. He sat down and flapped his hand at Bierce and Caputo.

"Drag up some chairs and let's get into this," he said.

He flapped among the untidy papers on his desk and found the report of the South Branch Park rape killing.

The memory of that thin young girl, kicked to death, was fluorescent in his mind, but he read the report from end to end before looking up. His mouth bunched, as if from inner pain, as he remembered the Medical Examiner saying the girl had probably been sexually used *after* she had been kicked to death. It was the little touches like this that curdled a man's heart. But that was not something he could say to anyone, not even in the soft, cradling hours of deep night when he and Sophie, his wife, lay in each other's arms in that closest intimacy of the wonderful *afterward* of love. No, he could never say this, even to Sophie; he could not taint her with it.

Was there no one? he thought, in despair.

He shook it off, and ignored the shadow that remained. That was something he would have to take care of later. Like the unfinished paperwork on his desk, he thought, deriding himself. A man could use derision as a spur to rouse himself.

He smoothed out the report on his desktop with the flat of his hand and looked up. The two detectives sat uncomfortably on hard wooden chairs across the desk, facing him. Bierce was dark, blue-eyed, black Irish, hot-tempered, a man who'd rather play a hunch than build a case brick by brick. Caputo was just the opposite, a cautious man who liked to see the ground ahead before he put down his foot, careful in judgment, uneasy if without tangible facts to hold in the hands of his logical mind.

Together, they made a good team; separate, they would be almost useless. Bierce would waste his energies chasing a hunch, and Caputo would be too cautious to get started. That was why Tutchek had teamed them. It was an experiment. He was not yet sure that it would work. If it didn't, he would have to transfer them to a different division.

"Well?" he said in an irritated voice. "How far have we gotten? Has the girl been identified?"

"Christ, Lieutenant," Bierce flared. "What's there to identify? Her face was kicked in."

Caputo was, as usual, more temperate. He took an eight by ten glossy photograph from an envelope and laid it on the desk before Tutchek. This was one of the photographs taken the night before by the Crime Lab upstairs. It was as stark as only a police photograph can be. In the harsh light of a flash bulb. It showed the skinny naked young girl sprawled on her back amid the short spears of grass, legs spread in horrible surrender, arms helpless, and the smashed face a highlighted nightmare. Caputo touched the photograph beside that ruined young face.

"Not her own mother, Lieutenant," his soft voice reproached. "Not anybody. Could you, yourself?"

Tutchek looked at the photograph. There had been a time, when he was first assigned to Homicide, that he'd have looked quickly away, but he had learned that this was an indulgence he could not afford. You had to look at things like this as you would look at any other bit of evidence. Objectively. It was not a mutilated dead girl; it was evidence, the thing that showed a crime had been committed. You couldn't look at it any other way. If you did, you were lost. So, you did it. But that didn't mean you had to like it. When you started liking it, you were lost too.

Tutchek studied the photograph.

"Did you check with Missing Persons?" he asked.

"Christ!" said Bierce. "It only happened last night—"

"We checked, Lieutenant," Caputo interrupted quietly. "They don't have anything. Like Ike said, it only happened last night. What can you expect? Later maybe."

Tutchek waved his bands in brusque apology. "I know, I know. I didn't think there'd be anything. I just asked. Do you mind, Goddamnit?"

They were taken aback at his sudden violence, and sat stiffer in their chairs.

Caputo said carefully, "What's there to mind?"

Both detectives sat with closed faces, waiting, as men do when a superior officers shows the teeth of his temper. Tutchek was not aware of this, and continued to study the photograph.

"I take it for granted they covered the neighborhoods on all sides of the park. Right?"

That was a question he needn't have asked, for covering the surrounding neighborhoods was a matter of routine. Still, there was more to it than that, actually. Tutchek knew the area. South Branch Park had been fashionable during the 90s, but had steadily deteriorated, and was now a tenement district, pocked with small shops, seven or eight haphazard factories that manufactured such things as paper hats or the crude plastic toys found in boxes of sugar-coated popcorn, and a half-dozen dreary taverns in which the customers sat hunched at the bar over their dismal glasses of beer.

These were neighborhoods from which violence exploded out of sheer hopelessness—not poverty, not injustice, not hatred or fear, just boredom. Senseless brutality. And that was the worst. You could find a motive in the others, but in the South Branch precinct, there was nothing but apathy. The inhabitants crept to work in the morning, crept home in the evening, ate, drank, slept, and crept out to work again the following morning, taking no joy in anything. The buildings had long been paintless, and no matter what color they were they all seemed gray, and the people—men, women, children—they seemed as gray as the rest of it. Their voices were gray, and there was seldom a shout or a laugh, and when they met on the street, they greeted one another with discouraging nods. Nothing was worth the effort. But there was violence there, nonetheless. Murder, and things worse than murder. This was the place in which a suicide would kill his entire family before cutting his own throat. The gray neighborhoods surrounding South Branch Park smelled of ancient evil and tired death.

So, when Tutchek asked if Bierce and Caputo had covered those neighborhoods to identify the dead girl, he was really asking if anything else had been uncovered—another death, a suicide.

Caputo said, "It's been covered house by house, Lieutenant. We didn't get a thing. They don't give a damn."

Tutchek said, "Yeah—"

He hadn't expected anything. The neighborhood had turned out last night to look at the battered girl because she was dead.

If she had dropped dead in the street, they would not have cared very much; it took a gaudy death to arouse their interest. But not for long, and certainly not in the bleak light of day. All right, the girl was dead. What difference did it make? They were all going to die sooner or later, and she had died sooner, that's all. Perhaps her father had done it, and tomorrow or the next day they'd find him floating in the river. Nobody'd be surprised; that's the way it went. They'd talk about it in mumbles for a little while, and maybe show ghoulish excitement at the moment, but, again, not for long. They were all going to die; it was only a question of when. And not too much of a question, at that. As Caputo had said—they didn't give a damn.

Tutchek thought of this, and shivered a little.

Caputo sighed. He looked unhappily around the small office, and finally he said, "If she's from that neighborhood, Lieutenant, we're up against a dead end. They'll never tell us nothing."

Bierce burst out angrily, "I'll get my hands on the son-of-a-bitch—" then broke off, red-faced in frustration, his knuckly hands knotting on his thighs.

Tutchek held up his hand, quieting them. "Wait a minute," he said, "wait a minute. You both looked at this photograph? Both of you?"

"Yes."

"Take another look. Forget everything else and just look."

Bierce and Caputo exchanged wary glances, and Tutchek said quickly, "No no. Nobody pulled a boner. Or maybe we all did. I was there myself, remember. And I might be entirely cockeyed. That's all I'm going to say. If I tell you what to look for, you'll see it, whether it's there or not. I want to make sure it's there. Or isn't. One way or the other." Aware that this must sound like babble, he grinned and handed the photograph back to Caputo. "Look at it again," he urged. "Both of you. I've known myself to be wrong, so don't worry. I don't want to talk myself into this. Look it over."

He pushed himself up from the chair. "I'm going to get a drink of water," he said. "I'll be back in a minute. Look it over while I'm gone."

He walked out of the office and into the deserted squad room. His legs didn't feel tired but, my God, they felt heavy. Probably cramped from sitting cross-legged in the chair. He went to the water cooler and on impulse, instead of taking a drink, he held first one wrist and then the other under the flow of ice water. It was like a refreshing message up both arms and across the back of his neck at the base of his skull. He let it run over his hands, and then held the cold wet palms to his broad, high-boned face. He did it twice and felt the tension seep out of him a little. Wound up, that was all. He'd been going at it hot and heavy; it was one of those days. He kneaded the hard muscles at the back of his neck, and rolled his head to free it of kinks. Then at length he drank three glasses of water and felt the sparkling cold wash through his heavy legs. Well, that was all he needed! Just to relax for a minute.

It just went to show. A moment ago he was dragging his caboose; now he was ready for anything. He'd have to remember that.

He went back into the office with a lighter step. Bierce and Caputo were sitting forward on the edges of their chairs, and Bierce's mobile face no longer looked weighted with frustration. Unconsciously, Tutchek made a mental note of that: Bierce showed himself too openly in his face. Something showed in Caputo's face, too, but you had to know him to note the difference.

Tutchek sat down. "Did you see the same thing I think I did?" he asked.

Bierce leaned forward as if to blurt something, but settled back and looked at Caputo. Tutchek noted that, too, and approved: Bierce realized he was sometimes too quick to talk, and therefore left most of the talking to his more cautious partner. That was good; it counterbalanced the open book of his mobile face. Yes, they made a good team. Or had the makings of a good team.

I'll have to keep this in mind, Tutchek thought.

Caputo placed the photograph on the desk. "Well," he said carefully, not because he was afraid to be wrong, but because he was methodical, "if she got her face kicked off there, Lieutenant, there should be blood all over the grass, and there ain't none. There should be blood all around, the way she was kicked. There should be blood all over her tits, and down her belly. She shouldn't be clean from the neck down."

"Her clothes were pulled off afterward," said Tutchek.

"Yes. But this is a fake, Lieutenant. This ain't no rape. I and Ike here worked on some of these kind of rapes, and we should of caught it last night, only there was too much going on, the crowds and all, we didn't catch it," Caputo was earnest, not excusing himself, but methodically pointing out why a mistake had been made. "This kind of rape, where the guy kills the girl first to give himself a charge, and then puts it to her, it never looks like this. I mean, they don't work that way. They mark up her tits with blood and smear it on her belly, and things like that. That's part of how they get their charge. Isn't that right, Ike?"

"Remember the one a couple years ago that put his initials on the girl's belly, Lieutenant?"

Tutchek nodded. "That was a bad one. He killed three little kids, all around eight or nine years old. But I missed that part of it this time." He tilted his chin at the photograph. "I was looking at something else. The grass. No blood."

"No blood," Caputo agreed. "It's a fake all 'round. She wasn't killed in the park, like we thought."

"But why shouldn't we think it?" Bierce was quick to defend himself. "Who'd come from all the way across the City or someplace to take a walk in the park? Or even for a ride in that cruddy park?"

"I thought that myself, Ike," said Tutchek mildly. "So forget it. We were all wrong. It was natural to think she came from that neighborhood, but thank God she didn't. That *would* be a dead end, as you said. This opens it up again."

"She was just dumped in the park," said Bierce.

"And there wasn't any rape, Lieutenant," said Caputo. "Not the rape it was supposed to look like. The M.E. said they did it afterward. I don't think the guy did anything. I think he tried to make it look like he did it, but Doc Knight said there was no semen, remember. It all adds up. She was knocked off someplace else, dumped in the park, and made to look like rape. So she must have been knocked off for some other reason. Why would anybody want to knock off a fourteen-year-old kid? Why?"

The question was a stone dropped into an empty well. The three detectives looked at one another, each hoping to find an answer in the other's face.

At length Bierce said, "Well, maybe she saw him pull a heist, or something." But that was lame, and he knew it. Still, it was something to say, to get the ball rolling. They couldn't just sit there and count one another's freckles. Bierce could not endure a silence.

Caputo said gropingly, "Let's put it this way. Maybe she had a fight with her old man, or something, and he didn't mean to knock her off, but then he saw she was dead, and dumped her in the park to get rid of her. It could happen."

Tutchek shook his head. "That's too fancy, Cap. And too risky. Where did he kill her? And how did he get her to the park? In a car? It would have to be in a car. Also, she'd have to have been killed in the car. I can't see anybody carrying the body around in his arms. She'd have to have been killed in the car and in the park. I can't see anybody driving around the city with a dead body in his car. What do you think, Ike?"

"Not in the park, Lieutenant. What would they be doing in the park? Not necking, for Christ sake. Nobody but a damn fool'd go in any park after dark. Especially that one. In the first place, it's too small. There's no place to pull off the road and park except those rhododendron bushes, and there's a three-foot ditch before you can get to them. There's not enough cover, anyway. Right, Cap?"

Caputo thought it over. "There are other reasons, too," he said.

Tutchek knew the other reasons and it was an effort to keep from stating them. Caputo's deliberation made him impatient to say. For God's sake, get moving, man! But he had to curb himself, for it was important to find out how much they had on the ball.

"What reasons, Cap?" he asked, and all but ground his teeth when Caputo changed position on the hard chair, crossed his legs, and appeared to think it over again.

"Well," he said, "it's one of the county parks. That means the County Park Patrol cruises through regularly. On top of that, South Branch Park is the point where three precincts meet, so patrol cars from all three precincts go through as part of the tour. Altogether, you can hardly go through the park at any time of day or night without seeing one cruiser or another. Nobody hardly goes in that park no more, except maybe as a shortcut. It ain't big enough and there's nothing there but that ditch they call a brook, a few oak trees, and those rhododendron bushes. The county keeps the crab grass mowed, but that's about all."

"And there's a city ordinance against going in a park after eight P.M.," said Bierce. "So what it comes down to is, you can't even use the park as a shortcut after dark without being picked up. Or standing a damn good chance of it. It's one of the few parks in the city where there haven't been any nighttime muggings. So even the muggers won't go in there. It's no better than an empty lot and everybody knows it."

"The *neighborhood* knows it," amended Caputo.

"That's what I meant," said Bierce. "So whoever knocked off that kid and dumped her in the park wasn't from the neighborhood. Nobody from the neighborhood'd take the chance. They'd rather ride crosstown and dump her in the river. It'd be safer."

"But somebody did take the body into the park," Tutchek pointed out. "Somebody did take the chance. Why?"

"He wasn't from the neighborhood," Bierce persisted. Caputo gave his chair a slight hitch a half-inch forward, as a pre-emphasis to what he was going to say. "There's only one thing left," he said. "He dumped her in the park because it was handy. He had to get rid of the body and the park was the closest. I don't mean they came from the neighborhood, either of them. I mean, it happened near the park, and that's why he dumped her there. It was handy. And maybe he didn't have any choice. He had to get rid of her right there or take the chance of driving through the streets and maybe getting stopped for a traffic violation. He could of got stopped for any number of reasons, and didn't want to take the chance. He had to get rid of her, and he did."

"Oh, here's something I meant to bring up," Bierce said suddenly. "We were talking to Doc Knight about this and he said he ran a blood test and she'd been drinking quite heavily before it happened."

Tutchek was raising a tired cigarette and his hand stopped six inches short of his mouth. He wanted to swear, but calmed himself with effort. "Why didn't you say that sooner, Ike?" he asked.

Bierce flushed. "It just came up, Lieutenant," he said. "We were talking about other things."

"Did he say she was drunk?"

"He just said she was drinking heavily."

"It's anybody's guess how drunk she was, Lieutenant," Caputo was always the conciliator, the middle-of-the-road peacemaker. "These days, even fourteen-year-olds can drink enough to sink the Irish navy and hardly show it. They start running the streets when they're old enough to walk. All the juvenile street gangs have debs. There's the DeKalb Barons down at The Point, for instance. You can't be a deb unless you get laid first, and you know how old a deb is, to start? Ten. Imagine laying a ten-year-old kid? But they do it. They do it all the time, and think nothing of it. They don't think anything of drinking. Some go on marijuana, some go on 'H.' And Christ, some of them are worn-out old bags before they're old enough to vote. But I'm not saying this girl was a deb. Sometimes kids from decent families are worse. These are just angles."

Tutchek thrust the cigarette into his mouth and impatiently slapped his pockets for a match. It was part of his job to talk over a case with the men working in the field—but it was not part of his job to sit around talking in a circle forever, just because they forgot to mention that the dead girl had been drinking heavily. Didn't they realize this was the hinge? That this one fact canceled out all other speculation? That if the girl had been drinking, her companion had also been drinking, and there weren't any clear-cut whys and wherefores when a drunk commits murder? And if there was one thing he certainly did not need to be lectured on, it was juvenile delinquency. He knew the situation far better, and in more detail, than Caputo, and he didn't need any kindergarten lessons. And too well he knew how easy it was to hide a bungled investigation behind that self-same juvenile delinquency bit. Furthermore, he had a half-dozen more urgent things to do than sit around having a *kaffeeklatch* with these two.

He picked up the photograph of the murdered girl, looked at it and snapped it down on the desk. "The important thing right now," he said decisively, even curtly, "is to get an identification. We can talk ourselves blue in the face, but unless we know *who* she is, we might just as well be forecasting the weather. The photographs are no help. Okay. But we do have one of the best police artists in the country, so let's use him. Let's see if he can reconstruct a face for us. How many photographs do you have?"

"Eight," said Caputo stolidly.

"All angles?"

"All angles."

The phone rang.

Tutchek said, "*Oh Christ!*" and scooped it from its cradle. "Just a minute," he snapped into it. Then crackled at Caputo, "Go up to the Lab and get the McGimp. I don't care what he's working on, bring him back down here. And, Ike, run downstairs and get us some coffee, will you? Make it black."

He turned back to the phone, not noticing how the men's faces closed and hardened at his peremptory orders.

"Lieutenant Tutchek, Homicide," he snapped into the phone.

"You're a fine one, you son-of-a-bitch," said a voice he recognized as that of Captain Jack Willis, Commander of the Twentieth Precinct house. "I thought you were going to send me some of your boys, or was that just for the Commissioner's benefit?"

"Oh, Jesus, I'm sorry, Jack. I've been up to my ears."

"I wish my ears were all I was up to in," said Willis bitterly. "Those puking cop fighters down here at The Point don't give a damn about our ears, however. We've just had a beautiful donnybrook down at the corner of Market and Peshine, and now I've got two more boys in the hospital."

"I'm sorry, Jack."

"Sorry my ass! Are you going to send me anybody, or aren't you?"

"Yes, sure. I said I would, didn't I?"

"Yeahyeahyeah. You said, he said, they said. Everybody says, but nobody *does*. Do you know what it means when a cop-fighting precinct gets out of hand? It means a cop can't go out of here on tour and be sure of coming back alive. When he walks the street, he's a setup for any cruddy son-of-a-bitch that wants to heave a brick at him from a rooftop. It means that if he tries to make an arrest, eighty-five crumbs will jump him from behind and try to beat out his brains with his own nightstick. It means that if we don't soon start getting some help down here, my boys are going to start wondering if anybody gives a good Goddamn. And if that happens, you can take police authority and piss it up a rope, and the hell with it!"

Tutchek bit back an angry retort. He had enough on his mind without this, but, still—or because of it—he could appreciate how Captain Jack Willis felt.

"I've worked cop-fighting neighborhoods myself, Jack," he said heavily. "I know what it's like. I'll send you two teams right away, though God knows I can't spare them. I have three major cases going right this minute. How about Harry Muir and Rory Scanlon? They've both worked The Point and know it inside out. But they're heavy-handed and you'll have to watch them."

"Watch them hell! I'll give them a sixteen-pound sledge and my blessing. Who else?"

"Lee McGuire and Joe Romaine. All right?"

There was a pause, and then Captain Willis said more quietly, "Those are four of your best boys, Ben."

"Not my best, Jack. They just happen to be best for The Point. They've worked down there, and they're tough, and can take care of themselves. If I sent anybody else, your cop fighters'd slaughter them."

"There's that," Willis admitted. "I want you to know I appreciate this, Ben. And I hope you don't mind the way I sounded off before, but we've got a bad situation down here, and it's driving me nuts. I'm just hoping to God there won't be a bad killing."

"Me too, Jack, me too."

Tutchek hung up, rested his big forearms on the desk, and drew a long breath. How could he have forgotten to send those men to Willis when he knew how bad the cop-fighting situation could be? Well, of course he knew why it had slipped his mind, but that was not an excuse. This was something that should have been taken care of immediately.

It wasn't as if he were merely doing Captain Willis a favor. Nobody was doing anybody any favors. It was reciprocal. The men he sent might be able to prevent a killing. His men were more experienced and better trained than the average uniformed patrolman, and more able to get at the leaders of these cop-fighting gangs that infested the rooftops. One killing would lead to another, and overnight Homicide could be caught in an avalanche of killings, unless something were done to prevent it. So this was what he had to do, even though it meant stripping the Division of four good men.

He called Policewoman Lund on the intercom and told her to detail Muir, Scanlon, McGuire and Romaine to duty in the Twentieth Precinct.

"But Detectives Muir and Scanlon are working on the Meade case, Lieutenant," she reminded him crisply.

"I know, I know. Tell them to turn it over to Bill Tussy and Gene Dode."

"Yes, sir. Lieutenant Gillespie and Detective Kitteridge are waiting to see you. You called them in for a conference on the Widdicomb drowning."

"Tell them to wait, damnit! No, no. I'm sorry. Tell them I'll be with them as soon as I finish with Caputo and Bierce."

"Yes, Lieutenant. But the newspaper reporters have been after me every fifteen minutes—"

"Not about the Meade case?" said Tutchek with quick alarm.

"No, sir. The rape killing in South Branch Park last night. They haven't asked about the Meade case or the Widdicomb drowning yet."

"Good. Tell them I'll have a press release on the rape case in about a half hour."

"What shall I say if they ask about the others?"

Tutchek groaned. He hadn't had time to think. "Tell them we've had only preliminary reports and are investigating. No, wait. I'll give you a handout on those together with the press release on the rape thing. The next time they ask, say everything will be ready in about three-quarters of an hour."

Tutchek put down the phone, but his hand lay heavily on it, as he remembered what Police Commissioner Willie Quinn had said that morning about "public relations". Commissioner Quinn did not want any more "negative public relations". When you got right down to it, what the hell was that supposed to mean? And just exactly how the hell was Homicide supposed to get away from "negative public relations"? Make every killing sound like a civic improvement?

Bierce came in with two quart-cartons of steaming coffee, and immediately behind him came Caputo with the police artist. Tutchek peevishly waved them into chairs while he phoned Doctor Knight, the Medical Examiner.

"Hello, Doc," he said when the Medical Examiner answered. "This is Ben Tutchek. I've got to turn out three press releases in the next hour. The Commissioner—"

"Yes, I've heard," Knight growled. "But if Commissioner Quinn thinks I'm going to be full of sweetness and light just because he wants to be re-elected, he's sadly mistaken. I'm doing the best I know how, but I can't bring the dead back to life, no matter how many votes it loses in the Third Ward come November."

"I don't think that's the point, Doc," said Tutchek stiffly. "The Department's been getting a lot of lousy publicity recently, and we're supposed to do something about it. Is there anything wrong in that?"

"Ah, you too, Benjamin, you too?"

"What?"

"Nothing, Ben, nothing. I'm tired, that's all. You're quite right. If I can tell Lazarus to come forth, I will, believe me. Now, what can I do for you?"

Tutchek gripped the phone. There were numbers of things he might say in answer—and in anger—but he let them slide. It was well-known that Doc Knight had a mordant tongue, and there were times, like this, when it was best to ignore it.

"I've been talking the rape case over with Caputo and Bierce," he said, "and we just can't see any rape in it all. It doesn't add up that way."

"I thought I made that plain last night, Ben," said Knight, surprised.

"You didn't, Doc."

"I'm sorry, Ben," the Medical Examiner sounded honestly contrite.

"Maybe I take too many things for granted. I think I said something about the child being used sexually after she was killed. I guess I was sleepy and didn't explain fully. And too, my examination was not so thorough as it should have been. The circumstances were difficult, but I won't beg off on that score. To be absolutely truthful, Ben, I didn't have any real opinion last night."

"Then what did you mean when you said she had been used sexually? You know what that means to me, but what's your definition of it?"

"I think it was probably done manually."

"To make it look like rape?"

"I'm sorry, Ben, but I am not qualified to give an opinion on the motive, Ben."

"You're right, Doc. I shouldn't have asked. That's our department. But let me ask one question. The basic thing in a sex killing is sex, not the killing. Killing is just the preliminary excitement. Right?"

"More or less, yes."

"Then if this were a straight sex killing, the man wouldn't have been able to control himself, would he?"

"It's not likely, but I won't answer that yes or no, Ben. I don't know the circumstances, so don't quote me."

"I won't, Doc. But off the record—?"

"Off the record, it was not a sex killing."

"Was the girl drunk? Now wait a minute, wait a minute. This is off the record. I'm not going to give it to the newspapers. You're so Goddamn suspicious, damnit!"

"Oh, come, come, Ben," the Medical Examiner chuckled softly. "You know I vote the straight-party ticket. I don't know what you're talking about."

"If ever you need a blood transfusion, Doc remind me to be a donor. My mother was Typhoid Mary. Was the girl drunk, or wasn't she?"

"Off the record, I'd say she was soused, not just drunk. If she were up on a hit-and-run charge, I'd say she was incapable of operating a motor vehicle."

"I'll put that in the press release, Doc. The girl was killed because she was incapable of operating a motor vehicle. Sorry, Doc. I'm tired, too. I've got the picture, and anything I tell the papers will be my own responsibility. Now what about the Widdicomb drowning? Have you seen a report on that yet?"

"Well, yes. Just a minute. I have it here. I think Harold Casperson examined her. Here it is—" there was a pause and Tutchek heard Knight mumbling to himself as he read through the report of Assistant Medical Examiner Harold Casperson. "Right forehead badly bruised, head gashed over the left ear, abrasions on left wrist, other contusions and abrasions—Hm. Found floating in the river. Automobile accident, Ben?"

"We don't know. Kitteridge thinks she was robbed, beaten up and thrown in the river. She was quite wealthy and probably wore expensive jewelry. It's Kitteridge's idea that she got those abrasions on the left wrist when they ripped the wristwatch off her."

"Well, yes. That could be. Just a moment— Let's see now, jewelry— pearl earrings, that's all. Here. Skinned knuckle, third finger, left hand. That sounds as if they pulled a ring off her too, doesn't it? You can lose a wristwatch in a motor accident, but not a ring. Not very easily. Looks to me as if someone pulled the ring off her finger. That changes things, doesn't it? I'd have called it a motor accident. But maybe your man Kitteridge is right, Ben. According to Hal Casperson's report, the ring was pulled off before she went in the river."

"Oh Christ."

"Sorry, Ben. But it still could be a motor accident."

"Yeah, sure. Let's forget the ring. Well, thanks, Doc."

"Ben—"

"Yeah?"

"On this Meade thing. I saw Herb Winkler's report and talked it over with him. There's not going to be anything about a gunshot in the report."

"But Herb said—"

"Herb's a good doctor. He knows his business. But he's excitable. He gets his back up when somebody contradicts him. And the way they tried to push him around in Meade's office this morning—well, that's no way to treat a boy like Herb. He'll have to learn to take it, Ben. If he didn't know his business—basically—I'd have booted him out of the office when he turned in that report today. There is absolutely no medical way of proving that a shallow wound of that sort was caused by a gunshot. Meade's doctor was right, and Herb was wrong. Nonono. Don't misunderstand me. Herb wasn't wrong when he said it could have been caused by a gunshot, but he was wrong to say that nothing but a gunshot could have made such a wound. As an example, and this is a medical classic, there was the Cladgett case in Linwood, New Jersey, three years ago. The man was examined by two qualified practitioners, one with a war record, and both stated positively that the man had been shot through the forehead by a .45 caliber bullet.

"But how did it turn out? Cladgett had been walking at the side of a marl road when a five-ton gravel truck passed. The rear tire of the truck flipped a pebble, and it went through Cladgett's head like a bullet. If the truck driver hadn't come forward later to say that he'd glanced in the rear-view mirror after passing Cladgett and saw him fall, the police would have arrested every man in South Jersey who ever owned a .45. They later found the bloodstained pebble, and that clinched it. So what killed Stewart Meade? A bullet? A pebble? A freak accident? I don't know, and neither does Herb Winkler. And so long as our medical reports are open to public inspection, we will not state that Stewart Meade was killed by a gunshot."

"Then what did kill him, Doc?"

"Cerebral hemorrhage. Caused by a head wound of unknown origin."

Some of the pressure went off Tutchek, but he was immediately angry with himself for feeling that way. But on the other hand, damnit, why shouldn't he feel relieved? Sure, it got Councilman Selig off the back of his neck, but that didn't mean he was playing ball with City Hall. The investigation would continue exactly as planned. Nothing was changed.

He glanced quickly at the three men sitting across the desk from him, but they were engrossed in the photographs of the murdered young girl, and apparently had been paying no attention to the conversation. Not that it meant anything, one way or the other.

"Well, we'll call it a cerebral hemorrhage for the time being," he said to the Medical Examiner. "But that doesn't change anything."

"Of course it doesn't," Knight barked. "Who said it did? Now is that all, I hope? I've got work to do."

"That's all. And thanks, Doc."

"I thought you'd thank me." Knight laughed sourly, and hung up.

Tutchek frowned, then shrugged it off. He had too much on his own mind without trying to figure out what was on Doctor Knight's.

Nine

He pushed the phone away from him and said impatiently, "Well, how are we doing?"

The police artist was a slight, pale man. His fair, thinning hair looked pink where the scalp showed through. He had the bemused air of a Sunday afternoon stroller through a museum of art, gently disapproving of everything he saw. But his smile was indulgent and remote, as if it really didn't matter at all.

His name was Hartley Malcolm, and he looked like the sort of person who would automatically be called Hartley. Not Hart, not Lee, nor any other nickname. He looked a little precious and languid, and really should have been called Hartley. Perhaps anywhere else in the world, except police headquarters, he would have been called Hartley, but the men who worked here were rough realists, and when they gave a man a nickname, it was usually because they felt it suited him better than the one sprinkled on him in baptism. So, in police headquarters, Hartley Malcolm was known as McGimp. The full nickname was Pimp McGimp, but you can hardly call a man Pimp to his face, and he was generally known as McGimp, or *the* McGimp. A clue to this, possibly, was in his eyes. They were pale blue, almost colorless, dreamy, ascetic, and just a little mad.

Still, he was one of the best police artists in the state, and at times more valuable than a camera, for he could *see* with an artist's perceptive eye, and a camera could only record. So, perhaps it was just as well that he was a little mad.

Except for one thing: he gave everybody the creeps.

He had two of the eight-by-ten glossies in his hand and he looked at them with the cultured appreciation of a connoisseur. "Beautiful photographs," he said, "beautiful. So sharply delineated, so descriptive, so immediate."

And that was what gave people the creeps. Other men might look at macabre photographs, such as these, and feel their stomachs churn, or stolidly, as possible, regard them objectively, but the McGimp always had something to say, and it was always something that set your teeth on edge.

"Come off it, for Christ sake," said Tutchek roughly. "I'm busy. Can you reconstruct that face, or can't you?"

"Oh now, come, please, Lieutenant," McGimp was maliciously reproachful. "I'm only a humble illustrator, not God."

"You're going to be even more humble in about ten seconds if you don't answer my question. We need a face for identification. Is it possible? That's all I want to know."

McGimp sighed and pretended to study the photographs with tranquil attention. This was an act. He had several acts. Sometimes he wept, and sometimes he derided in such a way that afterward you felt unclean and wanted to wash your ears, for having listened. He seemed happiest when he made you feel angry or naked or dirty.

Tutchek remembered this, and checked his temper. "Truthfully," he said, "I don't think there's much you can do. There's nothing to work with."

"Of course there's nothing if you don't know what to look for," McGimp snapped.

His almost childish vanity was always close to the surface, and he was easy to sting, when a guy knew how. It was the only way to handle him when he went into an act or a tantrum.

"Just what am I supposed to look at?" asked Tutchek carelessly. "Her dimples?"

"The bones, man, the bones. He broke her nose and tore up the flesh and kicked in her teeth, but he didn't change the structure of her face. It's still there, if you know how to look."

"Horseshit."

"I'll show you. Here ... She had heavy bones. All you can see is that she looked skinny, but the whole skeleton is heavy. This is a Slavic face. Polish, perhaps. The cheek-bones are high and broad. They pushed against the eyes and made them seem thin and squinty. A Slavic characteristic," he was trying to sound contemptuous, but his voice shook with the urgency to show that he knew more than Tutchek. "The nose was broad and probably tilted at the nostrils. Slightly porcine. The mouth was wide, quite wide, slightly V-shaped, sloping down to the ends. The underlip was heavy and may have seemed to pull down the upper lip, but the long V-shape was there. Because of the upper teeth. They're kicked in, but I can see. The upper lip will usually follow the line of the teeth, and the stubs of the teeth show a V-shape. And the two front ones on top were slightly protuberant. That would accent the V. This would give her an angry expression. Sexually exciting to men with primitive thresholds of tactile awareness," he raised a quick veiled glance at Tutchek's own broad-boned face and giggled. "The jaw is broken in three places and looks like a mess to you, doesn't it? Well, it's not. The basic structure is unaltered, my friend. The dangerous clown who snuffed out this brief candle did not know his business. You cannot alter structure by kicking it slightly to the right. He should have carried the bones off with him, to bury at the foot of a green bay tree. This was not a fragile, lady-like jaw, *Herr Leutnant*. It matched the rest of her and she had a heavy chin. Forgive me for seeming a latter-day Lombroso, but this was not an easy young lady to get along with. And now—" he flipped open his sketch pad with a flourish— "I will show her to you."

Tutchek saw Bierce and Caputo exchange grimaces and roll their eyes, and he felt an angry prickle of resentment. Couldn't the fools realize that there were some things you had to put up with if you wanted results? They knew the McGimp. They'd known him for years. They knew what to expect. *And* they knew how good he was, too, in spite of all his la-dee-da crap. Yet, if they had their way, they'd call him a friggin' fairy and hoot him out of the office, just because they didn't like the way he flounced.

Oh Christ! Tutchek thought, *and I'm supposed to run a division with lack-wits like those two!*

The McGimp's shrewd pencil flew over the rough surfaces of his sketch pad, and suddenly, out of the hieroglyphics of sharp lines and swift shadows, there was a face. McGimp ripped the sheet from the pad with another of his flourishes, and laid it on the desk in front of Tutchek.

"There you are, my friend. God could do better, but that's close enough," he said arrogantly. "Not a spitting image, I grant you. But then, ladies don't spit, do they?"

Tutchek straightened the sheet on his desk. Bierce and Caputo came automatically from their chairs to the ends of the desk, craning their necks for a better view. In those few minutes, the McGimp had really done a job. Whether or not this was the true face of the girl, it was still a face a man would remember. It was the face of a fourteen-year-old girl, all right, it's future character indicated, but not yet formed, but plainly shown, nonetheless.

It was the gaunt young face of early malnutrition but, as McGimp had said, the bones were heavy. It was a sullen face with a hint of violence in it, brutalized and defiant.

Tutchek felt a stab when he looked at it, for he had seen the faces of young Polish girls, heavy-boned faces like this, and he knew that the violence in this one might just as easily have been passion, and that the wide mouth might have been generous.

"Can you give me a side view on this, too?" he asked.

"I can do anything," McGimp jeered. "I'll put a crown on her head and make her Miss America."

"How long will it take you to do the front and side in ink? A week?"

"I'll give it to you in less than an hour," said McGimp furiously.

"I'll believe that when I see it."

McGimp sniffed and left the office, all but stamping his foot before he went.

Tutchek said to Bierce and Caputo, "Stay with him, and as soon as the drawings are done, run off a thousand copies on the photo-offset. See that I get a dozen of each. Distribute the rest to the precincts. Give the North Hudson Precinct a hundred. That's Polack Town up there, and we may get a lead."

"There are a lot of Polacks down at The Point, too, Lieutenant," said Caputo. "They work in the slaughter houses. Do you want us to leave fifty there, too?"

"Of course. What do you want me to do, lay it out precinct by precinct for you? Now get going. Circulate those pictures as fast as you can." And then, automatically, he added, "And report back to me."

Caputo said, "Yes, sir," in a wooden voice, and followed Bierce out of the office.

Ten

Tutchek rested his big forearms on the desk and closed his eyes for a moment. He opened them and shook his head to clear it of the encroaching drowsiness. Wouldn't it be wonderful to sleep forever, then lie back and take a nice long nap? He spied the two cartons of black coffee Ike Bierce had brought, and reached for one of them. His stomach turned over at the thought of taking anything, food or drink, but he swallowed the coffee in long, dogged gulps. It made him feel sodden but he knew it would keep him awake.

Slowly he reassembled his thoughts. Alec Gillespie and the others were waiting for him outside, but first he had to make a phone call. What was it now? Oh yes, the Meade case. It would be better for the investigation if he kept clear of the newspapers for the time being. Fooling around with a lot of reporters would complicate things, and it wasn't necessary. As it stood, Meade's personal physician, Dr. Coombs, could do the smoothest job of giving the news to the press. He did not like to handle it this way, he told himself, but it would help the investigation all 'round if the publicity were temporarily subdued. He looked up the number in the phone book, then called Coombs.

He identified himself and Coombs said, "Oh yes. What can I do for you, Lieutenant?" If the doctor had a warm bedside manner, this was not it.

"I have a report from the Medical Examiner's office, doctor, and it has been officially decided to list the death as a cerebral hemorrhage caused by a head wound of unknown origin."

"Oh." Coombs sounded startled, and when he spoke again, his manner was more cordial, "I agree with that, as you know, Lieutenant. I think that to make a more positive statement at this time would be most unwise. *And* might do a great deal of harm, especially if it had to be retracted later."

"No doubt. But you understand this can't be kept out of the newspapers. Do you think you can take care of that end of it?"

"You want me to release a statement to the papers?"

"Yes. I'll tell the reporters to get in touch with you for the medical facts. You were Meade's doctor, you have his past medical history—and they might question you about that—and you were the first to examine him after the death was discovered."

"That's perfectly true. I'll get in touch with Mr. Theodore LaFarge and we'll prepare a formal statement. I am somewhat acquainted with newspaper procedure, and I know the reporters will want as full a biography as possible for the obituary."

"Let me have a copy of that, too, will you? I'd like to know something about his background myself. Get it to me today, if you can."

"Of course."

"We're not dropping the investigation. That head wound has still to be explained. So if you come upon any information that might help, I want you to call me personally. You understand that too, don't you?"

"Oh perfectly, Lieutenant, perfectly. I'll do everything I can, be assured of that. And also I'd like you to know that I think you are acting most judiciously in this matter, and I'm sure that Mr. LaFarge will agree with me in that."

Tutchek said, "Yeah. Be sure to get a copy of Meade's background over to me this afternoon."

He hung up, not wanting to listen to any more of Coombs's bland assurances. He rested for a minute or two, took another swallow of coffee, and went out into the Homicide squad room, where Lieutenant Gillespie and detectives Kitteridge, Stephano and Koch were waiting for him. They gathered around the cigarette and cigar-scarred oak worktable in the middle of the room, and Tutchek said to Gillespie, "Now how far have you gotten, Alec? Give me the run-down."

"Well—we don't have too much yet, Ben," Gillespie slowly filled the crusty briar pipe, giving himself time to think it over. "The woman was examined by Hal Casperson. He said she wasn't killed by those blows on the head, but they knocked her out. She was unconscious when she went into the river and drowned."

"Did he agree with the holdup theory?"

"He's not in a position to say anything about that one way or the other, Ben, except that the scrapes on her wrist finger show that the wristwatch and ring were pulled off by force. Force was used. That's all he can say. And that's all we can say, at the minute."

"You've been working on it for hours, for Christ sake, Alec. We knew that much this morning. Did you get a positive identification?"

The three detectives looked sullen at this outburst, and Gillespie looked surprised, but did not reply to the rebuke.

"There was a label from the DeJongg Shop inside her evening dress," he continued in his even voice. "Kitteridge and Stephano took it to the shop. DeJongg told them that the dress had been sold to a Mrs. Helen Widdicomb, a regular customer. He verified this from his office records. Kitteridge described the woman to him, and he identified her as Mrs. Widdicomb. He said her address was twenty-seven Pomander Walk, where she lived with her widowed sister, a Mrs. Esther Langston, also a customer of the DeJongg shop."

"That's nothing but hearsay, Alec," said Tutchek, giving rein to his impatience. "What I want to know is, did you get a positive identification?"

Gillespie gave Tutchek's tired face a quick, narrow glance, and went on, "I'm coming to that, Ben. Stephano took DeJongg to the morgue after the body had been removed there, and he identified her as the Mrs. Widdicomb who had purchased the dress. She had been his customer for several years, so he was well acquainted with her. Stephano questioned him further, and he said it was believed that Mrs. Widdicomb was thought to be quite wealthy, and often wore expensive jewelry. He remembered a diamond and emerald wristwatch which she had been wearing for the past few months. He naturally could not say how much it cost, nor would he make a guess, but he did say it was obviously valuable."

"What did he mean by valuable?" Tutchek demanded, looking at the swarthy Stephano. "Two hundred? Two thousand? Did you ask?"

Stephano scowled. "Sure I asked," he had a rumbling voice. "I said, 'A couple thousand maybe?' And he said, 'At least.' But he's not a jeweler, so what else could he say?"

"Did he describe it?"

"He said it was round and about the size of a nickel, and had diamonds instead of numbers. The case and band were platinum. There was a round emerald where the case joined the band, and the band itself was set with diamonds. The band was about an eighth of an inch wide, and the platinum settings for the diamonds were square and linked or hinged together."

"Mr. DeJongg sure notices things, doesn't he. He did everything but appraise it. If you ask me, that's what he bases his fancy prices on when he sells a dress. What did he have to say about the ring?"

Stephano slid a wary glance at Gillespie, as if asking for support if Tutchek continued to question him in this hectoring way.

"He said it was an engagement ring," he muttered. "A big oblong diamond in a plain platinum setting. He knew something about diamonds and said it was worth five or six thousand dollars. She started wearing it about two months ago."

"Very observant is Mr. DeJongg. But that's business, I suppose." Tutchek did not realize he was hammering at Stephano; he was just impatient with these details, but knew they were important. "Did he know who she was engaged to?"

"No, sir."

"Did you ask?"

"Yes, sir."

"Did he have anything else to say?"

"No, sir."

"Okay," Tutchek turned abruptly back to Gillespie. "Now what about the sister? What's her name? Mrs. Langston? Did anybody get in touch with her?"

"Kitteridge tried, Ben."

"Tried? What do you mean, tried?" Tutchek stared at Kitteridge. "How did you try?"

Kitteridge was a lean, nervous-looking man, and he kept his hands out of sight below the tabletop, as if afraid they might betray his nervousness. But this was only a habit with him; he either used his hands volubly when he talked or, realizing this, self-consciously folded them in his lap to keep from waving them too much.

"I went to the house on Pomander Walk, Lieutenant," he said in a characteristic rapid voice. "There was nobody home but the maid, and I talked to her. She said Mrs. Langston went shopping before lunch and would probably be back in the middle of the afternoon."

Tutchek glanced at his wristwatch and was startled to see that it was four-thirty.

"It's past the middle of the afternoon now," he said. "Didn't you wait for her?"

Kitteridge's mouth tightened. "I phoned in, Lieutenant, and was told you wanted to talk to us here."

"I told him to come in, Ben," Gillespie interrupted. "You left word with Miss Lund that you wanted to see us, so I called him in."

"For the love of Jesus, Alec, why did you call him in before he talked to the woman? She was due back from shopping any minute—"

"I'd been waiting three-quarters of an hour by that time. Lieutenant," Kitteridge put in, defending Gillespie. "That was four o'clock, and the maid said it might be another hour. She said Mrs. Langston sometimes stopped off for cocktails before coming home."

"You should have used your head, man—"

"Wait, wait, Ben," Gillespie objected. "Let's hold everything for a minute. If you're going to blame anybody, blame me, not Kitteridge. I'm the one who told him to come in. You left a message with Miss Lund saying you wanted to talk to us, and I didn't think you'd call us in unless you had something we didn't."

"How could you think *I* had anything, Alec? I was working on the Meade case with Flavin and Gilman, and then I had to go over that rape in South Branch Park with Bierce and Caputo. Plus a half-dozen other things. So where would I get time to work on this? I asked you to meet me here because I wanted information, not a kaffeeklatsch."

"My mistake," said Gillespie shortly.

"All right, all right. Let's forget it. Perhaps I didn't make myself plain enough to Miss Lund. I'll be more specific the next time. Anyway, there's no harm done. We haven't lost anything except a little time," Tutchek delivered this half-apology with small, irritated gestures, which had the effect of making it sound like another rebuke. "Let's all calm down and see if we can keep this thing moving. Do you and Koch have anything?"

Gillespie looked a little pale and he took a long minute to re-light his pipe. His own temper had risen, but this was neither the time nor the place to let it go.

"Well ..." he said, steadying his voice. "There are three bridges over the river above the East Coast Fisheries, and she might have been thrown off any one of them."

"You'd be wasting your time unless you got a witness, Alec, and that's damned unlikely."

"I wasn't thinking of a witness," said Gillespie stubbornly. "I had the Belgrove Drive Bridge in mind particularly. There's very little traffic over it late at night, and we had a holdup there late in April. There's a bad curve just before you come to it. Cars have to slow down to ten, fifteen miles an hour. We tried to get more lights put up at the curve, but no dice. You know City Hall."

Tutchek did not react to the 'City Hall' bait, not even to make a sour joke. "Did you go there?" he demanded. "Did you find anything?"

"Yes, we went," said Gillespie wearily. "And no, we didn't find anything."

"What did you expect to find?"

"I didn't *expect* anything, Ben. I was just looking—paint freshly scraped off the handrail, blood perhaps, a bit of torn clothing, marks on the shoulder of the road where she'd been dragged, anything that might have been dropped. It would have been a help if we knew where it happened. That's what we've got stool pigeons for. Maybe we could find out who's been working holdups or muggings in that particular area. As it stands now, there have been muggings in the area of all three bridges, and that covers too much ground. If we can narrow it down to one we can start asking specific questions. And you know as well as I do, Ben, that a mugger will use the same territory over and over, and all it takes to turn a mugging into a holdup is a gun, and these days you can almost get a gun in a box of Cracker Jacks."

"You've got a lot of territory to cover," said Tutchek dryly. "There are three miles of river above East Coast Fisheries before you come to the city line. And if she wasn't knocked off in the city, you've got another twenty miles of river above the city line. You'd be weeks following that line of investigation. Unless somebody hands it to you on a silver platter."

"Do you suggest we give it up, then?" asked Gillespie in a formal voice.

"I suggest we keep it in mind," snapped Tutchek. "If we had a hundred men in the Division, I'd say go ahead. But we don't have a hundred. We don't even have twenty. Everybody's tied up, and on top of that I had to send four men to Captain Willis. And don't forget we're working on two other major investigations. We're shorthanded, Alec. We have to make every man count." Then, flatly, "I can't afford to have four men tied up in this Widdicomb thing, especially chasing down an idea that may or may not turn up a lead."

Gillespie was watching him intently as he hammered out the words, beating on the table with his huge fist to emphasize each point, and he saw the telltale pouches and hollows of fatigue and strain that were beginning to draw at Tutchek's face, pulling it down, making it look longer and gray and making the mouth seem pinched. He noticed, too, the jerky way in which Tutchek was beginning to talk, Tutchek who had seldom hurried his voice before. He saw all this with dismay, for there was nothing he could do to stop Tutchek from driving himself too hard.

He could be patient, and that was about all. Be patient, and take it on the chin for a while, and try not to cross Tutchek if he could possibly help it.

"You're right about our being shorthanded, Ben," he said. "How do you want this handled?"

Tutchek sat back in his chair and looked vaguely beyond them, thinking. "She had on an evening dress, so she must have been out with somebody last night," he said after a while. "I'll take Kitteridge and go see the sister. What's her name? Mrs. Langston? She should be able to give us that information. Also, we want a full description of the ring and wristwatch. We'll turn that over to the Pawnshop Detail in case somebody tried to fence it. Didn't it occur to any of you that she was probably out *with* somebody last night?"

There was a retort at the verge of Kitteridge's quick tongue, but Gillespie warned him to silence with a glance. "Yes, we thought of it, Ben, but it hasn't been verified yet."

"Didn't Kitteridge ask the maid?"

"She was only a day maid, Lieutenant," Kitteridge said. "She only works three times a week and wasn't there yesterday. But I did ask her and she said Mrs. Widdicomb mainly went out alone. The sister doesn't go out at night at all. She's a kind of invalid."

"Mrs. Widdicomb goes out alone at night and she's engaged to be married? That doesn't make sense."

"The maid said the man she's engaged to does a lot of traveling and is out of the city for weeks at a time."

"Why didn't you bring this up before?"

Kitteridge wanted to snap back, You didn't give me time! —but he remembered Gillespie's warning glance, and merely said, "I didn't get around to it. And anyway, the maid didn't really know anything."

Tutchek nodded. He was tired of this squabbling, and tired of trying to pull information out of them bit by bit. The thing to do now was keep it moving. He pushed himself up heavily from his chair.

"I've got a couple things to take up with Miss Lund," he said. "Then I'll go out to see Mrs. Langston with Kitteridge. I want Stephano and Koch to work with Bierce and Caputo on the rape case. McGimp is making some drawings to see if we can get the girl identified. That's the most important thing on our agenda right now, the way the papers have played it up on the front page. We can't let it stand still. It's too hot. The drawings are going to be run off on the photo offset, and I want them distributed to all precincts. I want Stephano and Koch to help get them out as fast as possible, and don't let anything interfere. When that's done," he paused, "... report back to me."

Gillespie said, "Sure, Ben. I'll take care of it. Is there anything else you want me to do?"

Tutchek's answer was like a slap. "No, just kind of look after the office till I get back," he said carelessly.

He left the four men staring at one another and plodded from the room to Policewoman Lund's cubicle outside the door. He told her to get out her notebook, and quickly dictated a press release on the rape killing. There was not much new to add to the story already printed, except that the police artist had reconstructed her face from photographs. Each of the reporters was to be given a pair of the drawings. He added a cautious note that police were investigating a possibility that rape had not been attempted.

"Now the Widdicomb drowning," he said tiredly. "Just give them the facts from the Crime Report and the Medical Examiner's report, and say we are investigating the possibility of a holdup. When they ask about the Meade death, tell them they can get complete information from Dr. Coombs or Mr. LaFarge of LaFarge Associates. Type them up and show them to Lieutenant Gillespie before giving them to the reporters."

He nodded meaninglessly and went back into the squad room. Kitteridge was the only one there. Stephano and Koch had gone and Gillespie was in the office. Tutchek trudged to the office.

"Miss Lund is typing up some handouts, Alec," he said. "Look them over before you let them go. I don't want any mention of an investigation in the Meade release. We'll come to that when we have something more definite."

"Sure, Ben. Do you want me to look over some of that paper work on your desk while you're gone? Weed it out a little, maybe?"

That was actually part of his job as administration officer, but Tutchek had not yet turned it over to him.

Tutchek said, "What? Oh. No, no. I'll go through it after I talk to the Langston woman. Just make sure there are no mistakes in the press releases."

He took his jacket from the nail in the back of the door and walked out, pushing his arms into the sleeves.

Eleven

Mrs. Esther Langston was lying unconscious on the sofa. She had fainted and slid from her chair to the floor with a small moan when Tutchek told her that her sister had been found dead. He had not been blunt, but there was no soothing way to break news like that. The maid was having hysterics in the kitchen.

"Shut that Goddamned woman up!" he roared at Kitteridge. "And get a glass of water or some smelling salts, or something."

It was ten minutes before Mrs. Langston recovered sufficiently to sit up. She was a tall, thin woman with the transparent complexion and pale lips of chronic anemia. Her pink-rimmed eyes rolled a little but she retained a grip on sanity.

"I'm quite all right now, Lieutenant," she said in a weak voice. "The shock, it was a terrible shock."

"But weren't you worried when your sister didn't come home last night, Mrs. Langston?" Tutchek asked.

"No, no, not really," her eyes wavered. "She ... she often went off for days without telling me anything."

"Did she go out alone last night?"

"Alone? Well—no, no. She and Charles Erdese went out to dinner. She and Charles are ... were engaged to be married. They ... they were very devoted. It was a very sudden engagement. Less than two months ago," her voice sounded a little wild but she did not lose control of it.

"Does Charles Erdese live here in the city?"

"Yes, yes. He, he has an apartment on Mt. Windsor Avenue, I believe."

Tutchek looked over his shoulder at Kitteridge. "Get in touch with him," he ordered, and turned back to Mrs. Langston. "We've been told that your sister was in the habit of wearing expensive jewelry. Do you know if she was wearing it last night?"

"She wore very little jewelry, Lieutenant. Very little. She never wore anything but pearl earrings and they weren't expensive. Oh yes, and her wristwatch. And naturally her engagement ring."

"It was an expensive watch, wasn't it?"

"Very. She paid thirty-two hundred dollars for it at Hoek and Sons on Webster Place, and *nothing* is inexpensive at Hoek's. She bought it right after she broke her en—" she pressed her pale lips together and looked unhappily down at the thin hands folded together in her lap.

"Broke what, Mrs. Langston?" Tutchek pressed her. "Broke her engagement? When was this?"

"It's something that happened last year, Lieutenant, and has no importance now."

"At this point, Mrs. Langston, nothing is unimportant. What about this broken engagement? Was it Erdese?"

"Yes. I don't know why the engagement was broken, except that they were both very strong-willed. Alice was always headstrong. However, that was when she purchased the wristwatch. She called it her consolation prize. She was very unhappy."

"Was there any trouble between them last night?"

"I have no way of knowing that, Lieutenant, but I'm certain there was not. They were to have been married in October after Charles returned from Brazil. He's a consulting engineer and travels extensively. Alice was looking forward to traveling with him later. They were very devoted."

Kitteridge appeared in the doorway to the hall where the telephone was. He shook his head and said, "I can't get an answer from the apartment, Lieutenant."

Tutchek looked sharply at Mrs. Langston. "Does Erdese have an office here in the city?"

"You—you don't think something happened to him, too, do you, Lieutenant?" There was horror in her eyes.

"We have no reason to think so, Mrs. Langston. But do you know his business address?"

"No, I don't ... but I think Alice wrote it in that little red-covered notebook beside the phone."

Tutchek said, "Thanks," and went out to the phone. He flipped the pages and found "Chas." listed at the top of the E page, and beneath that were two numbers. The HUdson 7-3310 would be the downtown exchange, and he called that. He was answered by an impersonal feminine voice, and asked for Charles Erdese.

"Mrs. Langston said I might reach him at this number," he said. "It's personal, and very important that I talk to him."

She evidently knew Mrs. Langston, for she said, "Oh dear, Mr. Erdese flew to Chicago this morning and didn't leave an address."

"Don't you have any idea how I can reach him? He'd go to a hotel, wouldn't he?"

"Sometimes he stays with friends or business associates."

"Did he go on business?"

"Oh dear, I wish I could help, but I don't know. He merely said he'd be gone several days, and that's all. Oh, just a moment. We did have an inquiry from Drexel Industries in Chicago, but Mr. Erdese turned them down. It was a large construction project in South Africa, but it would have meant spending two years there. Mr. Erdese may have reconsidered, but it's not likely. He doesn't accept such long range contracts."

"Doesn't he have a favorite hotel in Chicago? Most people do."

"Well—the Tuscany, perhaps, but not particularly. Oh dear, you must think me dreadfully inefficient, but Mr. Erdese doesn't really like *any* hotels. He's had to stay in too many. It's one of his jokes that he'd rather sleep on a sofa in someone's living room, but I think he means it. But if he did stay at a hotel, it would be on Lake Shore Drive. He'd insist on a view of the water."

"Well, thanks a lot. I'll see what I can do. My name is Tutchek, by the way. Ben Tutchek. If you happen to think of anything, you can reach me or leave a message at HUdson 7-0209." That was the phone booth on the first floor of Headquarters, and not an official number.

He went back into the living room. Mrs. Langston's eyes were enormous, and she watched him with wordless dread.

"We'll have to be getting along now, Mrs. Langston," he said. "I want to get a description of that wristwatch from Hoek and Sons. I'm sorry, but you'll have to go to the morgue to identify your sister. I know it's not easy, but it has to be done. Do you want Detective Kitteridge to go with you?"

"No, no. I—I'd rather go alone. I'll take a cab. Did—did you talk to Charles? Oh, how awful for him! He'll be heartbroken. He was devoted to Alice."

"You have enough on your mind, Mrs. Langston. We'll get in touch with you later."

He motioned to Kitteridge and they left quickly before her mounting hysteria burst upon them. It was a silent drive back to Headquarters.

Tutchek offered no information, but sat slumped in the seat beside Kitteridge, his chin resting on his chest, his eyes half-open. It was Kitteridge who broke the silence.

"Did you get a line on Erdese, Lieutenant," he asked finally.

Tutchek roused himself. "He flew to Chicago this morning."

Kitteridge whistled. "Just like that, eh?"

"It doesn't have to mean anything. He was always flying somewhere on business."

"But if he took the Widdicomb dame out, boss, why didn't he bring her home?"

"I don't know. Maybe they had a fight and she started for home in a cab. She might have picked the wrong cab, and Christ knows, there are plenty of wrong cabs in the city. According to Mrs. Langston, this wouldn't be the first lovers' spat they had. They were engaged last year and broke it off. She let slip that Erdese's got a temper."

"So maybe there wasn't any cab, boss. If he's got that kind of temper, well, maybe they got in a scrap and he took a slap at her and slapped a little too hard, then tried to make it look like a holdup."

"I know, I know, but let's wait till we talk to him. We can 'maybe' ourselves to death."

"Yeah. But that Mrs. Langston was lying by the clock, Lieutenant."

"Lying?"

"Well, maybe not lying, but she wasn't telling you everything. I had a feeling she was covering for Erdese. She damn near fainted a couple times while you were out in the hall phoning. I think she knew he'd skipped out."

"Did she say anything?"

"No, but she knew something about him. She started shaking like a leaf when you went out to phone. She was closer to the door than I was and must have heard something you said, because all of a sudden she calmed down a little."

Tutchek gave his shoulders an irritated shake. He did not want to hear any more of Kitteridge's wildcat hunches, and that's all this was, a hunch, and a far-fetched one, at that.

"The woman was hysterical, Kitteridge," he said. "Keep that in mind, will you? She's also anemic and obviously a semi-invalid. She wasn't pulling any cute tricks, man. She was just about to blow her top, and that's why I got out of there. Now come on, step on the gas, will you. I got a million things to take care of."

Back at Headquarters, Tutchek went straight to the Communications desk and dictated a pickup for Erdese to be sent immediately to the Chicago police, adding the information he had gotten from Erdese's secretary. He took care of this personally, while Kitteridge went stonily to the drug store down the street to get him a package of cigarettes and a bottle of aspirin.

George Gilman and Jeff Flavin were waiting for him in the Homicide squad room upstairs. It took Tutchek a moment or two to recall their assignments. The Meade case, of course. Gilman and a couple of appraisers had taken an inventory of that female stuff in Meade's apartment. Flavin had been working on the call-girl angle.

He motioned them to the worktable in the middle of the room and slouched down in the chair at the end of it, lighting a cigarette from the stub of the one he was just finishing. The smoke felt like bits of ground-up razor blades in his throat as he inhaled.

"How'd it add up, George?" he asked, at length.

Gilman had a long, blue-lined yellow pad on which all the items were listed, together with the appraisers' estimate of their probable cost. There were several pages of this.

Gilman made a little throat-clearing sound, as he usually did before beginning to talk. "Now I know you don't want all of this piece by piece, Lieutenant, so I'll—"

Policewoman Lund interrupted, calling from her desk, "Councilman Selig on the phone to talk to you, Lieutenant."

Tutchek said, "Oh hell," and lumbered across the room to a phone on one of the side desks. "Yes, Councilman ..."

"Listen, Ben I just called to apologize for flipping my lid this morning." Selig sounded like a contented cow who gave nothing but the Grade-A milk of human kindness. "I said a lot of things I didn't mean, and I don't want you to take them seriously. You know the pressure we are under over here at the Hall. But that's no reason for you and me to have a misunderstanding. I know I shot off my mouth and I want to apologize."

"We all lose our tempers sometime or other," Tutchek mumbled.

"I'm glad you take it that way, Ben. It wasn't actually anything personal. I would have blown up at Jesus Christ himself at that point. You know, the pressure."

"Yeah. The pressure."

"I'm glad you understand, Ben. And I want you to know I have every admiration for you and your boys. You're doing a fine job, and I know it. I was talking to Teddy LaFarge a little while ago and he wants you to know he appreciates the way you're handling the case. You've made a friend there, Ben, a good friend. Any time you want cooperation, he says, be sure to call on him. And that goes for me, too. Remember, everybody in the Hall isn't a horse's ass. We remember our friends."

Tutchek sat there for a moment after he had hung up. A spot of dull anger made his stomach feel a little sick. But there were too many other things to think about. He went back to the worktable.

"I don't want it item by item, George," he said to Gilman. "Just give me a general idea of how much he was spending on the girls."

"It wasn't as much as it looked, Lieutenant. A lot of it was nothing but flash. You know those gold cigarette lighters, lipsticks and compacts in Tiffany gift boxes. Well, the boxes were Tiffany, and that's all. The things themselves were only gold-plated or gold-washed. The cigarette lighters were worth twenty-five bucks apiece tops, the lipsticks about ten, and the compacts about fifteen. You know, the kind of stuff you'd give a dame if you're trying to make an impression but have no intention of going broke while you're doing it. I mean, for a guy with Meade's money. If *I* gave a dame a twenty-five-buck cigarette lighter, I'd be broke for the rest of the month. For Meade, it was just a lot of cheap flash. That part of it, anyways."

"What about the fur coats? There were three Persian lamb coats in the closet. Three different sizes. That didn't look like cheap flash to me, George."

"Well, there's all kinds of cheap flash, Lieutenant. You can give a dame a fur coat, and it's still cheap flash. From what Ed Lynch said—he appraised the coats—you can pay up to fifteen hundred or more for a good Persian lamb. But those coats, he said, were nothing but a lot of fur trimmings sewed together, and if Meade paid a hundred and fifty apiece for them, he paid a lot. That lace underwear is the same story—"

"Telephone, Lieutenant," called Policewoman Lund.

Tutchek swore and trudged across the room to the phone on the side desk. It was Captain Jack Willis, of the Twentieth Precinct house.

"I can't thank you enough for those boys you sent me, Ben," Willis sounded as if he felt like living again. "Muir and Scanlon made two pinches already—"

"Fine, Jack. I'm glad. And you're welcome. But I'm up to my ears right now."

"Sure, Ben. Take it easy man. I just wanted—"

"Tell me tomorrow."

Tutchek returned to Gilman and Flavin at the worktable. He hunched down in the chair and lit another cigarette. "Now where the hell were we?" he growled at Gilman. "Oh yeah, the Goddamned lace underwear. What about it?"

Gilman blinked. "Just that Meade didn't sprain his bankroll buying it, Lieutenant, that's all. It was okay, but nothing special. Ed Lynch called it department-store nylon. Altogether, Ed said Meade didn't put out more than seven hundred bucks retail for the whole works, and if he got a rate, which he probably did, it would be closer to five."

Tutchek looked incredulous, but before he could object, Jeff Flavin said, "That fits in with what I turned up, Ben."

"Let's hear it."

"I put Birdie Burdson on the call-girl angle. You know Birdie?"

Tutchek nodded. Yes, he knew Birdie. Birdie had been a con-man, one of the best—he knew them all—but old age and hard times had caught up with Birdie, and now he was a part-time bookie, tout, errand boy, but chiefly he was a fink. "Fink" was the contemptuous synonym for stool pigeon, which was hardly in need of a contemptuous synonym. Still, as finks went, Birdie was better than average, which was to say, you could trust him fifty per cent of the time.

"Birdie's all right if you watch him," Tutchek said. "But what's a broken-down con-man know about call girls?"

"Oh, he hangs around with them a little. He runs errands for them, and things like that, and they buy him drinks. He can still put up a pretty fair front when he's got a clean shirt. Anyway, they'll talk to him, and that's the main thing."

"The *main* thing is what they had to say about Meade. They knew him, I take it."

"They knew him, all right. He was a good steady customer. But he had no favorites. He played them all at one time or another. He'd stick with a girl for a few weeks or a month, then change to another. Now here's the thing, Ben, he used to be a spender. If he liked a girl and had her for a month or so, he'd give her a big flashy present when he changed over to another one. He paid one girl's rent for six months and that came to nine hundred dollars. He gave another a West Indies cruise and two hundred dollars' expense money. A show-off, you know? If he took them to a night club, he lent them flashy jewelry to wear. There was a diamond necklace, for instance. They all wore that. They called it The Headlights. That's what I mean by 'show-off'. Everything had to be flash. But according to Birdie, the girls say he spent plenty on them. He wasn't stingy."

"I don't get the show-off angle, Jeff. You'd think the president of a corporation like Meade-LaFarge would be too big for that kind of crap."

"LaFarge is the brains of that outfit, Ben. Meade was the greeter, the super-salesman. He could talk anybody into anything. For a while he had the girls thinking he was Mr. Fort Knox, but—"

"Lieutenant Stein on the phone for you, Lieutenant," Policewoman Lund called.

"Hell! Tell him I'll call back."

"But he said—"

"*I'll call back!*" Tutchek turned to Flavin, growling, "The Goddamned interruptions! Now what were you saying, Jeff?"

"Well, this follows what George just told you. Meade changed since last year. No West Indies cruises, no more expensive presents. He got so tight with his money that the girls started calling him the gold-plated Santa Claus."

"Maybe he started cooling off. He was in his middle sixties, remember. A man his age can't keep it up forever."

"No. That's what the girls were griping about. He was hot and heavy and always wanted more than his money's worth. Three or four times a week, the same as before. But he stopped spending the way he used to. Something changed him since last year."

"Maybe he got wise to himself," said Tutchek.

But that was too weak, and they all knew it. Once a spender, always a spender, especially the flashy ones like Meade. The three of them sat in silence, mulling it over.

"Guys like that don't suddenly up and start thinking of getting married," said Gilman, throwing the idea away.

"Here's an angle," Flavin offered. "Maybe he's been hooked by a real worker and's paying her bills. When you get up into the high-class glamor level, it runs into money."

"And he'd still be able to bang it out three or four times a week with the other girls?" Tutchek objected. "Nobody's that good. But here is something maybe we should look into. Is Meade-LaFarge in any kind of financial trouble? That'd put him on a budget quicker than anything. Let's look into both angles. They're both strong angles, and somebody felt strongly enough to break his head open. Take a shot at it."

Flavin's head jerked up, as if about to ask incredulously, "Tonight!" but he could see the answer and let the question go, unasked. Tonight. Right now. Tutchek seemed to have lost all sense of time, and was working 'round the clock. Which meant that everybody had to work 'round the clock, or brace himself for a blast. Although there was hardly a thing anybody could do before tomorrow.

There were not two steadier men than Flavin and Gilman in the Homicide Division, but they strode from the squad room with the hard-heeled step of men who were being driven unnecessarily.

Tutchek had not quite reached the door of his office when Lieutenant Stein stormed past Policewoman Lund, his face the color of clotted beets, but he stopped in mid-fury when Tutchek turned to him in haggard surprise. Tutchek had looked tired that morning in Mackenzie's office, but this was different, and Stein was shocked at the change.

"I'm afraid I've got bad news, Ben," he said, swallowing his anger. "The hospital called. Old Tony Scerbo just died."

"Scerbo?"

"That's the Park Liquor Shop robbery. He was the proprietor. Two punks held him up last night, took over two hundred bucks and a case of Scotch and beat him up. I got one of the punks—Poochy Ryan. We picked him up drunk and full of Scotch. His prints were all over the liquor shop, so he's tied hand and foot. We've been working on him all day, but can't get him to name the other punk. That's the big job now."

"OH JESUS CHRIST!"

"I know," Stein's dark Semitic eyes were full of pity, "Everything happens at once."

Tutchek compressed his mouth and straightened up, and Stein was astounded to see the vigor flow back into that broad, strained face. Tutchek had reserves of vitality he wouldn't have thought possible a moment ago.

"If the homicide rate were something we could control," said Tutchek in a new, crisp voice, "there wouldn't be any."

Alec Gillespie appeared in the doorway of the office, and Tutchek beckoned to him. "We got a new one, Alec," he said. "You might as well hear this because you'll be working on it. Give us the run-down again, will you, Saul?"

Stein quickly went over the facts of the robbery and the beating up of the old man, and the finding of Poochy Ryan that morning, dead drunk in his jalopy.

"The punk insists he was framed, but that doesn't mean a thing," he said. "His prints were in the liquor shop, the money was in his pocket, the case of Scotch in the car, and blood on his clothes. He's a stupid, vicious rat and thinks he's going to get away with it."

"Any other prints in the liquor shop?" Tutchek asked.

"Hell, yes. Dozens of them, all different. It's a shop. People went in to buy liquor and left their prints."

"What about the jalopy?"

"Now you're talking. We lifted a whole set of beautiful clear prints from the right door. Both hands. There's only one trouble. We checked with Records & Identification and they don't have the prints on file. The punk who left them doesn't have a record. So we still have to sweat it out of young Ryan. My boys have been trying to find out who he hangs around with, but so far it's no dice."

"What's his neighborhood?" Tutchek asked.

"He comes from The Point," Stein said bitterly. "He probably runs with the DeKalb Barons gang, and we'll never get anything from those rats, especially now that it's a homicide."

"The Point, eh?" Tutchek mused. "You know, Alec, I think we'll turn this one over to Harry Muir and Rory Scanlon. Nobody knows The Point better. I sent them down there to help Jack Willis, but we'll have to pull them out. He'll scream his head off but it can't be helped. I think the best plan, Saul, is to let them see what they can pick up on Ryan down at The Point. What do you think?"

"That's where they can do the most good. We can handle Ryan at this end. No sense wasting them on that."

"Okay. Handle it that way. Give them the run-down. And get me a full copy of the robbery report. Alec will work with you till I get squared away with some of that paper on my desk."

He swung into his office as if he were just starting, instead of just winding up, a grueling day. Stein and Gillespie walked out of the squad room together.

"Jesus Christ," said Stein, when they were outside. "What gives with Ben? He looked like walking death when I first came in."

Gillespie gave his head a worried shake. "He's been working his ass off for six weeks. It's beginning to show, I guess. It's a big job."

"Is he trying to do it all himself?" asked Stein shrewdly.

"He's been doing a lot," Gillespie evaded.

"I know. I was the same way, but not as bad, when I took over Robbery. Hell, nine-tenths of the commanding officers were the same way, when you come down to it. Afraid someone might slip up. I know. The first month I tried to do everybody's job. That's Ben's trouble."

"He works hard."

"Well, he'll snap out of it."

But they were troubled. They both knew that if Tutchek didn't snap out of it, Captain Mackenzie would take the job away from him.

The challenge of this new homicide had roused Tutchek from the bone-deep weariness, and he worked steadily at the mountain of papers on his desk. On top was the Lab report from Daly and Straub on Meade's shoes, clothing and suitcase. They had found no fingerprints but Meade's on the suitcase, and it was settled now that Meade himself had put the blood-stained shirt and jacket in there. *What the hell had the man thought he was concealing,* Tutchek wondered, *and why had he done it? Was there a chance that he had shot himself? That could be.* He made a note of that on his memo pad, and read the rest of the report. Tests showed that the stains on the knee of the pants had come from grass. Rye grass, summer grass. The earth found in the pant cuffs and on the shoes was a mixture of clay, sand, rotted maple leaves and dried sheep manure. Fertilized loam. Tutchek grimaced. Every garden bed in the city had just about the same mixture. He, himself, had the same thing around his rosebushes. Except for the rotted maples leaves. He had rotted birch leaves, because the tree overhanging his backyard happened to be a birch. He made a note of the maple leaves on his pad. That was the end of the Lab report. Not much help.

He put the paper aside and picked up the next one. He frowned. It was a carbon copy of Meade's biography. What the—oh yes. This was the obituary press release Dr. Coombs had promised to send him. He read it eagerly but his interest soon waned.

"Stewart Meade first became interested in investment real estate in Florida during the great boom of the 1920s, but realizing that this was a bubble about to burst, he returned to Hudson, the city of his birth, in search for sounder values on which to build his fortunes. It was in 1938 that he met Theodore LaFarge, then a young contractor."

And blah blah blah. The same old malarkey. Nothing in it to help anybody. Tutchek skimmed through the sheets, but it was the same from beginning to end, and he paper-clipped it to the other information on the Meade case.

Still, he had a sense of getting something done. It was better working on the paper at night. There were fewer interruptions. Kitteridge came in with his aspirin and cigarettes, and Tutchek sent him out to get a precise description of Mrs. Widdicomb's wristwatch from Hoek and Sons, and told him to turn it over to Pawnshop as quickly as possible before somebody tried to hock or fence it. Kitteridge was gone almost as soon as he had appeared, and Tutchek hardly noticed it as an interruption. He kept working over the papers, memos, letters, inter-department communications, as they came along, making notes and methodically laying the papers aside as he finished. Dinnertime passed, but he did not notice that either; he wasn't hungry. Alec Gillespie came in once to say that Muir and Scanlon had been notified of their new assignment and were working on it. Tutchek nodded vaguely and said okay, and Gillespie went away. By and by, Tutchek's eyes began to blur and it became an effort to read the papers. He sat back in his chair, yawned heavily and glanced at his wristwatch. It was quarter of one. He looked again to make sure it wasn't really five past nine, but the hour hand inexorably pointed to one. He was reluctant to give up, but his eyes actually were sagging, now that he knew the time.

It didn't look as if he'd made much of a dent in those heaped papers, but he knew he'd gotten a lot done. A few more good solid nights like this and he'd begin to see daylight.

He drove home and went to bed. The moment his eyes closed, he began to mumble and turn, and several times his wife bent over him and said worriedly, "Ben, Ben, what is it?" He awakened and said thickly, "Huh? Oh, I was dreaming, I guess." And when he closed his eyes, it started all over again.

Twelve

He was back in the office and at his desk at seven the next morning, after a breakfast of coffee (which he gulped) and eggs, bacon and toast (which he nibbled at, but did not eat. *You can't force yourself to eat when you're not hungry.*) At eight o'clock his intercom buzzed and Policewoman Lund told him that Sergeant Henry Bullen of the Seventh Precinct was there to see him. Sergeant Bullen, a gray-haired fatherly-looking man—a badly frightened father—came timidly into his office, clutching a newspaper in his right hand.

"What's on your mind, Sergeant?" Tutchek asked, much more briskly than he felt.

The sergeant swallowed as if he'd been holding a jigger of poisoned hemlock in his mouth. "It's this Meade death, Lieutenant," he stammered, showing the newspaper and Meade's picture on the front page. Then he blurted desperately, "He came to the precinct house yesterday morning to make a complaint about being hit on the head with a bottle of bathtub gin, he called it, and I thought he was drunk and talked him out of the complaint."

Tutchek came to his feet roaring, *"You what!"*

"Talked him out of it," said Bullen miserably. "I thought he was drunk. I could smell the liquor on him. I told him to go home and sleep it off. Here's the complaint I partly filled out." He laid the complaint form on the desk with a shaking hand.

Tutchek stared at it until his eyes felt as if they would explode. He raised his gaze to Bullen, unaware that Alec Gillespie was standing at the door, listening and watching narrowly.

"He told you he had been hit on the head with a bottle," he said in a dangerously thudding voice, "and you told him to go home and sleep it off. What else did he tell you?"

Bullen ran his tongue over fear-parched lips. "He said he found his wife in bed with this Wesley Buck in the Palm Terrace Hotel on Flagler Street and they were drinking bathtub gin and he threatened them with a gun and one of them hit him with the bottle. But listen, Lieutenant, then he said he was twenty-four years old when it happened. That's what made me think he was drunk. You could see he was in his sixties, he had white hair, and there he was saying he was only twenty-four years old."

"Goddamnit, the man had a hole in his head! He didn't know what he was saying, you damned fool!"

Gillespie saw the mottled violence in Tutchek's face, and thought it time to interrupt. "Now wait a minute, Ben," he said, going forward between Tutchek and the cringing Sergeant. "The man's got a point there. If Meade told you he was twenty-four years old, and smelled of liquor, what would you think?"

Tutchek's mouth writhed as he struggled to fight down his exploding rage. He turned and strode to the window at the side of the office, his fists tied in white knuckly knots.

"All right," he said at length, sounding as if he were strangling on the words. "He's got a point. But why didn't he try to find out what it was all about before sending Meade away?"

"Listen, will you, Ben? There's hardly a cop on the force who hasn't done the same thing time and again. You've done it and I've done it. Would you waste time on a drunk? Hell no. You'd tell him to beat it or you'd throw him in the can. The sergeant did the natural thing. And at least give him some credit for coming to us with the information. It might mean something."

Slowly, that terrible fury seeped out of Tutchek. He drew a hard breath. "Yes," he admitted, "I guess we've all done the same thing, more or less. This was a bad time to do it, though, Sergeant, but I won't hold it against you. Now let's calm down and see what we can salvage. You say he named a man called Wesley Buck and his own wife?"

Sergeant Bullen breathed again. "Yes sir, his own wife, not Buck's. He named them several times. He said they were the ones who attacked him. He might have been mixed up in other things, but he was very positive about that. He also said they registered in the hotel under the name of Wilfred Boyd. Here's something else he said, he said he caught them in a hotel room, then he said he was lying on the ground when he recovered consciousness. Then he said they were too confident, both of them. He made it sound like it really did happen the night before last. He said he saw her face in the moonlight."

"You know, Ben," said Gillespie, "it sounds to me like a mixture of something that *did* just happen and something similar that happened years ago."

"Yes, years. Bathtub gin—the 1920s. Say ...!" Tutchek reached out and picked up the copy of Meade's obit biography from his desk. He read the first sentence again—*Stewart Meade first became interested in investment real estate in Florida during the great boom of the 1920s.* And what had Meade told Sergeant Bullen? That he'd found Wesley Buck, a business associate, in bed with his wife in the Palm Terrace Hotel on Flager Street, drinking bathtub gin. There was only one Flagler Street that he knew of, and it was in Miami. It was more than a coincidence.

He looked up from the papers and quickly sketched in the facts for Gillespie. "Let's see if the Miami police have a record of any trouble between Meade and this Wesley Buck, or Wilfred Boyd, during the mid-1920s," he said. "If he did, Alec, and the facts tally with what Meade told Sergeant Bullen, we'll have to rule it out as something that happened nearly forty years ago."

"I'll have Communications put through a request to Miami."

"I'll do it. Now, Sergeant—" Tutchek addressed Bullen, "you're not going to be bawled out. You're not the only one who's ever turned down a complaint. Dozens of complaints are turned down every day—crackpots, drunks, troublemakers. We can't waste time on them or we'd need triple the Force. I don't want you to brood about it, or you won't be any good for anything. Now let's all get back to work."

Bullen said, "Thanks, Lieutenant," and walked a little straighter when he left the office.

Gillespie looked at Tutchek with open admiration. "That was a nice thing you just did, Ben. You saved his self-respect. Some of the bastards around here would have made him eat dirt."

Tutchek shrugged off the compliment. "He's a good man, or he wouldn't have come in the way he did, and Christ knows we can use good men. I wouldn't be doing myself a favor if I'd kicked his ass."

He glanced down at the mess of papers strewn untidily over his desk and felt sick at the thought of the hours of drudgery it represented. He no longer had any hours to spare. There were four major cases going—Meade, Widdicomb, the Park Liquor killing, and that fake rape. And, oh Jesus! the hundreds of details he had to keep at his fingertips. There wasn't any time for paper work. But that was Alec Gillespie's job. Alec was a steady man. He could handle it.

"Say, Alec ..." for some reason, it was hard for him to come right out with it, but there was no getting around the fact that he needed Gillespie's help. "Go through these damn papers, will you? Get rid of the sludge and the routine. I don't want to see anything unless it's important. I'm turning it all over to you."

"I'll take care of it, Ben."

"Good. That's a load off my mind. I'm going down to Communications, then I want to talk to Saul Stein about that Park Liquor killing. Did you get anything new on that last night?"

"Not a thing. And nothing new this morning, either."

"Well, if anything turns up on the other stuff, get in touch with me. You know where I'll be."

He left, and Gillespie began to transfer the papers from Tutchek's desk to his own. This was a step in the right direction, but how long would it last, he wondered. Ben was still charging around, doing everybody's work, and he might easily come back for the paper work the minute the pressure slacked off a bit. Wasn't Ben ever going to realize that an executive officer couldn't handle authority unless he was willing to delegate it, and let the men do the jobs they'd been trained for?

But maybe it wasn't as simple as all that, he thought gloomily; maybe I'd do exactly the same as Ben's doing. An executive job as important as Homicide was enough to scare anybody at first, and maybe you had to learn to trust yourself in it before you could trust other people with parts of it. There was the rub—trusting subordinates. God, the constant worry that somebody would pull a boner and mess up the works! Gillespie shook his head. He was content to remain Ben's administration officer; the command of Homicide was not for him. It was a rueful thing to admit, but Gillespie was more honest with himself than most.

Downstairs on the main floor, Tutchek spoke with Sergeant Daniel Ewing, who was in charge of Communications. He outlined the problem of the Meade-Wesley Buck trouble, if there had been trouble, back in the mid-20s, and told him to send a request-for-information-urgent to the Miami police.

"This is highly confidential, Dan," he emphasized. "I don't want any leaks."

"I'll put it through myself, Lieutenant."

"Good. Any answer to that pickup for Charles Erdese we sent to the Chicago police last night?"

"Nothing yet, Lieutenant."

"Call my office the *minute* it comes in, Dan. If I'm not there, give the information to Lieutenant Gillespie. Uh, by the way, do the newspaper reporters bother you much, Dan?"

"I'd chew the ass off the man who as much as opened his mouth to a newspaper reporter," said Ewing flatly.

Tutchek flushed, realizing it was not a question he should have asked. He should have said, "Keep it confidential, Dan" and let it go at that. Christ, he must have sounded like an anxious old woman.

He said, "Yeah, I know, Dan," and walked to the elevator. Ordinarily he'd have walked up the one flight of stairs to the second floor, but his legs felt like lead and there was a dull, heavy ache at the nape of his neck.

Lieutenant Stein was in a grim mood when Tutchek walked into his office. "We worked on that lousy Poochy Ryan half the night and wound up with precisely nothing," he said in a sour voice. "He clammed up and he's going to stay clammed up. That kind. Once in a while a dumb punk will pull a smart stunt, from his angle, only because he's too dumb to do anything else. It's bad enough getting stuck by somebody with brains, but Jesus Ever-loving Christ, it gravels my guts being stymied by sheer stupidity. If he said word one, Ben, just one word, it'd be an opening, and I could break him in half!"

"Maybe he's too scared to talk, Saul."

"Scared hell. I know when a punk is scared. He's too dumb to be scared. Talk to him yourself, if you don't believe me. He's in a cell on the fourth floor. Go ahead, talk to him. He'll make you a raving maniac in fifteen minutes. I couldn't do it. Harry Muir couldn't do it, and you know Harry. He can put the fear of God into a brass monkey. If you can do it, Ben, I'll pay for your bar mitzvah celebration."

"Maybe you should have talked to him like a Dutch uncle instead of turning Harry Muir loose on him."

"I did, Ben, so help me, I did. We tried everything, and I mean *everything*. I even showed him a picture of the Goddamned electric chair and told him how the smoke came up from the electrode on his head when they threw the switch. He didn't blink. Are you going to take a shot at it?"

"Might just as well, I guess."

"I'll have your oxygen tent ready when you're done."

Tutchek took the elevator to the fourth floor. The turnkey led him past the row of detention cells to an isolated one in a far corner of the room. The Ryan kid was leaning against the wall at the back of the cell, looking at nothing at all. He seemed almost relaxed, as if he spent most of his time looking at nothing, as if most of his life had been spent looking at nothing.

The turnkey unlocked the door and Tutchek went into the cell and sat down on the edge of the bunk. Ryan looked at him without interest. He was a chunky, muscular kid. Stein was right about the punk's stupidity. It showed. There wasn't a glimmer in that wide, pimply face, not even curiosity.

"What did you do after you left the Park Liquor Shop, son?" Tutchek asked, in unaccented tones; he was too tired to sound tough.

No answer.

"I'm not saying you killed the old man, son. But somebody did, and you were there last night. We have your fingerprints. Who did the job?"

No answer.

"And it was your car we found the case of Scotch in, son, and that case was addressed to the Park Liquor Shop. Somebody put it in your car. Do you have any idea who'd want to frame you?"

No answer.

"What were you doing in the liquor shop, son? Did you just happen to be buying a bottle when the holdup took place?"

Ryan's pale eyes shifted to several parts of the cell, but he did not answer.

"I don't care who killed the old man, son. If you did it, you'll burn. If somebody else did it, he'll burn. And if you helped him do it, you'll burn, too. If you didn't, you won't. And if we don't find the other guy, you'll burn, just because you happened to be there. That's how it stacks up."

Ryan licked his thin lips, but there was still no answer.

"Are you afraid to talk, son? Are you afraid somebody will do something to you if you talk? Were you recognized by the heister, son?"

Ryan could not keep his eyes still, and his face seemed to become a little narrower with a certain kind of primitive craftiness. A thought process was taking place in the murky soup of what might have been his mind. Tutchek had practically told him what to say.

"How did you happen to go into that liquor shop last night, son?" Tutchek held out the lead again.

Ryan swallowed, licked his lips, and made two starts before he finally said, "For a bottle. Like you said." He had a guttural, unformed voice.

"You were going to a party?"

"Yeah, A party. Me and—Uh, a party me and—uh, some other guys was gonna have. I was gonna take a bottle."

"Then what? You were buying this bottle?"

"Yeah. I was buying the bottle."

"That's when the holdup happened." Tutchek made it a statement, not a question.

"Yeah," Ryan's small eyes were bright with cunning. "This guy comes in and says, this is a stick-up."

"And he recognized you, son. That's why he had to frame you."

"Yeah, yeah. He knew me."

"If he knew you well, that was bad for you."

"Yeah. He knew me right away and that was bad."

"Yes, he had to frame you. But if he knew you right away, then you knew him, too."

Ryan stood with his mouth agape. He hadn't thought of that angle.

Tutchek did not press it. That was not the trap. That was only part of it. The trap, if it worked, would lie in what Ryan said without being prompted.

"But he had a gun and there was nothing you could do," Tutchek led him.

"Yeah. He had a gun on me. I was stuck."

"Then he pulled the heist and beat up the old man. He made you stand there."

"He made me stand there. He had a gun."

"But you got a good look at him. You can describe him."

"Yeah. He was a big guy," Ryan veiled his eyes and watched Tutchek from between slitted lids, to see how he was taking it.

"He was big," Tutchek encouraged him.

"Yeah, a big guy. Six foot. Husky. You know, a big guy."

"You know the color of his hair."

"Uh—he was a dark guy. He had dark hair. His face was dark. And his eyes. He was a big dark guy."

Tutchek encouraged him further, but Ryan's imagination flagged. He kept emphasizing that it had been 'a big dark guy.' He said it several times to make sure Tutchek got it. A big dark guy 'they mostly called Hype.'

Then Tutchek said, "You told Lieutenant Stein you were at a block dance in North Hudson. Hype was at the block dance. He comes from that neighborhood."

"No, no. He don't come from there."

"He comes from The Point."

"No, no," Ryan disagreed again, hastily. "He comes from another place. Newark."

"He was at the block dance with you."

"No, no. I wasn't at the block dance with nobody. Hype never goes up there. He don't like Polacks. He says they're fulla shit. He wouldn't go there anyways. They'd beat him up. He mostly hangs around Newark."

Tutchek left it at that. He said, "Thanks, son. We'll look around Newark for Hype." He went downstairs to the Detective Bureau on the second floor and stopped off at Lieutenant Stein's office before returning to Homicide.

"For the love of Moses," said Stein. "Your head is neither bloody nor bowed. Don't tell me you got a confession."

Tutchek half-haunched on the edge of the desk and lit a tired cigarette. "As a matter of fact, he told me one lie after another. If I'd tried to get the truth in so many words, he'd have stayed clammed up."

"I could have told you that, Ben. So what have we got? More lies."

"Wait a minute, wait a minute. There are all kinds of liars, Saul. A smart liar will mix in enough truth to keep you confused forever. But how does a stupid liar work?"

"His lies are obvious. He can be tripped up."

"That's right. If you ask him if something is black, he'll say no, it's white. If you ask him if it was long, he'll say, no, it was short. He tries to fool you in lying by opposites. That's how Ryan lied. I'd bet on it. He told me the holdup was pulled by a big dark guy, named Hype, who didn't come from North Hudson and didn't come from The Point, but came from Newark, and wasn't at the block dance with Ryan last night because he doesn't like Polacks. Now, I'll stake money on it that whoever helped Ryan with the holdup was the opposite of all that. I'd say the other punk was short, blond and on the skinny side. I'd say this other punk does come from the North Hudson neighborhood, *is* Polish, and was at the block dance with Ryan last night."

"It was the night before last, Ben. I didn't mean to interrupt, but let's keep the chronology straight. Where does this Hype come in? What's the opposite of Hype? Or is it a name Ryan just made up?"

"The night before last? I must be slipping—" Tutchek said vaguely, frowning. "But Hype. No, I don't think Ryan has the brains to make up a name like Hype. Did you ever notice that when these elementary liars need a name, they'll pick the name of somebody they don't like? I think that's what Ryan did. I think there's somebody named Hype down at The Point, and Ryan doesn't like him and—does this sound far-fetched to you, Saul? A minute ago I thought I really had something. Now it sounds like a lot of horseshit."

"It sounds all right to me, Ben. And don't call it far-fetched. Call it an educated guess. And God knows we have more experience with liars than anyone on the face of the earth. Except Congress. I think it's worth looking into."

"Well, we have to look into something, I suppose," Tutchek slid his haunch from the desk and started for the door. "Let me know if anything turns up."

Detectives Flavin, Caputo and Bierce were waiting for him in Homicide's squad room, and he said, "Be with you in a minute, boys," and continued to his office. The first thing he noticed was his desk, and the sight of it was like a breath of fresh air in stale lungs.

The snowdrifts of untidy papers were gone, and in place of them were the reports and other data of the four cases on which he was working, laid out in four neat stacks. He grinned at Gillespie.

"Why, you Goddamned old vacuum cleaner," he said. "I didn't think it possible."

"We'll keep it moving," Gillespie sounded pleased. He liked paper work; it was paper work that greased the wheels, if you didn't let it get out of hand. "But here are two things on the Widdicomb case you'll want to know. Chicago picked up Charles Erdese and are returning him on the three-thirty plane, here. I detailed Kitteridge and Meyn to meet the plane, and they'll have Erdese here about four. Here's number two—the Elmhurst police called a half-hour ago and said they found Mrs. Widdicomb's car in the river early this morning. Two kids were fishing and spotted it. It went through a wooden guard rail, over an embankment and down into the channel. This was on the straightaway on River Road and there were no skid marks and there was a moon that night, so visibility was good. So that means either the driver fell asleep at the wheel, or the car was driven into the river on purpose. There's a house a hundred yards up the road and the occupants say they heard the crash at eleven o'clock. They know it was eleven because the late TV news was just coming on."

"The car has positively been identified."

"Elmhurst checked with Motor Vehicle in Trenton and the license plates are registered in the name of Mrs. Helen Widdicomb, 27 Pomander Walk, Hudson."

Tutchek pursed his lips, trying to understand the significance of this latest find. Better let it wait until he talked to Erdese. He could beat his brains out on "ifs" and "maybes".

"Well—at least we know where it happened now," he said, still wishing it would fire something in his mind, but thinking was enough of an effort without straining. "Let's see, that River Road straightaway in Elmhurst is about five miles north of the city line, isn't it?"

Gillespie looked up at the city map taped to the wall above his desk. "It's closer to six, Ben."

"Did they find anything in the car that might give us a lead?"

"They haven't gotten it out of the water yet. That's the deepest part of the river. They're going to try to pull it out with a dragline, and if that doesn't work, they'll have to get a derrick. They'll let us know, but don't count on anything today."

"Well, that'll give us time to talk to Erdese. We'll see what he has to say. There's not much else we can do anyway."

"I had Miss Lund type up a memo. It's on the Widdicomb stack."

Tutchek said, "Thanks, Alec," and sat down at his desk. It was a relief not to be faced by all those ominous, unread papers, but the sight of those four neat stacks of reports made him feel as if he had termites in his stomach. Four stacks—four major cases. All he had to do was make one mistake and it would explode on the front pages of the newspapers. He couldn't afford any mistakes. *And there won't be any*, he thought grimly.

He looked out through the open doorway and saw the three detectives waiting to talk to him, and he raised his voice and called Flavin.

"I hope somebody's got good news, for a change," he growled, as the tall detective took the chair at the end of the desk. "I mean, something we can sink our teeth into."

"I've got something, Ben," said Flavin. "Good or bad, I don't know yet.

Meade's checking account is down to three hundred and some odd dollars."

Tutchek made a face. "That's something," he agreed, "But what?"

"This seemed to be a semi-business checking account. He had a purely personal account, but never carried much of a balance. He maintained about five hundred dollars. The other was a sort of private business account. Fluid cash for investments outside the corporation. In January he had thirty thousand in that account."

"Where'd you get all this? From the bank?"

"The bank. It wasn't easy, but LaFarge set it up. Remember last night we were talking about how Meade was economizing on his girl friends? We had two angles: he was either keeping a high-priced mistress, or Meade-LaFarge Associates was in financial trouble. I took the financial angle, and George Gilman's looking into the other. I went to LaFarge and laid it on the table. I expected him to scream but he didn't. He said we could run an audit on the corporation books any time we wanted. Meade was in charge of sales and promotion, and there was no possible way he could get his hands on corporation funds. What it came down to is that Meade was nothing but the frontman for the outfit. LaFarge took care of the real business. Then I asked him if he knew anything about Meade's personal finances. He didn't. So I suggested getting it from Meade's bank."

"I'll bet you had a sweet time without a court order."

"We had a hell of a time. LaFarge didn't even want to try, but he finally said he'd do it as a personal favor to you."

"To me!" Tutchek stared. "Why the hell should he do me a personal favor?"

Flavin looked surprised. "He said you'd done him one."

Then Tutchek remembered that telephone call from Councilman Selig. Selig had said something about LaFarge's being grateful for the way the police had played down the Meade case in the newspapers, and it had left a lousy taste in his mouth at the time. Now how about that! Bread cast on the waters, or something. Was it possible that this much good could come out of City Hall? Of course, it wasn't City Hall, or Councilman Selig, either. Though Selig must have given LaFarge some sort of pitch about 'our efficient and co-operative police department'. He wouldn't miss a chance like that to make a campaign speech. But how about that!

"I hope LaFarge doesn't figure on exchanging favors with me for the rest of his life," Tutchek grunted. "Still, if he helped, I'll keep it in mind. But a court order might have meant publicity. Maybe he thought of that, too. Anyway, he saved us time and trouble. How'd it go at the bank?"

"Fine. They were very co-operative. As a favor to LaFarge, they let me know. According to the records, LaFarge has been drawing money in five thousand dollar bites. He drew the money himself and took it in cash. In addition to that, he's been taking securities from his safe-deposit box. On July third, he cashed in ten thousand dollars' worth of municipal bonds. Altogether Meade has taken out sixty thousand since January, that the bank knows of. They're pretty sure he sold some of the securities through a broker, and nobody knows his broker, so we can't tell how much Meade unloaded since the first of the year."

"Is he a gambler?"

"I talked to Birdie again last night and he said Meade liked to take the girls to that gambling place of Lew Ricci's on Frelinghuysen Avenue once in a while, but he never dropped more than a few hundred bucks at the crap table."

"You don't get in that place unless you're a customer," Tutchek said. "Strangers and cops aren't welcome. Maybe he did his serious playing when he went without the girls. Is there any way of finding out?"

"With a Ouija board," said Flavin dryly. "Or if we're absolutely shot with luck, Birdie might pick up something, but I wouldn't bank on it. *Or* City Hall might help. Who sells protection over there?"

Tutchek grunted. "You can buy any kind of license in the City Clerk's office."

"Maybe we'd better forget the gambling angle, Ben. I talked to George Gilman on the phone a little while ago and he asked me to pass this along to you. He got it from Miss Burkhardt, Meade's secretary. Some woman has been calling Meade up pretty steadily the past few months. Miss Burkhardt doesn't know who it is, but it's the same woman all the time, and she always calls him ' Stewart dear'. La Burkhardt says she doesn't know what they talk about because Meade doesn't say anything until he hears the click of Burkhardt's extension when she hangs up. She says this is the only woman who ever called Meade at the office."

Tutchek listened intently. "Let's keep after that one," he said emphatically. "Now I think we're getting some place. If she's the first woman who ever called him at the office, she was leading him around by the nose. Hell, an expensive mistress could run through sixty thousand, and up, just about as fast as Lew Ricci's crap table. It's a stronger angle than I thought. Work with George on that. Wait a minute," he said as Flavin started for the door. "Here's something that came in this morning. I don't think much of it now, but you might as well know what it is ..." He told Flavin of the Meade complaint which Sergeant Bullen had turned away. "What do you think?"

Flavin shook his head and shrugged. "But that happened in Florida a long time ago." It seemed plain to him and he was puzzled why Tutchek took it seriously.

"Maybe not."

"But what would be the angle? Blackmail? For what? Did Meade kill Buck back then in Miami? Or the wife? That doesn't sound likely, Ben. Meade wasn't rational—"

The phone rang and Tutchek scooped it from its cradle. It was Kitteridge.

"They got the car out of the river, Lieutenant—"

"Just a minute, Kitteridge"—Tutchek looked up at Flavin. "Work with Gilman on that other angle, Jeff. Check back with me later. Now what about the car, Kitteridge?"

"They got the car out of the river. A work barge with a derrick did the job in thirty-five minutes. And listen"—Kitteridge was excited—"we found that wristwatch on the floor of the front seat. The catch was broken as if somebody pulled it off her. And we found her handbag *on* the seat."

"What about the diamond ring?"

"No ring. Not yet. Want me to stay with it?"

"Yes, but don't forget to meet that plane at three-thirty."

"But it's nearly two-thirty now Lieutenant."

"Then get down to the airport with Fred Meyn. The Elmhurst police can take care of the car."

Tutchek hung up and stared at the phone. Two-thirty? It couldn't be two-thirty. He'd gotten hardly anything done so far today ... He looked at his wristwatch. It was exactly two-twenty-seven. Where did the time go? It was flying by and nothing was getting settled. He'd developed some leads, but there was nothing solid, nothing you could really point a finger at. Two-thirty. There was a thin ache in his stomach and he was feeling jittery, and he knew what that meant—no breakfast, no lunch. He wasn't hungry, but knew he had to eat something. He'd eaten damned little yesterday, too. He hated to take the time, but if he didn't eat, the next thing would be a thundering headache. He got up reluctantly and reached for his coat, which dangled from the back of the door.

"I'm going to run down to the lunch room and grab a bite, Alec," he said.

"You're going to eat lunch?" Gillespie pretended surprise. "Forget it, Ben. You haven't eaten lunch for six weeks. Why break your record?"

Tutchek grinned but without much amusement. "My stomach thinks I seceded from the Union." Then he added, "If anything turns up, I'll be at the lunch room across the street."

But he didn't quite get there so soon, for Caputo and Bierce were waiting for him in the squad room. He nodded dully. The rape case. He waved his hand at the worktable in the middle of the room.

"Let's sit down," he said. Well, for Christ sake, he'd walked from his desk to the squad room, and he was glad to sit down again. What had Gillespie said? No lunch for six weeks. It hadn't been that bad, but Alec didn't know about the no-breakfasts and the no-dinners during that time either. Now it was catching up with him. From now on there'd be no more skipped meals. The resolve made him feel a little better and he roused himself.

"Did you distribute McGimp's drawings through all the precincts of the city, as I told you?" he asked.

Caputo said, "Yes, sir," and Bierce amended stolidly, "Not all of them, Lieutenant. You sent Stephano and Koch to help us and they took five hundred. We worked the north end and they worked the south."

There was a flatness in Bierce's voice that told Tutchek that Bierce did not want to be held responsible for anything Stephano and Koch had done in the south end of the city. Tutchek frowned over that. He knew the men might feel like that, but they didn't usually come out with it so baldly.

"Something eating you, Bierce?" he asked.

"No, sir."

"Did Stephano and Koch do something you don't like?"

"No, sir. I was glad they helped."

"Then why did you want to let me know that *they* worked the south end of the city?"

"Because they did, Lieutenant. Caputo and I worked the north end. Just in case you found out later, that's all. I don't want you to think we goofed on the job."

Tutchek growled, "Grow up, will you. Now what's on your mind? Otherwise."

Bierce leaned back in the chair and folded his arms across his chest. He usually sat back and let Caputo do the talking, but somehow or other, it was different this time. As if he'd made up his mind to keep his mouth shut. And keep out of trouble. Tutchek was annoyed, but let it go. Maybe this was Bierce's day for ulcers.

Caputo said, "Taking those pictures around and telling the story in every precinct house took a hell of a lot of time, Lieutenant."

"All right, so it took time. So what?"

"So long as you know, that's all."

"What's the matter with you two today? Didn't you get any sleep last night?"

"It's just that it took more time than we thought, Lieutenant. And we went back to the North Hudson precinct house today and spent some more time. That's Polack Town and you told us to give it special attention." Caputo warmed up a little and added, "We might have a lead there, Lieutenant."

"Good work." Tutchek said it self-consciously. "What is it?"

"It might not be anything, Lieutenant. We don't know yet. We talked to a couple of the precinct detectives, Goldstein and Zabriski."

"I know them. They're good men. I've worked with them before."

"So they said. Anyway, they kind of got a make on the pictures. It was that V-shaped mouth. You know how McGimp drew it in. I thought it looked a little too old for girl of fourteen, but the mouth was the thing that made Goldstein and Zabriski think they'd seen the girl around Polack Town. They think maybe it's a kid named Millie Salaski. She had a heavy mouth shaped like that, pushed out a little because of the upper teeth, like McGimp said yesterday. The rest of the face could be anybody."

"Has Millie Salaski been in trouble with the police up there?"

"No convictions, no arrests. But Zabriski and Goldstein say she's been getting away with it for the past four years or more."

"Uh-huh. Did she run with that kid gang up there? The Hudson Blues."

"Nope, and that's one of the troubles she was due for soon. She was a tough little bitch, Lieutenant. She was supposed to be too damned handy with the acid bottle. Or a switchblade. She didn't give a damn what she did. This is her reputation, anyway. She turned the Hudson Blues down and's supposed to have said they weren't tough enough for her to run with. Now they wouldn't let her get away with stuff like that for long, Lieutenant. They might not be as tough as the DeKalb Barons down at The Point, but they're a touch bunch of hunkies."

"If they're that tough, why'd they let her get away with it in the first place?"

"Did you ever see somebody after he got a face full of acid, Lieutenant? They left her alone. But for how long, is the question."

"Do Goldstein and Zabriski think they caught up with her? Is that the idea?"

"The only idea so far, Lieutenant, is that it *might* be this Millie Salaski. They're trying to check into it right now. We were working with them, but came in because you told us to report back to you."

My God, thought Tutchek, is everybody nuts today? Was this Caputo, the middle-of-the-road man, the conciliator, the one who always tried to smooth things over? He and Bierce had a definite lead up in North

Hudson and they should have stayed with it. If Goldstein and Zabriski had said the dead girl could be this Millie Salaski, they must have been pretty sure. They weren't men who went off half-cocked, and they knew their precinct like a book.

"Did they have anything else to say, Cap?" he asked, deciding to ignore their sour mood.

"Well ..." Caputo hesitated, reluctant to offer the precinct detectives' speculations "... they heard some talk that she was running with a gang outside Polack Town, and that's the one thing the Hudson Blues gang wouldn't take from her. Nobody in Polack Town runs with an outside gang if he wants to stay in one piece. That's what Zabriski and Goldstein are looking into."

"Then they must be sure the girl was Millie Salaski."

"They're checking that first."

"Good. Get back there now and work with them."

"And report back to you, Lieutenant?"

Tutchek sighed. Here it was again. "No," he said wearily, "no. Stay with it. If there's anything I should know, use the telephone."

After they were gone, he sat for a few minutes, resting his big forearms on the table. What was the matter with everybody, he wondered? The whole Division was acting as if it had a bellyache. Or maybe it was his imagination. That could be. He felt so tired he could hardly see straight. Maybe a little food would help.

On the way out, he stopped at Policewoman Lund's desk and repeated what he had told Alec Gillespie. "If anything turns up, Miss Lund, I'll be at the lunch room."

Then, finally, he plodded out of Headquarters to the Elite Lunch diagonally across the street. The bright blue-white fluorescence hurt his eyes and he took a side booth at the rear where the light was dim. A breezy red-haired waitress came to his table for his order.

"Hi, Lieutenant," she said cheerfully, "long time no see. For the luvva mud, wotcha been doing with yourself? You look like the morning after the night before. Just get back from a vacation?"

"How do you spell it, Mae?"

"You gotta watch them vacations, Lieutenant. They're killers. What'll you have? The beef stew's pretty good today. The chef put beef in it."

"Something a little lighter, Mae. Scrambled eggs, and coffee."

When she left to fill the order, he made some notes on the conversations he'd had with Flavin, Caputo and Bierce. He didn't trust his memory. There were too many things on his mind. The girl brought his plate of eggs, crisp brown toast and a cup of dark, steaming coffee. He put the notebook back into his pocket and took a sip of the coffee. It was strong and washed warmly into his stomach. He wanted to relax, and leaned his head against the back of the booth and closed his eyes....

A moment later, it seemed, the waitress was leaning over him, shaking his shoulder.

"Hey, wake up, Rip Van Winkle. You're wanted on the phone."

He said stupidly, "Huh?" and shook his head to clear it of sleep. "All right, all right. Where is it?"

"Back there where it always was, sleepy."

"Sure. Forgot where I was for a minute."

The phone was on the wall beside the kitchen door and he walked stiffly to it, his muscles cramped.

It was Alec Gillespie. "We're waiting for you, Ben. Charles Erdese is here."

"Already?"

"It's quarter of five, Ben."

"Quar—oh Jesus. I'll be right over."

The waitress was at the cash register and Tutchek flipped her a dollar bill on the way out, pausing to ask angrily, "Why didn't you wake me up before this, Mae?"

"You looked like you needed the sleep, that's why. And don't get sore at me. I'm not the one that's droopy."

Cut it out, cut it out, he told himself sharply; you're beginning to snap at everybody, calm down.

"Sorry, Mae," he apologized. "I'm sore at myself, I guess."

She smiled. "Ah well," she said, "we're all human."

Are we, he thought as he left, are we?

Thirteen

The Homicide squad room was empty, and Alec Gillespie was in the office with another man, a stranger. There was no sign of Wes Kitteridge or Fred Meyn. Tutchek went quickly into the office and closed the door behind him. He looked sharply at the strange man as he rounded the end of his desk and sat down. He saw a tall, slim man, dark hair frosted lightly with gray, strong-faced, which probably would have been even pleasant had it not been so deeply carved by sudden grief and the slack expression of shock.

"I'm sorry to bring you back to the city like this, Mr. Erdese," he said abruptly. "But you understand the circumstances. I don't think you want to waste time any more than we do, so let's get on with it. You were out with Mrs. Widdicomb on the night of her death, weren't you?"

"Yes," Erdese's voice was low, barely more than a whisper.

"What happened?"

"We—broke our engagement."

"You did? That was the second time, wasn't it?"

"Yes."

"Was there a quarrel?"

"Yes."

"What was it about?"

Erdese answered with difficulty, not wanting to talk about it, but knowing he had to. "The same as the first time, Mrs. Langston. Alice's sister."

"Mrs. Langston?" Tutchek's eyebrows lifted. "Why did you quarrel about her?"

Erdese shook his head, not in negation, but because it was a torment for him to sit here and be forced to talk about this. "Mrs. Langston is a semi-invalid," he said, "and has been for several years. She has no money of her own, and she lived with Alice. I have never believed, and still do not believe that Mrs. Langston is as ill as she pretends. When Alice and I were engaged last year, Mrs. Langston took to her bed, and Alice wanted to postpone the wedding until her sister was well again. I told Alice I thought her sister was shamming. She became indignant and broke the engagement."

"Did the same thing happen this time?" It was a trap question, for Mrs. Langston had not been in bed yesterday.

But Erdese shook his head again. "No, not quite. Alice had taken it for granted that Mrs. Langston would live with us after we were married. She was devoted to her sister and was convinced that Mrs. Langston needed her personal care.

"Mrs. Langston has a dislike for nurses, it seems," Erdese spoke bitterly. "I hadn't dreamed that Alice would want her sister to live with us. I'm sorry that I must say this, but I cannot stand the woman. She had fastened herself on Alice like a leech, and never intended to let go. I did not want her in my house after we were married. I was willing to spend any amount of money for her care, but I did not want her around. I should not have told Alice so strongly that I thought her sister a bloodsucking hypochondriac. I was wrong. There were better ways to have done it, but I was angry because Alice was permitting herself to be shamelessly used by that woman. That was when we quarreled."

"And broke the engagement?"

"Alice pulled the ring from her finger and gave it back to me. We were both angry, and she drove me home."

"Drove you home? In her car?"

"Yes, I don't own one. Because of business I'm in the city only a few days a month, and really don't need a car."

"What time was this, Mr. Erdese?"

"I got home about ten o'clock."

"Can you prove that?"

Erdese's head came up in shocked surprise. "You—you mean, you think I—I'm under suspicion?"

"It's not quite the same as being charged with a killing, Mr. Erdese. And if you can prove you were home in your apartment at ten o'clock, that all there's to it."

"Yes, I can prove it," said Erdese tonelessly. "The doorman saw me enter, and there was the elevator operator, too. It was slightly before ten. They go off duty at ten o'clock."

There was a quick nervous knock on the door and Tutchek snapped, "Who is it?"

Kitteridge's voice answered, "It's me, Lieutenant. Kitteridge. I've got Mrs. Langston here. I thought you might want to talk to her."

"Bring her in!"

The door opened and Mrs. Langston came unsteadily into the room. She was not sober, and the thick smoky odor of bourbon was almost an aura around her. However, she was not so drunk that she did not know what was happening to her, and her eyes were enormous and terror-stricken. Behind her, Kitteridge beckoned to Tutchek with a sideways dip of his head.

Tutchek said slowly, "Sit down, Mrs. Langston. I'll be with you in a minute." and went out into the squad room with Kitteridge.

"I spotted her for a drinker yesterday, Lieutenant," said Kitteridge in a fast low voice. "She had a breath and there was a bottle hidden behind the sofa. People don't hide bottles behind sofas if they're sociable drinkers. She's a solitary drinker and that means she's a chronic souse. You see how she is now. On top of that I found a half case of bourbon hidden under some clothes in the closet of her bedroom. There's your invalid that busted up the engagement, Lieutenant."

"What made you think of that, Wes?"

"I talked with Erdese before you came. Then I remembered the bottle she'd ducked behind the sofa when we were there yesterday. I thought, if she's a drinker, she'll be soused again today. And she was. I think she got soused every time her sister was out of the house, and she was soused the night her sister was killed."

"All right, but what's the point?"

"Suppose you had a sister you thought was an invalid and you came home unexpectedly early one night and found her drunk and saw all that liquor in her closet and suddenly realized your invalid was nothing but a common souse. And suppose you'd just broken your engagement for the second and probably the last time to the guy you love. Wouldn't you go off your rocker, Lieutenant?" Kitteridge paused, then said, "The Elmhurst cops estimate she went through that guard rail at ninety miles an hour. She just didn't want to live anymore."

They both started and turned as Mrs. Langston's hysterical voice skirled from the office. She was incoherent. Tutchek pounded across the squad room, followed by Kitteridge. Gillespie and Erdese were supporting the woman in the chair, and she was screaming. Her legs were outstretched and her heels drummed wildly on the floor.

At the sight of Tutchek's drawn harsh face, she shrieked, "It's not my fault, it's not my fault, I didn't do anything! I tried to stop her but she drove away like a crazy woman. I tried to stop her! I tried!"

Tutchek turned to Kitteridge, "Get her out of here," he said in disgust. "Take her home."

He sat down behind his desk and did not give her another glance as Kitteridge and Meyn eased her out of the office and through the squad room. Her sobs sounded like sick vomiting, and then the outer door slammed. Then Erdese left. Tutchek felt wrung out. He looked around the office and could still smell the sickening odor of undigested bourbon left behind by Mrs. Langston, and suddenly he had to get out of there.

He lunged to his feet. "I'm going to take a run up to the North Hudson precinct house and see how they're making out," he flung at Gillespie, adding his usual, "If anything turns up, you know where to reach me."

Gillespie looked after him sadly, then sighed and turned back to his paper work.

Captain Hoke Siemer, Commander of the North Hudson precinct house, came from his office with his freckled, meaty hand outstretched. "Well, I'll be a cruddy son-of-a-bitch," he roared. "If it isn't old Ben Tutchek himself in the flesh. How are you, boy? Well, I'll be damned. I haven't seen you since God's grandfather got married. How's it going, boy? Getting much?"

Tutchek shook hands, warming at Hoke Siemer's characteristic boisterous greeting. "How's it with you, Hoke?"

"I'll survive, I'll survive. But Jesus Christ, boy"—he peered into Tutchek's face—"you look like hell. That new job getting you down?"

Tutchek grinned a little. This was what you had to take from Hoke Siemer. He always spoke his mind, and you had to like it or lump it. But there was never any doubt of his honesty, and he was one of the most generous men on the Force.

"Well, we've been a little busy," said Tutchek. "We've got four major cases."

"Only four? Hell, boy, you should command a precinct house, especially this cruddy precinct. I get a dozen new ones every day. And just look at me, I'm getting fat on it. Spend a week with us, Ben. Homicide'll be a rest cure after that."

"I might take you up on that, Hoke."

"Sure, why not! The more the merrier. This is getting to be a regular Headquarters hangout anyway. A couple of Saul Stein's boys're nosing around out there—Alix Uri and Bill Hughes. Christ knows what they want. Maybe some of that nice blonde hunky pussy. Best in the world, Ben. You ought to try it sometime—"

Tutchek burst out laughing, and after a moment Siemer began to bellow and pound him on the shoulder. "You bastard," he said affectionately. "You *are* a hunky. Okay, what I said, still goes. But I should tell you. You probably invented it, you old stud."

"I'm just a guilty bystander, Hoke. How are Uri and Hughes making out, do you know?"

Captain Siemer wagged his grizzled head from side to side; he didn't know. "Oh, all right I guess. That was a nasty one, that liquor shop killing. Those cruddy punks kicking an old man to death like that. The pack we have up here is bad enough, but we haven't had anything like that. Knock wood."

"Did they go back to Headquarters? I wanted to talk to them."

"No. They moved in. They like it here. They went out with Goldstein a little while ago. They'll be back in a couple hours or so."

"Did you say Goldstein, Hoke? I thought Goldstein was working with my boys, Caputo and Bierce."

"Sure. He was. Him and Zabriski. But Zabriski's out with your boys now."

"I hope they'll be very happy together. All of them."

Siemer stared at him, his head cocked to one side. "What the hell's eating you, Ben?"

"Nothing. Not a Goddamned thing. But does Goldstein always switch around from one case to another like this? Does he get bored and switch over just to keep himself interested? One minute he's working on the rape killing, and the next thing I know, it's the liquor shop with Stein's boys. How can he keep his mind on things? I don't get it."

"How many cases do you have on your mind, boy?"

"That's not the point—"

"Or maybe you're trying to tell me how to run my house. I figure my boys know what the hell they're doing, especially Goldy. If he switched to Uri and Hughes, he's got a damn good reason, and I'll let him do it every time. It's his job, for Christ sake, not mine. If I tried to wet-nurse him every minute of the day, he'd never get anything done. If he falls flat on his face, I'll pick him up. The first time. And the second time. But the *third* time I'd boot his tail around the block to straighten him out. He hasn't fallen down the first time yet, so I let him alone. So make all complaints to me, boy. And if you want to make a federal case out of it, let's go in the other room and put on the gloves and I'll beat your brains out."

Tutchek said, "Ah, go to hell," half laughing, half angry. "When will Zabriski be back with Caputo and Bierce?"

"I dunno. About the same time, I imagine. Relax, boy, relax. They won't be back for an hour or two. Let's go out to dinner. It's after six o'clock."

"No, I'll wait here, Hoke—"

"And eat dinner later, eh? Sure—wind pudding with air sauce. Pull up your socks, boy. We're going out to dinner."

Tutchek went.

They went to a gaudy new diner on the Lynwood cutoff to the highway. "The food's crummy, but nourishing," said Siemer. He forced Tutchek to eat two bowls of thick pea soup. Tutchek would sooner have had diesel oil, but compared to the noise Siemer would have made had he refused, the soup was the lesser of two evils. It made him feel heavy and drowsy, so he had two cups of black coffee, which did not lighten him, but did take away the drowsiness.

It was seven-thirty when they returned to the precinct house. None of the detectives had come back yet, and in a little while Tutchek began to feel uneasy, just sitting there, and he called Alec Gillespie at Headquarters.

"Anything new, Alec?"

"Just came in ten minutes ago, Ben. From the Miami police. A Wilfred Boyd and a Vivian Marsh were convicted of running a real-estate confidence game in 1926. They drew two years each. The police were tipped off to the pair by a Sam Marsh, the woman's husband, who disappeared from Miami before the trial. Do you see a certain similarity in the initials of Sam Marsh and Stewart Meade?"

"Holy Christ!" Tutchek lurched up from his chair and gestured excitedly with his free arm. "That rips it wide open, Alec."

"Looks like it, Ben."

"This *is* it. Oh God, and we almost threw it away. When Meade spoke to Sergeant Bullen, he called Wilfred Boyd—or Wesley Buck—a business associate. That means he was running the confidence game with Buck down in Miami. Now stop me if I'm wrong, but everything points to this: Buck and Meade's ex-wife, or whatever she is, turned up in Hudson around the first of the year and began blackmailing Meade, and there was nothing Meade could do about it. He was sewed up and they made him pay through the nose. How do you figure it? On the evidence we have."

"The same way. But blackmailers don't kill, Ben."

"The evidence says he did."

"You mean Meade's statement to Bullen? You know how much that would be worth in court. The prosecutor wouldn't let it get that far. There's no case yet."

"I'll agree. There isn't a case yet. The first thing to do is see if we can find Buck and Meade's ex-wife. When Jeff Flavin calls in—"

"He's right here."

"Good. Tell him to get to work on it right now. Call in George Gilman—"

"He's here, too."

"Fine. Did Miami send a description?"

"Yes. And they're sending pictures by plane. But they won't be much good. They were taken almost forty years ago."

"Wire New York and the F.B.I. and see if they can help. Keep it moving, Alec. I'll be in as soon as I get finished here."

Tutchek sat down and replaced the phone in its cradle. He grinned and lit a cigarette. He was in a state of elation. His tiredness evaporated and now he felt as if he could go on forever. He knew Captain Siemer was watching him narrowly, but it did not make him feel uneasy this time. The Meade case had really begun to move, and that was the one that had worried him all along. But not because of City Hall, he told himself quickly. He knew that was only partly true, but that was over now. He'd never feel that unsure of himself again. Furthermore, it had been best to keep it out of the papers.

Goldstein, Uri and Hughes came in a little after eight. After shaking hands with Goldstein, whom he had not seen for a few months, Tutchek asked, "Is Zabriski coming in soon, Goldy?"

"He's right behind us, Lieutenant," said Goldstein. "He's giving us a couple minutes to get out of sight. He's got one of the Hudson Blues, and those kids are skittish when they see cops en masse. You going to stay with it, Uri?"

The blond, good-looking detective nodded, and Hughes grinned, "Alix is a better talker than me."

"Let's go, then. You want to listen in, Lieutenant?"

Tutchek laughed. He was feeling good. "Hell no," he said. "Just send me a letter, whenever you get time."

Goldstein led them, and Captain Siemer, down the hall to a small room. There was a long glass panel set into one wall and through it they looked into another room, now empty except for a small wooden table and several chairs. Tutchek did not have to be told it was a one-way glass panel. No one in the other room could look through it and see them in this room.

Goldstein whispered to Tutchek, "Zabriski has Karl Majeski, top man in the Hudson Blues."

"What's this all about, Goldy?"

"Shhhh—"

The door of the other room opened and the thickset Zabriski entered with a muscular boy of about seventeen, who had the Polish blond hair, gray eyes and high cheekbones. The boy strolled in with a defiant swagger, but his eyes were restless, betraying fear. Behind them came Uri and Caputo.

Zabriski said, "Let's sit around the table, Karl. This is just a friendly talk."

"Yeah, friendly," said the boy in a hard voice, "Friendly till you don't think you're getting the right answers." He sat down warily.

"You have nothing to worry about, Karl," said Zabriski.

"Now, you know Millie Salaski."

"What about her?"

"She wasn't a member of your club, was she?"

"No."

"Do you know what club she did belong to?"

"No."

"You were at the block dance the other night."

"You saw me."

"And Millie Salaski was there."

The boy tightened his mouth, but at length said sullenly, "You saw her, too."

"Who was the guy she was with, Karl? She was with a guy and you talked to them."

Goldstein whispered softly in Tutchek's ear, "Keep your fingers crossed. Zabriski is pulling a bluff."

The boy glowered, then mumbled, "She shouldn't of brought him."

"Why not?"

"He's a DeKalb Baron, that's why. We don't go down their territory, and they don't come up ours."

"So what did you do, Karl?"

"If you saw me, you know I didn't do nuttin'. I tole him we didn't want no trouble with the Barons, but some of our hotheads were drinking an' if he hung around he'd maybe get the shit kicked out of him."

"What did he say to that?"

"He got snotty. He tole me to stick it. But I'm trying to be nice. I say, Okay, you're tough, man, I won't argue. Maybe you're tougher than me and my brother, but man, there ain't nobody tougher than eight guys at the same time. So be a nice guy and get your ass out of here. I don't want no trouble."

"Did he leave, Karl?"

"He was still snotty. He must have been out of brains. All right, he was tough. There'd of been trouble. But Millie says, come on, let's get outta this cukey drag and have some kicks. He tells me to stick it again, then they go."

"They left together, Karl?"

"Yeah. He had an old Chewy. I followed to make sure."

"How'd you know he was a DeKalb Baron, Karl?"

"I seen him a couple times at dances in the Youth Center downtown."

"Do you know who he was?"

"One of the crummy Barons, is all. Millie called him ... uh ..."

Goldstein's lean hand tightened on Tutchek's forearm as the boy scowled, trying to remember.

Karl Majeski mumbled, "Butchy—Moochy—Poochy. She called him Poochy. That's when she said, come on, Poochy, let's get outta this cukey drag. Poochy."

Goldstein let out a long breath, but it was a moment later before Tutchek understood what he had just heard.

Detective Uri was asking in an engaging voice, "Was he a heavyset guy, Karl, muddy blond hair and a sort of pushed-in-looking face?"

"Yeah, that's him."

Goldstein plucked at Tutchek's sleeve. "Let's get out of here," he whispered. "It's all over but the shouting."

Outside with Hughes and Bierce, Goldstein told Tutchek how it had been set up. "Ryan was at the block dance. He told you that. He was a DeKalb Baron, and there are only two ways he'd come to a Hudson Blues block dance—with enough Barons to take care of themselves in a scrap, or with a girl from up here. He'd never walk in by himself unless he wanted to get slaughtered. The girl would be his protection. He must have thought she was a deb. Hughes and Uri told us about Ryan coming to the block dance. Then Caputo and Bierce came up asking about Millie Salaski. I mean, the dead girl who turned out to be Millie Salaski. It didn't take much thinking to put two and two together. Zabriski knows this precinct like the inside of his pocket, and he said none of the Blues debs would ask a mug like Ryan. They've got their regular guys in the gang. But a renegade like Millie Salaski would do a thing like that, if only for kicks. We asked around and several guys had seen Millie at the dance with a kid answering Ryan's description, but Karl was the only one who talked to them. As leader of the Blues, it was his job. And that's how we wrapped it up."

But it wasn't wrapped up. Poochy Ryan leaving the block dance with Millie Salaski was one thing, and Poochy Ryan killing Millie Salaski was something quite different. In his stupid way, he denied everything, and there seemed no way to tie him in with the killing of the girl.

Until Detective Uri, whose bright energy seemed limitless, snapped his fingers and said, "We must be out of our minds. Where did he put the girl's clothes? Where did he 'hide' the case of Scotch? The clothes were never found. Think it over."

They found the bloodstained clothes under the spare tire in the trunk of Poochy Ryan's car. This time he did not claim he had been framed. He blamed the girl for everything. She had pulled the holdup and killed the old man. (This was untrue.) Then, later, Ryan said, they'd gotten into a fight over division of the money. But he didn't kill her. No, sir. He just kind of gave her a little push—

And that did wrap it up.

Tutchek was so groggy from fatigue that he went into one of the unoccupied cells and fell into sodden sleep on the comfortless cot.

Fourteen

He was awakened at seven when the trustees came around with coffee and oatmeal for the prisoners in the tank and the detention cells.

One of them yelled in at him, "Come on, come on, on your feet, lame brains—*oh Jesus Christ!*"

He backed away from the cell as Tutchek sat up on the edge of the bunk and looked blankly at him with bloodshot eyes, his coat falling open to show the gun in its holster clipped to his belt. Disheveled and unshaven though he was, there was no doubt that he was a cop. He waved a limp hand at the frightened trustee.

"Bring that crap back," he growled, pointing his chin at the cup of coffee and bowl of oatmeal in the man's trembling hands.

The oatmeal tasted like wallpaper paste and the coffee as if it had been made from dried liver. It did not make him feel any better, only different. He stumbled out to the men's room in the hall, washed his face with cold water and gritty soap, and combed his hair. Then he went downstairs to his office, feeling as if he had risen from the dead, but just about. It was seven-thirty. He pulled over the battered old typewriter on his stand and slowly began typing up press releases on the Widdicomb case, then the mingled liquor store and rape killings. Alec Gillespie came in at eight.

Tutchek said, "I got tied up on that rape thing last night—"

"So I heard," said Gillespie warmly. "The boys did a nice piece of work on those cases."

"You're damned right. I'd like to get Goldstein and Zabriski down here in Headquarters. They're wasted out there in the precinct. Make a note of it, will you, Alec? Did Flavin and Gilman turn up anything?"

"We got a bite from New York. A Wilfred Boyd got caught running a con game three years ago. He drew a year. They'll have pictures for us this morning and George Gilman is going to pick them up."

Tutchek grinned. He was beginning to feel alive again. "Anything from Flavin?"

"Not yet. He was going to try to get in touch with his pigeon. Birdie Burdson. Birdie, being an old ex-con man himself, there's a chance he might know this Wilfred Boyd, or Wesley Buck."

"That's an idea. I hadn't thought of that. Did New York say anything about a woman?"

"Not a thing."

"Well, I guess we'll just have to wait till Gilman gets back with those pictures. There's not much we can do without them. I'll get these press releases out."

Fifteen minutes later, Policewoman Lund buzzed him on the intercom and said Captain Mackenzie would like to see him in his office. Tutchek swore wearily.

"Alec," he said, "finish up these press releases, will you? You know as much about the cases as I do, and they have to be ready by nine-thirty, ten o'clock, or the reporters'll be tearing the doors off the hinges. Foxy wants to see me and Christ knows when I'll get away. You can handle it, can't you?"

"Sure, Ben."

"And show Saul Stein a copy of the rape and liquor store thing before you let it go. His boys worked on it, and it's only fair to give him a look, in case he wants to add anything."

It wasn't really a meeting in Mackenzie's office, as Tutchek had expected. It was just a little congratulatory get-together. Mackenzie met him at the door of the office and led him in, slapping him gently on the back, which was a rare thing for Foxy.

"Nice work you and the boys did, cleaning up those cases yesterday," he said. "The Commissioner's here and wants to say a few words of congratulation himself, personally." There was a slight touch of amused irony in his voice.

Commissioner Willie Quinn took about an hour to say those few words of congratulation. Tutchek's fine handling of public relations, via the newspapers, came into it, with a few remarks on Tutchek's fine handling of the Meade case in the papers and, well, Tutchek was doing a fine job of handling Homicide, and he could just about write his own ticket.

"I need more men," said Tutchek, striking the iron while it was hot, for Quinn's irons sometimes cooled a little too suddenly.

"You'll have them, Ben. Do you have anyone in mind?"

"Two. Goldstein and Zabriski from the North Hudson Precinct. Without them we might not have cracked those two cases last night."

"You'll have them. See that Goldstein and Zabriski are transferred to Homicide, will you, Mac? Now, how is the Meade case coming, Ben?"

"I think we'll lick it, Commissioner. We got a nice break on it last night. Seems as if Meade and a man named Boyd or Buck were running a confidence game down in Miami during the '20s. Now it looks as if Boyd turned up in Hudson about six months ago and started blackmailing Meade. From what Meade's bank told Jeff Flavin, Meade paid out well over sixty thousand dollars since January."

Quinn stared at him, aghast. "A—confidence game. You're sure of that?"

"Positive."

"Does—would you say—does that affect Meade-LaFarge Associates?"

"Not a bit. Except for Meade's name. And *if* Meade was killed by his ex-partner in that con game, I don't see any way we can play it down."

"I wasn't suggesting that, Ben, but ... well, I'll trust your judgment. I have every faith in your judgment, Ben. I know you'll handle it to the satisfaction of all concerned."

"Thank you, Commissioner."

As he left the office he was astonished to see Foxy's left eye droop in a deadpan wink.

He hurried back to his office. He was beginning to feel the need to move faster again. Here it was going on ten o'clock, and what had happened so far? He'd been congratulated.

Jeff Flavin was waiting for him in the squad room and Tutchek got right down to business. There was no time to waste.

"Did you find out anything from Birdie last night?"

"A little, not much. He'd heard of Wesley Buck, but never met him. He knew or heard of most of the big time con men in his day. He said Buck was good, but not one of the best. Too greedy. He always tried for that extra dollar. For instance, Birdie said, Buck had the reputation that if the mark was good for a ten-thousand-dollar touch, Buck would try for eleven."

"That follows. If he was blackmailing Meade, if he was the one, he was bleeding Meade white. Good blackmailers don't do that."

"Yeah, their customers might get desperate," Flavin said significantly. "If Meade ran low on money and became desperate, he might go after Buck, mightn't he? With a gun, maybe. And in the mixup, Meade might have gotten shot."

"That sounds logical. But you know, Jeff, we're going to have a hell of a time proving that blackmail. Blackmailers don't give receipts and they don't accept checks. I think we're going to have some trouble tying Buck in with Meade."

"I might have an angle on that, Ben. Birdie says there's a retired con man in Jersey City he thinks knew both Meade and Buck when they were in Miami. That might help."

"Is Birdie getting in touch with him?"

"He's trying to get the address. Then he wants me to go to Jersey City with him. I'm to meet Birdie in a half hour."

"Good, good. Get in touch with me as soon as it's set."

"This might take time, Ben, especially if the guy isn't too anxious to help the police."

"There's that. But do the best you can, Jeff. We have to keep this thing moving. This is the kind of case that if we stand still, we lose ground. We have to move in on Buck before he moves out."

Flavin's brows twitched as if he were smothering a frown. He agreed, but was bothered by the over-urgency Ben was putting into everything these days. Tutchek was pressing too hard.

"I hear you were up all night cracking the rape case, Ben," he said. "Did you get any sleep at all?"

"If I did, it slipped my mind," Tutchek punched him lightly on the arm to show it was a joke. "Hell, I can go on forever, so long as a case is moving. It's the dead ones that kill me. Keep it moving, Jeff."

Flavin said, "Sure, Ben," but as he walked from the squad room he wondered how long Ben was going to able to run on sheer nerve. He'd watched him light a cigarette and there had been just the faintest tremor in his fingers when he raised the match.

George Gilman came in at eleven with the pictures of Wilfred Boyd, alias Wesley Buck. They were good clear police pictures, front and side views. They showed a quick-faced man with thin but intelligent eyes and a good chin, although the mouth looked a little too small and narrow. Still, with that face, Buck might easily have posed for a Man Of

Distinction advertisement. On the other hand, Tutchek chuckled, most con men could; that's how they made a living.

"But now," he said, more soberly, "the big job is going to be finding him."

George Gilman coughed. "Miss Burkhardt, that's Meade's secretary, recognized him as a Walter Babson, a personal friend of Meade."

"*What!*"

"Well, I remembered something on the way back from New York, Lieutenant. In the beginning Miss Burkhardt said there was a guy waiting to see Meade that morning he came in and dropped dead in his office. Then later after the excitement, or during the excitement, the guy disappeared. His name, she said, was Walter Babson. Then I got to thinking that this Boyd, or Buck, was a funny guy about initials. All his aliases have the initials W.B. A lot of crooks work like that. You know, they got monograms on their handkerchiefs or their pajamas, so they stick with the same initials in case somebody notices. So there were the same initials again, Walter Babson, W.B. So I stopped off at the Meade-LaFarge office and showed her the pictures and she said it was Walter Babson. I had my fingers crossed, Lieutenant, but it was almost too much of a coincidence, a Walter Babson—W.B.—being right there visiting Meade. It was a natural."

"George," said Tutchek, elation frothing inside him, "will you marry me?"

"Hell, Lieutenant, I'd like to, but I'm engaged to Commissioner Quinn."

"You can be a mother to me. By any chance did this wonderful Miss Burkhardt have Babson-Boyd-Buck's address?"

"No, but I got it anyway."

"Now wait a minute, George. Don't tell me. Let me guess. I have it—you put a new fuse in your crystal ball. But how did you get it?"

"I looked it up in the phone book," said Gilman, surprised.

That left Tutchek mute for several seconds, and at length he said, in a wondering voice, "I'm going to tell you something seriously, George. It would have taken me at least a week to have thought of looking it up in the phone book. Now just who the hell would think of looking up an ex-conman-blackmailer's name in a phone book?"

"But it stands to reason, Lieutenant. He's been living around here for at least six months and he must have needed a phone. The new phone book came out just a little while ago, so he was bound to be listed."

"I knew you'd tell me, George. But that's enough fooling around. Let's get down to work. Where does he live?"

"Thirty-one Oakwood Terrace. That's the Stone Bridge Section, near the park. All big houses up there."

"Well, he can afford a big house. Meade paid for it. Let's take a run up there and look it over. I'll take my own car in case we have to separate. I'll meet you on the corner of Mt. Windsor Avenue and Oakwood."

Tutchek was too preoccupied to give either Alec Gillespie or Policewoman Lund his usual, "Get in touch with me if anything turns up." He might easily have said that, for there was a short wave in the car. Later, he regretted not letting Gilman drive him. His eyes were very grainy and slow, and for some reason or other, the traffic was exceptionally heavy today and seemed to hurtle at him from all directions. Of course, he told himself, he hadn't gotten enough sleep last night, and that was the reason. He drove slowly and fretted all the way at the necessity of being so cautious. He felt gloomy. All day his moods had been changing swiftly from elation to depression. What a hell of a day!

He met Gilman on Mt. Windsor Avenue and left his car there, riding with George. They cruised slowly past number thirty-one Oakwood Terrace. It was a big yellow-brick house with wide grounds around it. Overhanging the sun porch at the rear was a tall maple tree, and along the house was a flowerbed, bright with zinnias. That was all Tutchek needed to see to settle it in his mind. The report sent down from the Lab by Bert Daly and Jerry Straub had said that the earth found on Meade's shoes and in the cuffs of his trousers was composed of clay, sand, fertilizer and rotted maple leaves. There was the maple tree and beneath it the flowerbed, which, like all flowerbeds in this area, was undoubtedly made up of clay, sand and fertilizer, in addition to the maple leaves. This could not all be coincidence. Everything fitted together too well.

They parked up the street in the deep shade of a wide oak tree and Tutchek took a pair of field glasses from the glove compartment of the car. They were there for just this purpose. Through them he scanned the windows of the house. Twice he saw a curtain shift and behind it moved the shadow of someone peering out into the street. He sat watching for a long time. After a while a newsboy came down the street on a bicycle, flinging papers on the front porches as he went. Tutchek saw the paper thud against the front door of Buck's house and fall to the mat. A few minutes after, the front door opened, a man appeared briefly, snatched up the paper, and vanished back into the house. But in that moment, Tutchek saw him clearly through the glasses, and he sat back in the seat with a small sigh. Gilman looked the question, and he nodded.

"That's our boy, all right," he said. "And judging from the way he acted, he's more than a little jittery."

"Maybe we should pick him up before he takes a powder," said Gilman.

"If he's jittery, he might run any minute."

"What would we do with him after we picked him up? Ask him if he blackmailed Meade? And what would we do if he said no? I want to nail him tight when I pick him up, George, not merely warn him. Remember, he ran a con game. He's not a punk. Con men are the smartest crooks of the lot. Listen. Suppose you go back to the Meade-LaFarge office and do a little more talking to Miss Burkhardt. If Buck was in the habit of 'visiting' Meade now and then, maybe she overheard something that might give us a lead. Look through his desk, go through the files. There might be something, there just might be something—" His voice trailed off and he stared vaguely through the windshield, depressed. He gave himself a shake. "Well, come on, let's go!" he ordered.

Gilman let him off at the corner and he trudged to his own car. He slouched down in the seat behind the wheel. Now what? He had to keep moving. Just as he told Jeff Flavin, if you stand still, you lose ground. Back to Headquarters and wait for the reports to come in? Or another meeting with Willie Quinn in Mackenzie's office? That wasn't moving; that was standing still. But of course—Meade's apartment. The case had gone ahead a long way since the time they first went through the apartment. Perhaps there had been a lead there then but they hadn't recognized it. The thing to do ...

He drove downtown to the Hotel Sutton, repeating over and over to himself, like a litany, the thing to do, the thing to do ... But he never did quite tell himself what it was, the thing to do. It was just the rhythm he was repeating, really. Counting sheep.

At the hotel, he went straight to Manthey's office and demanded the key to Meade's apartment, holding out his hand, waggling it impatiently. The manager took one look at his set face and handed over the key without asking any of the questions that quivered at the end of his tongue.

He went upstairs to the apartment. The air was hot, almost stifling, and stale. The air-conditioner had been turned off and the apartment had not been opened for days. The Venetian blinds were closed and the rooms lay in a humid dusk. He walked slowly the length of the living room, looking around to give himself a focal point at which to start. He stopped at the sofa to light a cigarette. He scratched the match, then stared at his hand, horrified. It was shaking so hard that it almost flapped in the air before his face, and suddenly he could feel that same shaking all through his body and down his legs. He sat on the sofa, putting out a quick hand to save himself from falling. He still did not realize that during the past six weeks, since taking over command of Homicide, he had driven himself so hard and so unremittingly that now he was finally at the edge of collapse. He muttered, "Sleep" thinking of the sleep he hadn't gotten the night before. But there had been six weeks of almost sleepless nights. He leaned his head against the back of the sofa and closed his eyes. He slept. But this was not ordinary sleep—it was the stunned sleep of exhaustion, and the hot, smothering air locked him in it.

Awakening was hard. He was like a drowning man struggling to reach the surface of the water. There was a faint humming sound and the air was cooler, and even before he opened his eyes, he realized someone had turned on the air-conditioner. It was another struggle to focus his eyes. Things had a tendency to swim and recede into darkness, and dark forms hovered over him. Slowly the dark forms took shape and he saw that they were Flavin and Gilman.

"What time is it?" he asked thickly.

George Gilman coughed. "It's four o'clock, Lieutenant." He sounded embarrassed.

"Oh hell," he groaned, weakly trying to push himself upright. "I've been asleep two hours."

Gilman coughed again. "That, uh, was yesterday, Lieutenant."

Tutchek gave him a blank look. "Yesterday? What do you mean, yesterday?"

Flavin touched his shoulder. "Maybe you'd better just lie still for a few minutes yet, Ben. You're worn out."

Tutchek lay back and did not object. He looked up at them without understanding.

"You came in here yesterday, Ben," said Flavin, almost as if talking to a child. "You haven't been asleep two hours. You've been asleep twenty-six hours. George and I were in earlier this morning, but we couldn't wake you up. The doctor said to let you sleep."

"Doctor?"

"He said you were just tired out and to let you sleep."

Now it began to come back to Tutchek. Not in a flood, but in little wisps and tatters of remembrance. Then his eyes widened and he cried, "Meade!"

"It's all taken care of, Ben," Flavin gently knuckled his shoulder. "We got Buck and the woman out of bed at seven o'clock this morning and wrapped it up while they were still groggy. That's the best time to get them, Ben—before they're awake."

"That's news?" Tutchek smiled weakly. "Look at me. Wait a minute. Did you say you wrapped it up? Is that what you said?"

"Signed, sealed and delivered. That friend of Birdie's from Jersey City helped. He was with us. He knew Meade, Buck and Vivian Marsh—Meade's ex-wife—in the old days down in Miami. He walked into the room, looked at the woman and said, 'Hello, Viv. Stewart told me you were in town.' We fixed up that speech beforehand. We thought if anyone cracked, it would be the woman. She did, and we got Buck out of the room fast. They do more talking when they're separated. She told us Meade came to the house last the night of the Fourth. They were out on the lawn in the back of the house. Meade threatened them with a gun and Buck tried to take it away from him and the gun went off. There were still some last-ditch fireworks going on here and there and the neighbors paid no attention to the gun. Meade fell down on one knee, but got right up again, and they didn't think he'd been hurt. It was quite dark back there. Then he turned around and left. Buck told the same story. The woman admitted the blackmail, and Buck had no choice. And that's it, Ben."

"How about that!" his smile was not his broadest, but it was real. "All wrapped up, and I had a nice sleep in the bargain."

They waited for him to get up, but he made no effort to rise, and finally Flavin said, "Do you want to lie there for a little while yet, Ben?"

"A little while yet, Jeff. Twenty-six hours' sleep—it takes time to wake up."

"We'll be back, Ben ..."

Tutchek closed his eyes, but opened them again when he heard the door close. He could have gotten up without trouble—he was fully awake and pretty well rested now—but he felt the need to be by himself for a little while yet.

And he wanted to think. There was something he had to think over. For some reason, his mind was clearer now than it had been in six weeks. Now there were those four last cases—the Widdicomb suicide, the Meade manslaughter, and those two bad ones—the liquor shop and the rape. He grimaced as he remembered how he'd gone charging around, trying to do all the work on all of them. And what had happened?

Kitteridge had cracked the Widdicomb suicide.

Flavin and Gilman took care of the Meade case.

Caputo, Bierce, Uri and Hughes, with the help of Goldstein and Zabrisi had done a wonderful job of tying up the liquor shop and rape killings.

But he had helped. There was no doubt about that. He'd helped—and hampered, too, he admitted ruefully. But he had helped. He'd talked things over with them, and, honestly, had kept the investigations going in a straight line.

But that was his job. That was what a Division Commander was supposed to do. And in the end (in spite of him, he admitted also) the men in the field were the ones who had wrapped up every case.

And that was the way it was supposed to be, too. He saw very clearly now, that if he tried to go out and personally solve everything that came in to Homicide, he'd be doing the men's jobs, and would only succeed in making a mess of it. And he had almost done that, too. He could go right down the list and remember how resentful the men had been. Even mild, conciliatory Caputo had rebelled.

But, by God, they had done their jobs in spite of him. (And with his help too, *they'd* have to admit. If it came to that. Which it never would.)

He let his eyes fall closed again. Not in sleep, but relaxed.

What was it Foxy Mackenzie had once said? Oh yes—an executive officer isn't a detective. He's only a foreman of detectives.

Well, from now on, it looked as if that was what he was going to have to be, nothing but a foreman of detectives. He'd have to get used to the idea. It would take time.

THE END

Lorenz Heller Bibliography
(1910-1965)

As Frederick Lorenz

Novels:
A Rage at Sea (Lion, 1953)
Night Never Ends (Lion, 1954)
The Savage Chase (Lion, 1954)
A Party Every Night (Lion, 1956)
Ruby (Lion, 1956)
Hot (Lion, 1956)
Dungaree Sin (Chariot, 1960)

Stories:
Backbite (*Justice*, Jan 1956)
Big Catch (*Justice*, July 1955)
Living Bait (*Justice*, May 1955)

As Laura Hale

Novels:
Wild is the Woman (Rainbow, 1951)
Lovers Don't Sleep (Falcon, 1951)
Kiss of Fire (Rainbow, 1952; reprinted in Australia as
 Kiss Of Death, Phantom, 1953)
Woman Hunter (Falcon, 1952; reprinted in Australia,
 Phantom, 1953)
Desperate Blonde (Beacon Australia, 1960)
Lessons in Lust (Beacon, 1961; re-write of *Woman Hunter*)
Sensual Woman (Beacon, 1961; re-write of *Lovers Don't Sleep*)
The Zipper Girls (Beacon, 1962; re-write of *Wild is the Woman*)
The Marriage Bed (Beacon, 1962; re-write of *Desperate Blonde*)

As Larry Heller

Novels:
I Get What I Want (Popular, 1956)
Body of the Crime (Pyramid, 1962)

Story:
Blood Is Thicker (*Guilty Detective Story Magazine*, Mar 1957)

As Larry Holden

Novels:
Hide-Out (Eton, 1953)
Dead Wrong (Pyramid, 1957)
Crime Cop (Pyramid, 1959)

Stories (alphabetical listing):
...And Death Makes Ten (*Detective Tales*, June 1947)
Another Man's Poison (*Shadow Mystery*, Apr/May 1948)
Any Corpse in a Storm (*Dime Mystery Magazine*, Aug 1949)
Anybody Lose a Corpse? (*Mammoth Detective*, Aug 1946)
The Big Haunt (*10-Story Detective Magazine*, Oct 1948)
Blackmail Means Homicide (*15 Story Detective*, Feb 1950)
Bloody Night! (*Dime Mystery Magazine*, Oct 1949)
Bodyguard (*Thrilling Detective*, June 1951)
Bullets for Beethoven [Dinny Keogh] (*Mammoth Mystery*, June 1946)
Coffin Key (*Detective Tales*, Oct 1951)
A Corpse at Large (*Ten Detective Aces*, July 1949)
Corpse in Waiting (*New Detective Magazine*, Nov 1950)
A Corpse to His Credit (*Dime Detective Magazine*, May 1947)
Criminal at Large (*Suspense Magazine*, Summer 1951)
The Crimson Path (*Detective Tales*, Sept 1947)
Cry Murder (*New Detective Magazine*, Oct 1952)
The Crying Corpse (*Ten Detective Aces*, Sept 1948)
Death Brings Down the House (*10-Story Detective Magazine*, Apr 1948)
Death Carries the Mail (*F.B.I. Detective Stories*, Aug 1950)
Death for Two! (*Detective Tales*, Dec 1952)
Death in Dirty Linen (*Shadow Mystery*, June/July 1947)
Death in Six Reels (*Doc Savage*, July/Aug 1948)
Death in Thin Ice (*Shadow Mystery*, Feb/Mar 1948)
Death Is Where You Find It (*Suspect Detective Stories*, Nov 1955)
Die, Baby, Die! (*Detective Tales*, June 1948)
Don't Crowd My Shroud (*10-Story Detective Magazine*, Dec 1948)
Don't Ever Forget (*Detective Story Magazine*, Mar 1953)
Don't Wait Up for Me (*Triple Detective*, Fall 1955)
The Eighteen Screaming Corpses (*Detective Tales*, Jan 1948)

The Expendable Ex (*Dime Detective Magazine*, June 1952)
Face in the Window (*Detective Tales*, June 1951)
Fall Guy (*Detective Tales*, Aug 1953)
Forger's Fate (*Dime Detective Magazine*, Apr 1951)
The High Cost of Chivalry (*Dime Detective Magazine*, Dec 1951)
Home for Christmas (*Thrilling Detective*, Dec 1947)
House of Hate (*10-Story Detective Magazine*, Apr 1949)
Humpty-Dumpty Homicide (*Detective Tales*, June 1949)
If the Body Fits— (*Dime Mystery Magazine*, Dec 1947)
If the Frame Fits— (*Detective Tales*, Dec 1951)
I'll Be Home for Murder! (*Detective Tales*, Apr 1948)
I'll See You Dead! (*Detective Tales*, May 1947)
In Her Mother's Best Bier! (*Detective Tales*, Dec 1948)
Keeping Honest (*Doc Savage*, Winter 1949)
Kickback for a Corpse (*All-Story Detective*, Apr 1949)
Killer's Kiss (*Detective Tales*, Aug 1949)
Lady in Red (*Detective Tales*, Oct 1948)
Lady-Killer (*Dime Detective Magazine*, Dec 1952)
Lethal Boy Blue (*Detective Tales*, May 1949)
Love Me, Love My Corpse! (*Detective Tales*, Aug 1948)
Make Mine Mayhem (*New Detective Magazine*, Jan 1949)
Man with a Rep (*Detective Tales*, Dec 1949)
Mayhem at Eight (*New Detective Magazine*, May 1950)
Mayhem's Mechanic (*Detective Tales*, Sept 1946)
Morgue Bait (*New Detective Magazine*, Dec 1951)
Murder and the Mermaid (*Dime Detective Magazine*, Oct 1952)
Murder Never Gets Too Old (*Private Detective*, Jan 1950)
Never Dead Enough (*New Detective Magazine*, Sept 1947)
Never Turn Your Back (*Mike Shayne Mystery Magazine*, July 1959)
Nightmare (*Detective Tales*, Oct 1952)
No Dead End (*Triple Detective*, Spring 1955)
On a Dead Man's Chest (*Thrilling Detective*, Apr 1953)
One Dark Night [Dinny Keogh] (*Mammoth Mystery*, Dec 1946)
One for the Hangman (*Suspect Detective Stories*, Feb 1956)
Operation—Murder (*F.B.I. Detective Stories*, Aug 1949)
Orphans Are Made (*Mobsters*, Feb 1953)
Out of the Frying Pan... (*15 Mystery Stories*, Oct 1950)
Port of the Dead (*New Detective Magazine*, July 1947)
Prelude to a Wake (*Dime Detective Magazine*, Feb 1952)
Red Nightmare (*Dime Mystery Magazine*, July 1947)
Sailor, Beware! (*Detective Story Magazine*, May 1953)
Save Me a Kill (*New Detective Magazine*, June 1953)

Self-Made Corpse (*Detective Tales*, Apr 1949)
She Cries Murder! (*New Detective Magazine*, June 1952)
Sing a Song of Murder (*Dime Detective Magazine*, Aug 1952)
Snow in August [Dinny Keogh] (*Mammoth Mystery*, Aug 1946)
The Spice of Death (*Private Detective*, Dec 1950)
Start with a Corpse [Dinny Keogh] (*Mammoth Mystery*, Jan 1946)
There's Death in the Heir [Dinny Keogh] (*Mammoth Mystery*, Aug 1947)
They Played Too Rough [Dinny Keogh] (*Mammoth Mystery*, Mar 1946)
This Shroud Reserved (*New Detective Magazine*, Oct 1951)
Those Slaughter-House Blues (*Mammoth Detective*, Feb 1947)
A Time for Dying (*Dime Detective Magazine*, Aug 1951)
Too Many Crosses [Dinny Keogh] (*Mammoth Mystery*, Feb 1947)
Tragedy in Waiting (*Invincible Detective Magazine*, Mar 1951)
The Trouble with Redheads (*Mike Shayne Mystery Magazine*, Apr 1959)
Two-Headed Killer (*15 Mystery Stories*, Feb 1950)
Undressed to Kill (*New Detective Magazine*, Sept 1949)
Vicious Circle (*Detective Tales*, Nov 1949)
The Voice That Kills (*15 Mystery Stories*, Aug 1950)
Wake of the Ermine Chick (*15 Story Detective*, Dec 1950)
When Cops Fall Out (*Detective Tales*, June 1953)
With Hostile Intent (*Fifteen Detective Stories*, Dec 1954)
With Love and Bullets! (*Detective Tales*, Feb 1953)
Written in Blood (*Ten Detective Aces*, May 1948)
You Can't Live Forever (*New Detective Magazine*, Aug 1952)
You Die Alone (*Fifteen Detective Stories*, Oct 1953)
You'll Die Laughing (*Detective Tales*, Oct 1950)
You're Killing Me (*Detective Story Magazine*, Sept 1953)

Dinny Keogh series:
Start with a Corpse (1946)
They Played Too Rough (1946)
Bullets for Beethoven (1946)
Snow in August (1946)
One Dark Night (1946)
Too Many Crosses (1947)
There's Death in the Heir (1947)

As Lorenz Heller

Novel:
Murder in Make-Up (Messner, 1937)

Stories:
Blood Money (*Suspect Detective Stories*, Nov 1955)
A Tasty Dish (*Suspect Detective Stories*, Feb 1956)
Twilight (*Short Stories*, Nov 1956)
The Hero (*Mystery Tales*, Dec 1958)
The Last Hunt (*Adventure*, June 1959)

As Burt Sims

Television Scripts:
1953: "Death Does a Rumba" (Season 2, Episode 12, *Boston Blakie*)
1953: "Island of Stone" (Season 2, Episode 1, *Chevron Theater*)
1954: "Tailor-Made Trouble" (Season 1, Episode 11, *Waterfront*)
1956 - 1959: Seven episodes of *Sky King*
1958: "Beautiful, Blue and Deadly" (Season 1, Episode 14, *Mike Hammer*)
1958: "Texas Fliers" (Season 1, Episode 18, *Flight*)

www.ingramcontent.com/pod-product-compliance
Lightning Source LLC
LaVergne TN
LVHW011928070526
838202LV00054B/4536